"I suppose I should take this time to thank you," she said, her lips stiff. "You've saved more than half the herd. I'm sure my husband will repay you for your efforts when he returns."

"Suppose I don't want to wait?" His voice was husky, caressing. "Suppose I want to be paid now?"

"You'll have to talk to Juan—"

"Juan, hell!" His voice was ugly now. "You know what I want! You want it too! You've been wanting it for a long time—"

His arms were around her, his hot mouth burning hers. For a moment, she yielded in shock, then she began to fight. The moment had come to deal with him. . . .

"Let me go," she said hoarsely. "In the name of God! Stop this! Let me go!"

He only laughed and held her more tightly, his hand going to the buttons of her shirt. She jerked backward, and the age-weakened material ripped. . . . "Little wildcat," he chuckled. "All right, if this is the way you like it—"

His blue eyes bulged as he felt the round muzzle of a gun against his mid-section. His hands left Tamsen's body and raised helplessly as he backed from the murderous expression in her eyes . . .

"If you lay hands on me or any of my family again, I'll kill you."

Books by Aola Vandergriff

Wyndspelle
Wyndspelle's Child
The House of The Dancing Dead
Sisters of Sorrow
Daughters of the Southwind
Daughters of the Wild Country
Daughters of the Far Islands

Published by
WARNER BOOKS

Daughters of the Opal Skies

by

Aola Vandergriff

WARNER BOOKS

A Warner Communications Company

WARNER BOOKS EDITION

Copyright © 1980 by Aola Vandergriff
All rights reserved.

ISBN: 0-446-81930-1

Cover art by Jim Dietz

Warner Books, Inc., 75 Rockefeller Plaza, New York, N.Y. 10019

Ⓦ A Warner Communications Company

Printed in the United States of America

First printing: May, 1980

10 9 8 7 6 5 4 3

For Ned Kelly
A figure in Australian history, one hundred years past

And Dusty
Whom I shall miss.

With special thanks to
Brian Peck: Australian Embassy, Washington, D.C.
The Australian Overseas Media Visitors
Liaison Officer, Canberra
and
George Ormrod,
Central Land Council, Alice Springs, New York
and
Especially Sandra and David

Daughters
of the
Opal Skies

Chapter 1

The dwellers of the Australian terrain fell silent when the man approached. Sweat-soaked, limping painfully, he crawled the last few feet to a rocky ledge where, lying prone, he gazed down into the valley below.

For a time, motion was suspended. Finally, reassured, small wild things returned to their usual occupations. A rainbow bird that had huddled on a dead limb at the intruder's approach spread its wings. Its golden underside glowed as it swooped in pursuit of a dragonfly.

After a pause, a bush rat ventured from its burrow and rummaged in the scrub, seeking breakfast. A stumpy-tailed lizard, ludicrous, bobbed by nature, scampered up to a booted moleskin-clad leg, pondered, and skittered across the barrier it presented. Then everything froze as the man spoke through clenched teeth.

"Squatters! Damn flaming bloody squatters!"

The people below were unaware of the watching eyes as they enacted a farewell scene. A tall man lifted a woman and a young girl into a horse-drawn buggy. A small group had gathered to see them off. Behind them a number of little white houses, sheds and buildings, formed a miniature town, tin roofs reflecting the strong light. Before the large house, a low rambling affair with a deep veranda, an enormous wattle tree towered. Here and there, pepper trees cast a deep shade, and several gums shone whitely. The Billabong creek, standing pools of water glistening in its almost dry bed, wound around the station like a frame, its perimeters delineated by dark salt cedar. Square man-made storage ponds studded the valley, sides diked high. Now, the water low, slick with moss, they shone like green jewels.

Behind the station, the land rose, forested for a space, disintegrating into mallee bush. Against a backdrop of dusty trees stood a leaning stringybark hut, surrounded by a falling-down sapling fence, mute reminder of the selector, who had settled to farm a portion of the valley, only to be squeezed out by a squatter who claimed property on both sides of him. The squatter, overextended, had sold the property to Daniel Tallant, making Tallant, in the watcher's mind, a man of the same breed.

His eyes roved moodily over the scene, taking in the numerous humpies of the aborigine employees across the river; the paddock of blooded horses; fat cattle in the distance raising a red haze of dust. Then they moved back to the people below.

"Bloody squatters!"

He raised his pistol and, resting it on one hand, drew a sight on the breast of the tall man in the buggy. He had no intention of firing. The range was much too far. And he had never killed a man.

When he did, it would be a squatter—or a policeman.

He shoved the gun back into his belt, wincing with the pain of his injured leg, damning his bloody luck.

Three nights earlier, he, his brother Dan, and their mates, Steve Hart and Joe Byrne, sat in a cave in the Wombat Ranges south of Greta and swore an oath of vengeance. They declared open warfare against the law that persecuted them, and the squatters who used the law

10

to drive the little man from the selections. To get even, they vowed to take from the rich and give to the poor.

The Bank of New South Wales at Jerilderie figured in their projected plans. He'd ridden there and looked over the lay of the land, managing to do so without being recognized and arrested. Then, as a bonus, he'd decided to survey the rich Opal Station on the Billabong. He knew an auctioneer who wasn't too particular about an altered brand.

But he'd flushed a brumby in the bush. As the wild horse flashed across his vision, his own mount reared, slipped, and went down, both of them injured in the fall.

His only hope now was to steal one of the animals from the paddock below.

The paddock lay in an exposed position. There seemed to be a large number of abos and jackaroos milling about. Some dogs too. He counted them. Four at least.

He pulled his coat collar up, shivering a little as the sharp wind of late May chilled a body damp with the sweat of exertion. Then he lay still, figuring the odds. He would make his move when darkness fell. It would be a long day.

For a time, the rainbow bird eyed him, head cocked a little to one side. Bright eyes watched from the bush rat's burrow. And the lizard sat, unmoving, carved from stone.

Then, apparently deciding this was only another wild creature like themselves, they began their foraging again.

Chapter 2

The cold wind didn't reach the sheltered valley where Juan Narvaéz assisted his wife Arab into the buggy. Then he handed ten-year-old Luka up to sit beside her mother, stepped up himself, and took his place at the reins.

Ramona Narvaéz, watching, felt her heart surge with pride. Papa looked so handsome in his trim black suit, his dark hair winged with silver. Mama, though she'd let herself grow soft and round with motherhood, was a picture in her forest green traveling costume. Her eyes were alight with anticipation. They were making for Wangaratta, where they would entrain for Melbourne. Arab would see her sister Em and Em's family for the first time in two years. Juan, of course, was going on business. Business that he was most maddeningly secretive about. While he was about it, the two sisters would visit, see the shops of Melbourne. And Em would be surprised to see how lovely Luka had grown!

With a gloved hand, Arab reached to touch her youngest child's pale hair. Then she felt a twinge of conscience at leaving her two other daughters behind. Pushing back the veil on the small hat that covered a mass of still-glorious auburn hair, she salved her feelings with a few motherly admonitions.

"Ramona, you will be a good girl? You will help Aunt Tamsen?"

"Yes, Mama. And please give everybody my love."

Arab wasn't listening. She was frowning at sixteen-year-old Missie. "Melissa Narváez! I said there was to be no more sulking! I explained why you couldn't go. This is a business trip—"

"You're taking Luka." Missie's face was flushed. "And Luka doesn't want to go."

"Luka's still a child!" Arab turned to her husband with an exasperated expression. "Juan, can't you straighten your daughter out? I can't leave her like this!"

Before Juan could speak, Tamsen moved forward, putting one arm about Ramona's waist, the other around Missie's. "The girls will be all right, Arab. I promise you. Just go, and enjoy your visit."

Arab's face cleared. "I know you'll take care of them, Tam. After all, they are almost as much yours as they are mine."

"Almost ez much, hell!" The words, pitched too low to carry came from the lips of Nell, the obese old ex-madam who'd been with the family all their lives. They were meant for the ears of Dusty Wotherspoon, the little ex-patriate Englishman with whom she had lived out of wedlock for more than thirty years.

"Now, Nell," he cautioned.

"Don't shush me, you leetle bastard. You know what I'm tawkin' about. Missie's the one Arab oughta took with her. She's a smart kid. Too smart fer her own good. An' she's strung up tighter'n a fiddle string. That girl needs some lovin' so bad she's gonna bust some day. Migawd! Arab shoved them two outta the nest when they wuz babies. Ramona's did awright. But that young'un needs some attention!"

It wasn't in Dusty to contradict his beloved Nell, but she was working herself into a state. "Tamsen tries," he said, his moustache quivering. "And," he added modestly, "I fancy myself as Missie's friend."

"Tamsen ain't her mother, dammit!" Nell paused, her face softening as she looked at the little man who'd loved her for so many years. "Ez fer you, you leetle sonofabitch, I bin watchin' you an' her! Figgered mebbe you wuz fixin' ter rob the cradle in yer old age."

Dusty's face flamed, his wispy white hair standing on end. "My word, Nell!"

Nell smiled complacently. She'd never doubted his fidelity. She looked at Tamsen, arms about her nieces, then at Tallant, absorbed in giving his brother-in-law last minute instructions. Damn shame they never had kids, when Arab had a couple to spare.

Dusty mopped his perspiring brow, glad that Nell's attention had been redirected. For a moment, he'd almost been prodded into telling her the secret he and Missie shared; of the project they were working on together. The thing was harmless enough. It kept the child occupied, and nothing would come of it. But he'd never thought his Nell might doubt him.

Jove!

There was a flurry of movement as Arab called a last farewell. Dan Tallant stepped away from the vehicle, and Juan saluted with his whip. They were off down the red track, soon obscured by dust. The group they left behind stood for a while in anticlimactic silence. Then Missie, with a sob, wrenched away from Tamsen and ran off to be alone.

Ramona moved to follow her, but Tamsen put up a staying hand. "Let her cry it out," she said softly. "I think she needs to be by herself."

Aunt Tamsen was right, of course. Ramona looked at the slender woman with loving eyes. The hot Australian climate, so ruinous to the women who inhabited it, had been kind to her aunt. She still had the figure of a

15

girl, her olive complexion was smooth, wrinkle-free; the mass of dark hair showed only an occasional silver strand. Dark eyes filled with understanding.

"I love you, Aunt Tamsen."

"And I love you."

"I still think someone should go after the child," Dan Tallant said, his eyes worried.

Ramona turned her scrutiny to her beloved uncle. He and her father were so different. Juan Narvaéz was handsome in a classic way, tall, slender, aristocratic. Dan was a man's man, from the top of his tousled head to the soles of his dusty boots. Broad-shouldered, hard-muscled, his open shirt revealing a tanned chest.

"I know where she is, Uncle Dan." And Ramona did.

Some distance away, on the banks of the Billabong, was a spot where salt cedar had formed a small ring. Here, Missie, suffering from her mother's rejections, both real and imaginary, would seek refuge. Here, in the dry season, she kept a small tin box that contained pages of scribbled paper—and a whiskey bottle. It was not for her own use, but to prime Dusty. The chronic little imbiber was the only intruder she welcomed. With his thirst satisfied, he would ramble on for hours about her Aunt Tamsen's past life; how she'd become a singer in a Texas cantina, to support her family; the way circumstances had driven her to become a madam in San Francisco, and later, on the Fraser River in the far north; about her romance with Dan—

And while he talked, Missie took notes for The Book. The Book that would make her famous one day. She wouldn't be like other women writers. She would publish it under her own name, a woman's name. Mama would be proud of her. Often, Missie sat and daydreamed of that day, imagining her mother's voice. "I knew you could do it, Missie. And I want to tell you something. I don't think you ever knew it, but I loved you most of all."

There was no daydreaming now. Missie had curled herself into a tight ball of misery in the gloomy salt-cedar shade, and was sobbing her heart out.

Melbourne had been only another beautiful shining bubble that burst when Arab decided she and Ramona were to be left behind. When the subject of the trip was broached, Missie had reached a peak of ecstasy, visualizing drawing rooms in which things such as worming of cattle and sheep-crutching were not mentioned. In which artists and novelists moved in a rarefied atmosphere to the genteel clinking of crystal and silver, and women were *listened* to.

She had even dreamed up a scene in which she met her own heroine, after whom she planned to pattern herself; Catherine Helen Spence—the shocking spinster of South Australia—author of *Clara Morison, Tender and True,* and *Handfasted,* denounced as calculated to loosen marriage ties, by the *Sydney Mail.* Miss Spence, to the horror of the Australian male, immersed herself in politics, spoke out for women's rights. Of late, she had been lecturing in Sydney—Melbourne.

In her dream, Catherine Spence would be speaking in Melbourne. They would meet, talk. And after some conversation, the writer would say, "Melissa, come to Adelaide with me, as my pupil. I forsee a great future for you."

Papa would be upset, of course. Perhaps, Missie dared to dream, Mama would cry. But in the end, they would see they couldn't possibly stand in the way of destiny.

But Mama had decided it was too much trouble to take the whole family. Only Luka was to go. Happy little

Luka, who wouldn't care one way or another, whose mind was like a vagrant breeze or a butterfly on the wing.

Lord, how she hated this place! The monotony of the endless days. The flies; the red dust that dulled the vegetation after the year's dry spring.

Dear God! To spend one's life with no one to talk to except family, illiterate jackaroos, wandering swagmen, abos—! It was all right for Ramona. Ramona loved Aunt Tamsen, maybe even more than she loved Mama. And she had all those animals she was always fooling around with. Motherless calves, crippled wild things she nursed back to health.

But she, Missie, had no one.

Wiping her eyes, she opened the tin box, forcing herself to go over the notes she'd collected on her Aunt Tamsen's life. She'd heard all writers had to suffer. Maybe it was true.

In the house at the station, Ramona was unusually quiet as she helped Tamsen scrub the big room that served as living room, dining room and kitchen, dividing the long house: the Narvaéz's quarters at one end, the Tallant's at the other. She carried the remainder of the lye water; first used for laundry; then to sluice down the floors; outside, pouring it at the foot of the wattle tree. Then she went to the dairy, a frame affair, covered with squares of sod, sides and roof, for maximum cooling. She turned the cheeses along one shelf, then eyed the crocks of milk on which a thick golden crown had risen. She would skim it later, just before she fed the orphan calves in their small pen. First, she had an errand to do.

Going into the house, she entered the dormitorylike room she shared with Missie and Luka. Taking off her gown and petticoats, she donned a man's shirt and trousers, tucking the trousers into a pair of heavy boots. Such unladylike garb had been frowned upon by Mama, but Tamsen had stood with Ramona in the argument. In the bush, such clothing afforded protection against the deadly snakes that infested the area: the tiger, brown, red-bellied black and mulga snakes.

Tucking her long hair into a wide-brimmed man's hat, Ramona returned to the kitchen. From a pantry at the rear, among the meats already cooked to prevent spoiling, she selected scraps that might not be missed, dropping them into a leather bag. It wasn't stealing, she told herself sturdily. Not when it was meant to save a life. Though if anyone found out she had taken it to feed a small dingo pup, whose mother had died, she'd be in for a scolding. Dingoes and kangaroos were the scourge of the station.

At last, mounted on Cloud, the spirited gray she'd received three years earlier on her fifteenth birthday, she rode along a gorge that led to the upper ridge.

Free of the house, doing what she loved best, she was still unable to shake her sense of depression. Acutely intuitive, she was always affected by Missie's emotional upsets. Her sister's torment pierced through to her very heart. But this was something more. It was like the feeling that came before a storm; heavy and brooding, a sense of electrical particles in the air, needing only to rub, one against the other, to crackle and burn. A feeling that something terrible was about to happen. She'd felt it for some time, hovering over all of them. She felt it now.

She turned in the saddle and looked back at the place that had been home for eight years. Opal Station, so named because they had seen it first at sunset, the glowing sky reflected in jeweled pools in the Billabong. In the abo settlement, she could see a thin stream of smoke and the figure of old Wyuna moving about; Wyuna, mission-taught, who ordered the lives of her people with the wisdom of a goddess.

The main house, surrounded by low rambling buildings, looked as it always did from this viewpoint. Beautiful and safe. Trees casting parallel lines of shadow in the late afternoon.

Smiling, Ramona shrugged off the feeling of doom that haunted her. She was having an attack of the vapors. It was probably due to the unseasonable vagaries of the year with its dry spring. In the meantime, she must hurry. The dingo pup was waiting for its dinner to arrive.

She buttoned the man's coat she wore against the chill, and rode on to the top of the ridge, unconscious of the eyes that watched her progress.

The man on the crest had lain there for hours, unmoving, watching the activity below. With each passing moment, his plan seemed more improbable. How could he, lamed as he was, get into such a populated area, steal a mount, and escape without detection? His only hope, if he were caught, would be to take a hostage.

He checked his gun carefully, and returned it to his belt. Then he saw the gray horse, with its rider, making its way upward.

He held his breath for a space when the rider paused as if uncertain whether to continue, then exulted as he came on. His bloody luck was in again.

With an indrawn breath of pain, he moved, crawling on his stomach, swearing silently as a clump of spinifex stabbed his hand. At last, he reached an outcropping of rock that marked the spot where his intended prey would emerge. Pulling himself into an upright position, he drew his pistol and waited, gauging the rate of approach from the sound of the horse's hooves.

Now!

He flung himself forward, reaching for the bridle, his weapon in hand. *"Bail up!"* It was the cry of the bushranger.

The horse reared, Ramona's hat falling away, loosing a

mass of dark hair as she fought to keep her seat. Swearing, her attacker jerked the brute to a standstill, then turned his attention to the rider.

"What the bloody hell!"

He saw a slim girl in man's clothing, eyes too big for her white face, a tiny tilted nose, a generous mouth.

Renegade though he might be, still he and his kind adhered to a gentleman's code. And he had never bailed up a woman before.

Chapter 3

The shock of having a wild-eyed desperado leap out at her immobilized Ramona for a moment. Then she slowly raised her hands and spoke, her mouth dry.

"Are you going to shoot me?"

The change in her attacker was amazing. The grimness faded from his eyes, and the flesh above a soft brown beard turned white, then was slowly suffused with red.

"No, Ma'am. I won't hurt you. I only want your horse."

Ramona's fears had fled. "Well, you shan't have him," she said tartly. "Now, if you'll take your hand off the bridle—"

The look of desperation had replaced his embarrassed expression. "I've got to have him! My horse is lamed—"

"Then come down to the station. My uncle will be glad to lend you one."

"I can't! My life wouldn't be worth tuppence down there! Damn it, don't make me have to hurt you!"

The pistol was pointing at her once more. The sight of the deadly black muzzle sent a chill up her spine. I've got to bluff it out, she thought. Dear God, I've got to bluff it out! She leaned forward, her voice low and scathing.

"Go ahead. Shoot! But remember, when you do, they'll be able to hear it in the valley. You'll never get away. You haven't got the nerve to shoot a woman, anyway."

His eyes blazing, he released the bridle and caught at her wrist. "You read me right," he said. "I don't shoot women. I've got a mother, and sisters. But I've got to get the hell out of here. If you don't go along with me, I'm going to yank you off that horse and tap you on the head with this." He gestured with the gun. "When you wake up, you'll have one helluva headache!"

"And before you hit me, I'll scream. Maybe I'll have a headache, but they'll be after you like a swarm of bees!" Ramona opened her mouth as if she would indeed alert the valley below.

"Wait! Listen!" In his discomfiture, the man let go of both wrist and bridle. Ramona chose the opportunity to wheel the horse away. The would-be thief ran a few stumbling steps, and fell down.

Ramona looked back, then reined in. Sliding from the saddle, she walked to where he struggled to rise.

"You're hurt." It was a statement, not a question.

"Just a sprain," he said, his teeth clenched. Then, surprisingly, a slender arm went about his waist. His own arm, on the hurt side, was lifted and laid across a pair of small shoulders. Ramona supported him until they reached a stone that would serve as a seat, and eased him down.

"We've got to get that boot off. It might be broken."

He shoved her away. "Leave it be! Get it off and I'll never get it on again. It's not busted. A bit crook, that's all. For God's sake, let me be!"

"I've got to get you down to the station. Aunt Tamsen's as good as a doctor—"

"Oh, lord," he groaned. "Can't you get it through

24

your bloody head! I can't show my face anywhere. The police are onto me. If I'm caught, I'll be shot—or else rot in gaol for a dozen years!"

"Have you—killed someone?"

"Not yet," he said ominously. "Look! Take your flaming horse! Go home! I'll get on mine and ride him until he drops. I'll crawl the rest of the bloody way! Just give me a chance. Pretend you never saw me. Now, go away!"

Ramona studied his mount. It grazed in a clump of acacia down a gentle slope. And it was limping badly. If it were ridden too far, it would be crippled permanently. She turned her luminous dark eyes on the stranger.

"You can't take my horse, but I will lend him to you."

The man's head jerked up with an expression of incredulity. The girl was serious. She meant what she said. After all his worry and scheming to steal a mount, the gray was being handed over and all he needed to do was say, "Thank you, Ma'am."

Minutes later, he was astride the animal, a leather bag of cooked meat in his hand. Upon learning that he hadn't eaten for several days, Ramona decided the dingo pup could afford to miss a day.

"I've never met a girl like you," the stranger said. "You won't turn me in?"

She shook her head. "You will bring him back?" She put her hand on the gray's flank and looked up at her rider with an expression that was half fear, half plea.

"This time, two weeks," he promised her. And he would. Never in his life had he failed to keep his word.

Ramona watched him go. She would say nothing about their meeting. She didn't want the newcomer killed—or for him to kill anyone from the station. She shivered at the thought that it might have been a man he'd waylaid. Her father. Uncle Dan. Dusty. All might have turned out differently then. She would have to practice a little deception, as she did with the dingo. In a way this man was like the dingo. He had the look of having been persecuted.

The problem now was how to get the lame horse down to the paddock without being noticed. Once there, it would be all right since no one would think to look at its brand. There, she could tend to its injured leg.

She knew the schedule at the station. She would wait for the hour when the jackaroos would be in the cookshack at their evening meal. Tamsen would be setting out food. Uncle Dan would be washing up—a cardinal rule for the men in the main house at the station. Dusty and Nell had probably eaten earlier, but would be settled into a companionable game of two-handed poker. The abos, if they paid any attention to the comings and goings of their employers' family, would say nothing.

When the time came, she caught up the injured beast and led it down the declivity opening into the valley. Everything went as she had planned. She was able to rub the horse's leg with liniment and return to the house with just enough time to wash up and change before the evening meal.

Normally a girl of healthy appetite, Ramona picked at her food. She wondered why she couldn't erase the bearded face of the man riding somewhere in the darkness from her mind. She was used to men, having fended off more than one of the young, unmarried jackaroos. Unlike Missie, she wasn't given to romanticizing. Yet his image stayed between her eyes and her plate. There was something different about him. And she didn't even know his name.

"Where did you go today, Ramona?" With a start, the girl lifted her eyes to Tamsen.

"For a ride," she said vaguely.

Dan Tallant put his fork down, a slight frown beneath his dark brows. "I'd rather none of you girls went too far afield."

"I'm careful," she said defensively. "I watch for snakes."

"I'm not worried about snakes. A hand from the Booradabie came through early this morning. A week or so ago, they lost a number of horses. Bushrangers. They say Ned Kelly's been seen in the vicinity.

Ramona kept her head down as her uncle explained that they were not to be frightened, though it was wise to remain close to the station. Young Kelly and his family had been the target of police brutality for years. The latest episode, which had occurred last month, might have been enough to drive him around the bend.

A probationary constable, Alexander Fitzpatrick, had imbibed too much. He got an idea to go to the Kelly house to arrest Ned's brother, Dan. There was an altercation in which Fitzpatrick claimed he was shot at by Ned Kelly, a Kelly brother-in-law, and a neighbor. Supposedly, young Dan stole his gun. And the policeman wove a yarn, saying Ned Kelly's mother, Ellen, had tried to kill him.

Everyone knew Fitzpatrick as a liar and a larrikin. And it could be proven that the bushranger was far away at the time. But, on his word, the law came looking for the Kelly brothers. They managed to escape into the hills. But the brother-in-law, the neighbor, and Ellen Kelly, a baby at her breast, were in prison, awaiting trial on the basis of Fitzpatrick's accusations.

"Dan!" Tamsen's dark eyes were starred with tears. "Can't we stop things like that from happening?"

Tallant shrugged. "Not while so many of the police are criminals themselves. Or while it's possible for squatters to trump up charges against the small farmer. There's the other side of the coin too, Tamsen. These bushrangers are looked up to, made heroes by a lot of people. We've got to keep our wits about us. One criminal act doesn't excuse another."

Ramona's voice, when she spoke, was hoarse and muffled. "Uncle Dan, have you ever met this—this Ned Kelly?"

"I've never met him, but I've seen him. A very good-looking young fellow. Tall, well set up. Brown beard. Nice eyes."

The girl's spoon clattered to the floor. She stood up, her mouth quivering. "I'm sorry, Aunt Tamsen. I'm not hungry. I think I'll finish up my chores."

She escaped to the dairy shed, where she stood skimming the golden clots of cream from the crocks, then putting them into another container with a blob of sour cream for a starter. In the morning, it would be sour enough to churn. She poured the milk into several buckets and carried them to the calf pen. There, she began with milk on a finger to induce each small animal to finally lower its head to drink from the bucket. It was a job she loved, even though she was often showered with milk.

Tonight, however, her heart wasn't in it. And she didn't sing as she searched nests for eggs deposited by dilatory hens. Ramona went to bed, but couldn't sleep.

When she finally dreamed, it was of a black and starless sky. And something in it was coming toward her, something she couldn't quite see. And when it neared, she saw it too well, in horrifying detail. It was Ned Kelly's face, older looking, a little worn, but relaxed and calm. It canted a little to one side, as if the invisible column supporting it no longer held.

But the eyes! The eyes! They were wide, without expression. Dead! And around the face the darkness! This was what she had felt, why he had haunted her—

She woke, her cheeks wet, and went to the window. Outside was the same familiar landscape. A cold wind rustled in the dry leaves of the wattle. From the creek came a rhythmic booming. Kangaroo. The insane laugh of a kookaburra rose over the other night sounds. Shivering in her thin gown, Ramona made her way back to bed.

A week later, a horse with the Booradabie brand was returned to its rightful owner, accompanied by a letter from Daniel Tallant. The animal had been discovered in his own paddock. God only knew how it had gotten there. But he was taking the advice the jackaroo from Booradabie had brought to him some time before, and doubling the guards around his own stock. They were armed, with orders to shoot to kill.

Chapter 4

May moved out and coldhearted June took her place. The air crackled with dry cold; frost, iron-hard, formed on the ground. The pools of water in the riverbed were glazed with ice. The crust on the square, man-made reservoirs froze each morning.

Ramona, to avoid having anyone notice the gray was missing, climbed to the cliff above the valley each day, afoot. The dingo puppy, warm from his small den in the rocks, licked her hand in gratitude for the bounty she carried, warming her freezing fingers.

Other than Ramona's daily excursion, the women remained close to the house, passing much of their time in mending, each with her own thoughts and concerns. Ramona had begun to fear Ned Kelly would not return. She had been frightened since the night of her dream, certain that he was dead. Even the roaring fire in the big fireplace along one wall failed to warm her. Finishing a hem, she looked at it critically, then tossed the garment to one side, reaching for another. Her own voice, when she spoke, surprised her.

"Aunt Tamsen—"

Tamsen looked up, her lovely face madonnalike beneath the softly drawn back hair. "Yes, Ramona?"

"Do you believe in second sight?"

Seeing the earnest expression on the girl's face, Tamsen took her time in answering. "I don't know, dear. I've never seen any proof—"

Ramona relaxed, and Missie entered into the conversation for the first time that evening. "I do. I read this story about a woman who dreamed she had blood all over her—" She paused, striving to untangle a length of thread.

"And then what happened?" Ramona asked.

"She killed her husband."

Seeing Ramona's stricken look, Tamsen said, hastily, "But this is fictional, isn't it? Only a story?"

Missie inclined her head, sullenly. She'd made a mistake trying to enter into the conversation. Aunt Tamsen made her sound like a fool. Well, she wouldn't try it again! How she longed for her private place in the salt cedar ring by the creek. It was the only place she felt she could be herself. Oh, if it would only grow warmer—

She'd done it this time, Tamsen thought to herself. For the first time since Arab left, Missie had opened up. And in her concern for Ramona, she'd cut her short, made her contribution to the conversation seem insignificant and silly. She hadn't meant to do it, but something had been troubling Ramona, lately, something so dreadful that the girl had circles beneath her eyes. She hadn't been eating. Probably not sleeping either. Not knowing her problem was what worried Tamsen. Missie's was quite clear; she was a middle child with a younger sister who was the center of her doting mother's attention.

Tamsen sighed. "The story sounds very interesting, Missie. Why don't you tell it to us? I'd like to hear it."

"I'm going to bed." Missie's voice was sullen. She put her stitching aside, stood, and left the room.

Tamsen looked at Ramona, bent to her own work, seeing the way her long dark hair fell forward, exposing the nape of a vulnerable neck. How fragile her niece was!

When she was Ramona's age, she was singing for money in a cantina in Texas, fighting off the advances of border ruffians, and all the while trying to keep Em and Arab from knowing what she was doing to put food on the table.

It hadn't been all bad. The sensation she'd felt, knowing she held a roomful of men in the palm of her hand! It sent a thrill through her even now—

Amused at herself, trying to quell the memory, she rose to put on the pot for a cup of tea. One of the old tunes ran through her mind. She began to hum it, unconsciously, a word or two slowly returning to her. Lost in her reverie, she assumed the pose of confident beauty that had been hers, head thrown back, arms lifted to an imaginary audience, hips swaying in a seductive way.

The sound of an indrawn breath stopped her short. Ramona was staring at her, wide-eyed. Dear God, what had she been thinking of! Her cheeks crimsoned.

"Aunt Tamsen! I didn't know you could sing like that!" Ramona's voice was filled with wonder and adoration. "Oh, Aunt Tamsen! You looked so beautiful! Please —sing some more."

Tamsen, still blushing, begged off. And after a cup of tea, Ramona went to bed. Tamsen sat quietly, waiting for Dan to come in. She'd had the growing feeling that Arab's daughters were not the only ones with problems.

Dan had seemed so nervous lately. Edgy. And he'd been home longer than he'd ever been during the dry. Oh, he'd made a token try at running the station just after they'd purchased it. But then he'd gone off opal hunting in Queensland. Opals had been her rival, here. True, they were lovely things with their hearts of fire, their flashing rainbows of sapphire, greens and gold. But they'd taken her man from her for months on end. They'd become a compulsion.

She sighed, thinking of the time he'd spent searching

other areas. He'd found black opals on a ridge near the coast; milky white ones with a gentle iridescence somewhere in the hot red center of the country. She could only hope they would one day become as valuable as he believed.

The gems were not entirely to blame, of course. Dan had always needed a challenge. Pitting himself against this raw red country was something he couldn't resist. Of all the men in the world, she had chosen one she had to keep letting go—because she loved him.

Now he was wanting to go again. She knew it from the way he guiltily tried to avoid conversation during the day; the way he made violent love at night, as if he needed this to remember.

He had not yet come in. She would go to bed. He would wake her with a touch. There would be no talking, then, only desperate, passionate protestations of love.

The bed was soft, but cold without his presence. She pulled his pillow close, cuddling it in her arms. Still, she could not sleep.

Nearby, there was another who shared Tamsen's wakefulness. In the circle of salt cedars, Missie's special secluded spot, an aborigine, strange to the area, squatted beside what appeared to be a shallow grave. In the rectangular hole he had dug lay the body of a woman, semiconscious, a baby at her dry breast. It mewled and whimpered, and finally twitched in fretful sleep.

The man and woman were of the same coloring; an inky black with an overlay of white delineating the fine facial bones. Their tawny hair was matted, bleached by the desert sun. Their story was a sad one.

On February 22, 1874, their people had attacked the telegraph station at Barrow Creek. They were driven back, but white men were killed. A force of police and white bushmen set out to avenge the dead, killing every aborigine they could find; man, woman, or child.

The man had fled with his father—all his uncles were known as father—to a peak in the Hart's Range, east of Barrow Creek. There, the greatest massacre of all had taken place. He had fallen with the others, a bullet in his shoulder. And a big-eyed girl, granddaughter of a nulungery, or medicine man, who had hidden in a cave with her grandfather, crept out to tend him.

The boy to whom she'd been betrothed as an infant was dead, as was the girl the wounded boy was soon to marry. The nulungery, knowing of his background, studied the signs and announced that they must marry, and leave the place of death.

Two fire sticks were tapped and placed before the young man. His bride came to him, and together they kindled a fire. They were wed. They went into the desert, leaving the nulungery behind, and became one of the wandering nomadic families, living on lizards, goannas, grubs, an occasional rat or dingo.

The dry spring took its toll in Australia's arid center. The woman gave birth. In search of food and water, they crossed salt pan and gibber toward the place of rivers.

Then, on a cold night, something had crawled into the woman's chest. He could hear it rattling there. And he knew he must find a nulungery: a medicine man who might send a lizard into her body to withdraw the evil; or, if a lizard were the culprit—a lizard, crystal, bone or charmed object—he would suck it out—

He had carried his wife and child for many miles. Then, meeting a black brother in the bush, he'd learned there was a small aboriginal settlement at the Billabong station. He'd brought her here, leaving her in this shelter, and crept toward the little cluster of humpies farther down the creek. Peering through a bush, he'd seen them;

his people dressed in soiled white man's clothing, a white man talking with them.

His heart thundering in his chest, he'd returned to the sick woman and the child. He'd done the best he could for them. He scooped out a long, shallow hole and built small smokeless fires in the bottom of it. When they burned to coals, he covered them with a thick layer of sand, making a warm bed on which to deposit her limp body. He lay the baby at her breast.

He should leave them here. It was the aboriginal way, to leave the helpless behind. But she had stayed at his side once. And to the aborigine, who had no concept of time, yesterday was today; today, tomorrow.

He did not know her name. She did not know his. Since that day when hills and rivers ran with the blood of their people, their names had not been spoken, nor had the names of the dead, thus giving them a double protection as they hid, not only from the white man's wrath, but from the spirits that surely roamed the earth seeking vengeance.

He was only Husband. She was Wife. And the baby was Child.

For a long time, he squatted at his wife's side. Frost settled on his black body, but he did not feel the cold. It, like heat, flies, hunger and thirst, was merely another thing to bear. Finally, his head fell forward, chin on chest, and he slept. He was still asleep when the sky turned gold with the morning.

When the first light touched her window, Missie was out of bed in a flash. Last night, she'd been sorry after she'd flounced off in a sulk, and she'd come back to apologize. She'd stopped short at the sound of Aunt Tamsen singing. Peeping from around the door, she'd seen her aunt, face glowing, posed as if for an audience.

A new thought had struck her. Maybe she had actually *enjoyed* that sinful past that everybody—except Dusty—kept so quiet about. It was like a revelation! Her Aunt Tamsen, who always seemed so one-dimensional! But was she *really?*

Missie was dying to get hold of her notes!

Donning a couple of flannel petticoats, a woolen gown and stockings, she managed to dress without waking Ramona and slipped from the house. Frost crunched beneath her boots as she walked through the sleeping valley toward the spot that was her own. Her cheeks were glowing in the sharp air as she reached the circle of cedar and squeezed her way to the center.

There she stopped, the breath leaving her body as though she'd suffered a blow. A—a grave! A dead woman and a baby! For a moment, she stood poised, blood pounding in her temples at the shock of what she'd stumbled upon. Then a trickling of sand into the grave brought her eyes upward. Beyond it stood a naked black man, his eyes wild, a spear raised to throw—

She opened her mouth to scream, but no sound came out. Her feet were leaden with fear, rooted to the ground, as determination formed on the aborigine's face and his arm drew back to drive the weapon home.

Then they both flinched at a small sound: a baby's cry, weak and pitiful. Missie tore her eyes from those of the savage and looked toward the grave. The child wasn't dead. It was moving. Dear God!

She whirled on the man. "Put that thing down," she said sharply.

Though he didn't understand the words, something in her tone made him obey. Exhausted, desperate, half sick, himself, he wavered for a moment, then backed away.

Missie dropped to her knees and gathered the baby

in her arms. "Poor little thing," she crooned. "Poor little thing!" Then the woman moved, and Missie touched her face. Despite the cold, it was burning to the touch.

She shook her finger at the woman's husband. "You stay here!" she said. Then she ran for the station, as fast as her legs would carry her, pounding on the first door she came to.

George Reade, boss cow-cocky, opened it to find the little girl from the main house, a black baby in her arms. He shook his head, dazedly, certain that he was still dreaming.

Much later, it was Ramona's turn to be surprised. She woke to find her bedroom full of people. George Reade was depositing a naked black woman in Missie's bed. Missie was holding a—a baby! And in the doorway, two red-faced jackaroos held an aborigine, pinioned by both arms.

With a gasp, Ramona slid down, drawing the covers up beneath her chin. Missie had heard her. She turned. "She's awfully sick, Ramona. I'm going to give her my bed. I'll find something to make one for the baby." She turned and looked toward the dark-skinned man, who stood, head down. "I just don't know what to do with him."

Ramona looked too, then averted her eyes. "For a beginning," she said tartly, "I'd send him to the abo quarters—to get some trousers on."

Chapter 5

A few days later, Ramona climbed the path that led to the top of the ridge. She was feeling easier in her mind about Missie. The girl had bloomed, taking a proprietary view toward the sick aborigine and her child. Missie had something of her own to love and care for.

Aunt Tamsen had been upset at first. Abo standards of cleanliness were not her own. But after she saw the invalid and baby, she recapitulated, helping Missie to put a tent over the bed, carrying steam kettles. The whole bedroom stank with a mixture of goanna oil and eucalyptus that old Wyuna brought in from the settlement. The treatment had been effective. But as soon as the woman was well, the room would have to be aired, the mattress on Missie's bed burned.

Ramona hoped it could be accomplished before her mother came home. Mama would have a fit at finding an abo in the bedroom her daughters shared. She was always so terrified that Luka would catch something.

She wondered where they would go, the man, woman and child. They were of a different tribe than the station people, being of the Kaiditj people at Barrow Creek, according to old Wyuna.

"Dem Kaiditj *myall*," she stated, positively. "Kill'im

white mans." She made a sign as if pressing a telegraph key. "We don't want nussing trouble here."

After tending the sick woman, Wyuna decided this particular group was, "Mebbe not so myall." The baby brought another change of opinion. "Dey mebbe-so good-feller."

Wyuna's attitude was very important. It would influence the rest of the local tribe. Uncle Dan and Papa could give the strangers permission to remain at the settlement, but the real welcome had to come from the station blacks themselves.

Ramona frowned, stumbling in her preoccupation. For Missie's sake, she prayed the newcomers would remain. But she had made herself a promise. She wouldn't let herself worry over anything that couldn't be helped. She would close her mind to those dark feelings of impending doom that had been troubling her. All she wanted now was the return of Cloud, her gray. Surely the man who took him would keep his word. And this was the day he'd promised to bring Cloud back. She'd counted and recounted, fearful of making a mistake. When she reached the top of the cliff, she was certain she had erred. There was no one to be seen. The dingo pup scampered from his hidey-hole, and caracoled about her feet, barking joyously.

"Will," she said, "I'm glad to see *you*." For once, there was no conviction in her tone.

Ned Kelly, unknown to her, had been waiting for some time. From his mother, he'd learned an important thing. "Never trust anybody, Ned, unless they're blood kin. Then be careful." Time and circumstances had proven her to be right. He sheltered the gray and a led horse in the copse and stood with them, watching as Ramona topped the path.

His heart bounded at the sight of her, yet he remained where he was, unmoving. He had been watching for a boyish figure clad in men's clothes. Instead, he saw a girl in a red woolen gown, a lacy shawl about her shoulders. Her skirts and hair were windblown. And she was just about the prettiest sight Ned Kelly had ever laid his eyes on. That fact held him in his place of concealment.

A trap, he thought. This was the way they would do it. The girl as bait to entice him from his hiding place. Then he would find himself surrounded—

After a few long moments he soft-footed toward her, eyes watchful, his hand ready for his gun.

Her first inkling that she wasn't alone came when the pup growled and slunk toward his den, with an instinctive distrust of humans, other than the one who fed him. Ramona whirled. He had come! Her face alight, she ran to meet him.

"Ned! Ned Kelly! You did come!"

He was stiff for a moment, then the tension went out of him. He grinned. "I see you've troubled yourself to learn my name."

"My uncle told me who you were," she stammered, cheeks crimsoning. "I mean, he described you—and I guessed."

His face went still. "He knows I took your horse? You told him?"

"Of course not!" She went on to explain about the rider from Booradabie, who spread the word regarding that station's stolen stock. He'd claimed it was done by the Kellys—

Ned's eyes were dancing. "Rumor," he sighed. "The Kellys are always blamed."

"Perhaps truthfully so," she retorted. "The horse you brought here carried the Booradabie brand! How do you explain that?"

"Fair caught," he admitted. "And by such a pretty girl. What have you there?" His eyes were on the string bag she carried. She opened it to show him, thanked by the delight in his eyes. Again, she had raided the pantry, bringing a number of sandwiches, a tin of biscuits, some dried fruit and a jar of cold milk.

The sun had warmed. There was no need for her shawl. She spread the feast on it and they sat together on a sun-warm rock. As they ate, she couldn't help thinking how boyish this so-called dangerous criminal was. By turns, he was brash, talkative—and shy.

In turn, new emotions plagued Ned Kelly. He'd grown up, seeing the kind of life his mother and sisters were forced to live. And he'd made a decision. There was no place in his way of living for a woman. There would never be.

But this was the way it might have been. He might have been an ordinary bloke, on an outing with a lovely girl, hoping for the opportunity to slide an arm about a slim waist, steal a kiss from a warm, soft mouth. At the thought, his body was racked with a yearning ache that he quickly subdued. What a bloody mess that would be! A bushranger and a squatter's daughter!

Ramona offered him another sandwich. He took it, cursing his trembling hands, conscious that she had been talking while his mind wandered.

She was telling him about the finding of an aborigine trio. He swore under his breath, and she stopped, looking at him in bewilderment. She couldn't know how he hated the black buggers—employed by the police, their tracking abilities had brought more than one bushranger to the rope.

"They ought to be killed off," he growled. "The whole flaming mob of them!"

"That's a dreadful thing to say," she gasped. "They're people! Human beings! And they've been persecuted—"

"You don't know what persecution means!" He was

standing now, the rapport between them gone. "The police have been at me since I was fourteen years old." He turned on her. "You're talking to a man who's been in jail. My brothers, uncles, friends! They've all been there! And now my mother, innocent of anything except loving her sons! She's in jail, waiting trial for a crime she didn't commit. They hauled off my brother-in-law, too. And my sisters are being harassed. Good God, don't try to tell *me* about *persecution!*"

His sudden movement, his angry voice, frightened away the sparrows that had clustered for the crumbs from their feast. The dingo had crept close to Ramona's skirts, but now he whimpered, slinking toward his den, stomach to the ground. Ned Kelly pointed toward the cringing animal.

"Look at him! Every man's hand is against him. There's a bounty on dingo scalps. Nobody ever told him, but he knows! So he belly-crawls into a hole! Well, by God, Ned Kelly won't belly-crawl for anybody—"

"Ned, please!" Ramona had risen, too. She put a staying hand on his arm, feeling the muscles quiver and bunch at her touch. "Don't spoil things. It's such a nice day."

At the sight of her upturned, pansylike face, the huge pleading eyes, the anger melted in him, leaving him weak in his bones. He was marveling at the power of a woman over a man as she drew him back to sit on the warm stone in the sun. For a moment he was unable to speak, then he drew a deep breath.

"Tell me about your family," he said. "What are your people like?"

She described her parents, now visiting in Melbourne with her Aunt Em. Her father was not the owner of Opal Station, she explained. He only worked for Uncle Dan and Aunt Tamsen, managing the place. She and Missie had been born in San Francisco, which made them Americans. Her little sister, Luka, was—well, *different*. She was born on the big island of Hawaii, at the height of a volcanic eruption. Sometimes Aunt Tamsen said she was the child of the Goddess, Pele—

As she chattered on, telling whimsical tales of her family, Kelly sensed the love in her voice. Apparently, Tamsen Tallant was the focal point of the station life, yet it was a close-knit group, living in comparative comfort in a raw land that didn't lend itself to a life of ease.

Ordinarily, he would have felt a grudge against people of this type; the grudge of the have-not against the haves. But Ramona led him so gently into the lives of those about her that he felt he knew them: studious, frustrated Missie; Luka, as lovely and elusive as a moonbeam.

So unlike his own family. He shut his eyes, seeing his mother's tired face, the hard lines that deprivation and sorrow had put around her mouth. His sister, Maggie, too young to be so careworn; six children, her husband in jail awaiting trial. And Kate—saucy Kate, her own lovely face smooth and hard. Kate could take care of herself. And she would never weep over any man.

A sudden cold wind rattled in the dry bush grass. A stirring whisper as of small dry bones. A pall had settled over the day, as if putting a period to it. Kelly stood once more. Picking up Ramona's shawl, he shook it free of crumbs and twigs, and placed it around her shoulders. Together, they walked toward the copse where the horses waited. Cloud nickered and nosed at Ramona. She put her arms about his neck, hugging the big gray with delight. Kelly could see the depth of her sacrifice in letting the animal go as she did.

"Thank you," he said huskily.

"Thank *you* for bringing him back."

For a moment, they were both quiet, realizing this was the moment of parting. Ramona broke the silence.

"Ned, I know I have no business to say this—but pretend I'm one of your sisters. Please—Please give up all these wrong things you're doing. Go in and give yourself up and stand trial for what you've already done. My Uncle Dan will help you. Maybe they'll let you go free on his responsibility—"

He stiffened at her last words. No man was going to go his bloody word on Ned Kelly's behalf. "Forget it," he said harshly.

"Think about it," she begged. "Maybe we can talk more the next time you come."

"There won't be a next time."

Ramona's eyes widened, her face going white. He regretted his rough tone. "There can't be a next time," he said, rather desperately. "Look, they've got my mother in jail. She's bound to be given a sentence when they have her trial. If she is, I'm going to pull off something big enough to have the whole police force looking for me. Big enough to have them all wanting me behind bars."

"But—why?"

"Then I'll send them a letter, offering to give myself up if they'll let her go. They'll never catch me, otherwise."

"Oh, Ned!"

For a moment, they stared at each other, her eyes wide with horror, his dark with a tragic determination. A cold wind shook the tree above them, showering down dry twigs and leaves. He raised one hand to brush them from her hair.

"Good-bye," he said.

Mounting his horse, he rode away. She watched after him, eyes brimming. The gray horse nuzzled her shoulder as the skies darkened and a crow flew, carking, before a sudden freezing gust. It was time to return home.

That night, she lay listening to Missie's sobbing. The aborigine man had built a wurley in the settlement, and

45

had come for his wife and child. It was better this way, Aunt Tamsen said. The woman, among her own kind of people, would recover more rapidly. But for a little while, they had been Missie's own, to love and to care for. Now only the faintest odor of goanna oil and eucalyptus remained to show they had ever been there.

Finally, Ramona rose and went to sit beside her sister, patting her quivering shoulders with loving understanding. She knew what it was like, this wrenching sense of loss.

She wished her mother would come home.

Chapter 6

Arab Narvaéz had no intention of returning home before she was forced to. When she arrived at Em's, gathered into her oldest sister's warm embrace, she forgot about Opal Station. It existed only in the back of her mind, like a bad dream. True, it was luxurious as outback stations went, but she had forgotten life could be like this: gentle, ordered. No fearsome aborigines just across the creek, curdling her blood with the sounds of their corroborees. No smell of livestock drifting on the wind. No dust, no flies—

Stepping back from Em, she'd looked at her daughter and down at her travel-soiled clothes, and burst into tears. "Oh, Em! Your house is so beautiful! You look so young—and look at us!"

Immediately, she had entreated Em to take her shopping, and she'd discovered the firm of Alston & Brown, at the corner of Collins and Elizabeth streets. She'd outfitted herself and Luka, using all the money Juan had given her, along with some borrowed from Em. He would be upset when he found out, but it was worth it. After all, Mrs. Emmeline Courtney was a pillar of society in Melbourne. They couldn't afford to be a disgrace to Em.

Now her old things hung in the back of the closet,

cleaned and pressed. She'd wanted to throw them away, but Juan had objected: "I like you in that," he said, pointing to an old woolen frock coat. "Besides, you'll need them when we get home. We can't afford too many new things."

But Arab was thrilled with her new purchases. She looked at them spread across the bed, her eyes shining. For today's outing with Em and Luka, she had chosen to wear a walking costume in mushroom-colored wool in a style known as "polonaise." The undersleeves, the piping at the seams and knife-pleated trimmings were of a soft russet that complemented her hair. The princess front of the dress was fastened to the knees with hooks and eyes, and there was no boning. Beneath it, she would wear a long corset to mold her figure into the day's fashion, and a bustle supported by layers of stiff frills mounted on a straight-fronted petticoat. To the left side of the waist, there was a small watch pocket, and in it she would place the fragile timepiece Em had loaned her.

When Em saw her sister fully dressed, she gave a low whistle of approval. "You look lovely. And so does Luka."

Arab smiled and turned to her youngest daughter. "Luka!" she exclaimed, in loving exasperation, "Luka, come here!"

The slim young girl was on her knees in a window seat, enthralled by the view from the window. She scrambled down and came obediently to her mother.

"You will wrinkle your dress," Arab scolded gently, straightening the short skirt hanging in pleats below a blue sash. The child's stockings were white to match her frock, her shoes French blue with pearl buttons.

A picture-book child, Em thought, watching mother and daughter. And Arab was both too loving and too critical of her. Her concern was due, of course, to the fact that Luka was "different." After the traumatic circumstances of her birth, the girl had developed slowly in the beginning. At ten, she was still like no other child. Em, personally, wondered if she weren't far more advanced. An ancient beautiful soul lay behind those long silver eyes that looked out upon the world with such wonder.

True, Arab had enrolled her in the Messieurs and Miss Roberts School of Dance immediately upon their arrival. And Luka had been sent home as unteachable. Questioning had brought forth the fact that she was graceful, light on her feet as thistledown, obedient—but when the music began, she did not conform to accepted patterns, preferring to weave patterns of her own. Arab had taken the rejection to heart. But was the child so wrong?

Seeing Em's eyes on her daughter, Arab flushed. "She *does* look all right? You *do* think it's wise to take her with us?"

"She looks wonderful. And of course she must go. She'll love Rippon Lea. And the Sargoods have ten children. She'll have a wonderful time."

The women pulled on their gloves and shepherded Luka to Em's carriage.

The curving avenue that led into one of the most beautiful homes in Melbourne, if not the world, was a bower of trees, flowers and fern. Luka leaned from the carriage, enchanted by the magic forest. The leaves were not even dusty!

From the shadow of oaks, elms, poplar, willows, starred here and there with more exotic trees, the carriage came out into the light. Before them, the women saw the large and gracious home of the Sargoods, with its polychrome brickwork and arched, stained-glass windows. Arab caught her breath. "Look, Luka! Oh, look!"

Luka was looking, not at the house, but at the lawns

of velvet green surrounded by flowers. As they alighted from their vehicle, they could hear the music of falling water somewhere in the distance.

Clinging to Luka's hand, Arab followed Em. They were ushered through an entry into a house of indescribable taste and beauty. After they were led to a spacious parlor, Em introduced Arab to their hostess who presided over tea and delicate refreshments. There were other feminine guests, all dressed in the height of fashion. At last, Luka was introduced to a girl near her own age and the two of them escaped to the green lawn, the flowers, to seek out the waterfall.

Arab could not remember when she had had a more enjoyable afternoon. In her heart, she ached to lead a life such as this. One of the guests was an accomplished pianist, entertaining her listeners as they moved quietly from group to group. And finally, Arab was approached by her hostess. "Your sister tells me you sing. Would you honor us?"

Trembling with nerves, Arab obliged, her sweet voice lifting in a simple ballad. After enthusiastic applause, she sang once more.

What would these people think, she wondered, if they knew she'd once been a singer and dancer in the troupe of the infamous Lola Montez? That she knew the words to songs far more torrid than this? Would they still accept her as they did?

And accept her they did. Oh, God! Not to have to go back to the tin-roofed buildings of Opal Station.

As she finished her third song, a whisper of movement caused her to glance in the direction toward which other eyes were turning.

Luka! Luka, wet and bedraggled, a dead frog in her hand and a beatific expression on her face. "I'm going to have a funeral," she said. "I've already dug the grave. Would you like to come?"

There was a stunned silence. Then Mrs. Sargood rose. "Of course," she said. "How nice of you to ask us."

Pale ladies followed their hostess as Luka led her to the lawn. In the middle of its velvet green was a tiny heap of earth. Luka wrapped the small dead creature in her sash, placing it in the hole. Then she said a few sweet consoling words and followed with a hymn, sung in a voice as soft and pure as moonlight.

When she had finished, Arab moved toward Mrs. Sargood. "I'm sorry," she whispered.

"There's nothing to be sorry for, my dear. You have a talented child, with a lovely voice. Do bring her when you come again."

"I've never been so embarrassed," Arab wept, when they reached home and Luka had gone to her room. "Em, I don't know what to do with her! She cries when an animal's sick or hurt—then seems almost glad when its dead!"

"I would say she's smarter than we are," Em snapped. "Do you like to see something suffer? Didn't you hear what she said? "I'm going to sing you into Heaven? Maybe we're the abnormal ones!"

Arab swallowed a sharp retort. It was clear that Em didn't understand. "She—Luka isn't like normal children, Em. I want her to be able to exist in polite society."

Delicate Em managed an indelicate snort. "You saw an example of polite society today. One great lady. One true leader. Mrs. Sargood. Everyone else was reaching for the smelling salts until she accepted Luka's invitation. A bunch of sheep."

The conversation broke off as the door opened to admit a laughing group. Em's daughters, Cammie and Vickie, were home from dancing class. Their arrival coincided with that of their father, Duke Courtney, accompanied by his son, young Scott, and Juan Narvaéz.

"Where's Luka?" Scott asked.

"Yes, where is she?" Vickie chimed in. Cammie's bright eyes scanned the room.

"She's upstairs, changing—" Arab got no further. A small figure appeared at the top of the sweeping staircase, clad only in chemise and drawers.

"Guess what!" Luka cried, her voice shrill with excitement, "Vickie's cat just had kittens in my bed!"

Scott raced toward the stairs, his decorously dressed sisters close behind him. Em looked at the stunned Arabella, her laughter bubbling. "I would say that Luka is a born leader."

That night, the mother and kittens sleeping in a laundry basket, the children abed, the ladies occupied with sewing, Juan and Duke Courtney adjourned to Duke's study. There, Juan signed a number of papers, made out in his and Dan Tallant's name.

"You don't have to do this, you know," Courtney said. "There's no reason I can't just give you what you need. Hell, I owe Tallant more than I can repay anyway."

"Dan insists—and I insist. We've always managed to run the station at a profit—until now. If only we hadn't invested in the freezing machine."

"If it had worked, you'd have been able to buy and sell me twice over," Duke reminded him.

It was true, Juan thought wearily. The machine, invented by Nicolle and Mort, had been erected on the margin of Darling Harbour where it connected with the railway; five miles of iron piping through which liquid ammonia was circulated. The idea was to freeze mutton and beef, transferring it to ships fitted for cold storage, for transport to England.

No longer would cattle have to be shipped alive to land, gradually emaciating, dying one by one. No longer would salt beef spoil, turning slimy in wooden kegs. It was a perfect solution for the cattleman and the shipper.

But on the first attempt, the machinery broke down aboard ship, the precious cargo lost. Though only Juan and Dan were aware of it, Opal Station, on the Billabong, was virtually bankrupt.

"You're not going to tell Tam and Arab?"

Juan shook his head. "Dan feels responsible for the whole thing, though I concurred in it completely. He has never been in debt before, and it's difficult for him to see it in its proper perspective. Since he won't tell Tamsen our situation, I can't tell Arab. You know how women are."

Courtney laughed. "Indeed I do. They would certainly confide in one another. But I know something else. Both Tamsen and Arab would take it like a couple of troupers."

Juan's shrug was indicative of his Spanish blood. "I agree. But you know Dan's pride."

"If I didn't," Duke Courtney sighed, "there wouldn't be all this damn folderol." He touched the papers before him. "And I still want you to make it plain to Dan that the money's his as long as he wants it. And the interest —hell, forget it! If you need any more, it's here."

"We will repay you within a year," Juan said quietly. "We're almost self-sufficient out there. The jackaroos work for little besides board. Dan figures his salary will take care of operating expenses."

"Explain this new job of his to me again. I know it's something to do with the railroad. But, good God! To be gone from his wife for a year!"

It was quite simple. Act Number 26 of 1876 had authorized the formation of a railroad from Port Augusta to Government Gums: two hundred miles of narrow gauge. The first phase had been completed. The rails had reached Wonoka, beyond Hawker, only last year. The second phase, Wonoka to Beltana, would stretch to Beltana by 1880, and on to Government Gums by October, 1881.

The short stretch of rail had fired the imagination of a group of businessmen. They envisioned a transportation system reaching from Adelaide to Darwin, connecting the southern part of the continent with the north. In order to get backing from England, first they had to perform a preliminary survey. They took up a subscription among themselves and hired Daniel Tallant. With his map-making skills and his knowledge of railroads and terrain, he could obtain the data they needed.

Duke Courtney put his head in his hands. "My God! It's equivalent to suicide! It hasn't been all that long since the Burke and Wills expedition! You know what happened to them!"

"It isn't as bad as it sounds. He will work out of the Alice Springs area. There's a telegraph station there, and a small town—Oh, maybe a dozen people—called Stuart. He will have an aide, an abo tracker, camels and cameleers—"

"What does Tamsen think of this?"

"When I left the Opal, he hadn't told her yet."

"The fool," Courtney said softly. "The goddam, stiff-necked, wonderful fool! Juan, I was going to offer you a job running some of my enterprises. Arab would be happier here, and we all love Luka. It would be good for Em. But right now, I think you'd better get the hell back, as soon as you can. Tamsen's going to need you."

Chapter 7

Winter had truly set in at Opal Station. There was a roaring fire in every bedroom to combat the icy wind that blew outside. Debris showered on the tin roof, and the main house creaked with the wind and the cold.

The girls had already retired, seeking the warmth of their woolen blankets, and Tamsen, clad in a soft flannel gown, was brushing out her mass of long black hair, preparatory to braiding it for the night.

Normally, it was a relaxing occupation, but her mind dwelt on the happenings of the last few days. George Reade, the head stockman, had been savaged by a stallion he was trying to break. Badly injured, he was taken across country and down to Melbourne by train. He would live, but he wouldn't return to work for a long time, if ever—

None of the jackaroos could take his place. Bob and Jim were old and ignorant, though obedient to orders. O'Brien drank too heavily. Matthews and Davis were fiddle-footed, always ready to move on to what might be greener pastures. Luke and John were little more than boys; from a family of starving settlers, they had cleared out so that there would be more food on the table for their younger brothers and sisters.

Together with the abos who were willing to work,

they were a motley crew. Dan had been busy from daylight to dark, just trying to keep them all in line. How would he manage now, with George Reade gone away?

Tamsen was also worried about both her nieces: Missie with her sullen silence, Ramona at the edge of her nerves. Who would ever believe that serene Ramona would burst into tears at a word?

Lord, she wished Juan and Arab would hurry home.

She brushed mechanically at her waist-length hair, her mind far away. It wasn't until Dan caught a fistful of it and pulled her head back to kiss her that she knew he'd come in.

The kiss was long and lingering. Then he placed a hand at either side of her head, forcing her to meet her own eyes in the mirror.

"Look at you!" His voice was husky. "Almost fifty, and you still look like a girl. Oh, God, Tam! How I love you!"

She put up her hands to cover his. They were cold and trembling. His face, reflected above her own, was pale, his eyes shadowed.

"You're half frozen," she said, alarmed. "I hope you haven't caught a chill. You've been working so hard. Go over by the fire and get warm. I'll be with you as soon as I braid my hair—"

His hand slid down the length of a silken strand. "Don't braid it, sweetheart. Leave it like it is. I like it this way."

Then his hands were under her arms, lifting her, turning her to face him, his eyes dark and intense.

"Tamsen?" It was a question.

The old familiar longing crept through her body, leaving her knees weak as she leaned against him, his muscular arms pressing her closer, closer, until they were one body, one heart, one pulse.

His hands went to the buttons at the high throat of her gown. It slipped to the floor, and he picked her up, carrying her, not to their bed, but to the sheepskin that lay before the fire. He put her down, gently, and stood looking at her for a long moment, seeing the way her dark hair fanned against the white of the soft wool; the reflection of light on a cream olive body, still slim and glowing with youth.

"Tamsen! Oh, God!"

She lay as she was, in a warm, drowsy state, enjoying even this—the waiting, while he undressed. Then she watched the lean bronzed body coming toward her. Her arms reached up to welcome him; to hold him close and warm his cold flesh.

Then he was no longer chilled, but burning against her as she gasped, pulse pounding in her throat. It's the same, she thought, as it has always been with us. Yet each time it's different—better—

"Dan, please—"

The same familiar urgent plea sounded. It was not her own voice, but a stranger's; a woman conscious of nothing but her need.

The fire flame flared and sparked, filling the room with dancing shadows that wheeled and spun against Tamsen's closed eyes. And then she rested, her cheeks wet against her husband's tanned chest.

For a long time they lay still, savoring their love. Then Dan sighed. "I love you, Tamsen. More than anything in the world."

"I think I'd die without you, Dan."

Was it her imagination, or had he stiffened against her? Tamsen slowly returned to a consciousness of an imperfect world. She knew this man; and she sensed he had something to tell her, something that would destroy the incomparable moment they had just experienced. Something she didn't want to hear.

57

With a dreadful need to postpone the thing—whatever it was he had to say—she turned to him, caressing him almost savagely in an attempt to rouse his passion again. He lay on his back, staring at the ceiling, his eyes dark and unseeing, unresponding.

Finally, she sat up, wearily pushing back her mass of tumbled hair, marveling at the steadiness of her tone as she spoke.

"What is it, Dan?" When he didn't answer, she said, "You're going away again. That's it, isn't it?"

He rolled onto his stomach with a groan, and she put a hand on his bronzed shoulder. "I'm sorry, Tamsen. Oh, hell! I'd rather be shot than have to tell you this!"

Slowly the story came out. He'd agreed to do some surveying for a railroad. He would be gone for a year, maybe two—

Dear God! In two years, she would be fifty, he would be fifty-six! Two years out of their lives! Two precious years! "I'm going with you."

"You can't, sweetheart. It'll be rough country, only men. No place for a woman. I'll be working out of the Alice; down to Government Gums, up to Darwin—"

Not only rough country, but dangerous country. "Dan, why are you doing this?" It was a cry of despair.

Again he tensed. Tamsen must never know he'd lost his shirt on the freezing machine gamble. He'd always taken care of her, and he always would. Yet he must give her an answer that would satisfy her.

"It's the—the challenge, I suppose. Doing the kind of work I like best. That I'm fitted for."

"There's the station."

"Hell, Tam! You know it's Juan who runs this place. And what do I do? I go off fossicking for opals. I need a job I can get my teeth into—"

It made sense, Tamsen thought wearily. And hadn't

she been through this before? Hadn't she seen the rest-lessness in Dan's eyes, seen him off with a smile—and welcomed back a rugged man who couldn't get enough of her? But those times were measured in months, not years.

Dan sat up, meeting her eyes at last. Tamsen quailed before the look in them. They were filled with pleading and pain. Something in him was forcing him to go, even though he hated to leave her behind. She could make his going bearable—or know she was responsible for his suffering.

"I can't say I like it, Dan," she said carefully. "But I've never fought anything you wanted to do. I'm not going to begin now."

His face cleared. "Then you'll forgive me?"

"There's nothing to forgive."

His arms went around her and he pulled her down to him in a state of exuberance. She fended off his embrace. She was tired. They finally rose from the sheepskin rug and made their way to bed. Dan slept. There had been so many nights of sleeplessness lately. But Tamsen lay awake, facing the lonely year or two that stretched ahead.

In Melbourne that night, Arab and Juan had almost duplicated the scene. It was Arab who initiated the love-making. She had begun to talk of their meeting, when he was a handsome young man in his uniform, a prince in her eyes, and she a member of the troupe of Lola Montez. From the moment they saw each other, in a Spanish Queen's garden where flowers bloomed to the music of singing fountains, they loved each other; two people en-closed in a glass bubble of enchantment that separated them from the rest of the world.

And suddenly, today was yesterday. He was the prince, she the young dancer who stole him from his realm. He held her, hearing the crystal sounds of falling water, the fragrance of blossoms filling the night air. This was not the mother of three children in his arms, but a dryad—a naiad—a nymph. And he made love to her, as he did on that first day they met.

Afterward, he lay quiet, her arm across his chest making a pattern of silver and gold in the moonlight. "What are you thinking?" she ventured.

"I was remembering the fountain at my home, the colonnades, the way we played together at night beneath the waterfall. The way you looked with the moon in your hair."

"We could have that again, Juan. We could build a home here. Em says you could work for Duke—" Her voice trailed off.

Juan was stunned for a moment, then he grinned in the darkness. Dios! The little minx! Of course her ardor, passionate though it had been, was a prelude to something. He'd come to know his Arabella very well. He didn't mind. The bribe she'd tendered was most rewarding.

"I'm afraid it's out of the question. I have my work at the station."

Arab evaded his reaching hand and flounced to the far side of the bed. He stifled his amusement at his beloved wife, spirited, so irresistible—so transparent. He didn't want her angry with him. And he was not above using a few tricks himself.

"I would move here in a minute," he said, "if the place weren't a pesthole of disease. They've had typhoid epidemics—and I understand there's a new case of small-pox reported on the docks, today. With Luka's delicate constitution—"

He paused. There was no need to go further. Arab sat upright, her red hair tumbling across her shoulders. "Smallpox!"

He turned comfortably on his side. "You'd better get some sleep. It's late." He knew Arab would lie awake worrying all night. It was sufficient punishment for her charming deceit.

He slept and dreamed. In that dream, he and Arabella were walking together in an enchanted garden. Bemused with love, they turned and fell into each other's arms. He lowered his head and sought the warm inviting mouth, but she turned away.

"I've got to pack," she said nervously. "We're going home."

Chapter 8

On the morning of the day that the Narvaéz family returned, Opal Station acquired a new head stockman.

Like most swagmen, he came afoot, walking unhurriedly. In one hand, he carried a tin billy, crusted black from the making of tea. In the other, a water bag. A round, oblong bundle strapped to his back held his worldly possessions.

Unlike the others, he stopped short of the station. Opening his swag, he took out a pair of moleskin trousers and a shirt, both glistening white, and shook them out, spreading them over a mallee scrub. On a flat rock, he set out razor, soap and comb. Then he proceeded to scrub himself from head to toe in one of the standing pools of the Billabong. As he shaved and trimmed his hair and beard, he considered a name for himself. Not a difficult feat for the self-styled, brainiest bloke in Australia. He finally settled on Arthur for a first name. It sounded genteel. L. for a middle initial. Arthur L.—Melvin, a corruption of Melbourne from which he'd departed in such unseemly haste.

Born in the wilds of the outback, he had first been known as little Mick, after Big Mick, his father, who was a former government man, or convict. Whether Big Mick escaped or served his time, his son never knew. All he knew was that the old man was "on the cross," and that he ran a small duffing yard for others like him, where cattle brands and earmarks could be altered on the sly.

How he and his old lady ever got together, the boy never asked. A romantic young schoolteacher, she'd taken up with a dashing youth, unmindful of his past. By the time Little Mick arrived, she was old and embittered. Yet, from her he'd inherited his insatiable desire for knowledge. After all, it was the only way a bloke could get someplace, being smarter than the rest.

From his father, he'd picked up a contempt for the law, and an eye to the main chance. He would confess to his drinking mates, that he was not a mug, but a spieler; that his talents lay in being able to charm the birds out of the trees.

A well-built, handsome man, with dark curling hair, he was completely amoral—and adaptable. He'd done a stint as an actor in Sydney—using the name of Geoffrey Kingman—until he was caught in a compromising situation with the starring actor's wife. Then he'd absconded with the company's funds.

When his money gave out, he presented himself to two doctors in Brisbane, telling them he had medical experience. Researchers from the Pasteur Institute, the doctors were attempting to develop a vaccine for cattle dying of pleuropneumonia.

It hadn't taken them long to discover he'd lied about his credentials, but in the meantime, he'd picked up enough medical terminology to establish himself as a physician in Melbourne.

He applied as a surgeon at Melbourne Hospital, built in Londsdale Street in 1846, through charity donations. Here, buildings were laid out in patchwork fashion; with the Public Library to one side cutting off most of the light and air. Surgical patients lay near the diphtheria wards and not far from the "septic" tents. Effluvia was pumped into underground tanks, then when the tanks were full, into the gutters along the street, where it seeped back into the wards.

Surgeons were scarce. Doctor Church, as Mick was known there, was an admirable addition to the staff. He emulated Jelly-Belly Jim Beaney, whose pudgy hands glittered with diamonds and rubies, as he operated in a bloody frock coat.

He didn't make too many mistakes, he thought now. No more than the rest of the flaming buggers who looked down their noses at him in the end. He couldn't have known that the last female he operated on was the wife of a prominent politico—or that the nurse standing by was her younger sister. Still queasy from drink, the night before, he'd severed an artery.

Outraged by his wife's death, the politico had gone to the trouble of looking up Mick's past. Finding no qualifications, other than a stint in jail, he'd given him the option of getting the hell out of town, or being tried for murder.

Mick was certain no one would testify against him. But the affair had received a lot of publicity. It was best to lie low for awhile. Besides, he missed life in the bush, it was in his blood. So he intended to try for a job at Opal Station. If there wasn't anything there, he'd go on to Booradabie.

Clad in his spotless white garments, he pulled on his latest acquisition, a pair of larrikin boots, their high heels not made for walking. He admired them for a moment. God, his old man would give his eyeteeth for a pair of these—

Then he tossed his soiled clothing into the bush, repacked the swag that held two more sets of white moleskins, and made his way along the creek to the station.

Dan Tallant sat on the corral fence, his heels hooked beneath a rail as he watched young Luke trying to break the stallion that had lost him his foreman. Though only a boy, Luke was perhaps the best rider among the jackaroos. But he wasn't good enough. Maybe nobody was. I would try it myself, thought Dan, but an injury now would cost me the railroad job.

Suddenly the lad lost a stirrup, and Dan leaped to the ground, shouting as he ran. For a moment there was a cloud of choking dust as the roan sunfished and Luke lost his hold, catapulting over the animal's head. The stallion reared with an almost womanlike scream, coming down with his punishing hooves as the boy rolled away.

Then Tallant had hold of the bridle. "Can't hold him much longer, Luke! Hurry!"

There was a sudden easing of the strain. The horse stood still, shivering. A newcomer stood at his other side. His weight had made the difference. Luke rolled under the fence and stood up, bruised, but with nothing broken.

"Hold him a moment," the stranger said. He vaulted into the saddle. "Let him go."

Dan obliged and stood away. The horse turned, baring his teeth, and the rider kicked him in the muzzle, a vicious kick that seemed to stun the animal for a space. Then the bucking began.

"Open the gate," the strange man shouted. Tallant complied, and horse and rider were out of the corral, riding hell-bent toward a grove of trees with low-growing limbs. Reaching the grove, the man in white gracefully slid one foot from a stirrup and lay, one knee hooked across it, along the stallion's side. Past the obstacle, he was upright once more, raking the horse's side with cruel spurs as they disappeared into the distance.

Luke's eyes were shining, his bruises forgotten. "Never seen nuthin' like *that* afore," he whispered in an awed tone.

"I haven't either," Dan confessed. "Maybe we ought to saddle up and follow——"

"He'll make it," the boy said with assurance.

"I think he will."

Within an hour, horse and rider were back, the stallion walking slowly, yielding to the rein. Reaching the corral, the newcomer slid from the saddle. The animal stood, head down, ribs heaving, dripping with sweat. The man was barely ruffled in his clean white clothing.

"Rub him down," he said to Luke. The boy, eyes worshipping, ran to obey. The stranger turned to Tallant.

"I'm Arthur Melvin," he said in a deep, calm voice.

"Tallant, here. Dan Tallant. I owe you my thanks. Where the hell did you come from?"

"I was coming here," Melvin said with a charming, crooked smile. "I walked in, saw what was going on and figured you could use a hand."

Dan mopped his forehead and grinned. "Sure as hell did. But what do you mean, you walked in?" For the first time, he saw the swag lying on the ground. He looked at the man, brows raised. He certainly wasn't representative of the swaggies who dropped by seeking a job or a handout, usually the latter.

Arthur Melvin, managing to look as embarrassed as his cocksure nature would allow, told Dan Tallant his made-up story. He'd purchased a small spread with what he was assured was a perpetual spring, built a small home, and stocked the place with cattle. The water had disappeared in the dry, and the bloody abos started one of their brush fires. He was wiped out. Looking for work.

Dan studied him. There was something about the

man that didn't quite ring true, despite the steady gaze of his light blue eyes. Still, he was a master hand with a horse. And he'd spoken to Luke with authority. And Dan needed a head stockman.

"Come on up to the house," he said. "We'll have a drink and talk a little. I might have something for you.'

When Arthur Melvin left the main house an hour later, he was euphoric. His luck was in again. The salary wasn't much, but he was to have George Reade's house, fairly comfortable looking digs. Best of all, Tallant was going to be away for a year or two. True, his brother-in-law would boss the spread in his absence, but from his name he was some kind of foreigner. There was always a way for a smart foreman to make a little pile for himself.

And the women! The youngest wasn't too much; too thin and intense for his taste. The dark-haired one had potential, but she needed a few years experience on her. But the Tallant woman was a classy sheila. What's more, she knew what the score was. He'd given her a look—the kind that only a woman of a certain type would recognize, and he'd seen her eyes widen and narrow as she studied him.

A bonzer babe. And with her ball and chain away for a long time, who knew what might happen!

From a window, Tamsen watched him cross to Reade's former home, his step a little swaggering. Then she turned to Dan.

"There's something about that man I don't like, Dan."

"He's perfect for the job, sweetheart. He's experienced, the boys will follow his orders. I've never seen his like on a horse—"

Tamsen shuddered, recalling the bold eyes that had touched hers in a blatant invitation, as if recognizing

68

something in her she thought she'd shed long ago. "I still don't think you should have hired him."

"Do you have a reason? Anything other than a hunch? I can tell him I've reconsidered, but I don't know what we'll do—"

What could she say? That she didn't like the way he looked at her? At her age? Ridiculous! It was probably all in her imagination. "I can't put my finger on it," she said feebly. "Maybe it's because he has—what the people here call a kind of *flashiness*.

Dan laughed at her. "Listen to you! You're getting to be a native. You're right. He *is* flash, but that shouldn't keep him from doing the job. Young Luke is already a devoted admirer."

"I suppose you're right. Forget what I said."

He hugged her close. "All I want is for my sweetheart to be well-cared for and happy—until I come home."

"I wish Juan and Arab would hurry home so you can leave," she whispered, her cheek against his beating heart.

"You're trying to get rid of me?" He held her away, his eyes daring her to say so.

"No. But the sooner you go, the sooner you'll be back for good. And it's safer travelling now than in the wet."

"I'll take care, sweetheart. Don't you worry."

She made an excuse to busy herself in order to hide her tears.

Her wish was granted that very evening. Long before the carriage bearing the Narváez family pulled into sight, old Wyuna came to the house to announce their arrival. Apparently, a cloud of dust, invisible to Tallant's eyes and Tamsen's, not only proclaimed a horse-drawn vehicle, but the number of horses and the number of occupants. When Juan, Arab in her mushroom-colored traveling frock, and Luka, adorable in a white sheepskin coat, hat, and matching muff alighted, it was to meet the combined force of the entire family.

Tamsen hugged Arab; Ramona and Missie fussed over Luka, and Juan give Tallant a nod that signified success. Dusty was overcome with emotion, and Nell practically blubbered as she went from one of the newcomers to the other, finally pumping Juan's hand vigorously.

"Dammit," she bawled, "it's good to see you home! I was feared Dan'd hightail it afore you got here. Skeert he'd leave us high 'n dry with that sonofabitch!"

Juan's startled eyes met Dan's. "I'll explain later," Dan told him. "Nell doesn't like our new foreman."

"What happened to Reade?"

"It's a long story. We'll go into it later. Right now, let's get you inside."

The carriage was unpacked, while Tamsen and the girls finished preparations for the meal they'd started when Wyuna sounded the first alarm. In the midst of the confusion, presents were handed out. A lapel watch for Nell. She attached it to her enormous bosom, straining her chins to look at it. A blue woolen scarf for Dusty, that matched his fading eyes. Bolts of material for Tamsen and the girls. A pipe for Dan.

The gifts distributed, they flocked to the table. Arab told excitedly of Em's house; the shopping in Melbourne; her visit to the Sargoods' mansion, Rippon Lea. Luka chimed in from time to time, telling of a lake with black swans, peacocks on a green lawn. Nell, pleased at having the rest of her adopted family home, kept interrupting with comments that sent them all into roars of laughter; while Dusty sat back, enjoying his beloved companion's wit.

No one noticed that Missie was unusually quiet.

70

Finally, during a lull, she blurted, "Did you bring me any books? Or the writing materials I asked for?"

Juan looked at Arab, his eyes questioning. She reddened under his gaze. She had promised, she knew. But the last of her funds had gone to purchase Luka's lovely little coat. And she had truly forgotten.

"I brought materials for new gowns," she said, a little sharply. "You'll be better occupied in sewing for yourself than scribbling all the time."

Luka's voice fell artlessly into the sudden lull, and the moment was glossed over. After the meal, Ramona went to tuck Luka into bed; the men retired to the office, outside, to confer about business; Nell, Arab and Tamsen cleared the table and did up the dishes.

No one saw Missie slip from the house. She crossed the almost dry creek to the aborigine village and went to the wurley occupied by the only friends she considered her own. She had even named them; the man was King, the woman Queenie, the baby, Princess.

The man and woman were outside, squatting by a small fire. Missie sat down on a log beside them. There was a time of companionable silence, then Missie said, "Could I hold Princess, please? Just for a little while?"

The woman looked into the girl's eyes and saw the trouble there. Silently, she rose and entered the flimsy structure, lifting the baby wrapped in a kangaroo hide. She carried her to Missie and placed her in the girl's arms.

Missie's quiet tears splotched the baby's soft fur robe. Everybody had someone. She could only borrow love for a little while.

Chapter 9

The family farewell dinner for Dan Tallant was a solemn occasion. Nell had attempted to brighten the evening with her own particular brand of bawdy humor, but it had been a miserable failure.

Dusty was very quiet. All the girls, Ramona, Missie and Luka, sat sober-faced and on the verge of tears. Arab clung to Juan's arm, secure in the knowledge that he would never leave her as Dan was leaving Tamsen. Juan wasn't the kind of man who needed a challenge to salve his ego.

Tamsen alone seemed to glow. Dressed in a gown that was old, but of a becoming apricot color, she had viewed her wan face in the mirror, then reached for a paintbox, dating back to earlier times. A touch of color on cheeks and lips, a dusting of tawny powder, made her look herself once more. Erect, smiling, she showed no sign that her heart was breaking.

Only Dan knew her appearance was a facade. When dinner was over, the dishes washed and put away, Tamsen remained in the kitchen, finding things to do long after the others had gone to their beds. When she finally joined Dan, he knew, intuitively, that tonight there would be no lovemaking. She seemed exhausted, drained of all

73

emotion. He settled for holding her, comforting her. She curled against him like a lost child.

Now, his sheepskin collar turned up against the biting cold of the gray dawn, swag packed, reins in hand, Tallant looked down at his wife. She wore a long black woolen cloak over her nightdress. Above it, her face seemed carved in marble. He bent to kiss her and she felt stiff and unyielding. Good God! If he'd killed her love for him—

To hell with the station! He'd sell out and meet his bills. Maybe Courtney would give him a job clerking in one of his stores!

"Tamsen—Do you want me to stay? You only have to say so."

"No, Dan. I'll never stop you from doing what you want to do." She smiled, painfully. "Not that I'm all that noble about it. I must admit I've looked forward to us getting old. Then maybe we'd have some years together. Dear God, I've even wished you'd get sick, or hurt—not much, just enough to keep you with me—" Her face twisted. "Let's not prolong this, Dan. I can't stand it."

He reached a hand to touch her cheek, then climbed into the saddle. "I love you, Tamsen."

Her haunted eyes met his. "And I love you."

Reluctantly, he turned his mount along the red path that led toward his destination. He didn't look back. He knew she would still be standing there, a frozen, wind-whipped figure, until he was out of sight.

At last, she turned to enter the house. Her eyes went to his empty chair at the table; the remains of the breakfast she'd made for him; a half cup of cooling coffee.

Automatically, she moved to the big tin pot on the back of the wood stove, pouring a cup for herself. She

74

whirled at a sound behind her, her heart pulsing in her throat. Had he come back?

It was only Missie, looking fragile and childlike in a long flannel gown, her small feet bare.

"Go back to bed, Missie. It's still early. You'll catch your death of cold."

Missie paid no attention to the steady voice. Her wide blue eyes were fixed on Tamsen's white face.

"Why did he leave you, Aunt Tamsen? How *could* he?"

Tamsen's first impulse was to lash out at the young intruder, tell her to mind her own business; to release her frustrations and ease her own pain. But she stopped herself. She knew the child meant well.

"Sit down dear," she sighed.

Missie seated herself primly at the table and folded her hands in her lap. Tamsen put a shawl over the thin shoulders and knelt to tuck the folds of the long gown about two small chilled feet. Then she poured a half cup of the bitter boiled coffee for the girl, lacing it liberally with milk, and brought her own cup to the table.

"You mustn't think less of your uncle, Missie," she said gently. "Some men—are different. Your father likes peace, orderliness, his family around him. Dan thrives on excitement, danger."

"You shouldn't have let him go! You could have made him stay home!"

"He's fifty-four years old," Tamsen said, half to herself. "Maybe that's part of it. He hasn't all that much time left for great adventures." Then, to Missie, "Don't you see? If I'd made him stay here, I would have robbed him of that. He was involved in political intrigue when I met him. It isn't generally known, but his work in Alaska helped the United States to acquire that country. He aided in rebuilding the south, after the war. And, maybe

75

some day, his work in Hawaii will bear fruit. We can't expect a man like that to just settle down, give up all that made him the man he is—"

"What about *you? You*'ve settled down. You sang and danced, had beautiful gowns and jewels. And your parlor for gentlemen made you rich. Why do you have to be a wife, when he can't be a husband?"

"Missie!" Tamsen was on her feet, blood pounding in her head. "What are you saying! What do you know about my life! Who has been telling you such things."

"You were an entertainer. You were a madam, and a—a damn good business woman! I don't see what's so bad about that! And I think it's awful of Uncle Dan to go off and leave you." Missie's chin trembled. She rose from her chair, stumbling a little on the long gown, and headed toward the door of the room she shared with Ramona and Luka, then turned to face Tamsen, her eyes brimming with tears. "I'm *never* going to marry. I'm going to be *somebody,* like you were—once!"

Dear God! Tamsen sank back into her chair, staring numbly into the depths of her cup. How had the child obtained such information! Certainly not from either of her parents. Arab and Juan would rather die than reveal Tamsen's past to their own young daughters. *Nell!* Tamsen's lips tightened. Nell was the only one who would describe Tamsen's career in a way that made it sound like something to be proud of. Nell was a late sleeper due to her old profession. But this was one day she'd rise at dawn.

Tamsen marched across the yard to the small house Nell shared with Dusty. She pounded on the door until the old woman, in a bedraggled pink silk robe trimmed with ostrich feathers, left from her palmier days, answered sleepily.

"Whut's the matter, Tam? Hell, it's still dark—"

76

"What have you been telling Missie about me?"

Nell blinked stupidly. "Missie? About you? Gawdammit, Tam, git to the point. Whut the hell you tawkin' about?"

"Somebody told Missie that I was an entertainer—that I ran a house! It wasn't Juan or Arab, that's for sure. Dan didn't—and I know I didn't. It's not the kind of thing to brag about—"

Nell was stunned, her face as red as a spanked baby, her expression hurt. "Hell, Tam! You know me better'n that!"

"Then—Dusty?"

Nell's laugh rumbled up from her huge frame. The thought of the wispy little man she loved gossiping was too ridiculous to be thought of. "He's more th' strong, silent type," she said with maudlin affection. "Never heerd 'im say more'n ten words at a time, less'n his gawdam tongue wuz oiled."

"Then, who—"

"I figger th' little brat was a-lissening sometime when she hadn't oughta," Nell said promptly. "She ain't whut you'd call nosey, but she's sure ez hell got a bump of curiosity. Left at loose ends like she is, nuthin' t'keep 'er occupied like, she's always around and nobuddy pays any attention."

The anger went out of Tamsen, leaving her limp. "I suppose you're right," she admitted. "But, oh, Nell—what do I do now?"

Nell shrugged. "Fergit it. The damage is done. Ef you don't make nuthin' of it, mebbe she'll fergit it, too."

Tamsen hugged her. "Oh Nell, forgive me! I'm sorry I woke you—and even sorrier I blamed you. I just couldn't think of anyone else who—"

"Aw," Nell said generously, "it's awright. Say, Dan took off, yet?"

Tamsen's arms dropped to her sides. "He's gone," she said, dully.

Nell patted her clumsily. "Ain't the end of th' world.' He'll be back. Got a purty girl a-waitin' fer him, ain't he?"

"Thanks, Nell. You get back to bed. I'd better get on over and start breakfast."

Nell saw her out with a broad smile that faded as she watched the lonely figure walk across the dark grounds. She loved Dan Tallant like a son. But he was sure one gawdam iggerant sonofabitch!

Determined to make the day a normal one, Tamsen set about her chores. First she passed the instructions Dan had left for Arthur Melvin on to Juan, so that he could convey them to the stock boss. Since Melvin was hired, she'd tried to keep out of his sight. She'd probably misread the glance he gave her at first meeting, but she instinctively distrusted him. Though, according to both Dan and Juan, the man was efficient at his job. Far better than George Reade.

That chore done, she turned to other tasks. But no matter where she turned, it was a day when everything went wrong. Arab burned her hand on the coffeepot. The bread didn't rise well, chilled as it was when Missie left a door open. The cream in the churn refused to make butter for several hours; then it didn't seem to be of its usual quality. Ramona reported that the cheeses in the milk shed appeared to be getting worm. Tamsen was preparing to put them into a pickle, when word came that one of the jackaroos had been injured.

Young John's wound looked worse than it was. He'd torn his wrist on a jagged branch. Five stitches with silk thread from Tamsen's sewing box set it right. But in the meantime, while Arab was busy mending a gown for Luka, the stew had burned—

It was late that night, and Tamsen was readying

herself for bed, when she remembered the cheeses. She was weary, but in no rush to crawl into a cold, lonely bed. She dressed again and went to the dairy house, wondering where Dan slept tonight. Probably somewhere in the bush, with only a small fire to warm him. Tears were icy on her cheeks when she opened the dairy door.

She lit a candle and began to work, lowering the cheeses into a salty brine, the enormity of Dan's absence finally beginning to dawn on her. Finished, she was reaching to extinguish the candle when she heard a sound behind her. She turned to find a figure in the doorway.

"Mr. Melvin! You—you frightened me."

"I saw you come out here, and thought maybe I might be of some assistance."

"I'm finished," she said coldly. "There's nothing more to do. So if you will excuse me—"

He didn't move, but remained leaning carelessly against the door facing, the white hat hanging by a cord around his neck framing his confident face. "I'd like you to know that I'm here—to help with anything you might need. I understand your husband will be gone for some time."

The inference in his words was unmistakable. "I believe you will have enough to do with your own duties. I'm quite capable of handling any situation, I assure you. Now, if you will step aside—"

For a moment, he stayed where he was. Then, sensing the anger in those magnificient eyes, he moved lazily. She was forced to brush against him as she passed, shoulders stiff, head high.

He closed the dairy door for her, his gaze following her as she marched across the yard. Damn, the girl had spirit! She was a thoroughbred, that one. But he'd broken thoroughbreds to the saddle before.

"Don't forget," he called after her. "Anything you need, anything at all—the offer still goes."

The door to the main house slammed behind her, and he chuckled. He wouldn't push it any further for now, but he'd given her something to think about. Dan Tallant was going to be gone for a long, long time.

Chapter 10

After the incident at the dairy house, Melvin's attitude toward Tamsen was most circumspect. If there seemed to be a slight exaggeration in the way he doffed his hat to her, there was nothing in the smiling pale blue eyes that suggested he considered her as anything other than the wife of his employer. As the weeks passed, Tamsen began to believe that, again, her imagination had been at fault.

September came, bringing the Australian spring. It would have been easy to be lulled by the soft blue days and the reappearance of bright, flashing birds, except that the station faced a very real problem. The water in the Billabong was fast diminishing; in the man-constructed tanks, it was dangerously low. But the very fact that water existed had drawn in a number of cattle, strangers to the Opal Station mob.

Among them were wild scrub cattle; cows with the Booradabie brand, the Wilga, Mairn, and Stevens brands; many of them with unbranded calves at their sides. They had come from the outer fringes of stations bordering the Murrumbidgee and the Murray; great sprawling stations, abutting the Opal. And, until the wet, the Opal could only support its own.

The answer was to hold a muster, asking the other

stations to cut out and brand their own, then drive them back into their own territory.

It was Arab's idea to make an occasion of it. The women of the adjoining places would be invited to accompany their men. A long, tin-roofed storage building could be cleared for dancing. They would barbecue several steers in charcoal pits. It would be the grandest party the area had ever seen.

Juan demurred, but not for long. His wife's shining eyes were not to be denied. As if it were already settled, she was planning where to bed down those who wished to remain for the night: women and children in the house, men in the jackaroos' quarters, or outside with their swags.

"I'll wear the gown I wore to the governor's ball in Melbourne," she said happily. "Luka has several pretty frocks. We'll make new gowns for Ramona and Missie— and you, Tamsen! That lovely tangerine shade I brought back!" She hugged her sister. It was impossible not to enter into her state of enthusiasm.

The muster was set for the first of November. Invitations were dispatched and accepted. Work on the party gowns was begun. The house was given a good turning out. Old Wyuna recruited several abo women she considered amenable to instruction, including Queenie, now completely recovered from her illness. Queenie brought Princess along, and Missie played with the baby while her mother worked.

The days until the muster were ticked off on a calendar in the kitchen-living-dining room. On the twenty-sixth of October, Ramona drew a line through the date, wishing it were over with. Despite her new gown and the excitement of festive preparations, she still had the feeling of imminent trouble. Perhaps it was the muster itself that worried her. Last year, one of the jackaroos had been gored by a scrub bull—

Her household chores completed, she went to check on a calf with a crippled leg. It was doing well. Then she moved to the small shed in which she'd set up a temporary hospital. Her newest patient, a crow with a broken wing, ruffed its feathers as she approached, making a threatening sound deep in its throat. But it made no attempt to attack her as she spread clean straw and fed it from her hand.

Next was the small joey she'd reared herself ever since its mother had been shot by one of the hands. For a long time it had lived in a leather pouch. Now it was in a box of straw in which she placed warm, wrapped stones at night.

Ramona caressed the animal's soft fur, her eyes filling with tears. Soon she would have to let him go. And her father was talking, only this morning, of organizing a hunt within the next few months. The long dry had brought an invasion of roos and dingoes to the station. Roos, feeding on the vegetation essential to cattle, were a menace, especially now since they converged on any area where there was water.

It wasn't fair, she thought sorrowfully as the little joey nuzzled at her hand. They were here first, the wild things. And they would be hunted down: this little fellow, the dingo on the ridge—

Leaving the shed, she looked upward, toward the crest. She had not taken the upward path for several days. The dingo was half-grown, now, and had taken to ranging. The last few times she'd gone, he hadn't appeared.

The rocky ridge glowed red in the sun. She had a sudden urge to ride toward it. Returning to the house, she dressed quickly in the men's clothing that served as her riding garb, then saddled the gray. As she rode up the narrow trail, scrub catching at her garments, her nerves were on edge. A feeling of urgency made her push her mount a little faster than was her custom. When she reached the top, she had an eerie feeling she was not alone.

Satisfying herself that there was no one there, she looked for the dingo. He didn't appear. Then she sat on the sun-warmed rock where she and Ned Kelly once shared a meal. Again, she had that prickling sensation that, if she turned, she would see him, hear his voice.

"I'm going to pull off something big enough to have the whole police force looking for me. Big enough to have them all wanting me behind bars."

Then he'd planned to offer his freedom in return for that of his mother. Word had already reached Opal Station that Ellen Kelly had received a sentence of three years in gaol, her companions six.

Where was Ned Kelly now? What was he thinking? What was he doing?

"Don't do anything rash," she whispered. "Oh, dear God! Don't!"

Putting her face in her hands, she cried. She cried for the sake of the dingo pup, the little joey—and Ned Kelly. For all the hunted.

Moments earlier, far from where Ramona sat crying, Ned Kelly, armed with a serviceable shotgun; his brother, Dan, carrying an old weapon tied together with string; and their unarmed mates, Joe Byrne and Steve Hart, crept through the bush toward a camp near Stringybark Creek.

The young outlaws had been prospecting in the rich creek bed. Kelly, himself, had redoubled his efforts since a friend brought the message about his mother's sentence, trying to work off the anger that burned in him like a slow fire.

Then, the previous day, he had come upon police tracks between Table Top and the bogs. Later in the evening, returning to the shelter he shared with the others, he found a different lot of tracks leading to a spot known as the Shingle Hut.

Two parties of police, apparently set to take Ned Kelly and his companions in a pincers movement. And there were eight of them, four in each party.

That night, the young outlaws dared not light a fire. They ate cold food and, slapping at mosquitoes, pondered on the best course of action. Joe Byrne and Steve Hart were, as yet, not wanted by the police. It wasn't known that they had joined the Kellys.

"You chums better smoke," Ned Kelly said suddenly. "Nobody's on to you. Get the hell out of here. Take to the bush."

Steve Hart looked at his hero with an injured expression. "What kind of bloody blokes do you take us for, anyhow? I'm in!"

Kelly's eyes moved from Steve to Joe Byrne, seeing the same implacable determination. "All right," he sighed. "Here's what we're going to do . . . ."

The plan was to bail up the police who were at Shingle Hut, take their weapons, and lie in wait for the other four. With luck, it could be accomplished without bloodshed. Bail them up and send them home with their tails between their legs.

Now all was working out better than Ned Kelly had hoped. Two of the police were gone from the camp, probably to reconnoiter. One of those left behind concentrated on cooking over a small fire. Another lay watching a beacon-fire blazing against a log.

Kelly's face creased in a tight grin. They would take them two at a time.

He moved closer. To one side a twig cracked beneath Steve Hart's larrikin boots, and they all · froze. There was no change in the scene before them. Evidently, the crackling of the bonfire had covered the sound. Still,

Kelly's face was wet with perspiration as he stepped from the dense bush.

"Bail up! Put up your hands!"

The man at the cookfire immediately complied. The other leaped for cover behind a log, his revolver instantly in his hand. He put his head up and aimed—

Ned Kelly's gun pointed true, then wavered. In his ears, he heard a woman's voice: *"Don't!"* He shook his head and his hand steadied. He pulled the trigger.

Never again, he thought, running his hands over the other policeman to make sure he had no hidden weapon, would he be able to claim he'd never killed a man. He sighed and faced his prisoner.

"I'll let you go free if you can get your mates to surrender and hand over their weapons."

Inside the hut they settled down to wait. Kelly pressed a palm against his left ear. A gunshot had never affected his hearing before. Now he had a ringing sound —no, not a ringing—more like a woman crying—

The sun had gone down on the ridge above Opal Station, the soft spring air replaced by a remnant of the winter's chill. Ramona mounted the gray and made her way down the path toward home.

Chapter 11

The morning of the muster dawned bright and beautiful. The majority of the guests had arrived the night before. Adam Jones of the Booradabie was accompanied by his wife Clara, his two spinster daughters, and young Adam, who was instantly smitten with Ramona's charms. From the Wilga came Mr. and Mrs. Smythe-Williams, an elderly couple. Robert and Beth O'Donoghue, in their thirties, with six children from two to ten, represented the Mairn. Several other smaller stations were represented; their men and women, awed at having been included among the owners of the big spreads, touched the elegant things of Opal Station with reverent, callused hands.

Only Leigh Stevens, from down near the Murray, failed to appear. His head stockman carried his regrets. He had been called away several days earlier; something to do with his status as a special policeman. He would try to make it if he returned in time.

It was impossible for one man to be missed. Each station owner had brought a number of jackaroos. Except for the main house where the women clustered, men were everywhere. Juan and the other male owners escaped to the jackaroos' quarters as soon as possible, in order to get away from the feminine chatter about clothes and children. Their own conversation had to do with water, the lack of grazing, the price of cattle on the hoof.

At last, the station slept, except for three men assigned to watch the whole steers roasting in their pits. The moon shone on a number of little hillocks that, at the cry of *muster-r-r,* rose to become men in the dawn, rolling their swags, heading toward the cookfire for their morning sustenance.

The jackaroos divided into groups, each taking a segment of the station's expanse. Small mobs of cattle would be located, strays circled and headed into the mobs, and finally driven by hallooing, yelping hands to a spot some two miles from the main house. Here, a deep gorge made a natural corral. The beasts would then be driven through a narrow yard in single file and branded with the appropriate brand. Calves were castrated, and cows with ingrown horns had them sawn away, the raw stumps liberally coated with tar to stop the bleeding.

From here, they would be driven through different gates, to separate each station's mob. And herein lay the danger. The hands were forced to accomplish this part of the operation on foot, inside the pens. It often took a tremendous amount of agility to avoid being trampled or gored by a fear-maddened beast.

By midmorning, the mobs were coming in. After a light lunch, the women took their place at the top of the gorge to watch their men at work below. Ramona, sickened at the sight of blood and burning flesh, chose to remain behind, but Tamsen, in her role as mistress of the station, was forced to accompany her guests.

The scene was one of chaos, red dust rising to the skies obscuring much of what went on. Only one figure stood out in the melee: Arthur Melvin, white-clad, seemed to be everywhere, cutting scrub bulls back into the herd, his stock horse wheeling to spring aside, wheeling again—

The present mob safely inside the main yard, he rode his mount upward and along a shelf, to descend beside the drafting gates where the cattle were sorted according to their brands. And, because Tamsen, despite herself, was watching him, she saw what happened. Her eyes wide with horror, she heard the woman beside her give a choked cry. "Sam! Oh, God!"

A bull had charged her husband. At first Tamsen could see a lanky figure running in the cloud of red dust, then he disappeared. He was down. The bull, head lowered, a snorting demon, came on.

The woman, a stringy whip-leather creature, typical of the small station wife, was on her feet, screaming hoarsely, Tamsen beside her.

Then the white-clad Arthur Melvin vaulted the fence. His bullwhip cracked, and the animal spun. Melvin stepped deftly aside. The whip sounded again.

As graceful as a dancer, Melvin led the brute away from the fallen man, pausing a moment before an open gate. As the bull charged, he stepped aside. The animal was now where he was supposed to be.

There was a ragged cheer as the small-station owner climbed over the fence. Arthur Melvin leaped over to join him. They shook hands. On the ridge, his wife sank back to her seat with a pitiful moan.

"A handy bloke, that one," she finally said to Tamsen, with a smile that revealed many missing teeth.

"He is," Tamsen admitted. She had to give Melvin credit when it was due. But she hated herself for the emotions the man aroused in her during his handling of the situation. For a moment, she had experienced an ugly need, a raw hunger—an attraction that was compelling and—horrible.

Dan! she thought. Oh, Dan, damn you for leaving me alone!

Knotting her hands into fists, she forced herself to endure the remainder of the afternoon.

By evening, the main job was finished. There were some stragglers, to be sure, but a few jackaroos would remain behind to finish up. Now, it was time for celebration.

The jackaroos retired to the Billabong, where they splashed and scrubbed the dust from themselves, dressing in their go-to-town clothing. The gentlemen made do with a shower system, newly installed outside the jackaroo barracks. It consisted of a perforated tin set into a roof-and-pole shed. Two grinning abo boys kept a bucket brigade going, pouring water into the tin from which it drained to sluice the bather below.

In the main house, the outback women were experiencing what was perhaps their most thrilling moment of the party. The water in which they washed was perfumed. And Arab had provided scented soap! The women, who had no finery to put on, who perhaps had never seen such clothing as Arab and her girls donned, displayed no jealousy. They were content merely to touch silk and velvet, to marvel at its softness.

"I can't wear my new gown," Tamsen whispered to Arab. "Look at them!"

Two women in homespun were marveling over young Luka's frock, the velvet ribbon that served as a sash.

"Don't be a fool," Arab hissed. "This is *making* their party! They expect it. They'll have something to talk about for a long time."

It made sense. Tamsen donned her new dress, soft tangerine velvet, falling straight in front, sweeping behind, with only the slightest suggestion of a bustle. Then she put her hands to her hair, arranging it softly about her face, the remainder in a coil held in place by a circlet of pearls.

She turned to face Nell. The old woman was rustling in purple taffeta with an alarming amount of bared bosom.

"Purty ez a speckled pup!" Nell surveyed her beloved Tamsen fondly. "Now I've got me somethin' t'say, an' I want you to lissen!" She shook an admonishing finger in Tamsen's face. "You ain't had no fun in a coon's age. T'night, you have yourself a good time. Fergit Dan. He ain't here, and it ain't yer fault. I ain't sayin' t'do nuthin' wrong, y'understand. But—hell—have yourself a fling!"

Tamsen smiled painfully. "I might just do that, Nell. Thanks—"

"Then stop holdin' up th' show. Git th' hell outa here. Us girls is all a-waitin' on yuh!"

Tamsen moved out of the darkened corner where she had dressed to meet the ohs and ahs of the assembled women. Then she led them outside and they walked, some of them self-consciously, toward the storage building. Made of saplings surmounted by a tin roof, it was open to the air. The waiting men sounded a cheer at their approach, and a fiddler struck up a foot-tapping tune.

Tamsen was seized by young Luke and whirled away. Behind her, the others met the same fate. The jackaroos were hungry for their company in an almost womanless land.

Tamsen moved from partner to partner as the tunes and tempo changed. The hodgepodge character of the country was revealed in its music: Irish reels, jigs, polka, schottiche, old English round dancing. Tamsen knew they were watched from the darkness by a multitude of eyes. Surely, the aborigines thought this was some kind of corroboree. And perhaps it was.

Finally, after a particularly strenuous reel. Tamsen begged off. She stood, her back to a pole, watching the

91

dancers with shining eyes. Young Adam Jones was certainly wooing Ramona. The child's face was crimson with blushes from his compliments. Missie didn't lack for partners among the jackaroos. And little Luka danced with the O'Donoghue's ten-year-old, moving gravely to a music of her own.

Arab was in her element. Juan's eyes, watching her, were proud.

Then Tamsen realized she had not been seeking out her loved ones, but looking for a figure that wasn't there. Why hadn't Arthur Melvin come? Her certainly knew he was invited— And why should she suddenly feel a pang of disappointment at his absence?

"You look very lovely, Mrs. Tallant."

The words, said softly behind her, made her whirl. A red guilty flush stained her cheeks, as if he could have known her thoughts were on him. The man was like an apparition, always appearing suddenly in the darkness, taking her by surprise.

"Good evening, Mr. Melvin."

"May I have the honor of the next dance?"

"Why . . ." She searched for an excuse, but did not find one. "I suppose so."

He inclined his head gravely, and left her. She saw him whisper something to the fiddler who nodded and kept on sawing away. Then he returned to Tamsen's side.

The dance ended in a stamping flourish that sent the participants, breathless, from the floor. Two dances of fast tempo had been enough for the moment; someone shouted for a break.

But the fiddler touched his bow to the instrument, drawing forth a soft, almost unbearably beautiful sound that moved gently into others. A waltz! Tamsen thought, dazed. Not the sort of thing for an affair like this at all.

Probably few of the guests had ever seen the dance before. Might even think it shocking—

Melvin was bowing. He extended his arm and led her to the center of the floor. There he bowed once more and placed a gloved hand—a *gloved hand!*—against her back. Keeping a decorous distance, he guided her effortlessly into the dance. She felt like thistledown, a veil of mist, as they glided, swirled and dipped, with the other guests as audience. There was a murmur as they began. *What a lovely gown! And isn't he the man who—.* But the comments died, breaths indrawn and held at the sheer beauty of the dancing couple.

The music ended to a hush, followed by a round of applause. "We dance well together, don't we?" he asked, his words covered by the sounds of enthusiasm. "Shall we try again?"

"No!" She must not be rude, so she softened her refusal. "No, please. I enjoyed it, but I'm tired."

His pale eyes gleamed as if he relished her discomfort. "Then we will walk for awhile, away from the crowd. I would much prefer it."

This man could be the devil, himself! He'd been most respectful towards her, but as they danced, she'd been conscious of the strong arms that held her, the taut body beneath that white clothing. She'd known what was in his mind—Dear God, she, Tamsen Tallant—forty-eight years old and happily married! To have such feelings about a man she didn't even like—

Arab's intervention saved her from an answer. She knew Tamsen didn't like to sing in public anymore, but —just this once? It was a means of escape.

First she sang a ballad that she'd sung so often in the old days; a song that, in her husky, breaking little voice, brought tears to every eye. She followed it with a saucy tune about a swagman, realizing, too late, that she

93

couldn't control the provocative movements of her slender body. She knew that Arthur Melvin missed nothing. His eyes held her own. A snake's eyes—

She was grateful when her song was interrupted by the sound of horses galloping into the yard. The fiddle died on a wailing note as all eyes turned to peer into darkness.

Leigh Stevens had arrived. Tired, grim-faced, unshaven, he had come with ugly news.

A group of police had attempted to arrest Ned Kelly. Kelly had shot and killed Constable Lonigan, and Sergeant Kennedy and Constable Scanlon soon thereafter. Only Constable McIntyre had escaped unharmed. The Kelly gang was armed—and dangerous. They were to be shot down like mad dogs if they were seen. And it was possible that they might range this far—

No one heard Ramona's small anguished cry. Young Adam Jones' attention temporarily diverted, she crept away. She went to the small hospital shed. There, in the darkness, oblivious to the damage she might do to her beautiful gown, she sank down beside the little joey's box, cradling her wet cheek against the softness of its fur.

Ned Kelly had kept to his promise. And now it was too late for him. Too late.

The party ground to a halt, the participants too shocked at the news to continue in their merriment. The women retired to the house, unnerved, and perhaps secretly titillated at the thought of being waylaid by a handsome bushranger on the way home.

The station owners, in the jackaroo barracks, laid plans to protect their property—and the virtue of their wives. Only at a large fire, around which the hands sat glumly, did another opinion come to light. Many of these men had tried settling on their own, or were the sons of such men. They knew what it was to be persecuted, driven from their small holdings by the more affluent squatters who impounded their cattle and accused them of depredations.

"He shouldn't of done it," old Matthew said, finally. "But I hope to hell he gets away."

Heads nodded in agreement with his words.

The Kelly gang, fleeing for their lives toward the Warby Ranges, had more friends than they knew.

Chapter 12

The muster over, Opal Station returned to a slower pace. It was one of the hottest Novembers in memory. The sun boiled down, turning the station grounds into hard-packed red earth. Occasionally, hot winds raised a dust that was even more unbearable than the windless days. Flies clustered wherever there was moisture; in the corners of eyes, the nose, on a perspiration soaked shirt. Queenie, with a palm whisk, became a permanent fixture in the main house, to "shepherd-im flies," as she described her function. Even the hoarse calls of the bright birds among the trees with their shriveled leaves seemed to rasp the nerves.

And each member of the family was on edge. Tamsen was filled with guilt at the emotions Arthur Melvin had aroused in her the night of the muster. It was sheer animal attraction, she knew. A base thing. Despite her colorful youth, she had never experienced such a feeling before. She felt cheapened, soiled—frightened.

Arab was at wit's end in regard to her daughters. Heat such as this could only breed disease, and her attention was focused on protecting little Luka. She'd forbidden Missie to go to the abo settlement, and the girl was morose and rebellious in turn. She had no idea what was troubling Ramona. Since the night of the muster she'd appeared to be in shock.

Juan Narváez faced an even graver problem. Water levels were still dropping. Even with the removal of strange animals from the station, it was clear it wouldn't support the mob it carried unless it rained. He might have to have some of the scrub stock cut out and driven down to Melbourne for sale.

Dusty's sudden illness interrupted the course of everyone's private concerns.

Nell brought the news to the main house one morning in mid-November, her heavy features quivering with alarm. "He wuz a-moanin' an' a-groanin' all night," she said. "I figgered mebbe he had snakes in his boots, but, hell, he ain't touched hardly a drop in a couple-a days—"

He hasn't been looking well, Tamsen thought. But she had laid it to the excessive heat. She followed Nell to the small house she and Dusty occupied and found the wispy little man in bed, his fragile body barely discernible beneath a sheet. She hadn't realized he was so small, that he had grown so thin. A dreadful fear twisted in her heart. Dusty was her oldest friend. He and Nell were growing old. She had never dreamed that something might happen to either of them. That one day they—just wouldn't be there.

Dusty pulled himself to a sitting position with only a fleeting grimace of pain. "My word, Nell," he said in a gently reproving tone. "Bringing a young lady into a gentleman's bedroom—it isn't done, you know."

"Oh, shut up you old fool!" Nell's face twisted in mingled fury, concern and affection. "You raised hell all night, an' you know damned well you did. Brung Tam over t'take a gander atcha. Me, I gotta git some shuteye sometime—"

"Are you ill, Dusty?" Tamsen asked. "I've heard there's a doctor at Jerilderie—"

"I'm sound as a dollar, Tamsen. Jove! This is much ado about nothing! A touch of the heat, perhaps. A small drop of medicinal whiskey, and I shall be up and about in no time."

"The hell you will," Nell roared. "You're gonna stay in that gawdam bed ef I gotta set on you."

"I'm only happy to obey your wishes, my love," he said mildly. "Now, if you will bring that drop I requested—"

Grumbling, Nell left the room. Dusty took Tamsen's hand. "There is nothing to worry about, dear girl. And a little rest never hurt anyone. But, tell me—how is young Missie faring?"

"Why, all right, I suppose—"

"Watch over her, Tamsen. She's a brilliant child. She needs more than her mother is giving her."

Tamsen went cold all over. It sounded like a death-bed request. "Dusty—"

She was interrupted as Nell bustled in, a bottle in her hand. "Here you are, you leetle sonofabitch. Go easy on it now."

Dusty tilted the bottle. Almost immediately his cheeks regained their natural color. "You're a good woman, Nell."

"Hell," she snorted, "I know it. Now, gimme that." She snatched the bottle out of his hand. "C'mon, Tam. Let's git outta here, so's the leetle bastard'll git some sleep."

"I thought perhaps we might talk over old times," Dusty said wistfully.

"Well, you thought wrong." Nell shepherded Tamsen from the house, to stand beneath the brittle leaves of an acacia tree. "Well, whadda you think?"

"I think he'll be all right," Tamsen said, a small note of doubt in her voice. "How long has he been feeling bad?"

"Ever sense last week when the mail come. Got hisself a letter from England. It give him th' staggers. Turned white ez a sheet. But he won't open his trap about it." She looked at Tamsen pitifully. "I bin thinkin'. You don't s'pose he's got hisself a wife back there, or somethin'?"

Now Tamsen could speak with assurance. "One thing I'm certain of, Nell, you're the only woman Dusty loves—or has ever loved."

Back to her old self once more, Nell preened a little. "I figgered as much," she admitted. "But you know how it is. Sometimes you git t'wonderin'."

"Yes," Tamsen said. "I know how it is."

Leaving Nell in a happier frame of mind, Tamsen walked slowly back to the main house. She'd been doing some wondering herself these last days. How could Dan have left her to face the long, lonely months ahead? Unlike Nell, she had a rival: Dan's freedom. He loved her—but he loved his freedom more. She almost wished it were a woman who was her rival. At least she'd be able to fight back—

A movement on the cliff wall caught her eye: a horse and rider. It would be Ramona. Every day since the muster, the girl had ridden to the top of the gorge, taking a picnic lunch with her—at least she had a healthy appetite. But when she returned, she always looked so sad and dispirited. No wonder, in this heat. And of all the places to go! It would surely be hotter up there than here in the valley.

It was almost as if she'd planned to meet someone —someone who never came. Tamsen frowned. The girl had showed no interest in the jackaroos, and there was no one else within miles who might prove attractive except

—her heart plunged—except Arthur Melvin. And he would surely have no dealings with a girl so young— would he?

Dear God, this was not *jealousy* she felt—

Of course not! She shrugged her thoughts aside as she entered the main house and set about the day's chores.

Dusty, true to his promise, was up and about within several days. A little pale and wan to be sure, but as lively as a cricket. Nell was elated at his recovery, though she still hovered over him like an adoring elephant. "He might have hisself one of them recollapses," she said.

Contrary to her morbid predictions, he continued to thrive. And when Juan Narvaéz stated his intention to drive a number of cattle to Melbourne within the week, he insisted on going along.

"But dammit, you can't!" Nell sputtered. "You bin sick!"

He granted her that. But he was well now. And the fresh air would be good for him. "Absence makes the heart grow fonder, old girl. And besides—" he searched for something to mollify her, "besides, I intend to seek out a physician while I'm there, and have a thorough check in order to ease your mind."

For Dusty, he was unusually adamant, and finally Nell grumblingly consented. It was Arab who raised an even stronger objection to their departure at this time. "You'll be gone at Christmas, Juan!"

It couldn't be helped. It was a question of selling some cattle to save the remainder. If they left soon, there was a chance of getting home in time.

Two days later, the cattle had been drafted; sorted into which would go, and which would stay. Juan had insisted on keeping the best of the breeding stock. Next spring's calves would make the difference between the station's success and failure. The mob to go was headed up, farewells were said, and the entourage moved off in a cloud of dust along the long red road.

Arab was sobbing openly. Missie's face was set in a mask of misery. She had gone to her father, privately, begging to be allowed to go along. He was appalled at her request. A young lady could not travel with a group of men, but he had made her a vague promise that they would try to arrange a visit at a later date. Missie had grown to distrust promises.

Tamsen was of mixed emotions. She was both glad and sorry to see them go. The tall white-clad figure of Arthur Melvin was among them. It was he who turned and waved—as if anyone cared!

At least she would be able to sleep tonight.

Chapter 13

The trip to Melbourne took a total of eighteen days. Two of the jackaroos had been left behind: Bob and Jim, the old men of the crew. The others were hard put to control the mob of half-wild animals that veered from the main body, mad with heat and flies, having to be driven back into the bawling dust cloud. At times, they seemed to move at a snail's pace. At others, when the cattle scented water, they moved in a great onward rush that was impossible to stem. Two were trampled when they thronged into the still flowing waters of the Murray. They were the only casualties, though the mob reached Melbourne gaunt, rib-thin.

Dusty was in the same state. His fair English skin was blistered. And the pain he would not admit to sometimes doubled him in the saddle. He kept his senses by setting himself a task; watching Arthur Melvin's every move.

He felt the chap was, as Nell would say, "a wrong'un." Normally spick and span, clean shaven in a country of bearded men, Melvin had allowed his beard to grow on the journey. It changed his appearance beyond belief. The first night out, he'd exchanged his white garb for a cowhand's rough clothing. He'd worn it since, sleeping in it, seeming to strive to be as rough and soiled looking as possible.

There could be only one reason for the man's altered habits: *He did not wish to be recognized in Melbourne!*

Dusty voiced his suspicions to Juan Narváez. Juan, worn and exhausted, shifted uneasily in his black-and-silver Spanish-style saddle. He had planned to turn the mob over to Melvin when they reached the outskirts of Melbourne, he and Dusty going straight to Em's for a hot bath and a soft bed. "The man's all right," he told Dusty. "He's good at his job."

The last night out, the jackaroos took turns at guard, shaving, trimming beards and hair, preparing to make a triumphant entrance into the city. Not so Melvin. Seeing him lying on the ground, head pillowed on his swag, Juan thought of Dusty's worries. What if he *were* wanted by the police? He might be picked up, and the station couldn't afford to lose an able man.

He walked to where the man lay, moonlight glinting in pale blue eyes. "You've done a good job," he told Melvin. "I can't afford to give you a bonus, but I can give you a few days off. When we get to Melbourne—you're on your own."

Was that fleeting expression one of relief? Juan sighed, thinking of Em's comfortable home. Well, after the long hot journey, a few more hours of work made little difference. He would handle the details of the sale himself.

The next night, a surprised Em opened her door to two travel-stained, weary men. "Juan! Dusty!" She threw her arms about Juan, and the smiling little Englishman. "Oh, I'm so glad to see you! Duke! Girls! Scott! Come see who's here!" She turned toward the rear of her house as she called to her family, then whirled at an odd choking sound: Dusty, his face the color of ashes, had crumpled to the floor.

For a time the household was in turmoil, a shaken Em kneeling beside Dusty, chafing his hands, while Duke Courtney held a glass of brandy to his blue lips. Juan hovered anxiously. "I shouldn't have allowed him to come on this trip," he said distractedly. "He hasn't been well—"

Suddenly the old man's eyes fluttered open.

"Balderdash!" he sputtered, softening the word with a weak smile. He inclined his head gallantly in Em's direction. "I was quite overcome at seeing one of my lovely girls again. My word, Em! You're more beautiful than ever—"

"And you haven't changed a bit," she scolded him affectionately, her eyes misty with tears. "We're going to get you to bed, then I'll call Doctor Lockesley."

They would do no such thing. A night of rest would put him right again. Finally they had to give in to his wishes, though Em looked in on him many times during the night. He seemed to sleep as peacefully as a baby, his open mouth revealing two missing front teeth below a scraggly moustache, his wispy white hair spread against the pillow.

He was still sleeping in the morning when Juan and Duke left for the cattle yards. When he finally came downstairs, he was his old jaunty self. Em fixed a late breakfast for him, and they sat long over their coffee as he told her news of the family.

"And Nell?" she asked.

"As lovely as ever," he said fervently.

"Dusty, why haven't you two married?"

"A sensitive girl like Nell likes to be courted."

Em suppressed a giggle, thinking of the romance that had endured for so many years. He was serious! And though the relationship between the gentlemanly little fellow and the bawdy old woman was irregular to her way of thinking, she could not condemn them. No two people had ever loved each other more. It would be unbearable if anything were to happen to either of them. The memory of the previous night was still in Em's mind.

"Dusty, I've been worrying about you. Would you please see a doctor—for my sake?"

He was planning on doing that very thing. Not that he needed a physician, but just as a precaution, don't you know. He also had a few errands to perform. Perhaps he might be measured for a new suit. Did Em think Nell would like him in blue?

"She would love you in blue."

Spurning Em's suggestion that she accompany him, Dusty set out alone for Elizabeth Street. Watching the frail little figure making his way down her walk, Em sighed. She'd forgotten how much she loved the little man who had been Papa's friend; and who had transferred his affection to all of them when Papa died. He was intoxicated much of the time, living with a woman who was not his wife—yet there were times when he'd been almost heroic in his efforts to watch over them: herself, Arab, Tam.

He'd been old as long as she'd known him. But now there was a difference. Now he looked as if a small breeze might blow him away, like a wisp of dandelion fuzz.

Chiding herself for her grim thoughts, she returned to her kitchen. A light lunch, she thought. But the evening meal should be a festive one. She had some New Zealand apples. And Dusty's English blood did not rule out a fondness for American-style apple pie. She set to work.

Dusty sauntered along the streets of Melbourne for a time, reveling in the sound of English voices. Jove, he thought. One day, this will be a city like London. He remembered Buckingham palace; being held once in royal arms. That picture was replaced in his mind by one of an ancient rambling house, with a mansard roof and turrets; ivy-covered, in the midst of green velvet lawns; formal gardens; sculptured hedges; a maze—

Second son, and demon rum, he thought, ruefully. But drink had sustained him, and he'd found Nell—

He wished he had a drink. For a space he thought about heading up Little Collins Street. But he'd promised to go to a physician, and a few days sobriety wouldn't kill him. He owed it to Em.

His eye finally found the shingle that proclaimed a doctor would be found within. He entered.

Some time later, he pulled on his shirt and buttoned it, thanking the medical practitioner for his thoroughness —and his honesty. "I wonder, sir, if you might recommend a solicitor?"

The physician gave him a name. "I think you're very wise," he told his patient.

Again, Dusty spent some time in a small office, surrounded now by dusty lawbooks, rather than medical tomes. When he emerged, he looked like what he was: an aging little fellow, a bit cocky, pleased with himself.

His next stop was at a jewelry store. Among other things, he purchased Maori-shell butterfly pins for Em, Arab, Tamsen, and an ornate locket for Nell. From there, he went to a photographer where, hair and moustache neatly combed, he sat stiffly posing while a man, head buried beneath a black hood, stood behind a black box.

Nell would like his portrait, in a locket against her feminine bosom.

He proceeded to a tailor shop, where he was measured, choosing a soft blue shade that matched his eyes. His final stop was at a stationer's. There he purchased an ample supply of paper and pens. He returned to Em's home, his face ruddy and glowing with good humor, arms laden with parcels, sniffing appreciatively at the odor of spice and apples that drifted from the kitchen.

"Well," Em greeted him happily, "you look as though you've had a good day!"

"A good day? Jove, it's been perfect!"

"You did go to the doctor?" she prodded.

"Of course I did. And if I may say so," he smiled modestly, "I came off very well. A perfect specimen of manly physique—for a man my age, of course."

"I'm sure Nell will be glad to hear that."

"Of course she will. By George, Em, do I smell *apple pie?*"

That evening, Dusty kept the young people giggling at the dinner table, with an unusual loquacity for him. Meanwhile, Juan and Duke Courtney discussed business. It would be several days before the auction of the mob they'd brought down would take place. Juan was beginning to worry that they wouldn't be home in time for Christmas. He had little appetite.

Dusty, in contrast, ate heartily. Here, in the bosom of Em's family, he felt warm and at home. And he had spotted where Duke kept his liquor. He might just take a bottle up with him to bed, to round off what had been a very successful day indeed.

Chapter 14

Christmas day was the hottest day of the year. Though the women of Opal Station had little hope that their men would return, they made every effort to make it a festive occasion. They'd brought in a cypress-pine, a small tree with dark green foliage they'd found higher up, where the creek bed was dry. Decorated with strung berries, scraps of cloth and colorful buttons, it made a creditable display. Arab, though none too housewifely, had indulged in a flurry of baking. The kitchen smelled of spice and fruit, but it also contained the heat from the stove, making it almost unbearable.

Taking the last of a batch of cookies from the oven, Arab covered them with netting against the flies, and mopped her flushed face. For the hundredth time, she asked, "Oh, Tam, do you think they'll make it home in time?"

"For pity's sake, Arab! I don't know!" Tamsen snapped. Then, seeing her sister's hurt expression, she melted. "I'm sorry, Arab. It's just so hot—these flies—and I was thinking of Dan." Her eyes filled with sudden tears, and Arab dropped the dish towel she held and put her arms around her sister.

"I'm sorry, too. I didn't think. Maybe he'll come home, too. Maybe—"

Tamsen shook her head hopelessly. "I'm not expecting him, Arab. There's no way——" She sat down at the table, her face buried in her arms, her slender shoulders shaking with sobs. Arabella stood beside her, tears streaming.

"What on earth?"

Tamsen's head jerked up and Arab whirled. Nell stood in the doorway, her beady little eyes suspiciously red. Then, without warning, she too began to cry, tears spurting outward in a silver shower. The girls moved to comfort her, but she shoved them away, blinking furiously.

"Helluva bunch we are," she grumped. "Bawlin' like a buncha sick calves. An' over some gawdam men, ain't got sense enuf t'stay to home where they belong."

Arab turned to lift the cookies onto a plate, her face still wet. "They're probably on their way now, Nell."

"I know that, but I can't help a-worryin' about that leetle bastard." Nell blew her nose. "They ain't a-gonna thank you fer snarglin' all over them cookies, Arab. So git th' hell over, an' gimme somethin' t'do. Ain't no sense in standin' around lookin' constipated."

The hours of the day dragged on slowly. Ramona went for her daily ride to the top of the gorge, despite the oppressive heat. She returned dispirited and pale. Missie was permitted to take the Christmas gift she'd made for Princess to the abo settlement. The tiny hand-sewn dress had been a mistake. The aborigine baby, unused to being encumbered, cried as she tried to fight free of it. All those hours of stitching, which Missie hated, gone to waste——

A melancholy group sat down to dinner that night. Bob and Jim had been invited to share their holiday meal, since O'Brien, the camp cook, was gone with the drive. They too were plunged in gloom. They'd found a dead cow in the largest water hole of the Billabong. It wore the

Timmons brand. Timmons, a small owner, had lost his whole mob just recently. Some kind of sickness that wiped him out—

"Do you have any idea what it is?" Tamsen asked, alarmed. "Is there any chance of our herd—?"

Bob and Jim exchanged glances. "Dunno," Bob said evasively. "Pulled it out. Figure that Melvin bloke'll know more than we do." They didn't want to mention the diagnosis they'd arrived at. Not on Christmas day.

"We'll have a funeral," Luka said happily. All day she'd been quiet, a sad little figure, sensing the edginess of everyone's nerves. Now they were talking about something she could understand, could help heal.

Arab flushed, but the jackaroos laughed. "Wait until we get it proper buried, little lady. We'll call you out."

"Promise?"

"Promise."

"I'll sing."

After the meal, the jackaroos returned to their barrackslike shelter. The women tidied up, debating whether to open their small handmade gifts, or wait until the men arrived, whenever that night be.

Tamsen settled the question. It wasn't fair to Luka. So, the dishes done, they settled about the little tree, opening gifts of crocheted slippers, embroidered handkerchiefs; shawls knitted for the coming winter; poems written by Missie, carefully printed by hand and illustrated; bookmarks—

They were so intent on making it a cheerful occasion that they didn't hear the sound of horse's hooves in the yard, nor the movement of men's boots coming up the walk. The door flew open to reveal Juan, Dusty, and Arthur Melvin.

Dumping the gifts from her lap, Arab flew into Juan's arms like an arrow. It took longer for the cumbersome Nell to get to her feet, but when she did, she enveloped the grinning Dusty in a bear hug. "You leetle bastard!" she roared fondly. "You made it!"

Tamsen, behind them, met Arthur Melvin's eyes. Clean-shaven, dressed in his immaculate whites, he stood behind them, his arms filled with parcels. "Won't you come in?" she said finally.

"Thank you." He placed the packages at the foot of the tree and went back for more. The heap grew higher with each trip. "It's the reason we're late," Juan apologized, gesturing toward the pile. "We bought some things, then Em loaded us up. Had to buy another pack horse. We've ridden more than eighteen hours straight. Dios, I'm tired!"

Tamsen busied herself setting out leftovers. There was nothing to do but invite Arthur Melvin to join the others at the table. After they'd eaten, he made no move to go, and took part in the opening of the packages as if he were a member of the family.

It was a glorious time. Luka was showered with gifts, among them a doll with a wardrobe sewn by her cousins Vickie and Cammie. For Luka herself, there was a blue velvet mantle, trimmed in white fur, and a frilly pink pinafore. She exclaimed joyously over everything, down to the ribbons that tied the parcels.

Ramona received a jeweled comb for her dark hair, a mirror, a wealth of soft materials. Her most prized possession was a box of watercolors. Just looking at it, she could see sunsets, flowers and trees, small animals. . . .

Missie accepted her presents without much enthusiasm until she came to an oblong package. "Oh, Papa! A book?"

He nodded and she unwrapped it with trembling fingers, then hid her face to hide her disappointment. *A Young Lady's Diary of Meditations*. A Bible verse and an admonition for each day of the year.

"Thank you, Papa."

It was only when she opened Dusty's gift of pens and paper that her eyes glowed. The look of infinite gratitude she turned on him was payment enough.

The "oh"ing and "ah"ing seemed to go on and on as each member of the family held their presents out for inspection. Nell was reduced to blubbering over Dusty's gift of a locket holding his own beloved picture. "Leetle sonofabitch," she choked. Under cover of Nell's emotions, Tamsen stared down at the last gift she had opened. A nightdress of sheer gossamer. It wasn't a thing that Juan would have purchased, or Dusty. Perhaps Em. But why would Em think that she—"

She raised her eyes and met Arthur Melvin's gaze, a wave of crimson touching her cheeks. Dear God, he knew what was in that parcel! He knew because he had put it there!

"I think we'd better get to bed," Arab said finally. Nell stood, agreeing. With a firm grip on Dusty's arm, as if he might try to escape, she led him from the house. Tamsen shooed Arab and the girls from the kitchen. She would remain to clear up.

Too late, she found herself alone with Arthur Melvin. Her face flushed again as she wondered if it were an accident—or if she'd unconsciously planned it.

"Thank you for your assistance," she said hurriedly. "Now, I'm sure you're tired after your long ride."

"I am, indeed," he said cheerfully. He went to the door and turned. His eyes were mocking as he studied her from head to toe, and she knew he was seeing her, not as she was, but in the misty gown.

"Tamsen," he said. At her involuntary movement, he added, "I think I've been here long enough to call you that. I hope you'll call me Arthur—"

"Of course," she mumbled.

"Then, Tamsen, I hope you've had a very merry

Christmas. And that the New Year brings you something better than you've ever had before."

He gave her an insinuating smile and stepped out, closing the door behind him. Damn him, she thought. Oh, damn him!

And damn Dan, for leaving her alone.

Chapter 15

The next morning began well. It was cooler, the screened windows letting in the sound of birds. And, except for Dan, they were all together. Arab's face was radiant, her hand going out to touch Juan every so often, as if to be sure he was there. Nell was rosy with smiles. Even Queenie, waving her palm frond to "shepherd-im flies," showed her white teeth in good-humored understanding.

Juan, himself, was relaxed for the first time in a month, he admitted. It wasn't only Christmas that brought them galloping home in such a rush. The Kelly gang had taken over Younghusband Station, and robbed the National Bank at Euroa. Desperate, running, there was no telling where they would strike next.

"Oh, Papa!" Ramona's voice trembled with her words. Juan studied his eldest daughter. It wasn't like her to be frightened.

"Don't let it worry you, sweetheart. There is a new Felon's Apprehension Act. If a man is declared an outlaw, anyone can bring him in, alive or dead. There's a reward of five hundred pounds set on each member of the Kelly gang, and I would imagine it will be increased after this latest escapade. Their activities will be ended before long."

Ramona looked down at her hands, clasped tightly in her lap. "It's all so awful, Papa."

"It is. I do not like to see men hunted like animals. But it must be done."

His daughter pushed back her chair and stood up. "I'm not hungry," she said faintly. "I—I think I'll go outside. But before she could move, there was a knock at the door. It opened on Arthur Melvin, his features grim.

"I have to talk to you, Mr. Narvaéz. We have a problem."

"Well, come in, man. Have some coffee. What's the matter? Surely nothing that cannot be—"

Melvin didn't move. He uttered the one word that struck deadly fear into a cattleman's heart.

"Pleuropneumonia."

The jackaroos, Jim and Bob, had suspected it. Mick Timmons had lost nearly all his mob to the dread disease, and had cleared out, giving up. But apparently one, perhaps more, had strayed here to die. This morning Melvin had examined the dead animal found at the water hole and made his diagnosis. Then he rode out among the station cattle. Many of them stood, heads down, shivering. Perhaps a quarter of them were already infected, two dead.

"Dios!" Juan and Dusty were on their feet. They left with Melvin and didn't come back.

Nell's jowls quivered. "What the hell's goin' on? They took outta here like their tails wuz on fire."

"If Melvin is right," Tamsen said dismally, "we're ruined. We'll probably lose every animal on the place." And as usual, she thought, Dan wasn't here to carry his share of the load. He was off to something more challenging. More *challenging,* for God's sake! A dry year, desperados ranging, the cattle dying! How much more challenge could a person want?

116

She looked numbly at the other women. "We'd better get the house in order, in case we're needed."

At noon the men had still not returned. After nibbling at a light lunch, Ramona saddled Cloud and rode to the top of the gorge. She had prayed that Ned Kelly would return, and she'd planned to plead with him, beg him to leave the country and start a new life somewhere. Somehow, she felt God would forgive him for the terrible things he'd done. But if he didn't stop now, who knew how many other people might die?

She sat on a rock, thinking of the man who once sat beside her. A man with a hurt boy's eyes; his mother innocent, in prison. And men were hunting him. Men who would be rewarded for putting him to death. She shuddered at that last thought.

As she rose to return to the valley, her eyes caught sight of something on a blade of dry grass: a crimson splash of blood. Her heart in her throat, she searched for more signs. Another spot—another—

The trail led to the den where the dingo pup had hidden. Bending, she could see him in there, dim though it was. "Come on out," she coaxed. "It's only me . . . ."

A low warning growl issued from its throat. Taking a bit of food from the pouch she carried, she held it out, invitingly. For a moment there was silence, then a whimper. The animal finally dragged itself into the light. A long wound gaped along its haunch, blood drying on the yellowish fur. The poor thing had been shot, not a fatal wound, but a painful one.

With a little cry of pity, Ramona put out her hand, touching the half-grown dingo. It yelped and spun, snapping, then ran off into the bush. She looked dazedly at her forearm. The pup's teeth had closed through the flesh, and her own blood joined the crimson splotches on the ground.

Tearing a piece from the tail of her shirt, she bound the wound tightly. She would return to the house wash it, and pour some brandy on the wound. But she would have to wear long sleeves until it healed. That would be hard to explain in this weather.

She rode down the cliffside, thinking of the dingo—and of Ned Kelly. If man hadn't hurt them first, they might never have turned on man.

Days passed, and Ramona's wound healed unnoticed. A pall had been cast over the station with Arthur Melvin's bad news.

Juan had come home the evening of the discovery, his lean face tense, dark shadows beneath his eyes. He had a decision to make. In Dan's absence, he felt Tamsen should have a hand in it.

It seemed Arthur Melvin was a man of parts. Prior to his unfortunate venture with a small station, he'd been one of a team of researchers in Brisbane, attempting to develop a vaccine for the very disease that threatened Opal Station.

"He swears we can inoculate the healthy ones, using a serum from those which are infected, and save some of them. I don't know. If we do nothing, they are certain to die from the disease. If we take Melvin's advice, they may die from the treatment. Or, if he's right, they may have a chance."

"Then we don't have a choice," Tamsen said calmly. "When do we begin?"

"Now."

For the next few weeks, Tamsen and Ramona were to live in the saddle, doing a man's work. Melvin didn't consider it wise to drive the weakened animals great distances, so they were vaccinated on the spot, wherever they were found. The men worked in pairs. The beasts were roped and bulldogged to the ground, one man pinning a thrashing animal's head while another proceeded with the inoculation. It was essential that each be marked for identification. Tamsen and Ramona took on that duty, trying to stay clear of flailing hooves as they bobbed each cow's brush off square with sewing shears.

It was a hot, dusty, grueling job. Everywhere cattle, vaccinated too late, were dying. There was no time to drag the carcasses away, to burn or bury them. The atmosphere reeked. Arab, in the house, went about with a cloth soaked in vinegar to her nose.

Maybe the cattle would all die, she thought, hoping somewhat guiltily that they would. Then perhaps Juan would take a job with Duke Courtney. They could live in a house that smelled of lemon wax and flowers. It would be better for Missie, For Tamsen too, she assured herself to assuage her conscience. It was terrible to know she was out there, she and Ramona, working like men. Both of them came in only to eat; dirty, worn out, sun-blistered. And just last night she'd seen a healed scar on Ramona's arm.

Tamsen was near exhaustion. First, they had gone in search of the large mobs nearer the station. Then they fanned out, finding smaller groups bunched in secluded hollows. Isolated on the far flung reaches of Opal Station, these beasts were not as yet contaminated. But it was only a matter of time before they would be. They too were inoculated as a precautionary measure.

In late January, they located a small herd of eight or ten that surely, except for a few singles, must be the last. They were situated in a little glade surrounded by tall cliffs, fed by a natural spring. There was no standing water; just a seep of damp that made grass grow lush and green; enough to keep the cattle from scenting water elsewhere. They would have to be vaccinated and driven out into the dry hot valley where the precious life-giving liquid was available, though in short supply.

One by one, the resentful beasts were brought to the ground; a jackaroo lying across an animal's head; Melvin inoculating; Tamsen dodging in and out to mark it as one that had received protection. Perhaps she was too tired, or careless because they'd reached the last of the herd. Whatever the reason, a flailing hoof connected with her shin. Grimly, she hung on, biting her lip until the blood came. The deed done, she hobbled to the black shade of a eucalyptus, and lay back in the soft grass.

"Are you all right?"

It was Arthur Melvin standing over her. She'd heard him tell Luke and Matthew to drive the herd toward the Billabong. And she dared not be alone with this man.

"I'm fine," she said, managing a painful smile. "Go on with the cattle. I'll just rest for a minute."

Looking down at her, Arthur Melvin came as near to sincere feeling as he'd ever come in his life.

For days, this woman had worked beside him without a word of complaint. Now lying at his feet, her hair dishevelled, face dirty, dressed in soiled ragged men's clothing, she was still the most beautiful creature he'd ever seen. What's more, he had a feeling a fire raged inside her. A fire that would burn a man to his very soul and drive him to heights of passion as no other woman could. Beneath the men's clothing was the exterior of a lady. And beneath that exterior, something wild and savage—

He swallowed, his big hands with their long tapering fingers clenching at his sides. "I'll wait for you," he said quietly. He lay down beside her.

Tamsen sat up. "We'd better go," she said in a nervous tone.

He was on his feet immediately, reaching a hand to assist her. For a moment, they stood looking into each other's eyes as if hypnotized. Tamsen moved first, trying to tug her hand free.

"I suppose I should take this time to thank you," she said, her lips stiff. "You've saved more than half the herd. I'm sure my husband will repay you for your efforts when he returns."

"Suppose I don't want to wait?" His voice was husky, caressing. "Suppose I want to be paid now?"

"You'll have to talk to Juan—"

"Juan, hell!" His voice was ugly now. "You know what I want! You want it, too! You've been wanting it for a long time—"

His arms were around her, his hot mouth burning hers. For a moment, she yielded in shock, then she began to fight. The moment she'd dreaded had come, and instead of the passion she'd feared, there was only revulsion. This was not Dan! Not Dan!

"Let me go," she said hoarsely. "In the name of God! Stop this! Let me go!"

He only laughed, and held her more tightly, his hand going to the buttons of her shirt. She jerked backward, and the age-weakened material ripped. He gave a muffled shout of triumph at the sight of golden flesh gleaming in the sun. She brought up a knee, and he evaded it.

"Little wildcat," he chuckled. "All right, if this is the way you like it—"

His blue eyes bulged as he felt the round muzzle of a gun against his midsection. His hands left Tamsen's body and raised helplessly as he backed from the murderous expression in her eyes.

She had shoved the weapon in her belt as protection against snakes. Almost too late she had remembered it. If he made one more advance, she had every intention of using the gun, and her face showed it. Her voice crackled like ice when she spoke.

"As I said, I wish to thank you for your assistance.

Now, you will return to the station with the rest of the *hands*. I would suggest you remember that's what you are, from now on. One of the *hands!*"

"Don't try to come the bloody lady over me," he said roughly. "You ain't no lady, by no means. A flaming tart, that's what you are!"

Tamsen sighed. He'd understood her from the first. "What I am makes no difference," she said. "If you lay your hands on me or any of my family again, I'll kill you." She meant it.

"Then why don't you fire on me?" he asked insolently, "if I'm such a danger to the virtuous women of Opal Station?"

She looked at him squarely. "Because Opal Station needs you. Your work has been more than adequate. And I plan to tell my husband so. Now if you will excuse me—"

She backed away, the deadly little gun still pointed at his chest, limped to her horse, mounted and rode away.

He watched her go, hands clenched at his sides, lips drawn into a snarl. The bitch! The snotty little bitch! He'd left the big time and taken on a menial job as a temporary measure. He'd have left here long ago if it hadn't been for her. Well, he wasn't leaving now. He intended to stay until he'd evened the score.

Chapter 16

That night, Queenie left the main house and headed back toward the abo settlement on the Billabong. She didn't fear the dark. She was at home in it as a cat, her bare feet knowing the feel of every stick and stone that led to the humpy she shared with her husband and baby.

Tonight, however, there was a different feel to the atmosphere. The rains January usually proffered had not yet come. But there was an electrical feeling in the air, a smell of ozone that haunted the aborigine woman's sensitive nostrils. Far off, there was a yellowish flicker of light that illuminated black clouds.

"Him feller show-off," she murmured to herself. It would not rain.

She crossed the yards, skirting the tin-roofed buildings, and reached the big tree that grew at the edge of the Billabong. There she paused, scenting danger. She stood transfixed for a moment, trying to determine its direction. When the hand closed over her arm, she set her lips against a startled whimper and turned to face her attacker.

"You ain't much," a voice growled. "But you'll do—in the dark."

Queenie was passive as big hands forced her to the

ground and roved over her, hurting, humiliating. One must never fight a white man. She'd learned that on a hilltop littered now with her people's bones. The frock she'd been given to wear in the big house was ripped, tossed aside. Then she felt his weight, endured his intrusion with a stoic calm.

"You flaming bitch," he panted, "help me!" He slapped his open hand hard against her cheek. Again—

For an eternity, she endured his furious attacks, his obscene caresses. Then he was gone, and she lay on the rocky, uneven ground battered, bruised, and alone.

At last she managed to stumble to her feet. Wrapping the remains of her frock about her thin, aching body, she made her way home. King squatted at a small cook-fire before the humpy. He raised his eyes, taking in his wife's appearance, then lowered his head in shame.

He knew. She did not have to tell him what had happened or who had done this thing. He knew. To a man who could track an animal by means of a broken twig or a misplaced leaf, the blond hair caught in a thread of Queenie's frock called out her attacker's name. An aborigine will share his wife with a friend, but this man Arthur Melvin was no friend. More than once, King had been the object of Melvin's abuse.

He could not kill a white man, but there were ways. He would wait.

As Queenie had predicted, it did not rain. But for days, the skies were sulphur-colored in the daytime, stormy black at night. Electricity crackled in the air; gusts of wind swirled at odd times, unroofing more than one metal shed.

Despite the weather, Ramona had resumed her vigil at the top of the cliff that overlooked the station. The dingo had gone. She felt he would not return. She had stayed away during the vaccination of the cattle, too busy to think. But now that it was done, her need to come here had become almost an obsession.

On the morning of February eighth, she woke at dawn after a restless night. Throwing a cloak over her nightdress, she saddled the gray and rode along the upward path, hating herself for the compulsion that took her on a fruitless errand. She reached the top and blinked her eyes at the sight of the tall figure who stood before her. It had to be a dream!

"Ned! Ned Kelly!" Without thought, she ran toward him, flinging herself into his waiting arms.

He held her and she could hear his heart beating. Then he put her gently away. "You mustn't, Ramona."

She reached up and touched a hand to his face, that remembered boyish face. It was the same, but the eyes were those of a stranger, dark and haunted, hard.

It is too late, she thought sickly. Too late.

He gestured toward the grove. In the dim light she could see four horses, three other men. Her heart beat in her throat as she looked at Ned Kelly with wide eyes. *The Kelly gang!*

"They won't hurt you," he said. "It's only my brother. My friends." His voice was suddenly tinged with bitterness. "I don't have many, you know."

She studied his face. "I'm your friend," she whispered.

"I know. And I trust you. I want you to believe in me. That's why I've come. I need your help."

"Anything I can do." Then her anguish erupted. "Oh, Ned! I know what you've done, and I'm sorry! But go away! Go someplace where you can start all over again, where nobody knows you! You can do it! You've got a whole life ahead of you—"

"I don't think so," he said. "I'm not even sure I'll see you again. That's why I've come. I brought you this." He placed a sheaf of papers in her hand. "If anything happens to me—I'd like this published. If you can't manage that, at least it will help you think better of me. And for some reason, that seems very important right now."

"Ned," she wept. "Oh, Ned!"

He placed his hands on her shaking shoulders. "I've got to go. Promise me you'll think about me sometimes —kindly."

"I promise, Ned! I promise!"

He brushed her cheek with the softest of kisses, like the touch of a butterfly, then walked to join the others at the grove. She watched, with tear blurred eyes, until they were out of sight. Then, scrubbing at her wet cheeks, Ramona sat down to read the papers he had given her. Evidently an open letter, it began, *Dear Sir*.

> *Dear Sir: I wish to acquaint you with some of the occurences of the present past and future.*
>
> *In or about the spring of 1870 the ground was very soft a hawker named Mr Gould got his waggon bogged between Greta and my mother's house on the eleven mile creek, the ground was that rotten it could bog a duck in places so Mr. Gould had abandon his waggon for fear of keeping his horses in the spewy ground he was stopping at my mothers waiting finer or dryer weather Mr McCormack and his wife hawkers also were camped in Greta the mosquitos were very bad which they generally are in a wet spring and to help them Mr. Johns had a horse called ruila cruta although a gelding was as clever as old Wombat or any other stallion at running horses away and taking them on his beat which was from Greta to the seven mile*

creek consequently he enticed McCormack horse away from Greta.

Ramona pushed her hair back from her damp face, puzzling over the rambling words with their lack of punctuation. It seemed Mr. Gould had sent the horse back to McCormack, whereupon the owner of the horse accused Gould of using it. Gould, in retaliation, had sent McCormack's wife a parcel containing a calf's private parts, asking Ned Kelly to deliver it. An altercation followed, and young Ned Kelly was sentenced to six months in prison—at the age of fourten.

The innocent rambling quality of the note, including all details, attested to its truth. Poor little boy, Ramona thought. Not much older than Missie! Poor little boy—

On the 29th of March, I was released from prison and came home Wild Wright came to the eleven mile to see Mr. Gunn stayed all night and lost his mare both him and me looked all day for her and could not get her Wright who was a stranger to me was in a hurry to get back to Mansfield and I gave him another mare and he told me if I found his mare to keep her until he brought mine back.

The mare, it developed, was stolen. Innocent, Ned fought arrest and was pistol-whipped. He was acquitted of being a horse thief, but was sentenced to three years in Beechworth Pentridge dungeons on a charge of having received stolen goods.

The note went on to tell of the illegal sentencing of his brother, Dan; of the way he'd found more than thirty of the Kelly horses stolen—by a constable—when he himself was released from prison; of the manner in which

127

he, Ned Kelly, had entered into the stealing of cattle and horses.

If a poor man happened to leave his horse or a bit of a poddy calf outside his paddock they would be impounded.

He named names, telling of as many as sixty cattle being impounded in one day, all belonging to poor farmers. And of how those farmers would have to either give the impounder a bill of sale, or borrow money to release their own stock.

And all this was the cause of me and my stepfather George King taking their horses and selling them to Baumgarten and Kennedy.

So, there it was! Persecution and its end result: unlawful deeds and justification. It was all there, an angry outpouring of a man's soul. Ramona read on, transfixed by the words. What she read next chilled her: a full description of the murders at Stringybark Creek, followed by Kelly's defense.

I would have been rather hot blooded to throw down my rifle and let them shoot me and my innocent brother. They were not satisfied with frightening my sisters night and day and destroying their provisions and lagging my mother and infant and those innocent men but should follow me and my brother into the wilds where he had been quietly digging neither molesting or interfering with anyone.

The details of the murders were chilling, but not as heart-stopping as the ending of the letter.

I give fair to all those who has reason to fear me to sell out and give ten pounds out of every hundred towards the widow and orphan fund and do not attempt to reside in Victoria but a short a time as possible after reading this notice, neglect this and abide by the consequences, which shall be worse than the rust in the wheat in Victoria or the druth of a dry season to the grasshoppers in New South Wales. I do not wish to give the order full force without giving timely warning. but I am a widow's son outlawed and my orders must be obeyed.

Ramona dropped the pages and buried her face in her hands. Dear God! Oh, dear God! Was there nothing she could do? She finally sat upright, gazing blindly into the distance, rubbing the scar where the dingo had bitten her. Well, there *was* one thing. The promise she had made to him. *If anything happens to me—* She hoped she never had to keep it.

At ten o'clock that night, Constables Richards and Devine of Jerilderie answered a knocking at their station door. In answer to their query, a muffled voice informed them that there was a fight at the Royal hotel and danger of someone being murdered.

Devine opened the door to find a gun pointed at his heart. Holding the gun was a tall bearded figure. Behind the figure were three more armed men.

"I'm Ned Kelly," the stranger said. "Bail up, or I'll shoot you both."

They locked the constables in an empty cell and stretched out on the floor to sleep. The next day, they donned police uniforms and surveyed the town, believed by the citizens to be the police reinforcements they had requested. Again, they stayed the night in their appropriated quarters. The next morning, they had their horses shod, telling the smithy to "send the bill to the government." For the police, he was happy to oblige.

Then they strode over to the Royal Hotel, took all its occupants hostage, went next door and robbed the Bank of New South Wales. Giving the account of his life, much as he had written it, to the more than thirty prisoners they'd collected in the hotel, Ned had one more task: that of presenting his written manuscript, a duplicate of the one he'd given Ramona, to the bank accountant, Edward Living, who promised on his life to have it published.

The telegraph line put out of commission, their prisoners ordered to remain where they were for four hours, the Kelly gang left Jerilderie. Only Ned paused for a moment, looking up with wistful eyes toward the spot where he'd talked with a girl at yesterday's dawn.

"Dammit, Ned," his brother exploded, reining back to join him, "we've got to smoke out of here in a bloody hurry! Come on!"

With a sigh, Ned Kelly turned his mount and spurred ahead, taking the lead.

Chapter 17

When the news of Jerilderie reached the station, Ramona was oddly comforted. The robbery itself was a criminal act, but there was no bloodshed. In fact, the prisoners, held in the hotel with free access to the bar, regarded the whole thing as a lark.

The law was less generous. Victoria and New South Wales joined together in placing an eight-thousand-pound reward on each outlaw's head, and summoning a special police force to comb the countryside. Rumors were rife. Members of the gang had been seen here, there. Black trackers, a contingent of the Queensland Native Mounted Police, were imported to aid in the search.

As time passed, Juan Narvaéz voiced his private opinion that the Kelly gang had used their ill-gotten gains from the Bank of New South Wales to flee the country. They would probably not be seen in Australia again.

Ramona's face glowed. "Oh, I hope so!" she said.

Arab looked at her oldest daughter in surprise. "Good heavens! One would think you were in sympathy with these outlaws!"

"They might change," the girl said doggedly. "In another place they would have a chance to start over."

Juan put down the month-old newspaper he'd been reading. "People like that never change, sweetheart," he said gently. "Ned Kelly was born to hang. We have to have laws in a civilized world; respect for the life and property of others."

"What about *his* life and property?" she shot back. "In prison on false charges when he was fourteen! And a policeman stole his horses—" She stopped. Her father was eyeing her strangely.

"When did you get to be such an expert on the Kellys, Ramona? I've never heard that story."

She flushed, thinking of the letter she had hidden away. "Maybe one of the jackaroos told me," she said evasively.

"You would do well to keep away from the jackaroos," Arab chided her. "They're a rough lot. I allowed you to help when the cattle had to be vaccinated, but that's over with. There's plenty to do in the house, and you must remember you are a lady."

Missie, itching to get hold of her father's newspaper, had been hungrily reading backward and upside down as he held it before him. She suppressed a smile at her mother's words. In telling Tamsen's life story, Dusty had carefully deleted all references to Em and Arab, except where they fitted the framework of Aunt Tamsen's spicy career. But lately, feeble and unwell, he'd dropped some pretty startling things. Cousin Martha, for example, married and living on a distant station, was an illegitimate child. When Tamsen was working at a cantina in Texas, two men, mistaking Em for Tamsen, had raped her—and Martha was the result.

And Mama? Mama was once a member of the troupe of the notorious Lola Montez, singing and dancing on stage like a—a loose woman. She'd performed before the Queen in Spain, and that was how she'd met Papa.

The McCleod sisters, as they once were, had never been ladies! Somehow, she liked them all the better for it.

Tamsen, seeing the expression that flickered across Missie's features, wondered at it. Later, watching the girl stretched on the floor, the coveted newspaper now in her possession, she was certain she'd misinterpreted that knowing look. Missie was just a dear, slightly neglected child.

And I'm a neglected wife, she thought sadly, as she cleared the table. She had had only one long letter from Dan. It enthusiastically described the camel he'd trained as his own; his liking for the Afghanistan camel drivers who plied their way between Alice Springs and end-of-track; the country with its amazing red gaps in the ranges; the oasis of Alice Springs.

"I intend to bring you here one day," he wrote. Then he went on to say that a complicated business of selecting alternate routes to submit to his backers had extended his stay. He would be away a little longer than he'd thought.

The letter ended with words of love that she read and reread, wishing she could make herself believe them. Somehow, they were not enough. She couldn't rid herself of a festering resentment that he had rushed off so eagerly, like a child playing games. At least she was cured of her unclean fascination for Arthur Melvin. But even that had been Dan's fault. He should have been at home to protect his wife.

Still, she had written, dutifully, keeping all mention of the problems at the station out of her letters. There was no sense worrying him. He couldn't do anything about them at a distance. She would just have to carry the burden a little longer.

If only it would rain! February had passed; March; April. Tomorrow would be the first of June. The first day of winter. The time for rain had gone by, and they faced another dreary dusty year. Despite the decimation of their herds—those driven to Melbourne for sale and others whose dry bleaching bones lay on the scorched land—

there was more work on the station than ever. The jacka-roos had been sent to dig out every spring and seep on the property in hopes of finding a steady supply of water for the thirsty cattle. In several spots they succeeded. In others, the levees they constructed with such effort surrounded only an area of wet mud in which the animals bogged down and had to be retrieved.

Each cow had to be treated with special care. There were few of them now, and all hopes rested on their calving in the spring. Minor injuries were carefully treated, on an individual basis. Major ones—broken legs, for example—brought butchered beef into the house, where the women worked long hours cutting it into strips to be sun-dried.

Juan, overworked, his aristocratic features showing lines of strain, was almost parsimonious in the way he insisted everything be used, nothing wasted. Arab was openly rebellious, especially when he cut in half the list of supplies to be ordered for winter. Tamsen worried, quietly. Had their losses been staggering enough to warrant such closefistedness? There was a great deal of money in the bank in Melbourne. Why did he not draw on that?

Juan was a proud man. He had made the station a success under his management. She would not demean him by asking questions. Whatever the situation, he would handle it.

Dusk approaching, Tamsen filled the oil lamps, hearing Arab's usual complaint that "In Melbourne, they have gaslights." Dear God, Tamsen thought, isn't anyone ever satisfied!

She stepped outside into the evening. It was still warm, despite the season. But the cold would come, and with it, its attendant problems.

In the far distance, dim shapes moved toward the Billabong: kangaroos. They were swarming now. And yesterday, a dingo had pulled down a crippled calf. If only they were into the business of kangaroo and dingo farming, she thought ruefully, they would all be rich.

Meanwhile, she must think positively. One day Dan would be home. She had only to wait. Em's last letter mentioned she would come sometime soon for a visit. The thought had cheered Arab tremendously. Ramona seemed more settled lately, no longer taking her solitary rides above the valley. And Missie was more content, always scribbling away on the sheets of paper Dusty had given her. Too, Queenie was clearly pregnant. Missie would have another black baby to tend—

Moments earlier, her work completed, Queenie had left the house. When she reached the big tree, she closed her mind and waited numbly for the assault that was sure to come. Grasped roughly and thrown to the ground, she felt nothing of the cruel treatment that followed. Finally, breathing heavily, Arthur Melvin drew away from her and rose, looking down at the body he had violated once again.

He was getting tired of this. It had never been good, anyway. Like making love to a dead woman. And now that she was pregnant, she revolted him. The thought that the child she carried might be his never crossed his mind. If it had, it would have made no difference. She'd been there when he needed a woman. He didn't need her anymore.

Tonight was the last time. He'd waited long enough for his revenge on Mrs. too-good-for-it Tallant. From now on, he intended to concentrate on that. He'd thought of catching her out, raping her. But that was too good for her, and only a temporary satisfaction.

He had other ideas. Watching the abo woman limp away, he stood, grinning to himself in the darkness.

Chapter 18

The morning brought a telegram, carried over as a favor by a Booradabie hand. It was a short note from Em, announcing their impending arrival at Opal Station.

Arab, remembering Em's lovely spacious home, panicked. Where would they put them all? The main house had only two bedrooms, and the girls' dormitory room, of course. How could they sleep a family of five, who were used to better things?

Finally Tamsen, exasperated, exploded. "For heaven's sake! This isn't the Queen of England! It's only Em. She's lived in a lot worse places than this!"

It was decided to move Arthur Melvin from the overseer's house into the jackaroo barracks. The house, built for their first overseer, a family man, had two bedrooms: one for Em and Duke, the other for the girls. Small Scotty could bunk down in the living-kitchen area.

"I don't think Melvin will be happy about this," Juan said gloomily.

"His happiness isn't our concern," Tamsen snapped. "He was down-and-out when we hired him. He's earning a good salary. He *is* one of the hands!"

Melvin moved his things without demur. But he had a notion that he was being shown his place. One more score to settle—

The whole house was turned out: bolts of velvet that had been meant for gowns were cut and hemmed into bedspreads; sheets were sorted and mended; the dust-caked curtains were shaken out and laundered; scrubbed floors were waxed with a mixture of wild honeycomb and kerosene. With a final addition of bright rag rugs scattered throughout and a fire laid in the fireplace, to be lighted when the guests arrived, all was quite presentable.

Tamsen made inroads on the precious supplies of flour and sugar, baking a quantity of delectable goodies. They would have to skimp later to make up for this extravagance, but for Em—it was worth it.

The Courtneys had taken the train from Melbourne to Beechworth. There, they had hired two wagons, one to carry the family, the other to haul the mass of staples Duke insisted on bringing along. "They'll have all that," Em insisted. "Wouldn't it be nicer to take them something different?"

He'd stood his ground, obstinately. The second wagon was laden with sacks of sugar, flour, potatoes, and dried beans. Em added several bushels of New Zealand apples; some pumpkins, marrows and onions at his request. In addition there was toffee, a number of spices and condiments—and, of course, gifts for everyone.

"We look like we're moving," Em laughed, her eyes sparkling. This was her first trip to the station. She'd wanted to come sooner, but her health had been delicate and had not permitted such a long journey. Then Duke had become so involved with his work that he'd been unable to get away. Too, the trip was easier now, the roads better traveled and dry, due to the long drouth.

Her enthusiasm faded as they neared their destination. At times, the dust was so thick that the horses strained at the traces. They jolted through dry creekbeds that would have been imposible in a wet year, but now only served to point up the heartbreaking dryness of the landscape. Em realized she had not seen water since they left the Murray.

"How can people live in this?" she asked, worriedly.

"They can, and do. There will be water at the station."

As they entered the fringe of Opal Station, Em was appalled. There was more vegetation to be sure, but it was so dry and brittle. And along their track lay a multitude of bleached skulls and bones. Her first view of the station, itself—tin-roofed buildings under a gray sky, set in a shrubless area of hard-packed ground—brought a cry of pity. Poor Arab! Poor Tam!

The station had known of their approach for hours. Old Wyuna had come to the house. "Feller come. Two wagon. Feller him this many." She held up five fingers, grinning with pride at being able to deliver the news.

Tamsen had never been able to figure how the aborigines managed it. A runner, perhaps? Signals from one group to another? Or an ability to read signs that a white man's eyes could not see.

At any rate, Wyuna's pronouncement sent the household into a flurry of activity. They were all dressed in their best and waiting when their guests arrived.

Tamsen and Arab forgot their dignity, running across the yard to greet Em like a couple of girls. Duke watched paternally as they indulged in joyous tears and babble of voices. Ramona and Missie came forth shyly to meet their city cousins, and young Scott swaggered a little for the benefit of Luka, his old playmate.

There was a hubbub as the jackaroos were called to unload the wagons. They carried the Courtney possessions to the house where they would sleep, and hauled off the supplies they'd brought to the storehouse. Seeing Tamsen's eyes as she watched the staples being unloaded, Em realized that Duke had been right. They were needed here. Perhaps they had not yet laid in their winter supplies. That would surely be the reason.

There was no dearth of food on the festive table they all sat down to. Em impulsively put out a hand to Duke, a hand to Arab, who sat beside her. Each reached to take the hand of the next, and soon they were all linked: a living circle; a circle of love. Em's eyes moved happily down the table, pausing briefly at Dusty's face. He looked so much older than he had in Melbourne; so tired. Sensing her gaze, he smiled at her. "Jove," he said. "This is good, being together like this!"

When he spoke he looked like his old self. Her returning smile was tinged with relief. It had only been her imagination.

After the meal, the gifts were opened and exclaimed over. But for Missie, the excitement of having guests was beginning to wear off. Once again, she felt like an outsider. Mama and Aunt Tamsen were wrapped in conversation with Aunt Em. Vickie and Cammie couldn't seem to talk about anything but clothes and boys. Ramona was polite enough to listen to them, but Missie decided she'd much rather be alone. She wouldn't be able to write today, not with all this intrusion. But she could read—

There was nothing left but the diary she received at Christmas. She'd just read Clara Morison for the fifth time. But anything was better than nothing. Taking the diary, she slipped from the house and made her way to the salt cedar ring on the Billabong.

One person saw her go.

Arthur Melvin leaned against the jackaroo barracks, clad in his immaculate white, rolling a cigarette. He lit it, then saw the girl moving stealthily across the yard. His eyes narrowed against the smoke. Then he laughed softly, tossing the cigarette to the ground and grinding it beneath his boot. It was time to put his plan into action—

Reaching her small enchanted hideaway, Missie

140

slipped through the salt cedar barrier and seated herself. She opened the diary, her mind still on the activities at the house. Why, oh why, did she always feel so much on the outside? Setting her lips, she forced herself to read; first the Bible verse, then the couplet that followed:

> *Young ladies voices should be soft*
> *As the sound of angel wings aloft.*

"Garbage!" she muttered aloud, turning the page.

> *Respect your mama, papa, too,*
> *And Heaven's gates shall open for you.*

"Trash!" She hurled the book across the small clearing and sat glowering at it, only to be shaken from her angry preoccupation by the sound of a masculine chuckle behind her. She turned to find Arthur Melvin had intruded on her private spot, the place where only Dusty was welcome. Her brows drew together in a frown.

Ignoring her irritation, he crossed the clearing and picked up the book, studying it, his brows raised. In a simpering voice, he read:

> *"A maiden's blush and downcast eyes*
> *Are more than beauty to man's eyes.*

"Good God! No wonder you threw the thing!"

Now Missie was laughing. His reading had been so ludicrous, his expression so horror-stricken. Her laughter rang clear and honest, and for a moment, her thin, rather hungry-looking features were almost beautiful. He looked at her with appreciation. This wasn't going to be so bad after all. The girl had possibilities.

In his rich, resonant actor's voice, he began to recite a love poem, one of the three he'd memorized to use if a romantic interlude called for it. Missie's laughter faded. She sat spellbound through his rendition.

"I didn't realize," she whispered. "I didn't know—"

"Didn't know that I was anything more than an ignorant station foreman. That's what you were going to say, isn't it?"

"I didn't mean—" she stammered.

"Don't let it worry you. You had no way of knowing anything about me. In fact, few people do." His eyes were somber. "I miss the discussions we used to have at the University, the lectures, the wealth of reading material. But it isn't the sort of thing one advertises in a place like this. Once I thought I'd like to write—"

"How wonderful," she breathed, her eyes shining. "Have you read Clara Morison?"

"Of course," he lied. "But it was some years ago. I've often wished that I had a copy—"

"I have one. I'll be glad to lend it to you." Her eagerness was almost pathetic.

"And I'll lend *you* a book of poetry," he said. The volume from which he'd learned the lines he quoted had come with him in his swag.

She leaped to her feet. "I'll go get my book for you now."

"Hold on," he laughed. "There's no hurry. If you go rushing into the house like that, there will be questions. I'd just as soon we kept all this between ourselves." His face twisted in mock deprecation. "I'm afraid your Aunt Tamsen doesn't like me."

"Missie looked down. She couldn't refute the statement. It was true. Aunt Tamsen didn't like him at all. She'd heard her tell Papa so.

"Suppose we meet here tomorrow, at about this time," he suggested. "You bring your book. I'll bring mine. I will read some poetry for you if you like."

"Oh, yes! Yes!" she whispered.

"Now it's getting dark. They may be worrying about you at the house. I'll go upcreek and circle back. You go on in, all right?"

It was an excellent plan. She watched him go, her heart lighter than it had been for a long time. She had somebody to talk to, someone who understood.

She returned to the main house to find she had not been missed. Em, Arab and Tamsen were still talking a mile a minute, trying to make up for the time they'd been apart; Vickie and Cammie were still on the subject of clothes and boys; Luka and Scott were intent on putting a puzzle together; Dusty and Nell sat kibitzing.

Missie slipped into the room she shared with Ramona and Luka, and searched in the trunk at the foot of her bed until she found the treasured book.

She would give it to him tomorrow. He would hold it in his hands, read it with those gentle blue eyes. And then they would discuss it together. He was an outsider, too. Just as she was. It was strange that it had taken them so long to find each other.

Chapter 19

The Courtney family was not to remain at Opal Station for more than a week. Duke's far-flung enterprises gave him little time away. But for that week, he reverted back to the two-fisted outdoorsman Em married.

Juan found some old clothing to replace his brother-in-law's expensive garb. The faded blue shirt, that opened to reveal a tan chest with curling golden hair, had been found in the harness room, along with the moleskins that molded to Courtney's muscular body. The shirt and trousers had belonged to a big jackaroo who had worked at the station for a few days and then taken off for Melbourne. The last they heard, he'd been jugged for brawling.

Juan grinned as Duke emerged in the rough clothing. He recalled how as a young man he was always ready to leap joyously into a fight. It had seemed a most unlikely union when he married flowerlike Em. But he'd certainly done well for her; striking it rich in the gold fields; discovering a talent for business. And surprisingly, he hadn't really changed. His speech was more polished, his clothing refined—but here, dressed as he was now, it was clear he was very much a man.

"Well, what the hell we waiting for?" Duke boomed. "Let's go!"

All day, they rode the environs of the station, Juan explaining the problems they'd had within the last year. Duke was silent, making no comment as he assessed the situation. It was a warm day for June, the sun shining. But the sunlight only pointed up the arid country; the depleted stock of lean-ribbed cattle.

When they returned to the station proper, they didn't go into the house. Instead they squatted on the far side of the jackaroo barracks, smoking. "Well," Juan asked finally, "what do you think? I'm too close to it . . ."

Duke stubbed his cigarette out in the dry red earth. "I think you've got a mess on your hands. A hell of a mess. First thing's water. You've gotta put down a bore—"

Juan shook his head. "There's no money."

"Damn it, man, I've got half the money in the world! If I can't—"

"Dan wouldn't stand for it. It may take years to pay you what we owe now. I'm counting on the spring calves."

"From the look of those cows, they'll already be dried beef when they're born," Duke drawled. "Now, suppose we do this. Suppose we go ahead and put a bore down and tell that stiff-necked sonofabitch after it's done."

"Thank you, but the answer is no. We'll manage. All we need is rain."

Two stiff-necked sonsofbitches, Duke thought wearily. "Well, it's your funeral. Now I've got another suggestion. I haven't brought this up, because I didn't know how you'd feel about it. But here it is.

He'd met a young Scottish gentleman at Government House. Denis Dugald was a younger son of Laird Dugald. The old man had prudently provided for both his boys. The elder was to take his seat in Edinburgh; the younger was given the country place, a large sheep and dairy farm in a quiet segment of the green hill country. Again wisely, Laird had given the lad, just out of university, a year or two to get the yen for adventure out of his system. Young Dugald was looking for a billet in the backcountry, where he might do some shooting.

"I hardly think it would pay—"

Courtney grinned. "Hell, man, you're not thinking. You've got a mob of kangaroos on your graze, eating their heads off. Emus, too. And you told me how bad the dingoes are—that you can't put out poison for fear of killing off the abos."

"But I don't see—"

"Then you're blind! Dugald only wants to hunt. Let the abos skin the kangaroos out in exchange for the meat. Their hides are worth from six pence to ten shillings on the market. Queensland pays 6 pence for the scalps. An emu produces six to seven quarts of oil when it's boiled down. And you'll get rid of the goddam dingoes. You don't have to do a damn thing. Don't see how you can lose."

Juan was silent for a moment, then he smiled, painfully. "I know now why some of us succeed and others fail."

"Bull!" Duke scoffed. "It would never have entered my mind if it hadn't been for young Dugald. But you'll have to realize the place will be a bloody slaughterhouse for a time. And the women won't like it."

"They will have to endure it," Juan said crisply.

"You'll do it, then? I can advance you the money for the bore and take it out in skins."

Juan shook his head. "We'll see if it works out, first. Then we'll talk." He smiled and extended his hand. Duke shook it, admiring the spirit of the man.

The plan, as Duke predicted, aroused a hornet's nest when it was mentioned at dinner that night. "Wholesale killing?" Tamsen said indignantly. "Here at Opal Station? I won't allow it!"

147

"I feel it is necessary," Juan said mildly. "It must be done."

"And I say it will not!" Tamsen faced him, anger blazing in her dark eyes.

"Dan left me in charge. I have managed this station for some time, and I will continue to do what I think best."

"And I am the owner's wife!" Tamsen said hotly. "I have a right to my opinions."

Juan sighed. "Yes, you have that right. But in this case they will make no difference."

"I can fire you," she blurted.

There was a long silence. Did I say that? Tamsen wondered. Dear God, I couldn't have said that! Not to Juan—

"As you wish," he said stiffly.

Arab, seeing a possible realization of her dreams, leaped into the fray. Clutching Juan's arm, she said, "You don't have to take this, Juan! We can go to Melbourne."

Em looked helplessly at Duke Courtney. "Duke, stop them! Oh, Lord! Don't let them quarrel."

The two adversaries faced each other, blind and deaf to the rest. Finally Tamsen's face crumpled. "I didn't mean that, Juan. I'm sorry—sorry. It's just that I don't like to see things die."

"The animals die, or the cattle. And with the cattle, the station dies. It's as simple as that."

"Then do what you have to do."

No one had seen Ramona's white face as she listened to the details of, what was to her, the planned murder of the animals she loved.

Missie wasn't present to hear the exchange. Leaving before dessert, she slipped into a cloak, her book beneath it, and left the house. Melvin was waiting for her in her secret place. She proffered the volume, wordless, as if she

148

were offering him her greatest treasure. He accepted it solemnly, as befitted the occasion.

"I will be very careful of it. I'll read it immediately and return it. But this—I want you to have it."

He handed her his volume of poetry. Last night he'd worked with it, bending the spine a little, leafing through the pages until they looked as if they'd been read again and again, turning the corners of a few down, as if to mark a spot. Here and there, he'd made a few notations on margins. Now it looked shabby, well-read, well-loved.

It was the nicest gift Missie had ever received.

He read to her for an hour. As the night grew colder, he didn't pause in his reading, but put an arm around her, pulling her close for warmth, as if it were a natural, unstudied action. She nestled there, her shivers leaving her to be replaced by another kind of trembling; a sense of wonder at the feelings blooming inside her like a rose. Was this what Mama and Papa felt for each other? Was this love? Weak with the emotions that were thrilling through her, she let her blond head rest against his chest. His heart beat in accompaniment to his words. Like music.

He had saved one particular romantic passage for a finale, but he stopped short. "I'm afraid you'd better get to the house," he said, concerned. "We can't have you catching cold."

"Just one more," she pleaded, as he'd guessed she would do. He grinned to himself, and in a thrilling almost whisper, read from verses that had fueled love's passions for centuries.

Neither of them guessed that across the clearing, in the tangle of shrub and saltbush, were a pair of watching, hating eyes. King had appointed himself guardian of young Missie. Knowing the man was here, seeing her approach, he had moved silently to squat in the shadows.

Not long ago, in this place, he had constructed a warm bed for a dying wife, a baby at her breast. And in this place, he had prepared himself to leave her and the child who could not survive her, in the manner of his people.

Then, a young girl had come upon them. Because of her, his small family had cheated the devil-devils that had threatened them. Now she herself was at the mercy of a devil-devil in human form.

His hand trembled on his spear, the knowledge of what the killing of a white man would bring still strong in his mind.

He would do nothing now. But he would continue to watch over her. And wait—

Chapter 20

The weather held through the Courtney's visit. Mild days and cold nights. On the unhappy day of their leaving, the sun slanted into the valley and the trees were full of squabbling birds with bright feathers.

"I don't want to go," Em said tearfully, embracing her sisters. "I've loved every minute of it!"

Arab too was weeping. She wasn't sure she'd be able to endure the long, monotonous days that would ensue after they were gone. "Come with us," Em said. "Juan won't mind if you visit for a month or two."

Arab shook her head. She had no wish to leave her husband's side.

Finally Duke managed to get his family aboard the wagon, allowing Scott to accompany the man who drove the second, now empty. Raising his whip in salute, he flicked the reins and they were off.

Once they were out of sight, Tamsen, who had managed to keep her composure, gave in to tears that silently streaked her cheeks.

Though of different dispositions, they had always been close, the McCleod sisters. Singly and together, they had been through enough adventures, enough tragic experiences, for a dozen women. And those experiences bound them together with a bond even stronger than blood ties.

When separation threatened, they clung to each other like children.

Even dear self-centered Arabella, Tamsen thought. Her constant chatter about living in Melbourne was only a dream. A dream in which they would all be together again, wear pretty clothes and go to parties. Nothing sad or ugly would ever touch them; the three dancing princesses—not even age.

Tamsen smiled wryly through her tears, thinking of her forty-ninth birthday in May. It had passed, unnoticed. Had it been an oversight? Or did Arab prefer to forget Tam was moving toward fifty?

"Sure ez hell hate t'see 'em go."

It was Nell's voice beside her. The big woman's face was blotched with red, her eyes glazed with tears she would not shed. She stood alone. Dusty had not come with her, and the Courtneys had gone to him to say good-bye.

"How is Dusty? Is he in bed?"

Nell nodded grimly. "Ain't doin' so good. Figger he don't count on seein' Em agin."

Tamsen flinched. "Don't say that, Nell!"

"Wisht I knowed what ailed th' leetle bastard."

"I still think we should get a doctor—"

"Won't have one, th' bull-headed leetle sonofabitch. Sez I'm too much woman fer 'im. Got 'im all wore out."

Tamsen chuckled. "He sounds normal, anyway."

"Not alweeze." Nell's face clouded. "Bin tawkin some like he's off his head."

"Delirious? Nell!"

The big woman's eyes evaded hers. "I didden mean that, eggs-actly. Hell, I dunno! Wants me to marry 'im, after all these gawdam years. All kinds of highfalutin flowery crap—"

Tamsen had been walking beside her as she lumbered toward the house she shared with the sick man. She halted suddenly at Nell's words. "Well, why don't you, if that's what he wants?"

"I ain't the marryin' kind," Nell said stolidly, her face mottled. "Neither's he. Fergit it." Then her eyes screwed up in a paroxysm of grief. "Naw, Tam. It ain't that. I don't want nuthin' t'*change*. I'm used to things like they is."

Dear God, Tamsen thought. She thinks Dusty is going to die! She put her arms about the grieving woman, feeling the trembling that shook the massive frame.

"Don't, Nell," she pleaded. "Don't!"

"Don't see why the hell not," Nell managed a sound that was half sob, half chuckle. "You girls has bawled all over me enuf times. Figger, gawdammit, it's my turn!"

Blowing her nose vigorously, she stamped ahead. They entered Dusty's bedroom to find the small man sitting up, a bottle in hand.

"Whereja find that damn thing," Nell bawled, wresting it from him. "Toldja t'lay off it until you was feelin' better."

"Jove, Nell! I only took a bit for medicinal purposes!" he said with an injured expression. "And I'm much improved." He flexed his thin arms to prove it.

Tamsen studied him. His eyes were faded, a little sunken, and he was very frail, of course. But at the moment he was quite himself. Evidently Nell thought so too, because she turned on Tamsen.

'You see," she said, aggrieved, "I toldja he was awright. But you hadda go making mountains outta gawdam moleholes!"

Raising her hands in a gesture of surrender, Tamsen left the small house and returned to the main one. Arab, Missie and Luka were clearing up the remains of the early breakfast they'd prepared for the Courtneys. Tamsen picked up a stack of plates.

"Where's Ramona?" she asked.

Arab shrugged. "I haven't the slightest idea. I haven't seen her since Em left. If it were Missie, I'd think she'd stowed away."

Missie smiled as if she had a secret. "I didn't tell you, Mama, but Aunt Em invited me to go. I said I'd rather stay."

"Well of all things," Arab gasped. "After all the fretting you did when I went with your father! I can't believe it!"

Missie's only answer was a repetition of that strange smile. Tamsen watched her thoughtfully. Little Missie was growing up.

Ramona had thought she'd get back before her absence was noticed. According to what she'd heard, listening to her father and uncle's conversation, the odious Scotchman might be here soon. Duke planned to contact him the minute he reached Melbourne. It left her little time. Under cover of the farewells, she had slipped away, going to the little hut where her wounded and orphaned wild things were kept. Opening the door, she spoke softly to the half-grown joey. He hopped to the door and waited timorously for further instruction.

"Come on!" she said, walking away. After a brief hesitation, he followed her.

Four miles up the creek was a spot where the roos came to drink. A spring on the banks above drained into the creek, making an almost permanent water hole. Here there was still a bit of grass for grazing. The only hope for her pet was to have him mingle in with a mob of his own kind. Papa would never allow her to keep him. When the hunter came, he might not find this secluded place. And if he did, he could only kill a limited number of animals at one time. Perhaps her joey might escape. It was a gamble, but it was all she knew to do.

She reached the spot, waited until the little roo

nibbled at the grass, then began to run. Though she fairly flew, she heard him bounding after her. She stopped and led him back to the place where she wanted to leave him. Again, she tried to escape, with the same result.

Finally, she put her arms around the soft brown furry creature and wept. "You've got to stay here! You can't go home with me! Please—oh, please!"

He only cocked his head at her, his intelligent eyes stating that he liked this game, whatever it was.

At last, she gathered an apron full of pebbles. Walking backward, she pelted him as he moved toward her. He paused, his paws dangling, as he tried to puzzle out his beloved mistress's behavior. He moved. Again, she pelted him. Again, again.

She finally managed to leave him, a small bewildered creature, sitting like a statue while other roos moved in around him.

She sobbed all the way home.

That night, Juan informed Arthur Melvin that he must remain in the barracks. A member of a noble Scot's family was to occupy the overseer's house within a few weeks. Without meaning to do so, he gave Melvin the impression that he was to be displaced by his betters: another insult to be mulled over and eventually avenged. It left a bitter taste in the mouth of the son of a schoolteacher and a small-time outlaw. But he didn't intend to let it push him into revealing his hand.

He had seen the girl again that night and had been pleased with the way things were going. Well. Almost too well. He had read to her for a time, and then she had declared her love for him. Gently, he had put her off. No, he had told her. She couldn't love him.

She was too young. She couldn't possibly know her own mind. And he'd sent her to the house for her own protection. He chuckled now, thinking of his cleverness.

Missie had returned from their tryst, love-dazed and bewildered.

That night, while she dreamed of love and marriage, a little house, children of her own, Ramona cried herself to sleep. Tamsen tossed with an unbearable need for Dan's arms around her; Nell hovered over Dusty's sleeping form; and Arab quarreled far into the night with Juan, begging him to move them all to Melbourne.

Only Luka slept the sleep of the young and the innocent.

The next afternoon, the weather changed. An icy wind blew, bansheelike, around the small station, reddening the sky, clawing at the tin roofs with dirt and debris. Cattle crowded in fence corners, turning their tails to the wind, and wild creatures sought shelter in the rocks on the cliffs above. The wind cut to the bone. No human dared venture out into the storm.

The family clustered around a roaring fire, wearing shawls against the chill that crept in from every crack in the walls and floor.

The abos across the river, huddled in their humpies, endured the weather stolidly. Like the heat, the wet, the dry, this was a part of living.

In the salt cedar ring by the Billabong, trees bent beneath the screaming wind, dry twigs scattering across the empty space.

Duke and Em, returning with their family to Melbourne, peered at the storm through a window, thankful that they'd made their train.

Chapter 21

In late August, old Wyuna bustled in to announce the coming of "two-man funny-feller." For once, she was almost too late with her pronouncement. Arab and Luka were napping; Ramona and Missie were off someplace. Only Tamsen, who was kneading bread in the kitchen, received Wyuna's news. She hardly had time to finish and clean the flour from her hands before two horsemen entered the yard, the hooves of their magnificent mounts clanging on the iron-hard earth.

She opened the door as they dismounted, shivering a little, hoping the chill didn't get to her rising loaves. It was clear these were the guests Juan expected. The first, obviously Denis Dugald, was a towering youth, his big frame clad in an expensive English tweed. He was incredibly handsome, she realized, as he removed his cap to reveal waving hair the color of burnished copper. The cold had laid a splash of color along strong cheekbones, and his eyes flashed with an appreciation for a pretty woman as he smiled an engaging smile.

"Mrs. Narvaéz?"

Tamsen had decided to dislike the boy since the day Juan first mentioned him. But a softness crept into her voice, despite herself. "I'm Mrs. Tallant."

"Thank the guid Lord," he said fervently. "This will

be Opal Station then. I feared we were lost!" He turned
to his companion, a small man in black, wearing a small
round hat and carrying—of all things—a set of bagpipes
cradled in his arms. "Gie me that, Boswell. Gae back
doon the road and lead the wagon in."

His man obeyed him instantly, and Tamsen was left
with a young giant holding Scottish bagpipes at her door.
"The mon who brought our things dinna know the way,"
he said good-humoredly. "He's back a wee piece."

"Come in," Tamsen said graciously. "When they
arrive, I'll show you to your quarters. You will take your
meals with us, of course."

He was delighted. Within minutes he'd made himself
at home in the kitchen, his feet—enormous, to match the
rest of him—thrust out to the fire. Before his companion
returned, he had eaten half an apple pie and consumed a
pot of coffee. He'd also put in a bid for a hot buttered
loaf-end when the bread was done.

He was handsome, charming, and utterly endearing.
Tamsen had a hard time remembering the awful thing
he'd come to do.

It was brought home to her the moment Ramona
entered the door. The girl's face went white as she saw
the young man lounging before the fire.

"Ramona," she said helplessly, "this is our guest,
Mr. Dugald. Mr. Dugald, this is my niece, Ramona Narvaéz."

"Denis," he said rising. "Call me Denis." He extended his hand and Ramona ignored it.

"How do you do, *Mr. Dugald*," she said icily. She
swept past him and entered the room she shared with
Missie and Luka, slamming the door behind her. Denis
Dugald looked at the door in amazement, then at his
extended hand.

Tamsen's face was flaming. The girl had been bla-
tantly rude. It wasn't like her. "I'm sorry, Mr.—Denis—

but Ramona is rather sensitive. She knows you came here to hunt—"

His bewildered face matched her own in color. "But hunting's a *sport*. In England, gir-r-ls ride to the hounds. And Courtney thought it was needful here—"

"It is," she sighed. "But the very idea of killing—"

"I wouldna like the lassie to think me a mur-r-rder-er. They are only animals."

"So are people," Tamsen snapped. She turned and began, furiously, to wash up the dishes.

Young Denis Dugald sat quietly, trying to readjust his thinking. From the time he was a wee lad on a bit of a pony, he'd ridden with his father, shooting hare, pheasant, fox. He could hear his father's voice now. "Well done, lad!"

He'd ridden to the hounds when he was at school in England. There had been the exhilaration of flying across green slopes, Lady Moira beside him. Moira, whom he'd thought of taking to wife when he decided to settle down.

But Moira had never stirred him as that first glimpse of this bonnie lass, her hair all tumbled—and a look of hatred in her big wide-apart eyes.

Perhaps later, when he had the opportunity to talk to her—when he could control the brogue that the excitement of arriving here had put on him—he could explain.

He no longer felt at home in the cozy kitchen. He was glad when the wagon arrived and they were shown to the small house that was to be his during his stay. It too was bright and homelike. But there was no woman in it. No smell of baking bread. Young Denis Dugald, who had never known his dead mother, suddenly felt terribly alone.

Dinner that night was even more awkward. First he met a small, mannerly Englishman who was apparently recovering from an illness. By his side was a most amazing woman with an incredible vocabulary. Poor Boswell's ears might be permanently crimson. Denis was unable to ascertain their relationship to the family. The lass, Ramona, was also there. He found it hard to swallow beneath the weight of her accusing eyes.

The next sister, Melissa, didn't seem to be impressed by newcomers one way or another. She ignored them all, ate hastily, snatched up a coat and left the house.

The little one, Luka, managed to destroy his dignity. He dressed for dinner this first night. How could he have known they'd never seen kilts? She'd burst into giggles, insisting on knowing what he wore under them.

Then Narvaéz brought the conversation to hunting. He asked what sort of weapon Dugald had. A Winchester repeater? He was unfamiliar with the weapon. How many times did it fire? Could the hunting begin tomorrow? He would go with him on the first hunt. And he would assign two abos as helpers. King was a good man, a tracker. And he might try Gheera, one of old Wyuna's grandsons. He could skin out the pelts in the field.

Only Denis noticed when Ramona left the room. He knew she wouldn't return until he was gone. So, with the idea of getting an early start in the morning, he made excuses for himself and his man.

He walked toward the small house, head down, lost in thought. It was a moment before he realized that the usually silent Boswell had spoken to him.

"What did you say?"

"T'was nought, lad. 'Tis nae for me to make joodgments."

"She is beautiful, isn't she." Dugald spoke in a low voice, half to himself.

Boswell wore a startled expression. "T'was the auld woman I made mention of. Her tongue would shame the deil, himself!"

Dugald laughed, and clapped his servant on the back. " 'Tis a new country, with different ways. We may speak in the same manner before we retur-r-n hame."

Boswell lifted his eyes to the night sky. "May the guid Lord forbid," he said piously.

True to his word, Dugald made an early start in the morning. First there was breakfast at the main house. The lassie for whom his eyes searched did not appear. Later, Ramona watched through the window as the men checked their guns, discussing their merits before they mounted. Then she turned to Tamsen.

"I hate that man," she said angrily.

"Do you hate your father? He's going shooting, too."

"Of course not. He wouldn't do it if Mr. Dugald hadn't come!"

"Juan's killing the animals because it's something that must be done. Denis is doing it because it's something he's *always* done. He doesn't see any wrong in it. Ramona, please try to understand."

Ramona didn't answer. She leaned her forehead against the window, seeing her little joey as she pelted it with pebbles. Then, in its place, was the face of Ned Kelly, with its wounded eyes.

The world was nothing but a place for men and guns.

A shot sounded in the distance. She clenched her hands and shivered as another came. Another. She suffered for all the hunted things who had no place to hide.

The shooting went on, interminably. As the year deepened into Australian spring, a warm blood smell seemed to hang over the station. The men were sickened, but they proceeded grimly with their task. Denis Dugald's young features gained a new maturity. Sometimes, raising his rifle, Ramona's face came between him and his target. Once, he lowered his gun and wiped his eyes. Then he raised it again and fired, his jaw set. This was no sport, as he'd thought it would be, but he'd made a deal and he would stick with it.

At the dinner table, the conversation was steered carefully from any mention of the day's work. Tamsen encouraged Denis to talk of home. Oddly enough, it was of the farm that he had the most memories. He hadn't been too happy at the thought of being pressed into the life of a country squire, but now he was homesick.

He talked about the dike that separated the farm from the forest; covered with wild roses, campion daisies, forget-me-nots, foxgloves—and Scottish bluebells. He told of cutting peat and riding far to a bog, where it was cut into neat squares and stacked to dry. It was impossible to describe the warmth of it, the scent of it burning.

He talked of the people who dropped by the farm; peddlers with needles and ribbons, pots and pans, or heavy baskets of fish. And the gangers searching for work or a wee bit of food and bed for the night.

Then there were the special times. On Hallowe'en, the boys blacked their faces and went from house to house begging toffee, carrying hollowed-out turnips carved with faces and with candles to light them. "Then we dooked for apples," he said solemnly.

Luka's laughter chimed, Tamsen and Nell joining in. Juan, striving to keep a straight face, explained to the embarrassed Scotsman that the word was *duck*.

Ramona, sitting in a corner near the fire, found herself mellowing in the warm family atmosphere, and fought against it. If he were not a bloody murderer, she thought forlornly, she might even like him.

He was off on another tale, telling of the fun on Hogmanay, New Year's Eve. There were parties then. If a black-haired boy were the first foot across the threshold at midnight, it brought luck to a house. "I didna hae black hair," he said gloomily. "I had tae settle for the mistletoe." If a lass were bold enough to snatch a kiss, the lad must give her a pair of gloves. If the lad were first, she gave him a tie.

Ramona's lip curled. "I imagine you received a lot of ties," she snapped.

Denis jumped a little in surprise, flustered at the unexpected sound of her voice. "Ay," he said, blushing. "Oh, ay."

Ramona returned to her stitching, jabbing a finger until it bled.

The talk eventually turned to the aborigines; their origin in what they called the Dreamtime; the way they identified with trees, rocks, water holes, believing them to be one with an ancestor who performed some creative act at that point. Certain spots where sacred corroborees were held must be avoided. However, one day Denis might have the opportunity to watch a playabout. These were a sight to behold, the women squatting, chanting, each beating time with two boomerangs. The men, naked and painted, leaped and bounded in a wild and violent manner, their ferocious shouts blending with the wailing of the women in a most awesome manner.

"Forgive me, sir," Boswell said modestly. "Speaking of the blackfellows, they hae many dingoes at their settlement. We were woondering—?"

"Leave them alone," Juan said promptly. "They value them. And they eat the pups, keeping the numbers down."

Boswell turned a little green at the thought. Denis frowned. "I hope I didna get one today. "He came tae me, like a wee guid doggie. I reached tae touch him, and he growled and clacked his teeth. I hated tae do it, but he was that fierce. T'wasna the fierst time for him. He had a long weal along his flank where some other body had potted him."

Ramona stood, her sewing falling to the floor. She

walked straight toward Dugald and pushed up her sleeve, revealing the mark the dingo had left so long ago.

"I have a scar, too," she said savagely. "Why don't you shoot me!"

Whirling, she left the room. Arab rose. "I don't know what's got into that girl," she said helplessly. "I'll go in and talk to her."

It was Nell who stopped her. "If I was you," the old woman said tartly, "I'd leave her the hell alone!" Arab faltered for a moment and returned to her seat, but the camaraderie of the evening was gone.

Chapter 22

As Ramona lay wide-eyed on her bed in the main house, Arthur Melvin took his leave from young Missie. Tonight, he had permitted himself a chaste kiss on her cheek. He walked back to the jackaroo barracks, damning himself for the surge of need that had quaked through him at the time.

He would have to watch himself. He'd moved so cautiously, leading the girl into infatuation step by step. With word and inflection, he'd managed to turn her from her family, showing that he understood her, though no one else did; that he appreciated her mind. If he had to discuss that damned book she'd loaned him once more, he'd lose his bloody sense. And though he'd enjoyed showing off his actor's talents in reading those simpering flaming poems, he was getting fed up with the whole thing.

He entered the hated barracks, and went into the cubicle he'd partitioned off for himself. Not that it did much good. He still had to endure the snoring, the smells; the perspiration and unwashed feet.

He lay down on his bed, arms beneath his head, and stared at the ceiling. He needed a woman. He'd known that tonight when he'd let a skinny little chit of a girl get to him. And he had to be careful. The time wasn't right, and the stakes were high. Sometime after Christmas, he intended to be living in the main house with a dutiful little wife. And thanks to Missie's chatter about the book she was writing, he knew enough about the Tallant bitch to make a little blackmail pay off.

In the meantime, he had a problem.

Shifting his position, he thought of the black girl across the river. Submissive, uncooperative, she hadn't been much. But at least he'd found a release. His practiced eye had determined that she would be due in a couple of weeks. Then there would be a time after that—

No need to even think about it. He'd strolled through their camp today, and found nothing else to interest him. Unless, of course, he got desperate enough to try old Wyuna. His mouth twisted wryly at the thought. Tonight he'd kicked the hell out of the abo, King, when he found him snooping around the clearing before Missie arrived. That seemed to help a little. Tomorrow, he just might do it again.

Meanwhile everything was moving without a hitch. For a time after the Dugald bloke arrived, he'd had a few shaky moments. Much as he disliked him, he had to admit he was a good-looking devil. Young, too. But the coming of the Scot had made no difference. Proper besotted, young Missie was. He smiled smugly. He hadn't lost any of his old charm.

He let his mind wander back to the abo girl.

He had no way of knowing that he was wrong in his calculations. At that moment, in a small humpy quickly erected at a distance from the aboriginal settlement, Queenie was bearing a child. It was a month early, due perhaps to the severity of the winter—or the potions Wyuna had given her in those first months; potions that had failed to dislodge the baby from her womb.

Wyuna was with her. King squatted, spear in hand,

at the edge of the clearing. To go any nearer was tabu. Waiting, he mulled over the things Wyuna had told him about the baby's conception.

The aborigines believed babies were born because spirit children from another life entered the mother's womb. Or they were possibly made with the help of the Rainbow Snake, or the moon. His own opinion had been that his wife had walked under a tree, where, as everyone knew, spirit babies waited.

Wyuna snorted at his naiveté. "Him-wife walk under tree, but white devil-devil proper dere, no mistake."

Mission trained, having seen half-castes born from such unions, she proceeded to instruct him in the way of such things.

Confused, shaken to the roots of his belief, he squatted, unmoving even when he heard the brief cry. After a few moments, Wyuna waddled toward him, along the path.

"Devil-devil, him," she pronounced. "I fix."

She returned to the hut and he remained where he was, aching from the beating he'd taken at the hands of the man who had violated his wife. Only his staring, red-rimmed eyes showed the extent of his anger and grief.

Within two days, Queenie was back in the main house, at her task to "shepherd-im flies." Princess played happily in a corner. But there was no small black infant in its bark coolamon. Missie, who had been awaiting the event, was astonished.

"You've had your baby, Queenie!" she said. "I'm so glad! Was it a boy or a girl? Why didn't you bring it? Can I go see—"

"No baby," Queenie said placidly, waving her palm frond."

"But I thought—"

"Baby go dreamtime."

The baby was dead. Missie's eyes filled. "Oh, Queenie, I'm sorry."

Queenie did not reply, but continued at her task, her black face inscrutable.

Two days later, Denis and Boswell returned from a hunting trip, white and sick. They had shot several dingoes that were nosing about a hole in the rocks above the riverbed. Then, checking to make sure there were no pups inside, they unearthed a grisly sight: a newborn baby, its head lolling to one side as if its neck had been broken. They had buried it there, heaping the grave with stones to keep predators away.

No one saw the way Missie shrank, her face seeming to shrivel like that of an old woman. Juan's face was ashen. "It would be Queenie's," he admitted. "The aborigines often dispose of an afflicted baby—"

"This little fellow seemed perfect to me," Denis said. "Though he did seem to be a half-caste. He was quite light in color."

"That could be a reason. Many of these people have white blood in their background. Possibly a throwback to a generation or more—"

Arab's eyes were dilated in horror. "Killing a baby! Dear God, Juan, it's murder! You've got to do something."

Juan threw up his hands. "What in the hell do you expect me to do! These people don't think like we do! Dios! Do you think I can force them to keep a child they don't want! Should Queenie be put in jail? Hanged, just because she's a poor ignorant girl with nothing to go by but what her people have been doing for years?"

"Don't shout at me," Arab said, her lip trembling.

He put his arms around her. "I didn't mean to shout. But this makes me sick. Think of doing away with one of our own. Ah, Dios!"

There was a white ring around his lips. Arab pulled herself together. "I think we could all use a cup of tea," she said quietly. She led the men into the house.

Missie ran. She wasn't conscious of where she was going until she found herself at her destination. The magic circle surrounded by salt cedar had lost its enchantment. The cedars were sparse after the winter winds and the long dry. They cast little shade. A late sun burned into the clearing, pointing out a faint rectangular outline—the place where King had made a warm bed for his dying wife; where Missie had found them. She had taken the little family for her own, loved them.

Now she knew that she'd never really known them. Not at all.

She was still in the clearing when Arthur Melvin arrived, finding her tear-stained, dust-streaked, looking more like a punished child than a young woman. Heedless of propriety, she flung herself into his arms. Dressed in his clean white clothing, he suppressed a shiver of distaste and held her away to look anxiously into her swollen eyes.

"What is it, little sweetheart? What have they done to you this time?"

He listened patiently as she sobbed out the story of how Queenie had had her baby, and of the thing Denis Dugald had found beneath some rocks above the riverbed. He hid his only emotion, a sense of relief. No one would ever recognize anything of himself in a black woman's child. He had to give Queenie credit for some sense.

"Then, she killed her baby?" He managed to put incredulity into his tone. "But why?"

"I don't know," Missie wept. "Denis said it looked like it might be part white."

"Then that's it. Damn the woman, hanging around the jackaroos like she did! I've told her more than once to clear out!"

Missie drew away. "The jackaroos! Oh, Arthur, none of them would—"

He smiled down at her fondly. "Little innocent! You don't know anything at all about men, do you? Most of them will take advantage of anything that's freely offered."

From the aboriginal camp upriver came a monotonous, chanting sound. As it rose in volume, it was accompanied by the beat of boomerangs striking together. Then there was a shrill, high-pitched, unholy shriek as the men joined in.

A corroboree! Dear God, a corroboree! When a baby had been murdered—

A scent of decay hung in the air. Skins from yesterday's hunting, blood from today's. Murder, death! Blood, dust! Dying cattle! Heat! Murder! The words hammered at her brain to the tempo of chanted words and clashing sticks. A scream—

Her face blank with shock and horror, she stood still for a moment, then clutched at Melvin's shoulders with frantically clawing hands.

"I can't stand this anymore," she cried. "Oh, Arthur, I can't stand it! Take me away! Oh, God, please take me away!"

Much later, having calmed her, he sat holding her like a child. His voice was hypnotic as he talked to her; making promises he had no intention of keeping. They would go to Melbourne, he said. Or Sydney. Or even to Adelaide, where her heroine, Miss Spence, lived, if she wished. There would be books, lectures, plays. And they would live happily ever after.

But first, he said sternly, came marriage. He had never really loved before. It must be done right, or not at all. Could she keep calm, trust him for just a few more days? And keep their secret until the thing was over and done?

She could do anything, as long as their life together lay at the end.

Downriver, the corroboree had grown to full volume. But Missie no longer heard the savage music. She rested her head against Arthur Melvin's heart, its beating making a music of its own.

Chapter 23

When Arthur Melvin presented himself to Juan Narvaéz, asking for a few days leave, Juan was almost tempted to deny his request. Ever since he had been forced to move the man into the jackaroo barracks to make room for Dugald, the man had been behaving strangely. Nothing he could put his finger on, really, but his manner seemed to fall just short of insolence.

Probably he was reading something into the man's character because he didn't like him. And, he had to admit, he had certainly earned his leave. He told him that he could go.

After Melvin had ridden off, Juan was sorry he hadn't asked him to wait a few days. A rider brought in a letter from Em, and it contained exciting news. Cammie was getting married. The groom-to-be was a fine young man from a good family. The wedding was set for the first day of the New Year. There was so much to do, so many preparations to make in such a short time. She needed another woman's help. If only Tamsen or Arab could come—

Arab's eyes brightened for the first time since the discovery of the dead child. "I could take Luka," she said. Then the brightness faded. "Tamsen is the one who should go."

Tamsen, standing behind her, shook her head at Juan. The episode of Queenie's baby had turned Arab into a bundle of nerves. She'd been unable to eat. Last night, she hadn't slept. She could use the time away.

"You could all go," Juan said uncertainly. Denis, Boswell and I can eat with the hands. Maybe Nell—"

"Nell can't cook worth beans," Tamsen said. "Besides, she's got her hands full with Dusty. And I'm certainly not going to turn Denis and Boswell over to O'Brien's cooking. No, Juan. You go with Arab, and take the girls."

Juan resisted, declaring it would be impossible for him to remain in Melbourne for a month. But Arab's eyes looked so desperate. Finally, beseiged from all sides, with offers from Dugald and Boswell to take over his duties, he gave in. Ramona refused to accompany them. She had her chores, and after all, she'd never known Cammie that well. Missie, too, begged off on the trip, with the excuse of staying behind to help Ramona.

Tamsen felt a sense of relief as she watched the buggy containing the members of her family draw away. Juan had worked too hard for too long. He was worn thin. And Arab would return with her spirits renewed. With Melvin gone too, there should be no problems. And maybe January would bring the blessed rain.

She hugged Ramona and Missie to her. "We're going to do just fine, aren't we?"

"Just fine," Missie echoed, unable to hide a triumphant smile.

For the next few days, young Denis was too occupied with station affairs to do any hunting. Without the sound of shooting punctuating the long hot afternoons, Ramona was lulled into a feeling of security. She watched him on the long evenings as he talked of fishing in the Firth of Clyde; of small Scottish towns that sat still while the world passed them by; of men from Spain who sold oranges at three for a penny; of foreign fortune-tellers; Italians with barrel organs and monkeys; a trained bear.

"I'd love to see those things," she burst out.

He looked at her oddly. "Perhaps someday you will."

Tamsen noted the girl's blush and wondered. They seemed so right for each other. A pity he was so wild about hunting.

Like him or not, Ramona found herself dressing for the evening, studying her gowns to see which complemented her olive skin, her misty dark hair. Dugald took no note of what she wore. He was too enchanted with the way her eyes were set in her young face; the tiny tilted nose; the wide mouth that seemed made for kissing. He thought of Hogmanay, and mistletoe.

More or less restricted to the station proper because of his duties, he insisted on taking on some of the heavier work himself. Ramona, accustomed to carrying heavy buckets of grain, rebelled at first. But as time went on, she began to enjoy his gallantry. Everyone had always taken her work for granted. Now she had someone who appreciated her, helped her. Missie wasn't much help, always drifting around in a dream. Probably writing in her head, Ramona thought, indulgently.

Then, one night as she milked, her head resting comfortably against a cow's warm flank, she was aware that she wasn't alone. When she left the barnyard, strong hands reached out to take the brimming pails from her.

He carried them to the dairy house, where she strained them and poured them into clean crocks while he lounged against the door. A little flustered, she turned to skim the previous day's cream.

"I like to watch this," he said, a little hoarsely. "I remember when I was a little lad. We had a dairymaid who was kind tae me. I followed her at work, pretending she was my mother."

"I'll bet your mother didn't like that."

"I dinna know. I never had one. My mother died when I was bor-r-n."

She turned with a little cry, wiping her hands on her apron. "I'm so sorry!"

"It makes nae difference now. I dinna remember her." His expression belied his words. He looked hungry and forlorn.

As she searched for something to say, there was a voice behind him, out of the darkness. "There ye are, lad!" It was Boswell. "I've been sear-r-ching for you. The mon, King, hae found us a mob o' the roo-beasts, four miles up creek. Shall we see tae them in the mor-r-ring?"

"Ay, mon! First light. Are the goons cleaned? Ready tae go?"

"Everything is in or-r-rder," the manservant said modestly.

Her head whirling, Ramona pushed past them and ran to the house. They'd found the spot where she'd left her pet joey! They'd kill him for sure, now! Unless there was some way she could stop them. But what could she do? Numbly, she helped Tamsen get the food on the table, burning her hand as she emptied a kettle.

"Let me see that," Tamsen said. Ramona jerked away. "It's all right," she said, her eyes brimming with sudden tears. "Leave me alone."

When everyone was seated at the table, Ramona made an excuse to leave the house. She'd left something undone in the dairy room, she said. It would only take a minute.

Once outside, she went directly to the house that had once been the overseer's. The object she looked for was nowhere in sight. Opening the door of one bedroom, she saw a neatly made bed, a pair of small polished shoes sitting beneath it: Boswell's room, obviously.

She turned to the second bedroom, Denis Dugald's room. Here the spread was rumpled as though someone had napped for a few moments after it was made up. There was a dent where a head had rested on a pillow. Clothing was strewn about. As upset as she was, there was something endearing about the chaos.

In the corner of the room, she found the Winchester repeater that was Dugald's pride and joy. Boswell had spoken the truth. It was well-oiled and gleaming.

She carried it outside, and shoved the barrel beneath the flat stone that served as a threshold. Then, using the stone as a lever, she pulled with all her weight against the handle of the gun.

She had been gone from the main house more than the minute she'd promised. Five minutes passed. Ten. Fifteen. At last Denis rose, his face red with embarrassment. "I canna eat while a wee lassie's laboring," he stammered. "Maybe I can gie a hand at whatever she must do."

His excuse was so transparent that Tamsen hid a smile. "Hell, yes," Nell boomed knowingly. "Give the little lady a great big hand!" Tamsen silenced her with a look. "Gawdammit, Tam," Nell grumbled. "Ennybody kin see which way the wind's ablowin'."

"He can't," Tamsen said. "Neither can she. Let's let them find out for themselves."

The dairy room was dark. Denis peered inside. "Ramona?" he said her name softly. She wasn't there. It didn't seem possible that he could have passed her on the way out. These long summer nights still held enough light to see by.

Puzzled, he turned toward the main house. As he passed by his own sleeping quarters, he heard a grating sound. He frowned a little, thinking of the abos, a door that wouldn't lock. He moved toward the sound on silent feet.

It was the lassie. But what was she doing? Guid God!

"Ye fule!" he roared wrathfully. "Ye silly wee fule! What are ye doing to ma goon!"

She jerked at his shout, feeling her elbows clasped roughly in big hands. He lifted her off her feet, tearing her grip from the weapon, and set her aside.

"A—a snake went under the threshold," she offered weakly. "I was trying to kill it."

He paid no attention to her as he pulled the weapon free, his hand caressing the bowed barrel as if it were a wounded thing. "Ma goon," he kept saying. "Ma puir wee goon!"

Then, with a wordless growl, he threw the gun aside, and snatching her up under one arm, opened the door with the other. She fought and kicked to no avail. Inside, he pulled out a straight chair and sat down, bending her over one knee, pinning her flailing limbs with the other. His hard hand came down, again and again. Unable to move, she shut her mouth tightly and endured the humiliation.

When he was done, he set her on her feet, a hand at each shoulder bruising her collarbone. "I'll teach ye tae spoil a man's pr-r-operty," he growled. "Ye'll pay for the day!"

Without warning, his mouth came down on hers, hard and burning. For a moment she fought to turn her head, then her mouth softened, lips parting in answer to his kiss. She swayed forward, aching to feel the length of him against her, dazed with the pounding in her breast.

With an effort, he managed to put her from him, his eyes blazing as he said, "Ye'll no touch ma things again, ye understond!"

With a small whimper, she whirled and was out the door, running across the space to the main house. She burst through the door and ran to her room, oblivious to the shocked expressions around the supper table. How dare he! Damn him!

Tamsen rose to go to the girl. She'd looked terrible. Dishevelled, her hair fallen, her face crimson. But before she could move, Denis Dugald walked in.

"She didna need ma help," he said shortly. "I've come for ma supper."

He seated himself and reached for a biscuit, ignoring the silence of those around them. Spreading it liberally with butter and jam, he took a bite and swallowed.

"There will be nae hoonting in the mor-r-rning, Boswell. Ma goons out of or-rder."

"I cleaned the thing," Boswell said, with an injured expression.

"Ye shouldn' hae leaned it against the wall. It gie a warp to the bar-r-rel," Dugald said, twin spots of anger still burning in his cheeks. He helped himself to some potatoes. "And bye the bye, mon. Take care when you return tae the hoose. There's a snake oonder the thr-r-reshold."

Chapter 24

In the days that followed, the open enmity between Ramona and the young Scot became an uneasy truce. They were forced to work together from time to time, and they did so with as few words as possible. The memory of that night, culminating in a kiss, was foremost in each of their minds in spite of their attempts to forget. If a touch was necessary as they worked, carrying feed and water, doctoring a sick animal, they both recoiled.

Missie, lost in a dream those first few days after Arthur proposed, finally began to return to reality. There was much to do. Her clothes were to be gone over, cleaned, mended, and packed in a trunk ready to be moved. And there was the book she was working on. Dusty had supplied her with priceless information, but he rambled a lot in his tales. There were gaps that needed filling in the information she'd compiled. She'd better get some answers now, she thought with a feeling of loss. She might never see her old friend again.

For the moment, Dusty's health had improved. Nell refused to allow him any exertion, but he often sat beneath a big tree where he could watch the station at work. He was delighted to have Missie join him. He hadn't seen much of the girl lately. Too, she was always kind enough to bring him a drop or two for the thirst he'd developed over the years.

Each night, Missie prepared a list of questions. Each day, she managed to sort what she needed from the chaff of his memories.

"When I publish my book, Dusty, I'm going to dedicate it to you!"

He smiled, tousling her golden curls. "My word, Missie, that is a compliment to be treasured."

He watched her cross the yard, thinking a little sadly that it was good she didn't know how fragile her dream was. For one thing, the stories he told her about Arab's, Em's and Tamsen's past, true though they were, would undoubtedly prove too shocking for this era.

Too, she had little chance of becoming a writer at all. One day she would meet some young man and fall in love, marry and raise a family. But someday, she would happen on some old pages written in the past—and remember him.

He wondered if he should have tried to discourage her in her obsession. Then he knew he could not have. It gave the girl something to do when she needed it.

Nell walked out to join him, sniffing a little at the alcoholic smell of his breath. The leetle rascal snuck him a snort, she thought, grinning a little. Well, hell, he was lookin' better anyways.

She put her hand on his shoulder, following his gaze. It moved from Missie walking toward the house to Ramona and Denis, working together, carefully maintaining a distance of at least four feet as they carried water to the chickens.

"Jove! I would think the girls would take more interest in young Denis—"

Nell snorted. "Some men's got it, some ain't. They ain't all like you, you leetle sonofabitch!"

Dusty smiled with modest pride. As usual, his Nell was right.

"Don't be so gawdam smug," she said, slapping him playfully on the shoulder. He looked up at her affectionately, and they laughed together.

Meanwhile, Ramona, having finished her chores, was preparing to return to the house. Dumping her pail into the tin trough that watered the chickens, she hung the bucket on the fence and turned to depart.

"Wait," Denis said, a little harshly. He quieted his voice to a more polite tone. "Please wait. I'd like tae talk tae you."

Repressing her impulse to inform him they had nothing to talk about, she faced him stiffly. He looked at her for a moment and sighed.

"I canna talk wi' ye like this, nae wi' your wee face closed against me. Ma Scot's toongue gets in ma way. Weel ye walk wi' me?"

Finally, she nodded. But she kept her distance from him as they walked up the nearly dry creekbed, away from the station buildings. As they walked, he cursed himself for a fool. He was still angry about the Winchester, but the way he had punished the girl was unforgiveable. As for the kiss—it had been impulsive. He preferred not to think about that.

If Juan Narvaéz had been home, he would have left on the spot. But he'd promised to look after things, and he was committed. There was no point in living in a state of open warfare. The fact that he wanted the girl's liking most desperately, he concealed from himself.

Finally, he stopped. "This is as guid a place as any."

Ramona walked to a tree at the edge of the creekbed and leaned against it. He followed her, putting one hand on the trunk beside her. She felt trapped, a little smothered by the pulse beating in her throat. "Well?"

"I'm asking ye tae forgive me," he said huskily. "I had nae call to treat you as I did."

"If you expect me to apologize for ruining your gun, I won't. I would do it again."

How bonny she was, with the red in her cheeks, those dark eyes sparked with fire. Within her family, he knew she was regarded as a quiet, docile girl. Denis Dugald had reason to think differently. He had a sudden urge to kiss her until she couldn't breathe—

But that was not what he'd brought her here for. He took a deep breath.

"Then, when I get a new goon, I shall hae to keep it in a safe place, lassie."

Ramona's eyes brimmed. "Why don't you just go away."

He stiffened. "When your father returns, I will. There are other stations. Though I admit there's no challenge in hoonting the wee beasties as I've doon. Per-r-haps I'll offer ma services tae the police. I've been told of the mon, Kelly, who—"

Ramona's hand flashed out, leaving a red welt imprinted on the face above her own. With a twist, she was around him, free of the imprisoning arm, and she ran along the creekbed, skirts flying.

His hand to his stinging cheek, he watched after her. There was no pleasing this one. He'd apologized. When she told him to go, he'd said that he would. His Scotch stubbornness came to the fore.

He was done with trying. But he would not let her run him off. He'd be domned if he would!

He returned to the house and lifted Juan's old single-shot from its brackets on the wall. Then he walked back up the creekbed.

Ramona heard the shooting later, and bit her lip. She knew the sound of Papa's gun. Her only consolation

184

was that it fired just one bullet at a time. She tried to close her ears to the sound.

Near the end of December, Arthur Melvin returned to Opal Station. He had gone from town to town, checking out the churches and missions. It wasn't until he reached the Murray that he found what he wanted. A small brush-arbor revival was being held in the countryside. On its fringes, men from isolated stations were engaged in talking and heavy drinking, while their women, hungry for hope, listened to the preacher harangue. Melvin took his seat among them, listening for several weary hours as the man lashed out against aborigines, whom he called sons of Cain; against pleasure, all of which was sin; against lust, adultery, fornication. His sermon was liberally laced with a dosage of hell-fire and brimstone. As he talked, Melvin figured his man.

A lanky unkempt fellow, with a mass of bushy black hair that he tossed like a willow in the wind, he had one walleye that belied the fanatic sincerity of the other. As he passed the collection plate, he laid a heavy burden of guilt on his listeners. When one of them fell into a fit, jerking and twitching, inadvertently revealing her boney knees, he had to hide a grin.

No doubt about it, Melvin said to himself. A kindred spirit, though in a less attractive package. He reminded him a bit of his old dad. He didn't look like a bloke who'd be averse to making a bit of change.

As he'd suspected, the Reverend Elizar Tuggs was an easy man to deal with. He was proud to do his part in uniting two young people in holy wedlock. His one eye attested to his sincerity, while the other gleamed at the offer Melvin made him in return for his coming to Opal Station.

He asked no questions regarding the odd arrangements. They rode across country in relative silence until they neared the station. There, Preacher Tuggs was to make camp and remain until Melvin came for him.

Wyuna, as usual, sped to the house to make her announcement: "Two feller come." When only Melvin appeared, Tamsen concluded that the aborigines did make a mistake occasionally. Or perhaps Wyuna was getting old.

Facing Melvin, she felt the old dislike bristling. Clean despite his journey, smooth-shaven, his eyes bland, he looked so sure of himself. "You're back a little early," she said. "I suppose you wish to resume your duties?"

He waved her question away. "I'll take it easy today. I have an important matter to attend to tonight." He didn't look at Missie, who trembled at his slight inflection on the last word. "Why don't we talk it over tomorrow?"

"I don't see that there's anything to talk about. Either you intend to work, or you don't."

He smiled enigmatically. "We'll see," he said. Then he left the house.

Missie had been stirring a pot on the stove. At Melvin's arrival, she'd left her task. She watched the man walk away, a mingled wave of love and fear making her shiver. Her life was going to change. She would be leaving her mother, her father, her sisters—Dusty, Aunt Tamsen—

A smell of scorching filled the air. "Missie!" Tamsen said crossly. "Can't I trust you to do *anything?*"

Missie's face closed as she lifted the pot and set it in a pan of cold water. Soon all this would be behind her. She would make herself a name for something she could do well.

Tonight, Arthur would be waiting.

Chapter 25

When twilight fell, Missie flitted like a small white butterfly toward her secret place beside the Billabong. She'd worn her only white gown; a child's frock really, since it was two years old. She had let down the hem with fumbling, inept fingers, and let out a few seams in the bosom. In a little bag, she carried a wispy veil, constructed of mosquito netting and lace she'd removed from a petticoat. There was also a nosegay of silk flowers she'd extracted from her best bonnet. She would look the part of a bride.

She pressed through the salt cedars, nervously expectant. He was not here as yet. As time passed, she grew more and more worried at his absence. What if she'd misunderstood his message? Suppose he didn't come—

Melvin had ridden upcreek to where Preacher Tuggs waited. Leaving his campsite, they rode to a reasonable distance, then dismounted, walking the remainder of the way. No need to have those damned abos announce their arrival.

When they reached the hideaway, Missie was waiting. Hearing the sound of their boots crunching on the gravel, she had a desire to flee. Then she thought of those idyllic nights, the love poems. A shout rang from the abo camp downriver, and she shuddered, remembering the dead baby. Arthur would take her away from all this.

She carefully fitted the veil to her blond curls, and held her nosegay, trembling, as they approached: Arthur tall and handsome, accompanied by a lanky walleyed man in a rusty black suit. He carried a Bible in his hand.

Melvin didn't look at his quivering girl-bride. He moved to stand beside her. "Come on, Tuggs," he ordered. "Let's get this over with."

The minister tossed his hair back from his forehead, and began to read the ceremony in a high, nasal voice. Above, night birds cooed and chuckled. A small animal moved in the brush. It should have been most romantic, Missie thought, dazed. But it suddenly seemed wrong! Wrong. In a small voice, she heard herself making the proper responses.

The groom did not kiss the bride. Instead, he shoved a number of clinking coins into the preacher's hands.

"That's it. It's over. You can clear out. Try not to make too much noise until you're on your way."

Then the Reverend Tuggs was gone. She was alone in the salt cedar circle with a man who was her husband —but who suddenly seemed a stranger.

"Mrs. Melvin," he said in a rough, triumphant voice. "Mrs. Arthur Melvin! What will those stuck-up sonsofbitches have to say to this?" He laughed with an ugly elation, his laughter somehow more frightening than his words.

"We'd better go tell them." She backed away. "I must get my things—"

His hand shot out, gripping her shrinking shoulders. "No, you don't! We've got to make this bloody thing legal!"

Ripping at her gown, he pressed her backward. She

fell to the ground and he was down with her, crushing her breath from her body, clawing, bruising, hurting hurting hurting—

It wasn't Missie he attacked so violently. It was Tamsen. Tamsen, who'd thought herself too good for Arthur Melvin. Her features took the place of blond Missie's as he violated her, cruelly, brutally.

She was sobbing, semiconscious, when he rolled away and hauled her to her feet.

"Now, we'll tell them," he said, grinning with malicious satisfaction.

In the main house, Tamsen and Ramona were alarmed at Missie's long absence. Her nightly excursions had rarely lasted more than an hour. Even those had ceased of late. Now it was after midnight, and she still had not come in. There were so many things that could have happened; she could have fallen. A poisonous snake—

Tamsen went to her room, got her small pistol, and dropped it into her pocket. "I'm going out to look for her," she said, her face determined.

Ramona demurred. "I think we should wake Denis and Boswell."

"I'll try by myself, first," Tamsen said wearily. "There's no sense spilling our family problems into a stranger's lap."

"Denis isn't a stranger," Ramona blurted. Her face crimsoned as Tamsen looked at her with raised brows.

A knocking at the door interrupted them. Not a genteel knock, but a hammering that brought Tamsen's heart into her throat. Missie! She thought. Something has happened—

The opened door revealed two people: a swaggering man in white moleskins; a thin girl-child in the pitiful remains of what had once been an attempt at bridal finery.

"Dear God," Tamsen whispered, "Missie! Oh, dear God!"

Melvin shoved his battered, tear-stained bride forward. "Meet the Missus," he said with an insolent smile.

"You're lying," Tamsen spat. "You—You—!"

"I think sonofabitch is the word you're looking for, Ma'am." He gave her an exaggerated bow. "And if you think I'm lying, ask my wife. The ceremony has been performed, and," he smiled, savoring the effect of his words, "the marriage consummated. I believe this makes you—my auntie? Aren't you going to welcome me to the bosom of the family?"

"Get out of here." Tamsen said in a deadly voice. "Get out of this house!"

"If I go, my bride goes with me."

"No," Ramona said suddenly. She moved in front of Missie, covering the shivering body with her own. "Leave her alone!"

Melvin swung a muscular arm, slamming Ramona into the wall. He grabbed Missie by the arm, twisting it cruelly. "We're not wanted here. Come on—"

Tamsen's hand touched the chill steel of the weapon in her pocket. She drew it, pointing it steadily at the man. "Let her go—"

"You wouldn't dare shoot me," Melvin taunted. "Not now!"

Tamsen aimed deliberately and fired. A bullet whipped through his shirt sleeve, penetrating the outer arm. Eyes wide with shock, he released Missie, clapping his hand to the wound. The immaculate white shirt was stained with crimson.

"Take one more step and I'll kill you," Tamsen said

through clenched teeth. "Ramona, take your sister to her room!"

Missie, barely conscious of what was happening allowed her sister to lead her away. Tamsen held her ground, gun raised and pointed at Melvin's heart.

Melvin stood still for a moment, his eyes wild with anger. "You win this time," he said finally. "But I'm not through. You know that."

"And I intend to remain armed. *You* know *that*. You are not to show your face here again. If you do, I'll shoot you like a mad dog! If I don't, Missie's father will."

"Maybe I can make him see reason," Melvin sneered. "I know a lot about his precious wife's past. She was a stage tart, wasn't she? And you, my dear, you were—"

She raised the pistol again, and he departed, trying to move without unseemly haste. He brushed past Denis Dugald as he went, the young Scotsman dressed haphazardly, Juan's rifle in hand, as he ran toward the still open door.

He burst in, finding Tamsen sagging against the table, a smoking pistol at her side.

"I heard the shot," he said. "Is there na trouble?"

"Oh, Denis, Denis!" She dropped the gun and let him take her, holding her close as she sobbed out her story. "Denis, I don't know what we're going to do."

He patted her, clumsily, thinking how this family's hurts had become his own.

Later, Missie, bathed, her bruises rubbed with the precious emu oil, was put to bed. Slowly, her mind began to function, trying to find some rationalization for what had happened. She was Arthur's wife. She had taken vows in the sight of God. And he hadn't meant to hurt her. He'd probably been nervous, knowing what kind of reception the announcement of their marriage was bound to receive.

"We're not wanted here," he'd said. "Come on—"

And Tamsen had shot him.

The memories of those romantic nights, the words of poetry like honey on his tongue, the gentleness of him— all these came back to her, blotting out the rest. Slowly, Tamsen evolved as the villainess of the piece.

The next morning, she was sullen and silent, turning her face away, refusing to answer Tamsen's questions. "I'm Arthur Melvin's wife," was all she would say. Ramona received the same treatment.

By afternoon Tamsen was at her wit's end. Arab and Juan should be notified, summoned home. Yet the news would cast a pall over Cammie's wedding. By the time someone rode to the telegraph office at Jerilderie, the telegram was sent and received, it would be nearing the date.

She conferred with Denis and Ramona; they agreed it would be best to wait until after Cammie's wedding. And they would keep Missie's secret to themselves until her parents were informed. There was no need to upset Nell and Dusty. The little Englishman might not weather the news.

When Tamsen left Denis and Ramona to go see to Missie, Ramona reached to touch the Scotchman's hand. "Thank you," she said.

He looked startled. "I dinna do anything to be thankit for."

"Thank you for being here," she whispered. Seeing his eyes fixed on hers, she rose hurriedly. "I must go help Aunt Tamsen."

Missie bided her time. That evening, hearing them all at the supper table, she climbed from her bed, tottering on her stiff limbs. Going to her trunk, she took out

192

her little volume of poetry, the notes for her own planned book, and two gowns, making the whole thing into a tight bundle, and tying it neatly with an old sash. She slid the window open carefully and dropped the package to the ground. Then she eased herself over the ledge, scraping both wrists in the process. Still in her nightdress, shoes pulled over stockingless feet, she ran, with a peculiar hobbling gait.

Dusty, having had had no appetite this night, had forced Nell to go to the main house for supper without him, explaining that it was too hot to eat. He sat now beneath the big tree, enjoying the evening, until she returned.

Half dozing, he jerked awake at the sight of a small figure, running across the yard. Missie? Carrying a bundle—and in her nightgown? He started to call after her, then chuckled, remembering the imagination, the mysterious ways of youth. Jove, he kept forgetting that Missie was still a little girl.

Arthur Melvin was waiting in the salt cedar circle just as Missie had somehow known he'd be. He'd washed his wound in the creek, managed to bind it with a strip of his shirt, and used the remainder for a sling. Since the night before he'd moped in the sheltered spot trying to plan his best method of revenge. His eyes widened at sight of Missie. She had come!

Seeing the pleasure in the eyes of the big man who stood, like a wounded hero, his bare upper torso shining in the last ray of the setting sun, Missie's heart caught in her throat. It had been right to come! Right! How could she have ever doubted him?

Forgetting the fear and pain of the previous night, she ran to him. He held her with his one good arm, murmuring soft endearments, his mind working at top speed.

"We've got to go," she whispered. "Hurry! When they find I'm gone, they'll be after us."

He smiled oddly. "Then we'll have to create a little diversion, won't we. We'll give them something to keep them busy."

Chapter 26

The aborigine, King, squatted on the edge of the Billabong, gazing morosely into the dusk. The woman had been cross since the birth of the devil-devil's child. Despite Wyuna's explanations, he still had haunting doubts. The spirits here were not their own. They were far from their tribal territory, lost in the dreamtime of the ancestors of a strange tribe. He felt his own spirit slowly withering. He needed to renew it with the visions of trees and stones that were so closely allied with his own creation.

He had spoken to the woman, hinting at the need for a walkabout. She had refused in a sharp voice, unbecoming to a married woman. But perhaps in their own country, she would walk beneath a tree, or near a totem with a gentler spirit. There would be another child, and her disposition would heal.

His sharp ears caught the sound of movement far up the creek. An animal coming for water? He stood, spear in hand, and moved toward the sound on silent feet, his weapon at the ready.

He stopped and stood still, blending with the darkness of a tree behind him. Young Missie, his blessed savior, emerged from the spot where she had first found him and his family. With her was the devil-devil, shirtless, his arm bound. He led the girl to the other side of the creek, his voice carrying clearly as he said, "Wait, I have something to do."

He returned to the bank from which they'd emerged, took his wounded arm from the sling, and crouched by a low shrub. King could not make out what he was doing until he saw the small glow that erupted, enveloping dry vegetation in flame.

"No," the girl screamed hysterically. "Oh, my God, Arthur! No!"

The big man sped from the conflagration he'd started. Reaching Missie, he slapped her brutally across the face. Her arm twisted behind her, he led her away.

King stood poised for a second, indecisive. A black-fellow must not kill a white man. The lesson was engraved too deeply in his mind. At last, he whirled and ran for the station.

The family was sitting quietly at supper, Missie's absence having been explained to Nell as a touch of illness.

"You don't look too good, yourself," Nell boomed. "In fack, you an' Ramona look like hell. Hope it ain't nuthin' ketchin'."

"I don't think so," Tamsen said quietly. "It's the heat, I'm sure. Ramona, maybe you should check on your sister."

Ramona rose obediently and entered the bedroom. In an instant, she was back. "She's gone, Tamsen! Oh, God, he's got her!"

"Who's got her?" Nell's face was a mask of bewilderment. "What the hell you talking about?"

Denis was on his feet, heading toward the door, when it flew open. Nell shrieked at the sudden appearance of a wild-looking black man, spear in hand. She was certain that they were all about to be massacred. But

King stopped short and faced them with a kind of dignity.

"Him-devil-devil," he said, searching dumbly for words. "Missie take'im. Make'im fire—"

The smell of smoke reached them now, and they could hear the crackling of flames.

Denis turned to a pale Ramona. "Go to the barracks. Tell the boys to wet down the buildings. I think we're safe here, except for the trees, and they stand away. Tell Bob to bring axes and saws to the middle of the area. Have Jim get sacks and wet them. Nell, get Dusty—"

Nell was pointing from the doorway. "There he goes, the damn fool! Runnin' straight fer the fire! He's lost his gawdam mind! Somebody stop him!"

After that first sight of Missie, Dusty had drowsed again. The scent of smoke roused him. He looked around, blearily, for the source, then caught sight of the red flames licking in the distance. They were near Missie's clearing. Oh, my word! Missie! Missie!

A surge of adrenaline lifted him to his feet. He began to run, as fleet as a young boy, his worn-out heart galloping in his chest. "Missie! Missie!" Crying her name, he dashed into the flames.

Denis Dugald, at Nell's cry, had emptied the contents of the water pail over a cloak he'd snatched from a hook. Then he, too, ran, vainly trying to keep sight of the fleeing figure. Damn, how the old boy could go! He was a few feet behind him when he disappeared into the fire. With a hiss of indrawn breath, the Scotchman strengthened his resolve—and followed.

He found himself in a clearing, a fiery ring surrounding him. In the middle of the clearing stood Dusty, staring blankly about. And the old man's sleeve was afire.

Throwing the cloak about the frail figure, Denis

lifted him and ran back through the flames. He carried him to the house and deposited him on a bed, leaving him in the care of the weeping Nell. Then he returned to the serious business of fighting fire.

It was the dry hard-packed earth of the station that saved it. The area was an inferno as the fire swept around it on all sides. A few horses were rescued from the paddock and led to the center of the cleared area, where they snorted and plunged in fright.

With a thunderous roar, the flames poured down the valley like water in a funnel. The stock to the east were doomed: cattle, kangaroos, and dingoes perished. Even the hardened jackaroos blinked back tears that were not entirely due to smoke as they went about, beating out small danger spots.

Finally, they all stood watching numbly as the devastation moved on. The tin roofs of the houses were blackened with smoke, but they still stood. The big trees had been felled and dragged away. Smoke still rose from the fringes where the fire had begun. They were trapped in a circle of fire and ash. But they were safe. There was nothing more they could do.

While Tamsen and Nell saw to Dusty, Ramona bandaged Dugald's burned hands, tears falling on them as she worked. "I'm sorry," she whispered.

" 'Tis the best balm ye could put tae them," he said gallantly.

She looked up at him, eyes swimming. "Denis do you think that Missie—?"

He folded his arms about her, pulling her close to his charred shirt front. "Missie is safe, Lassie. Dinna fret. We'll find her."

Dusty, too, kept calling for Missie. Miraculously, he'd suffered no burns, but it was clear he was in pain. He finally subsided when Tamsen said, "Missie's home, Dusty. She was tired. We put her to bed." She hated herself for the lie, but it seemed to calm him. Leaving him to Nell's care, she went outside and wept shamelessly. The hopes of Opal Station had died in the fire. Missie was gone.

She wished she had killed Arthur Melvin!

In the morning, when the ashes had cooled, she would set the jackaroos to searching. It might be possible that the abo settlement survived. If the fire hadn't swept the other side of the creek, Missie might be safe.

Only yesterday, she had debated about wiring Arab, spoiling Cammie's wedding day. And what she had to tell her now was so much worse!

Her daughter missing. Maybe dead. Dear God, if only Dan were home! He would know what to do. And he'd left her alone to cope with drouth, pestilence—and now this! It was unfair! Unfair!

When morning came, the smoke had thinned enough to show that the other side of the creek was untouched by the fire. A black ribbon along the banks showed that the aborigines had beaten out the flames that had touched on dry grass. Life at the settlement seemed to go on as usual, except for a few curious glances in the direction of the station. The abos were used to fire. They had lived with its dangers for many years.

Tamsen went to enlist their aid in searching for Missie. They came willingly, walking through the still-hot areas on bare feet, not even feeling it.

The girl was nowhere to be found. But one of the Abo men did retrieve a bundle containing clothing, a sheaf of scribbled paper, and a poetry book, inscribed to Missie with words of love—from Arthur Melvin.

It was Denis Dugald's idea to enlist the aid of King. An expert tracker, he would be able to follow the pair, since it was clear they had escaped the blaze. But another trip across the creek proved fruitless. According to Queenie, King had gone walkabout.

Defeated, Tamsen returned to the station, only to be greeted by more bad news. Nell appeared at the door, her face crimson, eyes screwed up like a child's. In a shaky voice, she told Tamsen that Dusty was "bad off." "Leetle bastard finally give in when it come to gettin' a sawbones. Now, he's askin' fer a gawdam preacher too. Sez he's gotta get somethin' offen his mind."

"Oh, Nell!"

The two women clung to each other for a moment, then Tamsen went in search of young Luke, the best rider among the hands. Giving him what he claimed to be the fastest horse among those they had salvaged, she sent him on his way.

Luke was only too glad to be of service. Since he'd come to Opal Station, he'd been possessed of an adolescent adoration for Tamsen Tallant. He'd seen her unhappiness when her husband went away, and he'd nursed a secret grudge against the man: leaving like that in a time of drouth. He'd watched Tamsen working like a man during the pleuropneumonia plague. And now, after the fire, she looked dead-tired, ill. She needed her husband home, by God! And Narvaéz, off frolicking in Melbourne, ought to be out looking for that Missie girl, himself.

Reaching Jerilderie, he rounded up a doctor and a minister, as he'd promised to do. Then, passing the telegraph station, he paused, setting his young jaw. Perhaps he could be of some *real* help.

Motioning for the two other men to wait, he felt in his pockets for the remains of last month's pay, and entered the little office. "I want to send two wires," he said. "One to Melbourne, t'other to Alice Springs."

Chapter 27

While Luke was sending his telegrams, King was closing in on his quarry. On the night of the fire, he'd guessed, accurately, that the buildings of the station would be saved. Crossing a burning belt of vegetation, he had returned to the aboriginal settlement where, with his fellows, he helped put out small grass fires. When he was certain that his people were out of range of the blaze, even in the event of a wind change, he went upcreek, to the spot where Missie and the devil-devil had disappeared in the brush.

Even in the dim light of dawn, their trail was clear to his practiced eye. The man's tracks were far apart, the girl's reluctant, digging in, dragging back. He followed them for five miles, to a site near a small spring, where two horses had been tethered. Someone had camped here some time ago, and had not bothered to hide the traces of his occupancy. His spoor was older, leading in another direction, his mount poorly shod. The print of the devil-devil's larrikin boots was plain. Here he had mounted the other horse, taking the girl up before him.

King studied the hoof prints. He knew the animal. A big roan from the station. He followed its tracks, hardly slowed as they led into brittle vegetation. Each broken twig told an instant story.

On foot, he traveled swiftly across the rough terrain. Here the horse had left the valley, scrambling upward with its double load, slipping and sliding until it reached the top of the escarpment. Its spoor continued on across a high plain that dipped into another valley.

The black man ran on, like a well-oiled machine, his body glistening in the intense heat. Trained to the rigors of the desert, he felt no need for food or water. Hunger and thirst were unthought of in his intense concentration.

He came upon a clearing. Here, sixty miles from Opal Station, they had camped for the night. From the look of the prints, the girl had tried to escape. A trampled space showed where the devil-devil had caught her. Here, there had been a thrashing of bodies. King's keen eye noticed a single blond hair twisted in a broken twig on the ground. He stared at it, his face impassive, his eyes glowing red as he thought of what had happened to his own wife.

He slaked his thirst at a brackish water hole, and, curling like an animal in the mallee scrub, he slept for two hours. He came instantly awake at the time he'd set himself, and searched through the brush until he found a pink, thin-shelled lowan egg. Piercing the shell with a sharp stick, he ate it raw. Refreshed, he was ready to follow once more.

This day, he ran for more than eighty miles. The tracks now showed the horse was faltering. There were deep marks where it had lunged as the devil-devil put the spurs to it. The trail continued on through dark rock-filled gullies, across dry plains and creeks, through punishing scrub.

At nightfall, King rested again. Here there was no water. He coiled his black body between two rocks like an inky shadow and waited until the morning.

Now the trail led along the base of an escarpment,

rising steadily higher, seeming to disappear into a wall at the foot of twin pinnacles. King sensed he was nearing the end of his quest. Spear in hand, he followed the spoor. The tracks led to a fissure in the wall, just wide enough to admit a horse and rider. The way was deep in sand, an indication that, in the rainy season, pouring water from the pinnacles above created a small creek. The corridor curved and turned. And finally King came to its end.

He looked down upon a little river-fed valley, a hut with a sagging roof, rail fences grown up in grass. He allowed a dim memory to intrude into his concentration. His fellows had talked of places like this, where a man's stolen cattle were taken and rebranded. It had been a tale of disbelief. Aboriginals did not own property, they did not take one from the other. When they had food or skins, they shared.

But this was clearly one of those places. Everything attested to it. Squatting behind a rock, he settled down to watch.

An old man came out of the hut, followed by a younger man. The devil-devil. King watched with burning eyes as they cut two horses out of a decrepit paddock and saddled them. He was prepared to flee should they come his way. Instead, they rode off in the direction of the river.

King eased himself up. Like an animal, he ran from rock to rock, from one patch of scrub to another, seeking cover as he made his way down into the hidden valley. Reaching the hut, he peered into an opening that served as a window. There, seated at a table littered with dirty dishes, her head buried in her arms, was young Missie. No one else was in the single room.

King slipped to the door and opened it. Missie raised her head at the sound. Her face was drawn, her soft hair matted, her eyes blank with shock.

"King!"

"Missie—come along King." His mouth worked with the unfamiliar words.

She was across the room in a rush, clinging to him. "Oh, King! King!"

This was not fitting. There was another rule. A white man might touch a blackfellow woman, but it was death for a black man to touch a white woman. He took Missie's wrists and put her gently away.

"Him come?"

Missie's features were suddenly pinched. She had been dreaming of escape. But now that help was at hand, she knew she couldn't take advantage of it. She thought of the horrors of the previous night; of the way she'd tried to stifle her moans, so the sounds of what Arthur was doing to her wouldn't carry across the room. She'd heard that filthy old man, his father, laughing from his bed. And then there had been that ultimate sickening revelation when Arthur growled, "You're not even as good as that bloody abo, Queenie!"

But she had married Arthur in the sight of God—for better or worse. And she could never go home now, disgraced, degraded. Not to the same house with Ramona and little Luka.

She raised a small drowned face to King. "No," she choked, "I can't." Seeing his puzzled expression, she tried to explain, knowing it was of no use. Finally, she pushed hard against his naked chest with both hands. "Go! If he comes back, he will kill you! You've got to go! Oh, God, please—"

He nodded gravely, and within moments, he melted away into a world of grass and scrub and trees, making his way back to the corridor that led into the valley.

There, he squatted for two days, watching.

He watched Missie in her tattered nightdress, carrying pails of water, her thin shoulders bent. He saw her washing men's clothing at the river, spreading them to dry. He saw the old man grab her, the way she struggled to free herself of his grasping hands, and the devil-devil coming upon them, knocking the old man to the ground.

After the encounter, they seemed amiable enough. The men walked off together, the devil-devil's arm draped across the other's shoulder.

At night, he was suddenly alert, his acute hearing picking up the thin thread of a woman's scream.

He'd had enough of watching. Taking a branch, he carefully swept away the tracks he'd made in the sandy corridor. Then he went along the winding trail that led down the escarpment, back in the direction from which he'd come. There, he sat and thought awhile, his hand darting out to catch a stumpy-tailed lizard that had come within his reach. Tearing at it with his hands, he removed the tail fat, eating it raw.

He had made his decision. He would continue on his walkabout. He would return to his tribal ground, where his dreamtime ancestors held sway.

He ran for a little more than a week. And finally he reached the place where there was a mountain of black-fellows' bones, where the creeks had once run red. Here was a cave where the nulungery had lived. It was the old sorcerer himself, who had advised the boy and his wife to run, far from the newly dead that haunted this place.

He entered the cave and found the sorcerer was still there. King squatted silently beside him. Finally, the old man spoke. "You are here, my son."

"I am here, my father."

"The scent of the white man is upon you."

"The scent of the white man is upon me."

"You have come for my help?"

"I have come for your help."

After some discussion, King drew a line on the earth at the cave's mouth. It pointed directly in the direction from which he'd come. Rummaging beneath a heap of dried grass, the old nulungery drew forth an emu bone, pointed at one end. There was a string of human hair fastened to the other, and a charm bag of paper bark. Drawing the string taut, to improve the force of his spell, the ancient, white-bearded man began a chant in a reedy voice—in English, since it would touch a white man.

Kill devil-devil. Kill devil-devil. Make him deadfellow: Pull away his fat, make his bone fellow—

The chant went on, repeated when the last line was reached. King, watching the old nulungery, wondered if his powers had failed with age. But when the sorcerer was done, he put the singing bone away carefully.

"When it is finished, I will tell you. Sleep, my son."

In the hut in the hidden valley, Missie worked and slaved, enduring her husband's brutal lovemaking, her father-in-law's obscene advances, stoically. Arthur had decided, since he was between jobs, to go into business with his father. The rail fences mended, they began herding cattle from outlying ranches into the valley. There, brands and notched ears were altered.

What they were doing was wrong, but Missie couldn't help being glad when they left, sometimes to be gone for several days at a time. She hadn't much with which to busy herself. In their hasty departure, she had dropped her little bundle with the precious volume of poetry and the notes for her own book. She had found some of her husband's old schoolbooks in a box in a tumbledown shed. In his absence, she would get them out and read them, trying to imagine him as a little boy. If she could only create some affection for him—

Returning early, one day, he found her at it and

threw the books into the cookfire. The books that had been his mother's.

Deprived of reading, she took to walking. She spent much time at his mother's grave, a mass of piled stones, not too far from the house. She wondered what the dead woman had been like; how she had endured a life like this.

On the day Missie learned she was pregnant, she showered the stones with her tears.

Chapter 28

At Opal Station, they waited grimly for the arrival of the doctor—and a minister. Dusty asked, alternately, for their presence, and for Missie. They were forced to keep up the fiction that, "Missie just stepped out," "Missie's asleep," "Missie's working in the dairy room." Dusty listened, smiled, and slept. He had no idea that there was nothing left of the station but acres of charred land.

When the doctor finally arrived, he was ushered in quickly. In too short a time, he was out again. "There's nothing I can do for him," he said candidly. "He says he doesn't need me. He needs you, Reverend Ainsworth. He would also like a drink, and it can't hurt him at this point. So, Ainsworth, if you don't mind—"

The preacher, reluctantly carrying a tumbler of whiskey, entered the room and closed the door. In a few moments, a strange expression on his face, he opened it once more and beckoned to the gray-faced Nell. He closed the door behind her.

"Aunt Tamsen," Ramona whispered fearfully, "you don't suppose—"

"I don't know," Tamsen said. Only the strength of her will held her up. She was drawn with fatigue. "We'll have to wait."

Denis Dugald's big hand closed over Ramona's, and

she let it stay there, drawing a sort of comfort from his warmth. Then they all jumped as they heard Nell's booming roar.

"Hell, yes, I do!" the old woman shouted. And later, "Gawdammit, I said I do! Enny more fool questions?"

Reverend Ainsworth opened the door once more, his expression even more peculiar. He swallowed, and said, "They would like the family to come in now."

Tamsen moved toward the door, Denis behind her, supporting Ramona. They found Dusty sitting up, a red spot on each pale cheek.

"Lookut th' leetle bastard," Nell said fondly. "Grinnin' like a gawdam ape. Hell, Dusty, go ahead. I'll let you spill th' beans."

"Ladies," Dusty said primly, and looking toward Denis, his moustache twitching in a smile, "and the gentleman, of course, I would like you to meet my wife."

Nell held out her pudgy hand on which a gold ring gleamed. "Had it in his pocket ever sense that trip to Melbourne," Nell beamed. "Kin you beat that? Leetle sonofabitch!"

Dusty extended his empty glass to his glowing bride. "I believe," he said modestly, "the occasion calls for a drink."

During the remainder of the day, his health seemed vastly improved. When he asked after Missie, it was necessary to invent a larger lie. Adam Jones and his wife Clara had dropped in during Dusty's illness. Missie had gone home with them, for a visit with their daughters.

"It's just as well," Dusty said. Then his look of disappointment faded. "She will be pleased to hear the news, I'm sure."

Tamsen did her best to make Dusty and Nell's wedding day a festive occasion. She managed a wedding cake, of sorts, and prepared a roast with yorkshire pudding, the way Dusty liked it. Dusty had his meal on a tray, and the others carried their plates in to join him. It was a short celebration, for they didn't wish to tire him.

When it was over, Denis returned to his own house with a plate of food for Boswell, who had felt his presence in the sickroom might be too much. Tamsen and Ramona excused themselves and went to the kitchen to wash up the supper things. Nell and Dusty were left alone together.

"Nell," Dusty said, "I want you to look into my coat pocket, and see if you can find a folded paper there."

"Sure," Nell said cheerfully. Checking the charred garment he'd worn when Dugald carried him into the house, she found the paper intact.

"Put it in a safe place," he said feebly.

Nell looked around. They'd put Dusty in Tamsen's room. Tam had taken over Missie's empty bed. But there was Tamsen's old cashbox, memento of bygone days. Well, what the hell, if it made him happy—

She opened the box, lifted the drawer, and slid the paper into the empty space below. Then she went to sit beside her bridegroom. Tousling his white hair playfully, she gripped his emaciated hand in her big paw.

"Dunno why we didn't do this sooner. Hell, it feels good, bein' legal an' all."

"I am a lucky man. Oh, my word, I am! Married to the loveliest creature in the world—"

"Aw-w, yer butterin' me up. I got th' best of th' deal!"

He pulled the hand that held his to his lips. "I'm very happy, Nell. But I'm also quite weary. Why don't you lend Tamsen a hand. I'll just rest a moment. I shall be waiting for you."

"Sure," Nell said again. "It's bin a big day."

Tucking the sheet carefully under her new husband's chin, she beamed at him and lumbered out. She was no help in the kitchen. Too filled with her own joy, she

211

dropped things and generally got in the way. But Tamsen and Ramona didn't mind. It helped to keep their thoughts from Missie.

"I'm gonna be th' best gawdam wife that ever wuz," Nell boasted. "We got lots of good years ahead of us. You notice how much better he looks?"

He did, indeed, the women agreed.

"Mebbe I better take a gander at him, anyways," Nell said worriedly. She tiptoed to Tamsen's door and opened it, peering inside, her face clearing as she turned away.

"Sleepin' like a baby," she said. A tear glistened on her broad face and she scrubbed at it with her sleeve, sniffing, her features flushed with embarrassment.

"Hell, Tam, ain't no use pertendin'. Leetle devil had me skeert fer awhile. Figgered he was done fer, fer sur." She blinked and managed a watery smile. "Mighta knowed you couldn't keep a good man down! Mebbe he worked it all out so's we'd git spliced. Wooden put it past the leetle fart."

She tried for an air of belligerence, but failed, her face softening. "It was kind of romantick, at that," she said, unable to hide a satisfied grin. "Say, Tam, did I ever tell yuh how we got t'gether in th' first place?"

She had, but Tamsen listened as she recounted it again, visualizing the fresh-faced, pink-cheeked Englishman, somewhat less than sober; the obese, flashy woman Nell must have been in her early thirties. Nell had been dealing in a shady establishment. A drunken loser had insulted her and Dusty, a stranger, had sprung to her defense.

"That's where he lost them two front teeth," Nell said complacently. "I whupped hell outten th' drunk an' took Dusty home. Let 'im think he done it. Bin t'gether ever sense, 'cep'n when he went back east that time an' come back with you. Leetle devil was pissed off, wantin' to git married—" Her face twisted painfully.

"I was a goddam fool. Wish t'hell I'd had th' sense God give a duck! All those goddam years—"

"I've never understood why you didn't marry him," Tamsen said.

Nell flushed again. "Well, hell, Tam, lookut me!" she said with a brutal frankness. "Dusty's a gennulman. Never would talk about them folks of his that kicked him out, but I guess they was some punkins in England. S'pose he decided t'go back? Er s'pose he woke up one day an' took a good look at what he was hitched to; a tough old bitch that lived rough and cussed like a goddam trooper. Tam—Do you s'pose you could help me clean up my langridge?"

Ramona stifled a giggle, but Tamsen managed to keep a straight face. "I'll try."

Nell mopped her perspiring brow. "Thanks, Tam. That takes a helluva load off my mind."

She polished her ring on her apron and admired its glow. "We ain't missed much," she said softly. "We had everthing but kids. An' you girls sure ez hell made up fer that."

"Nell." Tamsen dropped her dish towel and put her arms around the old woman who had been more than a mother to her in her own peculiar way. "I love you, Nell!"

After an affectionate embrace, the prickly old woman pushed her away, blinking to hide her tears. "No sense gittin' sickenin' about it! Them dishes done? Hell, I got a husban' t' look after. This here's my wedding night!"

Beaming, she waddled toward the door of the room where Dusty slept.

Tamsen walked to the outside door, opened it, and stood for a moment, looking up at the stars. Dusty's

213

miraculous recovery, Nell's happiness, had taken a great load from her mind. Still, there was Missie. She wondered where the girl was; if she were seeing these same stars; if, in spit of Melvin's brutality, she could still love the man. The thought of Missie out there somewhere, alone with him, made her shiver.

A low sound, halfway between a sob and a groan, erupted from Dusty's room. Nell?

Whirling, Tamsen turned and ran for the bedroom door. She hesitated for a moment, then threw it open.

Dusty slept peacefully, his blue eyes closed, mouth a little open beneath the straggly moustache, white hair spread against his pillow. But Nell—

Nell was pasty faced, her eyes like raisins set in a sagging dumpling.

"Nell—?"

At Tamsen's voice, the dreadful face came to life. For a brief space, the dull eyes flickered with emotion; a devastating grief sparked with anger.

"Leetle bastard done went an' died on me," she said in an expressionless tone.

"Nell—no!"

"Hell, I know when a man's dead! Now git th' hell out and leave us be! I got th' right—th' right—"

Her voice caught on a choking sob, and she buried her face in the sheet that covered the recumbent form, her heavy shoulders shaking as she wept, shuddering with harsh retching sounds.

Tamsen backed away stiffly and closed the door behind her. Outside, she stood numb and tearless, unable to comprehend her loss. She was conscious only of a vast aching void. A part of her life had been torn from her. She would never be quite whole again.

More than Papa, she thought dazedly. She had loved him more than Papa. And poor Nell! Dear God, on her wedding night!

Finally she pulled herself together and moved like an automaton to fill the coffeepot. It was going to be a long night. She would not alert the others. This night belonged to Nell. She would wait here on the fringes of Nell's grief, until she was needed.

Tamsen covered her ears against the sound of Nell's weeping. Around her, the shadows created by the flickering lamplight moved in nightmarish patterns on the walls.

It was nearly morning when the door to the room creaked open. Tamsen lifted dull eyes to see Nell in the doorway; a strangely altered Nell. She seemed shrunken; her gray features looked as if they had melted together.

"You kin see 'im now, if you wanna."

Tamsen followed her to the place where Dusty lay, dressed in the blue suit he'd had made in Melbourne. He looked serene lying there, his hair combed neatly, his hands folded across his chest; prepared for burial by his wife's loving hands.

"Looks good, don't he?" Nell's tone begged for recognition of her efforts.

"He looks wonderful," Tamsen choked. She fled in search of Denis Dugald. A box must be constructed. The funeral would have to be held today. Ramona must be told—

That afternoon, they stood at a graveside, Boswell trying to support the sagging Nell while a flustered Denis made an attempt at a funeral service. His brogue thick, voice stumbling, he read a passage from the Bible.

"Ashes tae ashes, doost tae doost," he ended, closing the Book.

Dusty would have enjoyed Denis' efforts, Tamsen thought, as she watched the dry red earth shower down upon the box. She had stood dry-eyed through the service, her mind in the past. Dusty had been Papa's new-met friend, his drinking buddy. Together, they had lazed through the hours at a wagon yard in St. Louis. Then, after Papa's death, Dusty had seen Em, Arab and herself through to Texas. He'd taken her to meet Nell, who'd given her a much needed job in the cantina at Magoffinville. He'd stood by them all for more than thirty years.

Now, only she, of the three sisters, stood here to say good-bye to him.

And Missie was gone. Oh, Missie! How a last sight of you would have gladdened his heart!

It was over. She moved toward the faltering Nell and guided her back to the house. The old woman lay down on the bed where Dusty had lain, and slept, exhausted from her emotions. Tamsen, worried, kept checking on her. Finally she found her awake, staring at the ceiling.

"Is there anything I can do?"

"I want t' see that Ramona girl."

"She—she's a little upset. Do you feel up to—?"

"Dammit, send 'er in!"

Tamsen watched nervously as Ramona, red-eyed and on the verge of hysteria, went into the bedroom and closed the door behind her. She wasn't there for long. In a short while she left the house and did not return for some time. When she did, she went in to Nell.

Tamsen, making up the beds in the dormitory room, flinched as the front door slammed. She went into the large room. Nell's door was open, the woman gone.

Alarmed, Tamsen rushed outside and looked toward Dusty's grave. Nell was there, down on her knees by the soft earth. Tamsen took a step forward, then stopped. It was better not to intrude on her sorrow.

Nell was only there a moment. She rose, dusted her hands, and waddled back toward the main house. Tamsen ducked inside so that Nell wouldn't know she had been watching over her. She was glad to see that a little— though not much—of Nell's color had returned. She was going to be all right.

She's stronger than I am, Tamsen thought. If I could only face up to it! Oh, God, if I could only cry!

That evening, Nell safely abed, Tamsen walked to Dusty's grave. And she saw what Nell had done on that earlier visit.

Somehow, somewhere, after the long dry, Ramona had managed to find a single flower. Ensconced in a whiskey bottle, it bloomed at the head of Dusty's resting place.

Tamsen drew a shuddering breath and the healing tears began to fall like rain. The small symbol of Nell's love, so appropriate for Dusty, made his death seem real at last. A nightmare no longer. Tamsen fought her way back to the pain of reality.

She cried for Dusty, who was dead; for Missie, who had disappeared; and, finally, for herself, because Dan had left her to face these horrors alone.

She cried because, sometime in these last few days, a Christmas had come and gone, unnoticed.

And she cried for Nell, a widow on her wedding day.

Chapter 29

On January first of the New Year, 1880, Em adjusted her daughter's veil, her eyes misty. Within a few moments, Cameron Courtney would become Mrs. Charles Courtney Ellington. A robust girl, she seemed almost fragile in the gown that Arab, with her innate sense of style, had helped her to select.

"She's lovely." Em's oldest daughter Martha, who had arrived at the last moment with her husband, Peter Channing, and her children, looked at her sister in admiration.

"You look beautiful, too," Em said.

In her pale yellow gown, dressed for her role as matron of honor, Martha seemed a different person from the worn young mother who had arrived the previous evening. The filmy chiffon dress gave her an air of frailty. Gloves concealed her work-worn hands.

"Are you happy, Martha?" Em asked impulsively. "I know you and Peter work too hard. If you'd let Duke help—"

"I'm happier than I've ever been in my life," Martha said, her eyes shining. "Peter's a fine man, a good father. And it's good, working together."

Em looked away, ashamed of having questioned her. She recalled the days when Martha was small, when she and Duke had little besides what they wore on their backs. She wouldn't trade those memories for anything in the world. And Martha and Peter had a stable beginning in their small, remote station above Adelaide.

Still, it was so surprising to see Martha in the role of a station wife. Martha, who had once been a defiant youngster; whose attempts to take Dan Tallant's affections from Tamsen had caused so many problems. Martha, who had stowed away on a ship bound for Hong Kong; and sometime during the passage, had been married to Peter by the ship's captain. A far cry from today's ceremony—

Em's thoughts were interrupted as Martha's daughter, Petra, burst through the door, stopping with a cry of delight at sight of the bride. Petra was a winsome youngster, despite her odd, Oriental features that had always led Em to believe she was not Peter Channing's child.

Petra carried a message: Aunt Arab said it was almost time for the ceremony to begin.

Downstairs, Arab Narvaéz was surveying the scene with pride. Em had declared she could never have managed without her. It was Arab who had done the elegant little place cards that graced each plate at the sit-down dinner that would follow the ceremony. She had also set up tables to display the gifts to their best advantage, careful to place cards with the donors' names at each one. And she had coped with the late arrival of the Channings last night, and even helped deal with a case of bridal vapors.

Yes, she had helped.

She smiled at Juan, placing a gloved hand fleetingly on his knee. He was so handsome in his dress clothes. And he was beginning to look rested. Surely, he would see this was the kind of life they should be living.

The music paused and began again. At its cue, Em entered, head high, cheeks flushed pink. The groom's parents were distinguished looking, but his mother not so lovely as Em.

Then Scott and Luka. Luka, in soft blue, a silver sash to match her slanting silver eyes; her hair a cascade of palest gold that brought a gasp from the onlookers. For once, her wayward, dancing feet moved to the music as she glided forward, her small hand in the curve of young Scott's arm. Before the altar, they separated. She moved to stand beside a tall basket of flowers, their freshly sprinkled petals forming a charming frame for her angelic face.

Then Martha in yellow, on Peter's arm; Vickie in rose, her escort the groom's brother, a mannerly boy. And then, at long last, the bride.

Seeing her, floating like a gossamer cloud, held to earth by one hand tucked into Duke Courtney's arm, Arab thought of her own wedding. Had she ever been so young? So beautiful? Her eyes misty, she stole a glance at Juan. He was looking down at her with eyes that were dark pools of love and remembering.

Theirs had been a garden wedding. There had been the music of a fountain, bright birds flashing, threading through the trees in iridescent embroidery.

With an effort, her gaze returned to Cammie. The minister, one of the most respected in Melbourne, was intoning the words of the ceremony. Cammie's responses were soft, barely audible; the groom's fervent. A ring was placed on a slim finger; a veil lifted softly to reveal the pretty face it had concealed. A gentle kiss—

Then the music changed, striking up a joyous note. The young couple moved triumphantly down the aisle, their smiling faces attesting to their happiness.

After a session of kisses and congratulations, the wedding party moved to the long banquet room. Seated at a table set with fine china, gleaming with silver, the company toasted the bride and groom. Finally, the festive meal at an end, the couple stood together to cut their wedding cake. Under cover of the resulting confusion, Juan turned and brushed his wife's cheek with a kiss.

It wasn't long besfore the bride, turning to throw a kiss to the guests, tossing her bouquet straight into Vickie's arms, lifted her skirts to run upstairs. Em followed to do her last duty for her daughter. She would help her dress for going away.

The gentlemen retired into Duke's study where they would partake of cigars and brandy. Arab led the ladies of the party into the small parlor, where they would survey the wedding gifts. Moving from a silver carafe to fine linens, to a set of hand-painted lamps with porcelain bowls, Arab could not help thinking how incongruous these things would appear at Opal Station: this set of silver flatware with its ornate handles; the porcelain statuette; the delicate hand-blown glassware.

Her jaw set as she moved among the expensive things, pointing them out to the admiring women. Her girls would have weddings like this! All of them! She would see to it, no matter what she had to do!

Reaching the last of the gifts, she turned to a small, magnificently carved table. Here she had placed the telegrams and letters of congratulation that had been received from Sydney, from Adelaide, from the wide spectrum of Duke Courtney's business acquaintants. They had been opened, but were as yet unread. Time had not permitted it.

"This one is from the Governor," Arab said. "And this, from the manager of one of my brother-in-law's representatives in New Zealand. This one—" She paused. Jerilderie? And it was addressed to Juan! *"Come home,"* it read. *"Everything is burned up. Your daughter missing in fire. A Friend."*

Arab read it once, uncomprehending, then again. With a low moan, she wilted, slipping to the floor.

Martha was on her knees instantly, checking for a pulse. "Luka," she ordered, "get your father! Hurry!" Luka, her silver eyes blank with fear, obeyed.

Em, hearing a buzz of excited voices below, hurriedly straightened Cammie's traveling gown. "Off with you. Charles is waiting on the back stairs. Go, before they learn you're not coming down."

Cammie hesitated for a moment, then ran.

Em wiped her eyes. Arab had thought arranging a wedding was such fun. Wait until one of *her* daughters left home! Then the shoe would be on the other foot!

She went to a rear window. The carriage was moving out, Cammie cuddled against her new husband. Em would have to go down now and tell the guests the wedding couple had departed. She took a last look at the carriage rolling off in the distance. Then she left her daughter's room and closed the door gently behind her.

As she descended the stairs, she was startled by what she saw: Arab lay stretched on a couch, her glorious hair in disarray; Juan, surrounded by a mob of excited guests, was trying to pry a piece of paper from her clenched fingers.

Retrieving the paper, Juan read it. He went white, then faced the bevy of women, their men crowded into the doorway behind them.

"You will have to excuse us. My wife has received bad news. She is not well."

Martha took over. "The banquet room is cleared by now. If you will follow me—"

The room emptied, Juan showed the wire to Duke and Em.

"It could be some kind of ugly joke," Courtney decided. "Do you know anyone who would do a thing like this?"

Juan shook his head.

Duke Courtney set his jaw. "Em, get some brandy

into Arab and get her to bed. We're going to check this thing out."

The Melbourne telegrapher made the wires sing. He finally reached Jerilderie. Yes, they had taken the message there. It was sent by a young man named Luke, a hand at Opal Station. He had come to Jerilderie to enlist the services of a doctor and a minister. Yes, there had been a fire. He'd heard of several small stations being destroyed. But aside from the wire, he knew nothing of what had happened at the Opal.

Juan blanched. "It's true. Tamsen wouldn't have had the boy wire us if it weren't bad. *Your daughter!* Dios, man! *Which daughter?* And Luke was sent for a doctor and a minister? We're leaving tonight!"

Duke caught him by the shoulders. "Use a little sense, friend! That wire was sent some days ago. Going off half-cocked won't help! You can't move Arab in the state she's in! Wait until morning! We'll all go. You and **Arab** go ahead, the rest of us will follow as soon as I gather some supplies. They may be needed."

The two men returned to find the house empty of guests. Good manners had dictated that they take their leave as soon as possible, due to the circumstances. Em had not given Arab brandy as Juan suggested. Instead, she dosed her with laudanum, left from an amount prescribed when young Scott had suffered an earache. Arab slept, her face ravaged with tears, one hand still clenched as if holding the telegram.

Em met her husband and Juan Narvaéz at the door. She didn't need to ask any questions. Their expressions told her the message had been a true one.

"Juan and Arab are leaving for home in the morning," Duke told her. "We'll follow later with Luka. I want to get some things together: food, clothing, medical supplies."

Em shrank. Her daughter was here! Her grandchildren! And they could only stay three days. She'd been looking forward to some time with them. But this—

Martha came forward. "I didn't want to tell you until after the wedding," she lied, "but we'll have to leave in the morning, too, Peter thinks we should get home."

Em put her arms around her daughter and began to cry.

Later, packing for the trip they would take on the morrow, Em thought of Cammie. She would be aboard ship by now, moving toward some unnamed enchanted isle they'd chosen for their honeymoon. At least they'd fled before Cammie learned the tragic news. Whatever they found at Opal Station, for Cammie this would be a day to remember as one of happiness.

Chapter 30

In the morning, Juan and Arab boarded the train for Wodonga. There they would rent horses, faster transportation than a hired buggy, which sometimes bogged down in the deep, furry dust. Luka was left to travel with the Courtneys who would be a day or two behind them, when the next train ran. Arab, still persuaded that her last child's nervous system was delicately balanced, wished to learn the true status of affairs at Opal Station for herself before subjecting Luka to anything that might shock her sensibilities.

Too, the girl would only have slowed their progress.

Arab chafed at the slowness of the train; the necessity to ferry over the Murray's now-shallow waters, once they were on horseback. She insisted on riding hard and fast, angry when Juan forced her to break the journey twice at night. Painstakingly, Juan explained over and over that the horses must rest; that they couldn't take such pushing in the heat; that traveling at night over rough trails wasn't wise. A horse might fall and break a leg. There was also the fact that she hadn't ridden for a long time.

"I can do it," she said stubbornly.

That night, stopping at a small bush hotel, he tried

227

to help her dismount and she toppled into his arms. He half led, half carried her inside, where, getting a room, he bathed her face with cold water. She had lost her hat and veil along the way, and her creamy, sheltered complexion was blistered and crimson. He was certain she'd be unable to travel the next morning. Perhaps he should go on ahead, and she could wait here for the Courtneys and the wagons.

She was up and dressed and waiting for him at first light, her face swollen from the severity of her sunburn. A few coins persuaded the wife of the hotel's owner to part with a slat, calico bonnet she'd just finished making, and a length of mosquito netting which Juan swathed about his wife like a shawl; it would offer some protection against the flies that constantly tormented them.

"I must look terrible," she whispered. "A fright!"

"You could never look a fright," he said gallantly, though he did have a temptation to laugh. She looked like a naughty little girl, playing dress-up. *Little girl.* A pang struck him as he thought of Ramona and Missie—*Ah, Dios, which one had he lost, and how?*

Though he could guess at the effort it cost her, Arab set the pace once more.

That night, they made Wilga Station where the elderly Smythe-Williams couple took them in for the night. The old woman clucked over Arab's condition like a mother hen.

Yes, they had heard about the fire from one of the Mairn hands. The Mairn, he'd told them, was wiped out. He'd also said there was some trouble on the Opal. But they'd been worried about leaving their own place—

"It's all right," Arab told the apologetic old woman. "I understand."

The next morning, they left the Wilga. Now Arab began to hang back. Juan pulled up. "Are you all right?" he asked.

"I guess I'm stalling," she admitted. "I keep thinking of the girls. Whatever happened, I feel like it's my fault. I haven't been a good mother—not to Ramona and Missie. I keep thinking of all the things I haven't done—and now it may be too late. I've been wondering which one, and what happened. I couldn't stand to lose either of them. I feel so guilty!"

"*You* feel guilty? *Dios,* Arab! *I* should have been there! Instead, I left everything on Tam's shoulders. I hadn't even thought about the station for days—until this. Maybe if I'd been there—If anybody's to blame—"

Seeing the pain in his haunted eyes, she reached out a hand to clasp his. "Maybe the best thing to do is just wait until we find out what's ahead of us. I—I love you, Juan."

They rode on, each trying to keep from thinking. When they turned into the valley, they found the same familiar red road leading through scrub. There couldn't have been a fire. Their information had been wrong, wrong—

Then they rounded a curve. Ahead of them lay the aborigine station, untouched. Across the creek, Opal Station lay in the midst of ashes and cinders, smoke-blackened, denuded of trees.

"Oh, my God!'

Arab reeled in the saddle, then stiffened her shoulders and dug in her heels, spurring her mount to a final burst of speed.

Wyuna's announcement that, "two-feller come," had brought Tamsen to wait at the door of the main house. That morning, she had ridden out with Denis to see if any cattle might have survived in hidden pockets. They had found the valley devastated, except for one small mob grazing across the Billabong.

She hadn't had time to freshen up. Her clothing was black with soot, her face smudged. Normally, she would have rushed to change. But news of each approaching rider brought a surge of hope that Missie might be returning.

Lately there had been a stream of refugees from on down the valley. She would feed them and send them on. She shaded her eyes with her hand. These were coming from the wrong direction, but the woman wore a sunbonnet. Small settlers, she guessed. Probably they'd skirted the fire, coming along the ridge above—

"Put the coffee on," she called over her shoulder to Ramona. The sentence ended in a stifled sound of recognition as the woman's bonnet fell back, Arab's glorious hair gleaming in the sun. Arab! Juan!

She ran to meet them, then faltered as she thought of what she had to tell them. Arab remained in the saddle as if frozen, and Juan dismounted and came toward Tamsen.

"We got your telegram," he said. "Which one of the girls—Have you found her?"

Telegram? "But I didn't—!"

She was cut short as Arab made a small whimpering sound. Ramona had appeared in the doorway. "It's Missie," Arab cried. "Oh, God, Juan, it's *Missie!*"

She swooned in the saddle and Juan and Tamsen rushed to her aid. Between them, they were able to carry her into the house. There, she clung to Ramona and wept. It was some time before they could get through to her. Missie had not died in the fire. She had just—gone away.

"I—I don't understand."

"Missie eloped with Arthur Melvin," Tamsen said finally.

Slowly, the color returned to Arab's face. "They're married? Are you sure?"

"He brought a minister back when he returned from his leave. It had apparently been planned for some time."

Arab's weary brain was spinning. She was unable to

230

hold to a thought. This was not what she wanted for Missie, this marriage to an older man. But Missie was alive! Alive! That's all that counted for now.

"Surely Missie would have told someone—Dusty and she were close. He would have known she planned—"

"That's another thing, Arab," Tamsen said gently. "I have to tell you before you see Nell. She and Dusty were married several days ago. He—He died that night."

Arab had been jerked from one emotion to another without having time to recover. Missie had been dead. Now, she was alive and married. Her beloved friend Dusty was gone. Arab put her hands to her face, tears dripping from between her fingers. "I don't know," she said in a thin voice. "I don't know anything. I just don't know—"

Tamsen put her shattered sister to bed and tended her until she slept. Then, leaving Ramona to watch over her, she beckoned Juan outside. They walked a distance from the house while Tamsen searched for words. Juan anticipated her.

"You've always been honest with me, Tamsen. Now, I want the truth."

Dully, she recited the details. Melvin had tried to attack her, some time ago. She'd held him off at gunpoint, and he'd carried a grudge. His wooing of Missie was probably a means of revenge.

She told of the way he'd brought the girl to the house after the ceremony. Missie was dazed, battered, incoherent.

"He wouldn't go, so I shot him." she finished, simply. "I aimed for his arm. I wish I had killed him."

Then, the next night Missie slipped out and went to him. Evidently they had a rendezvous in a clearing up-creek. The bundle she'd taken with her—clothes, books, papers—was found there.

They fled the station, but first Melvin completed his revenge, setting the fire burning.

Juan's eyes were hot with fury. "Dios!" he spat. His old accent returned as he spoke through clenched teeth. "I'll keel him! The sonofabeetch! Ah, Dios!" He turned on his heel and Tamsen caught at his sleeve.

"You've got to think of Arab first, Juan! And there's no use looking for them. I've tried!"

"The man, King—He is a tracker—"

"King's on walkabout. It's useless, Juan. All we can do is pray that Missie will leave him—and come home."

Juan slumped, looking suddenly old. "I prayed that my girls would be safe; that neither of them died in the fire. Perhaps it would have been better that way." He turned away to hide his grief-ravaged face. "I should have been here—"

"I was here," Tamsen pointed out. "And I didn't know what was happening."

He put his hands affectionately on her shoulders. "My poor Tamsen. You have been saddled with all our burdens. You've had to face Missie's problems, the fire, Dusty's death. I should be comforting you."

She looked up at him, her eyes too large for her small, smudged face that had lost its lovely coloring. For a moment, his concern for her touched the iron core of will that had kept her upright through a series of disasters.

"I am all right, Juan."

"Arab does not have your courage. I would suggest we keep the—details from her. Let her believe what she wishes to believe. Em and Duke are on their way here, with Luka and their children."

It was agreed that the whole truth should also be kept from Em. Dusty's death would be enough of a shock. Duke would be told the true story. He might have an idea that would help.

Now there was nothing to do, except see what could be salvaged from the fire. First, he would like to visit Dusty's resting place. Tamsen pointed it out to him, and he walked toward it. He stood there for a long time, his hat in his hand, his head bared to the glaring sun. He had been gone when he was needed. He'd lost the station, his own daughter—and he'd lost his old friend.

He wished a man could cry.

Chapter 31

Em and Duke arrived with their children and a wagonload of supplies. The sight of the burned station was a shock, even though they'd known what to expect. What they had not been prepared for was the tragic news of Dusty's death. Em could not accept that he was gone. He'd been a fixture in their lives for so long, fading away these last years, but *there*. It didn't seem possible that they could go on without him.

The bad news was balanced with good. Arab had recovered from her shock, and had begun to view her daughter's elopement in a romantic light.

"You know Missie's always been different," she told Em placidly. "An imaginative child. I had hoped for a wedding like Cammie's, but this is the sort of thing Missie would do." She had been noticing Ramona and young Denis. Perhaps she might be able to plan a real wedding one day, after all.

Ramona, overhearing her mother's chatter was miserable. If Mama only *knew,* she thought. The memory of her sister on that last night, bruised and bleeding, was almost more than she could stand. Melvin, boasting that the marriage had been consummated! It had been more like rape!

She walked outside for a breath of air. The brightness of the sun made her squint as she gazed off into the distance at barren land. *Oh, Missie. If only you would come home.* A soft tap on her shoulder startled her and she turned to see Denis' handsome face.

"Such a frown," he teased, coming to stand by her side. "A copper frae your thoughts."

"I wasn't thinking," she lied. "It's the sun. It's so bright."

"The soon should always shine bright frae a bonnie lassie." His big hand swallowed hers, and he smiled down at her.

"That wasn't true, Denis. I was thinking about Missie, wondering if she's all right. Do you think she'll ever come back?"

"If she wants tae coom, she will. We dinna ken what's in her mind. The marriage may wor-r-k oot."

Ramona shook her head. "You didn't see her. You don't know."

Denis had been a comfort in these last days. On New Year's, Hogmanay, as he called it, he had hung mistletoe in the doorway and startled her with a kiss. Chaste as it was, it gave her a strange feeling, as if the blood were rushing to her head, making her dizzy, her knees weak. He had held her for a minute, his blue eyes almost black. Then he released her.

"Ye owe me a tie," he said. "Would ye like tae try frae a pair of gloves."

She'd laughed off his suggestion, knowing that if she kissed him again she might give away her feelings.

She was attracted to him; she admitted that. Of late, she'd had strange dreams that brought her upright, blushing in the darkness. Probably Missie had had those same dreams, and she had married a man who didn't love her.

When her body threatened to betray her, Ramona fought to keep her emotions under control. Denis was the only available man; that was all there was to it. She wanted to be held, to feel his kisses, his warmth. But she could never love a man of his interests. She recalled the slaughter of the kangaroos and dingoes, and shivered.

"Listen," Denis said.

Small Luka was singing. Her voice dipped and soared, beautiful, unearthly, with a sound of birds and bells. It came from the direction of Dusty's grave.

"What is that?" Ramona asked, puzzled. "It's not a hymn."

Denis laughed. "The tune's *The Wearing of the Green,* but I dinna recognize the wor-r-rds."

They walked toward the sound, the words becoming clear.

"They're in Jerilderie town, my boys, and we shall take their part. And shout again, 'Long may they reign, the Kellys, Byrne and Hart.' "

"Dear God!" Ramona whispered.

"As high above the mountaintops so beautiful and grand Our young Australian heroes in bold defiance stand—"

"Luka, where did you learn that song?"

The young voice continued to the end, despite Ramona's interruption. *"In bold defiance stand, my boys, the heroes of today. So let us stand together, boys, and shout again 'Hurray!' "* Finished, she beamed at her sister.

"Scott taught it to me. Everybody in Melbourne knows it. I thought Dusty would like to hear it."

Denis Dugald was glowering. "Tis a hor-r-rid thing tae make her-r-roes of a lot of domn bluidy mur-r-r-derers. I dinna like tae see a wee lass sing a song sooch as that! Her-r-roes, indeed! They should be hangit, the four of them!"

"You don't understand." Ramona's face was crimson. "These men, they were driven to be what they are.

237

And those who admire them are the same kind of people, persecuted, imprisoned at every turn."

"I hae no patience wi' the lawless."

She put her hands to her hips. "Then you'd be willing to kill Ned Kelly, if you had the chance?"

"Perhops!" He grew uneasy at the girl's expression and tried to turn it into a joke. "But ye forget. I hae nae goon."

Ramona turned and went back to the house. He watched after her, puzzled. He could understand her sympathy for the animals. But this obsession with an outlaw—Ramona was not the hero-worshipping type. And there was nae way she could hae known the mon!

"What's the matter with her?" Luka asked. "Didn't she like my song?"

"She liked it. Ay, I think she liked it tae mooch," he said dismally. He walked back to the house he shared with Boswell, nodding to Juan Narvaéz who stood talking to Duke Courtney near the dairy shed.

The two men had just shaken hands on a deal. After a few terse questions, Duke had assessed the financial state of Opal Station. Then he had offered Juan a position in one of his companies in Melbourne, should he wish to take it.

Juan turned the offer down. He owed it to Dan to salvage what he could here. And there was always a chance Missie might return.

It was the answer Duke expected. He tried again. Since Juan was empowered to handle Tallant's affairs, he could negotiate another loan. Would he consider *that* option?

Again the response was negative. Again Duke Courtney was not surprised. He had deliberately saved the third alternative for last, knowing it was the best way to handle a proud man.

He had been reading of a new type of cattle; an

improved, hardy breed. He'd been wanting to experiment with them, but had no time to run a station of his own. He'd broached the subject to young Peter, his oldest daughter's husband, but his station was small, and he preferred sheep.

Opal Station was ideal for his purposes. With Juan's permission, he would stock the place, put down a bore, and make a few other improvements. In return, they would work out a profit-sharing method.

"On this?" Juan said, gesturing toward the charred land.

"The fire was a blessing in disguise. With the scrub gone, after the rains, the grass will be knee deep. Hell, man, I'm getting the best of the deal."

"It doesn't look like it will ever rain again," Juan said dismally.

"It will." Duke Courtney grinned. "It will."

They shook hands on it, Juan feeling a new sense of confidence. Duke Courtney had a way of making things happen. If he could only solve the problem of Missie . . .

Nell joined them in the afternoon. She had kept pretty much to herself since Dusty's death, and they'd left her to her sorrow. But her girls were all together, and she wanted to see them. She looked old, gray-faced, her chins wabbling, as she marched determinedly to the main house. "How the hell are you?" she boomed, averting her gaze from Em's tear-stained blue eyes.

There was a lull as the group tried to think of something to say. It was broken by Luka, who threw herself into Nell's arms. "I sang a song to Uncle Dusty today. He liked it."

"How the hell you know that? He say so?" Nell was dry-eyed, but her mouth was trembling.

"Luka!"

"Leave 'er be, Arab! Well?"

"He didn't exactly say it," Luka said. "But I heard it inside my ears. He said, 'Oh, my word! You have a voice like your mother.' Then he said, 'Tell my wife—Oh, I forget the rest. But it doesn't matter,'" she said comfortably. "He doesn't have a wife, so I must have heard wrong. Would you like to hear my song?"

Nell, stunned, nodded mutely, and Luka began at the beginning of the dozen verses some unknown admirer had penned about the Kelly gang.

The melody carried outside to where Denis Dugald and Boswell worked at moving their gear to the jackaroo barracks, so the newcomers would have a bed for the night. It touched a sore spot; Ramona's change of attitude toward him still rankled. For a time, he'd believed she might be receptive to his attentions. But if words over an unknown, murdering outlaw could come between them—

There was nothing more for him here, now that Narvaéz was home. Maybe he *would* offer his services to the police.

In the main house, Luka finished her song, and Nell led the applause. "Say," the old woman said, "do you remember the time Dusty—" She followed it with a story that had them all laughing. Tamsen came up with another. Nell's color finally returned. She seemed her old self once more.

Except for Denis Dugald's set jaw and Ramona's quietness, the evening that followed was a pleasant one. When everyone had said good night, Nell tramped to the house she had shared with Dusty, her step a little lighter.

She went inside, closed the door, and spoke to the darkened room.

"Awright, you leetle bastard," she said affectionately. "I know yer still hangin' around. Figger yer keepin' a eye out t'see how I'll ack, now I'm a merry widder."

Inside her head she seemed to hear a dim chuckle. "Jove, Nell! Oh, my word!"

She clapped her hands to her ears. "Well I'll be gawdammed," she said. "It works!"

Nell was done with her grieving. As long as she could talk about Dusty—and tell him off once in a while, like she used to do—she figured he'd never be very far away.

Chapter 32

The wire sent to Daniel Tallant at Alice Springs didn't reach his hands until late in January. The officer-in-charge at Alice Springs, seeing the urgent nature of the message, had relayed it to Darwin. But it had crossed paths with Tallant, who was already on his way back to central headquarters.

He had been away for three months and was anxious to return. The hellhole that was Darwin had been nothing but trouble. First, one of his aides had strayed too close to ocean's edge and had stepped on a stonefish. Then, his other aid had contracted some tropical ailment that made him unfit to travel. It was evidently contagious, since it struck both Tallant and Said, his camel driver, three days out of Darwin.

Only the stolid aborigine who walked, untiring, at the head of the line, remained well.

They had tried to beat the wet as they crossed the swampy lands of Northern Australia. But it had caught up with them when they reached the fringes of desert and gibber. For a time they had labored through mud in which the horses sank to their bellies. Dan and Said, waist-deep in mud, struggled to extricate them, heaving, tugging, coaxing. A pack horse had to be shot and left where it was, only its head visible in the slippery sea the landscape had become.

Numbly following the line of telegraph poles that stretched across the terrain, it was two days before Tallant realized they had left the wet behind them. Now came the problem of water for the animals. Salt pans shimmered in the distance, invitingly. Aware of their treachery, Tallant held grimly to his course, the sun beating down, drawing every drop of liquid from his whip-thin body.

It was madness to travel across the gibber at this time of year. Two months might have made the difference. But he would rest for a time at Alice Springs. He would make up his reports. And then he would go home.

On this whole journey, he had been seeing Tamsen's face before him, her eyes accusing. The scheme to replace the money he'd lost without telling her had seemed so simple at the time. Not until he was at the point of leaving did the enormity of it hit him. He'd been gone before, months at a time, and she'd forgiven him. But the months had stretched into more than a year.

He would never leave her again, not if she still cared. Please, God, let there be letters waiting at Alice Springs—saying she still loved him.

Light-headed, dizzy, he reeled in the saddle. He was growing old, he realized. He'd had enough adventure for one lifetime. The present money crisis ended, the station should make a comfortable living. He and Tam would grow old together.

After a day without water, they slept in the shelter of a mass of tumbled rock. Dan tossed feverishly, his thirst unaccountably confused with his need for Tamsen. He woke, searching for her, calling her name. Toward morning, he lay awake for a long time, shivering now. There was a chance he might not make Alice Springs, he

244

admitted to himself. He'd been a goddam fool! Tamsen! Tamsen! Standing over a campfire in the wagon yard in St. Louis, her dark hair swinging. He'd loved her then. He loved her more over the years. Beautiful Tamsen, wife and mistress, who stirred him as no other woman had ever done—

He slept, imagining her cool fingers against his burning forehead. "Do you feel well, Dan? Would you like a drink of water?"

"No," he said in his dream. "I want you."

He woke in the morning. The sun was already high. And their aborigine guide was shouting. Reeling to his feet, Tallant went to the spot where the black man crouched and jabbered, pointing at a procession of ants moving from a crack in the rock wall of the gorge. Dan stared for a moment, puzzled. Then he could see what the abo saw. The ants that emerged had swollen bodies. That could mean only one thing.

Going to his horse, he took the miner's pick from his swag, and brought it back to the spot. Then he hammered away at the crack until a small seep of water was revealed. He followed the aborigine's example, soaking up the water with pads of dried grass, getting a few precious drops of liquid.

Cupping a wet grass pad in his hand, careful to avoid dripping any of the precious liquid, Tallant went to where Said lay, tossing in delirium. He held it to the man's cracked lips, squeezing the moisture into his throat. Said's condition had worsened during the night. He was unable to travel.

Dan's head throbbed. Perhaps if he tied him to the camel's back? No, that would be torture. They would have to wait here until he recovered sufficiently. At least there was water.

All day, he laved the sick man's face. Said, muttering in his native tongue, did not know him. Tallant cursed himself for having brought so few supplies. He had thought to travel fast and light. If the wet hadn't caught them, they would have been in Alice Springs by now. Obsessed with the need for water, he'd almost forgotten there had been no food since the previous day.

Getting his rifle, he found he was too weak to hunt. He found a spot where he could watch the rock face. Maybe a wallaby would appear, but it wasn't likely. Here, in this dead land, there was nothing. A dingo appeared on the rocks above, laughing down at him, and he sighted, levering the weapon. It shimmered and disappeared. A figment of his imagination. He sighed, put the gun away, and brought another pad of grass to Said, who pushed it away.

That night, the abo caught a lizard. He built a fire and, with many trips to the reservoir, managed to squeeze enough water into the pan to boil it until it made a broth. Tallant was unable to force any of it down the sick man's throat. It dribbled from the corners of his mouth. While the abo chewed away at the creature, Dan made himself drink a cup of the broth, though he had no appetite. He put back Said's for the morning.

He awoke to a cloud of suffocating smoke and got to his feet, calling for the aborigine: "Neenan!"

There was no answer. Choking, his eyes burning, Tallant stumbled to the spot where Said lay. There was no pulse. The man was dead.

And the aborigine, Neenan, was gone. He had lighted the fire, covering it with wet pads of grass to confuse the dead man's spirit, and fled. He would be pursuing a tortuous path over the desert now, in order that the spirit would not find him. Dan Tallant wouldn't be able to find him, either.

He returned to the fire, kicking the grass away, and

heated last night's broth. The thought of eating repelled him, but it would give him strength. Then he dragged the body of the dead Said close to the rocks and covered him with smaller stones that he managed to roll down with the aid of his pick.

He went to the camel. "Hooshta!" he commanded.

Protesting, the animal rose, rear end first. Dan, holding the strap that was fastened to the camel's nose ring, mounted his emaciated horse and rode on toward Alice Springs.

Days later, he staggered through Heavitree Gap. When he left, the town of Stuart had been set in a bower of wild flowers and ghost gums, surrounded by purple hills. Now, in the dead of a dry summer, the beauty of the Alice was hidden by a film of red powdered dust. But he had reached his destination, even if he was too worn and ill to feel any sense of triumph. Since this morning, he'd been on foot. There had been water in the MacDonnell range, but his horse had died before they reached it. This morning, he'd abandoned the exhausted camel.

With the single-mindedness that had brought him this far, he moved through the sleeping town. There was no one in sight, the ten or eleven inhabitants having chosen to remain indoors until the sun was low. Black flies clustered around Tallant's burning eyes, his nostrils, his ears, making a polka-dotted effect on his shirt. He'd long since given up trying to brush them away.

He crossed the dry, winding Todd River and moved, one foot following another, to the spot where the Alice Springs telegraph station sat on high ground above the spring in the riverbed; in the sandy stone country of the MacDonnells.

Ernest Flint, the officer-in-charge at the station had seen many derelicts stumble in from the desert, but none in as bad shape as this one. He looked at Tallant curiously, not recognizing the man, though they were face to face. When Dan spoke, he was on his feet in a flash, leaving his key.

"Good God, man! I'll get you to your bed. You need medical atteniton."

"I want my mail," Dan said through stiff lips.

"Later. Let me call Sam. He'll take over here, and I'll have a look at you."

"I want my mail."

Sighing, Flint reached into a box and drew out a sheaf of papers. "There you are. Now, come—"

Dan looked at the messages he held in his hand. Two letters. A telegram.

He unfolded it with thin, burned fingers. The letters danced before his eyes and he shut them tightly and read it once more.

Flint caught him as he pitched to the floor.

Within minutes, he was carried to the small house he had occupied when he was working at the Alice. Gentle hands removed his tattered clothing, washed the wasted body, and lifted it into bed. He had not regained consciousness.

Flint, returning to the station, damned himself for being seven kinds of a fool. He'd forgotten about the wire, though he himself had sent a copy to Tallant in Darwin. Evidently the man had not received it there.

He read it again: *Station destroyed. Fire. Missie maybe dead. Dusty dying. Wife needs you.*

News like that was a helluva shock for a well man, let alone one in Tallant's condition.

Carefully tended during the remainder of the day, given small sips of water, small sips of broth, Dan regained semi-consciousness. Flint, encouraged at his progress, left him for the night after he'd fallen into a natural-looking sleep. He had no way of knowing that the man's temperature would rise, that the message he'd received

248

was burned into his brain along with the compulsion to keep moving—keep moving—

Tallant awoke in the cool room in the middle of the night. Coolness. The hot months must have passed. He'd slept through them. And there was some reason he had to head along toward home. Some reason.

A portion of his subconscious mind told him to move craftily, in case someone tried to stop him. Why they would, he didn't know. The clothes he'd left behind were in the closet. Where were his boots? No matter, there was another pair. Stealthily, he dressed himself.

His horse was dead, he remembered. He had to ride a camel. He stole outside, blind to the sight of a paddock filled with fine horseflesh, and moved on to an enclosure where the camels were kept.

Free from pursuit, he mounted. He must follow the telegraph line, he thought dizzily. The telegraph line—.

He rode all night and through the next day. Part of the time he slumped forward in a daze. At others, he felt wildly triumphant. He had conquered the need for water, for food. He had beaten the desert. It had done its worst.

Oh, Tamsen! Tamsen!

Into the next night, the next day. Follow the line—

Again, he had reached barren land. Gibber and sand. Gibber and sand. The sun beat down mercilessly. His hat had fallen away and the sun burned into his brain. Suddenly the camel surged into a back-breaking trot. It scented water. The small pool, surrounded by scrub, lay a little to the left of the telegraph line. It was a small oasis fed by a seep. Dan remembered it now.

He slid from the camel's back and lay flat, drinking the brackish water, scooping it over his feverish face.

Rest awhile, he thought dimly. He would rest, and then he would go on.

He found a spot in the sparse scrub and stretched

out, face turned to the sky, lapsing into unconsciousness.

He was still there, hidden, when a camel train bound for the north arrived. It had been a rough journey, even for the desert-oriented Afghans who manned the train. Delighted at finally reaching water, they didn't notice the new camel that joined the spare animals following those laden with packs. Filling their skin bags, they moved on.

Dan woke to darkness. It was night. No, he could still feel the rays of a setting sun slanting across him. He sat up, blinking, bewildered at the darkness. He rubbed at his eyes, slitted them toward the late sun—

Good God! He was blind!

A wave of panic shot over him, making his heart pound furiously. He forced himselsf to calmness. It was nothing permanent. A touch of sandy blight, perhaps. It was not uncommon in the desert. But he couldn't remain here like this.

The camel! If he could catch the camel and mount it, the animal might take him back to the Alice.

He listened. There was no sound of the camel's tinkling bell. Perhaps he was deaf, too. He clapped his hands, grateful for the noise they made in the stillness of the desert.

The camel was gone. He had no way of finding it. He would have to make the rest of his way on foot—on foot—

But where was he?

The shock of his blindness brought on a moment of brief lucidity. He remembered following the telegraph line. His keen surveyor's mind calculated the place where the camel had left the track, triangulating the spot. Finally, he began to crawl. Within fifty feet he came up against an object.

By accident or design, he'd found a telegraph pole.

He could not go on. The chances of locating the next would be a million to one. Better to die here.

Dammit, he wasn't a quitter! And Tamsen needed him! He wouldn't give up! He slumped against the pole, holding to it as if it were a lifeline, his mind working frantically. There *was* something he could do! Something—

He remembered a man they'd brought in to the Alice Springs station several months ago. The sight of him had been shocking. Laid out on the station floor, he was a mummified thing of brown leather; a bundle of sticks in men's clothing; eyeless, where the ants had gotten to him, lips drawn into a hideous grin—

He'd been found like this, at the foot of a telegraph pole. Oh, God!

And Flint, the operator at the station, had said something. He'd said—

It came to him like a revelation, like the voice of God, Himself.

"The damn fool! We would have found him and brought him in if he'd had sense enough to cut the wire. Didn't he know we have to check out every break?"

Without letting go of the pole, Dan scrabbled about with one hand until he found a sharp stone. Holding it in his teeth, he began to climb, his body trembling with the effort, desperation giving him strength.

Reaching the wire, he sawed at it grimly, hearing a pinging sound as it parted. Then he let go, sliding down to lie in a heap at the pole's base.

When he woke, it was truly night, and he was shaking with a chill. He knew he had to make it back to the water if he were to survive until help came. Removing his shirt, he tied it to the pole and crawled back in the direction from which he'd come.

"I tried, Tam," he whispered. "I tried."

Now there was nothing to do but wait. If help didn't come, he would die. And if it weren't the sandy blight that was affecting his vision, if he were truly blind, he'd be better-off dead.

His strength spent, he lay down and gave himself up to his feverish dreams. He wasn't alone. Tamsen was there, her long hair flowing free. And they made love beside the opal-tinted waters of the Billabong.

Then an ant crawled across his face. In his delirium, he reached a hand to brush it away, touching empty sockets where his eyes had been. And he knew, without seeing, that the hand was mummified, a thing of brown leather extending below the sleeve of his faded blue shirt.

He sat up, crying out, and a nightbird took wing at the sound.

"Tamsen," he called. "Help me! Oh, God, Tam!"

Chapter 33

The Courtneys' stay at Opal Station lasted little more than a week. Em insisted that Tamsen return with them, but Tamsen refused. Both Em and Arab, not knowing of Dan Tallant's reasons for going off as he did, leaving his wife behind, couldn't help sympathizing in sisterly fashion. Tamsen was so thin, so haunted-looking. She'd been through so much. Dan should have been at her side.

All that opal hunting, Arab said scornfully. And now this! Dan's junketing around in Alaska and Hawaii might be forgiven. He'd done that work at the request of the government of the United States. You'd think he'd remember all the suffering *those* assignments had caused his wife, not to mention the rest of them. But no, he was just plain fiddle-footed! And poor Juan was working himself to death, running the station for him.

Em was inclined to be more open-minded. Still, Tamsen was her sister. It hurt to see her so drawn and sad-looking. If Dan were only more like Duke! Duke had been an adventurer, too, but marriage had changed all that.

Their sympathy took shape in the form of commiseration. "I know how you feel, Tam. If only Dan had been here." "If there's anything Duke can do to talk Dan into settling down—"

Every word was a twist of the knife in the raw wounds of Tamsen's feelings. She ranged between anger at her absent husband for putting her in a position where she was an object of pity, and a need to justify his position. But after all, how could it be justified? Facts were facts. Dan had wanted another fling at adventure, and he'd left her behind.

"It would do you good to come to Melbourne," Em coaxed. "You deserve a change as much as Dan does."

"You certainly do," Arab chimed in. "And if I were you, I'd meet some other men! Show Dan he can't just leave you sitting in one spot and expect you to be there when he decides to come back!"

"Arab!"

Arab shook her red curls. "I don't mean do anything *wrong,* Tam! But it might make him open his eyes!"

It might at that, Tamsen thought forlornly. And the promises Em held out to her, of dinner parties, the chance to buy some pretty gowns, were enticing. Too tempting for an old woman who would be fifty in May.

No, she was married to Dan Tallant for better or worse. And she loved him, despite his apparent neglect. And she was needed here.

As much as Tamsen adored her sisters, she found herself avoiding them. She made frequent trips to Nell's small house, using the pretext of cheering the old woman's spirits. But it wasn't Nell who needed cheering, she thought forlornly, but herself. She had never adjusted to the fire, Missie's disappearance, Dusty's death. She found herself clinging to Nell's normalcy like a drowning woman.

It was the weather, she thought as she manufactured an errand to the dairy room. And in those dry years before, the air was heavy, filled with dust and static electricity. Clouds gloomed on the horizon, but never fulfilled their promise. She pushed back her hair, feeling it crackle beneath her fingers. If this kept up, she thought glumly, they would all begin to glow in the dark. She puttered about for awhile, and finally forced herself to return to the main house.

Em and Arab were in Arab's bedroom. Not wishing to be included in their tête-à-tête, Tamsen went quietly into her own, and, leaving the door ajar for coolness, stretched out across her bed. The murmur of voices grew louder as the girls returned to the central room, and Tamsen realized she'd been put in the awkward position of being an eavesdropper. They were talking about her.

"She does look tired," Em was saying, "but it's not all Dan's fault. We've always let Tamsen carry more than her share. Look at the way she's helped you with your girls. You'll have to admit she practically raised Ramona and Missie."

"Maybe she had too much of a hand in it," Arab said with a touch of jealousy. "I thought I could trust her to watch over the girls when we came to the wedding. And look what happened! She lets Missie run off and get married!"

Arab was blaming her! Tamsen sat upright, her hands knotted into fists. Blaming her! When she'd faced down a man, shot him, had the station burned about her!

"You're being silly, Arab," Em said crossly. "You know good and well Tamsen didn't *let* anybody do anything! She'd give her life for any of your daughters! For any of us, in fact! Just look at the way she works here from morning until night—"

"I work, too!"

"Well, I only wish she'd go to Melbourne with us. Maybe you'd appreciate her more!"

"I didn't mean to put Tam down, Em," Arab said in

255

a small voice. "I don't know what's the matter with me. Maybe it's the weather—"

"I'm cross, too," Em admitted.

But their last words of mutual apology didn't reach Tamsen's ears. Her brain was still seething with the shock of those earlier words. *I thought I could trust her—And look what happened!* Dear God! Dear God!

Finally getting herself somewhat under control, she knew she could not walk out into the room and face the speakers. Not after what she'd overheard. Emulating young Missie, she backed out of her window, managing to scramble to the ground. Then she walked at a swift pace up the burned valley, ignoring the damage to her skirts as she tried to force down the anger that blazed inside her.

She had worked in a tawdry cantina to support her sisters. Later, she tried other means, and, failing, became the madam of a house of ill fame in San Francisco. Then both of them, finding what her work actually was, had looked down on her! It was like that now. Not knowing what she'd suffered, what she'd endured, Arab had made a judgment and found her lacking.

For two pins she'd march back there and tell her the truth! That Missie's elopement was not a romantic escapade by any means, but more likely a tragedy.

No, she couldn't do that. But there was something she could do. She could accept Em's offer, go home with her for a couple of months, and let Arab handle her own affairs. She'd soon learn there was more to do than keep Luka immaculate, and sleep with her beloved Juan!

And maybe that remark of Arab's about meeting other men wasn't such a bad idea! Dan Tallant could learn a lesson, too! She was tired of looking after everyone else's needs. Starting now, she'd look after herself!

Gown soiled, face smudged, eyes suspiciously bright with some indefinable emotion, Tamsen returned to the house. She announced that she would be accompanying the Courtneys to Melbourne.

The morning they left was dark and lowering. Red dust swirled and the glow of lightning glinted on tin-roofed buildings and along the top of the gorge. All night Arab had told herself stoutly that it was good for Tamsen to have a vacation. Now, the house would be occupied by the Narvaéz family alone. But when the time came for Tamsen's departure, she longed to beg her to stay. How in the world would she ever manage to get along without her? She opened her mouth to speak, but the wind blew her words away. The wagons moved off, and she stood for a long time, watching after them, the gritty dust scouring her tender face.

Finally, the small group broke up, Nell returning to her house, Juan to the jackaroo quarters with Dugald and Boswell. Arab and her daughters went into the house, now solely the Narvaéz domicile. The table was littered with dishes from the travelers' early breakfast. Dust seemed to be blowing through every crack, and settling. The water pail was empty. She had forgotten to set the coffee-pot on the back of the stove, and there was a smell of scorching grounds.

Grimly, she set to work, thanking her lucky stars for Ramona, who knew the order of things in the kitchen. It seemed inconceivable that Luka did not know how to dry a dish! It was time she learned.

By evening, Arab was tired and cross. Dinner was less than successful, though Juan, Denis and Boswell tried to soothe her ruffled feelings. What right did Tamsen have, running off to Melbourne, leaving her with all the work?

That night, at eight o'clock a miracle occurred. The atmosphere, after crackling all day with friction, suddenly erupted. First, there was a wind that clawed at the house, carrying dirt and ash before it. Then lightning rolled along the roofs, and zigzagged down from rolling clouds to strike the cracks like rifle shots. And then the hail came.

Ramona ran from the house. A broody hen had nested in a fence corner and there were small chicks clustered beneath her wings. Denis Dugald followed Ramona, one arm above his head to protect it from the pelting hail. Together, they managed to rescue the hen. They scrambled for the chicks, with which they filled Ramona's apron. Then they ran for the shelter of the dairy house as the deluge struck.

Settling the hen and her babies in one corner, they returned to the door to face an unbelievable sight. The station yard was a sea of running mud—for the first time in three years.

"It's raining!" Ramona's face was wet with rain and tears of joy. She raised an ecstatic face to Denis: "It's raining!"

He reached out to her, hugging her. It seemed natural for them to hold tightly to each other, sharing a blissful moment. And even more natural for him to touch her soft parted lips with his own. A touch that turned into something more urgent, a thing of mindless passion, as he lifted her to hold her against his lean hard body, kissing her, his mouth hot against her own; against her throat, against the smoothness of a shoulder as his big hand drew the material away.

Shocked at his own actions, he dropped his arms for a moment, stepping back. This was the girl he was going to marry! "Ramona—"

Released, she regained her senses. With a little cry, she was gone, running toward the house through the downpour of rain.

He watched her go. She was like a small wild thing. Timid and shy. And he had frightened her. But he had learned one thing. This was the girl he wanted. He would have to go carefully, keeping his emotions under control, until he convinced her of his good intentions; that he wished her to become his wife.

Ramona reached the house, her eyes large and luminous, her cheeks crimson. Arab took no note of it. She was too disturbed at the mud the child had tracked in. When Juan entered, a little later, his feet were muddy, too. But there was no scolding him. Her husband was too euphoric about the rain to hear a word she said.

Chapter 34

Tamsen did not enjoy her journey to Melbourne. Arab had looked small and pathetic in that final farewell. She had not meant the things she said, not deep inside. Arab was not like Em. She'd had hardships when she was a girl, things so terrible that she'd closed her mind to them. And because of those hardships, they'd all spoiled her; Juan, Ramona, Tamsen, herself. If everything didn't go as she wished, it had to be someone else's fault.

What if Missie comes back, Tamsen thought uneasily. And what if Arthur Melvin is with her? Could Arab cope?

Nonsense! She would have to! And she had Juan. Juan would kill him. When would she ever get out of the habit of thinking her family couldn't get along without her?

It hurt to see the loving glances Em and Duke exchanged. They brought back memories of Dan. It was hard to talk with Vickie, who had reached a rather silly boy-crazy stage. Tamsen couldn't help comparing her with Ramona. Young Scott chatted endlessly of the merits of cricket and rugby, of which Tamsen knew nothing.

Another devastating thought had struck her as they traveled. She'd had no word from Dan in months. What if he decided to surprise her and come home. She would not be there.

When they reached Melbourne and Em's lovely house, Tamsen felt like she was in an alien world. But she'd made her decision to come, and she would stick with it. Her first act, however, was to send Dan a wire. She pondered over the wording of it. There was no point in worrying him over things that couldn't be changed at a distance. Finally, she wrote: *"All going well. Visiting Melbourne two months. Wire here. Love you very much."*

Two days later, she received an answer. *Thanks for information. Enjoy yourself.* There was no personal message, only his name.

Tamsen was devastated. Such a cold response! Was there another woman she wondered? Or was it just that he didn't want her anymore?

All morning she stayed in bed with a thundering headache. When she rose at last, she insisted on a shopping trip. Em accompanied her into town where she purchased two bright modish gowns. "Now," she asked her sister with a brittle smile, "when do the social events you promised begin?"

Within ten days, the charming Mrs. Courtney's sister, Tamsen Tallant, was the talk of Melbourne. Such a beautiful woman! That lustrous dark hair, and those enormous melting eyes. And such wit and talent. Tell me, have you heard her sing? Tamsen heard the talk and gloried in it. It soothed the pain that was always within her, deep inside. There had been no other word from her husband. It was if he wanted to forget she existed.

Within three weeks, Tamsen was setting the trend in fashion. The Melbourne of the day was a combination of the overdone and the dowdy, utilitarian garb. With a natural flair for style—and the figure for it—Tamsen sent young girls and stout matrons scurrying to dressmakers.

For the ball at Government House, she found a bolt of gold tissue fabric imported from the Orient, and, with Em's help, constructed a gown that would have feminine society on its ear for days. In the usual crush that attended governmental functions, she glowed like a small slender candle. She sang, at the governor's request, and the ballroom was hushed and still. Graciously refusing an encore, she exulted, realizing she had lost none of her old ability to hold an audience enthralled. She went to the dance floor, whirled from one pair of arms to another, still with that wonderful surge of power.

"You are something of a witch, you know."

Tamsen, jerked from her thoughts, looked up into a pair of warm gray eyes. Somehow she had changed partners without even noticing. The man who guided her now was tall, broad-shouldered, with startling eyes in a tanned face that displayed a dimple as he smiled down at her.

"I'm sorry. I didn't understand."

"I said you are something of a witch. You put us under a spell with your singing. I am still under your spell."

Though his words were flattering, his expression said he was unmistakably sincere.

"Why, thank you. I don't believe I caught your name."

The name was Ian Gregory. He was an emissary of Her Majesty, the Queen, here to study the financial and political situation of Australia. Before he had a chance to continue, she was swept up by another partner. She smiled back at him, ruefully. "I'm sorry. I promised—"

He bowed and went in search of Em, wife of his good friend Duke Courtney, and the sister of this enchanting creature. Finding her in conversation with several ladies, he waited politely until he could draw her aside. With some adroit questioning, he managed to piece together a profile of Tamsen Tallant, and to form an adverse opinion of her husband. Em, beaming with pride at her sister's success, could not conceal the note of sympathy that crept into her voice at her sister's lonely lot.

"Then we must see that she enjoys her stay to the fullest," he said with determination. "I'm sure you have an invitation to the gala at Rippon Lea next week?"

Em did.

If she did not think him presumptuous, he would like to offer himself as her sister's escort. Since he was known to be a family friend, it should not be considered matter to set tongues wagging. Especially if they arrived as a foursome and under such excellent chaperonage. Of course, she must consult her husband and the lady, herself—

Armed with a half-way promise and an invitation to dinner at the Courtneys' the next evening, Ian Gregory found himself a station against a wall, from which he could watch the slim figure moving like a golden flame.

That night, in the privacy of her room, Em broached the subject of Ian Gregory with a hint of concern. "You know what he's like, Duke. In the two years he's been here, every girl, every spinster, every eligible widow has been after him. And he's managed to shrug them all off. I think he's *smitten* with Tamsen."

"Don't be ridiculous, sweetheart! The man can't be past forty. And Tamsen's only two years younger than you are."

"You're saying she's old? That a younger man can't fall for an older woman? That one isn't attractive after a certain age?" Em's voice held a dangerous edge.

"Hell, no!" Duke was suddenly alarmed. He silently cursed himself for putting his big foot in his mouth. "Or, maybe yes. You, Tam, and Arab are exceptions to the rule. Tamsen still looks like a girl. But, Em, she's *married*. And she loves Tallant—"

"Does she? How long can a woman love a man who goes off and leaves her for years at a time?"

"But Em—" He paused, on the verge of telling her the truth; that Dan had taken his job to avoid financial ruin. "Even if the fellow is 'smitten,' as you say, Tamsen's got a head on her shoulders."

"I'm still not sure it's the right thing to do," Em said worriedly. "We can't let her get involved with Ian."

"Suppose we just mind our own business. The general idea is to give Tamsen a good time while she's here. God knows, she deserves one. And if having an escort to a party or two will help, I don't think it should be up to us to say yea or nay."

"I suppose you're right," Em said reluctantly.

He rolled to his side and pulled her against him. "Now, will you please come here and be quiet? I happen to *like* older women, and I'd like to work out a few problems of my own."

Afterward, close and warm against him, Em felt comforted. Dan was gone, but his love and Tamsen's had been like this—and Tam wouldn't be apt to forget it.

The next morning, learning that Ian Gregory was coming to dinner, Tamsen felt a slight stirring of her pulse. She had not forgotten those warm gray eyes, or the way his brown hair fell over a boyish-looking forehead. A few questions elicited the fact that he was a widower, his wife having died shortly after their marriage some twenty years before. And that he had a reputation for being totally disinterested in marrying again.

"How sad," Tamsen said. But in her mind, she could hear a deep, sincere voice saying, *"You are something of a witch."* She had felt the thrill of having made a conquest.

You are a silly woman, she scolded herself. Why would a man like that be attracted to a woman on the brink of fifty!

When she dressed for dinner that night, she purposely chose a modest gown of black velvet; it had a fichu of white frill, and full sleeves drawn in with cuffs of the same frilling. In comparison with the image she'd presented at the ball, Tamsen looked small and nun-like. Em looked at her appearance with approval. It was clear Tamsen had not set out to attract Ian Gregory. She felt even more at ease.

She had no way of knowing that the sight of Tamsen in her demure black gown would strike Gregory like a blow to the solar plexus. In the golden gown, she had been vivid, exciting. But in the dark one, she had a wistful beauty that her dress could not add to, nor detract from; the small olive face gently touched with a natural peach bloom, mouth full, sensuous, a little sad; eyes huge and searching from beneath long black lashes.

Though he was imperturbable, impeccably correct in his manner, Tamsen felt his hands tremble on hers as he took them in greeting, bowing over them. In turn, she felt like touching the hair that glowed bronze brown in the candle's light.

Dear God, what was happening to her! She'd been drawn, briefly, to the evil in Arthur Melvin. Now there was something in this man that exerted a magnetism she felt tugging at her. Perhaps the days of the cantina girl, the madam, weren't behind her as she'd thought.

Sensing her nervousness, he dropped the hands he'd held for perhaps a fraction too long, and began a round of small talk that put her at her ease.

At dinner, he drew her into conversation about her life on the station. It seemed impossible, he thought, watching her. He'd met many of the outback people before. Their women showed signs of a rigorous life in a climate unkind to its feminine population. They were old before their time, withered by sun and blowing dust. Today, at a chance meeting, Duke Courtney had seemed

266

to make a point of mentioning the lady's age. As if it made any difference: A woman like this one was ageless.

As he took his leave that night, he invited his host, hostess, and her sister, to a play on the following evening. As a foursome, of course, he hastened to explain. Em accepted for them all, after only the slightest hesitation. After all, where was the harm?

That night, Tamsen realized she hadn't thought of Dan all day. And when she slept, it was not of Dan that she dreamed. There were a jumble of erotic scenes in which she was first in Arthur Melvin's arms then lying close to Ian Gregory.

She woke, her face flaming, and sat up, her hands clasped about her knees as she tried to unravel her tangled emotions. Finally, she buried her face against her knees, and wept. She could not go on like this!

She rose and dressed. Under pretext of doing some shopping, she went to the telegraph station and sent a wire to Alice Springs. *I need you,* it stated simply. *I want to join you there. I love you.*

That night at the play, Tamsen was cool and remote. Em, relieved, gave her attention to the action on stage; but Gregory guessed that something troubled beneath Tamsen's exterior. He took his cue, directing most of his comments to Duke, treating the two women with courtesy. Returning to the Courtney home, he declined an invitation to come in for a few moments. There would be time, he thought, as Tamsen disappeared into the interior of the house. There would be time.

He did not see her the next day, nor the next. Tamsen, with the excuse of a headache, refused to attend any functions. She remained at home, her eyes darkly shadowed, her small face pale, as if she were waiting for something or someone.

It wasn't until the third day that the wire she expected arrived. She was alone in the house. Em having taken Vickie to her dancing lesson, Scott off with his friends. She unfolded the message with trembling fingers, praying that it would contain a word or two of love.

There is nothing for you here, it read. *Do not come. I repeat. Do not come.* There were no words of affection. He had signed his full name, *Daniel Ward Tallant*—as though it were some kind of a business deal he was rejecting—some kind of a business deal!

There is nothing for you here. The words danced before her eyes. Nothing. Nothing, after all these years.

So this was what it felt like: a wrenching pain followed by a dreadful emptiness. An emptiness that would never be filled.

Chapter 35

At Government House, Ian Gregory had been unable to keep his mind on his work. The vision of a small oval face kept coming between his eyes and his papers. Finally, he gave up, walking to the window where he peered moodily out at the scene below. His eyes narrowed at the sight of a little figure in a crimson cloak.

It couldn't be!

Shoving his papers into a drawer, he left his office, taking two steps at a time. He approached the woman and she turned to face him. It was Tamsen Tallant! But a Tamsen he had never seen before. Her eyes glittered as if she had a fever, her cheeks held a hectic, abnormal flush. The hands he took in his own were burning.

"How nice to see you," she said in a high, unnatural voice at his greeting. "I was walking by—"

He thought of the scene from his window. She had not been walking, but waiting. She was lying, but it made no difference. The important thing was that she was here. Then a thought crossed his mind. It might have been someone else she waited for.

"You are meeting someone? You have an errand?"

She shook her head.

"Then do you mind if I walk with you? I've had enough of paperwork for today."

She studied him with an odd, assessing look. "I would love your company. I have missed you these last days."

His heart leaped, but he hid his feelings. He crooked his arm, and she rested her small hand in the curve of it. As they walked, she chatted feverishly for a time, as if she couldn't bear an instant's silence. She's in shock, he thought. He'd seen similar symptoms in a friend who'd returned from service in India. Gradually, his own calmness had a soothing effect on her. But he sensed that her tears were close to the surface.

"I should like to take you to dinner tonight," he said quietly. "Perhaps if Duke and Em—"

"They have a previous commitment. But I am free."

"As far as the proprieties—" he began uneasily.

She shrugged. "If you are concerned with them—"

"I am only concerned with your reputation. The gossips—"

Her reputation! *Her* reputation! Tamsen Tallant, ex-cantina girl, ex-madam—and soon to be ex-wife. She began to laugh, her laughter verging on hysteria. He watched her uncertainly, wondering what he should do. Then she wiped her eyes and smiled up at him, speaking in a normal voice.

"Forgive me. I was laughing at a—a private joke. Something I remembered. It was rude of me. In regard to your invitation, I will be happy to accept, unless it might damage your own good name. As I recall, it is never the gentleman who receives censure."

"Then, if you do not mind that tongues will wag—"

"I do not mind."

The dinner was only the first of similar occasions to follow. Heads turned to watch the small woman in apricot velvet and her tall, gray-eyed escort as they dined by candlelight. Afterward, they danced until nearly dawn. Returning to Em's home, Ian Gregory bowed over Tamsen's hand and released it lingeringly. Then he bade her good night, his behavior most circumspect.

Em and Duke had returned at midnight, and Em was frantic. She had insisted on waiting up, her nerves ragged, her temper edgy. When Tamsen entered, Em flew at her in a rage, built up after long hours of worry. Tamsen's appearance, her none-too-modest gown, sparkling eyes and disheveled hair added fuel to the fire.

"My God, Tam! Where have you been! I've been worried sick!"

Tamsen was noncommittal as she drew off her gloves. "Dinner. Dancing."

"Don't you realize what you're doing? You're going to be *talked* about! Melbourne is like a small town! A married woman doesn't go about with an eligible single man! Your name will be ruined!"

"I've never been overly concerned with my name, Em. You know that." Tamsen's voice was small, icy.

"Then think of Dan's name! Dear God, Tam! Think of Dan!"

"Why should I? He doesn't think of me."

Em put her hands to her spinning head. "Then promise me this will be the last time, Tamsen. I can make some excuse—You had some business to discuss with Ian. Duke was to meet you, but—"

"Do not make excuses for me. I am responsible for my own actions."

"Evidently you are not," Em snapped. "I forbid you to see Ian Gregory again. Do you understand me? I forbid you!"

"Then you are telling me I'm not welcome here? That I should go home?"

Em sagged. "No, Tamsen. I love you. I want you to have a good time. And I know how you must feel with Dan gone for so long. That's what frightens me. I'm not going to say any more. Except, please be careful."

"I will be, Em." Then she said, obscurely, "I don't believe in making the same mistake twice."

Em went to bed, twisting and turning until finally Duke sat up with a sigh. "Talk it out," he said. "Then maybe I'll get some sleep. I have to be at the office in the morning."

Em poured out all her worries. There was something going on between Tamsen and Ian. They'd been out almost all night. There would be gossip—

"Let's take one thing at a time. You've been fretting because Dan went off and left Tamsen behind, saying she needed to enjoy life a little. Wasn't that why you invited her here?"

"Yes, but—"

"And as far as the talk is concerned, Tam has never let that sort of thing bother her."

"But Duke, she's my sister."

"And a person in her own right. Hell, Em! I remember a woman who offered to go with me; who said she'd follow me if I took off—with marriage or without. What would your gabby friends say if they knew that? And she was *Tamsen's* sister!"

"Duke!" Em's face flushed as she recalled the day she'd practically forced a young miner into returning her love. "You shouldn't bring that up. It isn't fair."

"What if you had it to do over again?"

"I'd do the same."

Seeing his pretty wife in the dim light, her gold brown hair tumbled about her shoulders, Duke groaned and reached for her. She was still the minx who had trapped and tamed him, the woman who touched him as no other ever had. In the ecstasy of his caresses, the culmination of their lovemaking, Em forgot Tamsen and her problems. Finally she slept, and Duke stared wide-eyed at the ceiling. If there was anything in what Em said, he owed it to Dan to talk to Tamsen. He would watch the two tomorrow night at Rippon Lea, and draw his own conclusions as to their developing relationship.

Gregory called for the Courtneys the next evening in a closed carriage, bearing Her Royal Majesty's insignia. He was handsome, correct in his evening garb. Tamsen had dressed almost too simply for the occasion, in a gown the color of autumn leaves. She was certainly not trying to attract attention, Duke thought. And Gregory, handing both women into the carriage with a courtly gesture, seemed to make no difference in his attitude toward either of them.

Though Em was a little cold and stiff, it was a pleasurable drive to Rippon Lea, where lights glowed through stained-glass windows making colorful patches on the lawn. There, tables had been set up against a background of flowered borders, and from one corner, where the musicians had been situated, drifted the strains of soft music. Several of the younger guests were already dancing. The others drifted among the tables, the women like bright butterflies.

Bright butterflies! As his mind made the analogy, Duke Courtney's eyes turned toward Tamsen. The little devil! She had set fashion's pace, all the ladies to emulate her colorful gowns, and tonight she had reversed the field. Dressed in her simple autumn-colored gown, the other women appear gaudy, overdone. His lips twisted in amusement.

Tamsen and Em left their escorts to speak to friends among the people beginning to throng the lawns of Rippon Lea. Duke talked quietly to Ian Gregory for a time, discussing the cattle he'd had shipped to Opal Station. His friend displayed a genuine interest. He did not behave like a man who had anything to hide. When the dancing began, Gregory did not monopolize Tamsen. If there were

273

any wagging tongues tonight, Duke thought, the couple's behavior would surely still them. He went in search of his own wife, intending to have a good time.

It was an enchanted evening. Tamsen moved from one pair of arms to another, enjoying the strength of the Australian men who swung her from her feet; the grace and manners of the English; the blarneying tongues of the Irish as she turned their compliments prettily. Dancing; light refreshments. Dancing; a midnight supper. More dancing—

Then Ian Gregory was her partner again, keeping flawlessly in step as he guided her toward the edge of the pool, far from the house, across the green lawn. Here, the swans slept, heads beneath wings. Here, an arched bridge raised, crossing a stream to the path leading to a waterfall.

Shakily, Tamsen realized that they were alone. The music from the party was soft, filtered through leaves. Voices were muted. And Ian Gregory's gray eyes seemed almost black as he looked down at her.

"I've been wanting to kiss you all evening," he said huskily.

"Then, why don't you?"

The arms that went around her trembled as he sought to repress his desire. He kissed her gently, then lost all restraint, straining the slender body against his own as his mouth caught fire from hers. He was startled for a moment at the violence of her passions as she returned his embrace, melting against him, seeking his lips with an answering fire. Good God, he'd never known a woman could be like this.

What he didn't know was that, for a moment, she was in her husband's arms. That it was the face of Dan Tallant above her in the darkness. Hold me, Dan, a voice whispered in her brain. Don't ever leave me—

Gregory picked up the slight figure and carried her

274

to a tree's shadow. There, he placed her gently on the grass, kneeling beside her.

"I want you. You know that. But I want you for always. I want you to be my wife." His hand went to the bosom of the autumn-leaf gown, feeling the pulsing of her heart. "Tamsen?"

She turned her head, wearily, to avoid his eyes. He wasn't Dan. She could not go on pretending. "I'm married," she said dully, "and I'll be fifty years old soon."

"I know that. And it doesn't matter. From what I have learned, your husband has deserted you. A marriage can be undone!"

"Can it? Can it ever? Oh, Ian, I don't know."

He lay down beside her, putting her tear-stained cheek against his shoulder. "Don't think about it tonight, little sweetheart. Just leave it to me. I'm going to love you, take care of you for the rest of your life."

It was good to be held and comforted, but was it enough? Could she lie beside him, like this, every night of her life—pretending he was someone else? It wouldn't be fair to him! It wouldn't be fair.

"We'll talk about it tomorrow," he said softly. "But for now, we'd better get back before someone notices we're missing. Besides, I'm not certain I can trust myself any longer."

He helped her to her feet, and brushed at her rumpled gown. With another gentle kiss, he led her back over the arched bridge, away from the music of the waterfall.

Neither of them realized their absence had been noted. Duke Courtney, standing at a table, glass in hand, had watched Gregory dance his sister-in-law across the lawn. Then, he had seen them disappear among the trees. Stealthily, he had edged backward, skirting the fringes of the cleared expanse. Reaching the bridge, he halted. Good God, he was not his sister-in-law's keeper! To

Courtney, an honest, forthright man, spying was inconceivable. But so was marital infidelity. Tamsen was Em's sister, wife to his good friend.

He waited where he was, trying to convince himself that the two were merely walking together, that nothing immoral was in either's mind. He was still there, indecisive, as the couple emerged from the secluded spot. They paused a moment, Ian removing a blade of grass from Tamsen's hair. She laughed softly, and reached to touch the dimple in his cheek. A gesture of affection.

Duke Courtney was taut with anger, the instincts of his youth—to lash out with his fists, beat Ian Gregory to a bloody pulp—strong within him. He held his breath until the wave of uncontrollable fury passed. To submit his wife to the sight of a brawl on the grounds of Rippon Lea was unthinkable.

He would have it out with Tamsen when they reached home.

Chapter 36

If the ride from Rippon Lea to the Courtney house was a silent one, Em, Tamsen and Ian Gregory saw nothing significant in it. They had all been up late the previous night. And again, it was nearly morning. Tamsen sat quietly, trying to sort out her feelings; Ian still savored the delights of their brief rendezvous; and Em yawned, trying to hide it behind a discreet, gloved hand.

Reaching his own door, Duke Courtney was out of the carriage, handing his two charges down before Ian could move. "No need to stir yourself, Gregory," he said tersely. "I will see them in. It's late."

He cursed beneath his breath as he fumbled for his key, the fury that rode him making him inept. At last, he ushered the women inside. "Em," he barked at his surprised wife, "you will go to bed. Immediately. Tamsen, I will see you in my study in five minutes. Be there!"

He strode into the study and slammed the door behind him. Though he was no longer a hard-drinking man, he poured himself a glass of brandy with shaking hands, downing it. Then he poured another, whirling to glower at Tamsen as she entered. She reddened under his gaze, seeming to wilt, then raised an imperious chin.

"You have something to say to me?"

"You're a goddam fool," he said thickly. "And so is Ian Gregory. That makes a pair of you."

"I don't know what you're talking about!"

"The hell you don't! Don't lie to me, Tamsen! I used to have a lot of respect for you. Even when you were a madam, you ran a clean house—and you managed to keep your own skirts clear. But to act like a goddam whore—"

Her face blanched, but she met his eyes steadily. "I've done nothing wrong. But if I do, it's my business."

"Is it! When I brought you here? When you go sneaking off in the bushes with a man who was my friend? God almighty! To do this to Dan!"

"Before you start judging," Tamsen said, her voice ragged with anger, "maybe you ought to have all your facts straight. The truth is, Dan doesn't give a damn!"

He sat down behind his desk, and leaned toward her, an authoritative figure. "And maybe you need a few facts, Mrs. Tamsen holier-than-thou Tallant! I know you think you can justify your behavior by saying Dan's been away a long time. But there are women who've waited for their men a lot longer than a year or two!"

"But—"

He silenced her with a warning hand. "I've never betrayed a confidence before, but I'm going to now. It's better than letting you betray your marriage vows! Now, damn you, listen!"

He told of Dan's flier in the refrigeration scheme. "He lost his goddam shirt," he said grimly. He went on to tell of the loan he'd made to Opal Station; of the way Dan had his checks sent to a Melbourne bank for current needs. He didn't take the job because he wanted it, but because he had to.

Tamsen's white face was splotched with red. "It

278

won't wash," she said. "Even if your story's true, Dan was still wrong. I'm his wife, half of the marriage. I should have been told. We could have worked things out together."

"Dan's a proud man."

"And I'm a proud woman."

"Women should be protected."

"Women should share—in the bad times, as well as the good."

Duke slumped in his chair, staring dismally into his glass. "Oh, hell, Tam! That still doesn't make what you're doing to him right!"

"Maybe I can make it right," Tamsen said in a remote voice. "Wait here a moment."

She left the room and was back within moments. She placed two telegrams before him. "The first is the answer to one I sent when I arrived in Melbourne," she said, still in that distant tone. "Prior to this, I hadn't heard from him for months. You will note there is no personal message. The second is an answer to a wire I sent after meeting Ian Gregory. In that wire I had asked permission to join him in Alice Springs. Now, if you have no objections, I will say goodnight."

She left the room and Duke stared at the papers before him. *Thanks for information. Enjoy yourself.* And the second, *There is nothing for you here. Do not come. I repeat. Do not come.*

What the hell was wrong with the man!

Ah, God, poor Tamsen! No wonder she'd gone off the deep end! He thought of the way she'd looked at the station, concerned over Missie, shattered by Dusty's death, her surroundings a stretch of ash and cinders.

Maybe Tallant didn't want to air his personal feelings in a wire. Perhaps he'd sent a follow-up letter to explain his curt dismissal. He would wait and see.

A week later, he sent a telegram of his own. *Tamsen needs reassurance. Advise you provide if you wish to save marriage. Immediate reply requested.*

The answer he requested did not arrive. Courtney's objections to Tamsen's affair with Ian Gregory were not mentioned again.

The gossip about the pair, rife at first, gradually died down. Duke Courtney was a very important man. Few dared to cross him, since he was influential in the mercantile trade. Ian Gregory was an emissary of Her Majesty the Queen, and therefore well-known in political circles. Tamsen's name remained on guest lists, despite the private feelings of more than one hostess. And Tamsen and Ian attended every function as a pair.

But as the days passed, Ian began to grow impatient. He had remained faithful to his dead wife for twenty years, immersing himself in work as a substitute for his masculine needs. And now, like a miracle, he loved—Ah, God, he loved! He urged Tamsen to file for divorce, to set her own mind free.

Tamsen held back. Though she'd told Duke his betrayal of Dan's confidence made no difference, she couldn't help thinking of what Dan would find when, and if, he returned. The station burned, Dusty dead, Missie gone. The cattle with which he'd hoped to repay Duke decimated through fire and disease. He'd clearly inferred that he didn't want her. Yet it seemed poorly timed to divorce him now, when he was in such bad shape financially. Perhaps she should let him make the first move.

Tomorrow was her fiftieth birthday. Ian had planned a private party for the two of them, at his bachelor home: candlelight and wine.

He would declare his love for her, take her in his arms, kiss her. And, alone together, really for the first time, the inevitable would follow. Did she want it to happen? Sometimes she thought she did. At others, she found the idea repellent. Now it seemed to make no difference.

She entered the empty house. Duke would still be at work. Em, Scott and Vickie were gone. Tamsen had the notion that Em had been avoiding her of late.

The Scarlet Woman, Tamsen thought, smiling a humorless smile. She placed her reticule on the small glass-topped table that graced the entrance, and drew off her gloves. At that moment, her eyes fell on a telegram, a wire from Alice Springs.

She'd read it twice over before she realized it was addressed, not to her, but to Duke Courtney. And it wasn't from Dan, but from someone named Flint.

Do not know how much you understand situation. Concerned. Informing you without Tallant's knowledge. Use information as you wish. Tallant sick, blind, despondent. Possibly suicidal.

Dear God! Here was the answer! Dan, too proud to tell her they were penniless—and now, too proud to tell her he had lost his sight! Damn him! Oh, damn him!

In the same breath, she said, "Help him! Oh, please, God, help him!"

She paused, but only for a moment. Then she went to her room and drew out two riding habits, boots, a heavy cloak. Anything else she needed, she would pick up on the way. She didn't dare wait until Em and Duke returned. She knew they would try to prevent her from going without a male escort.

Before she left the house, she stopped at the glass-top table, picking up the telegram that Duke had not yet read. Thrusting it into her pocket, she replaced it with a note that read, simply, *"I'm going home. Thank you for everything. I love you all.*

She sailed for Adelaide, where she boarded the train

that would carry her as far as the end-of-track. As she listened to the steady rhythm of the train, she thought of Ian Gregory. At about this time, in Melbourne, he would be waiting for her at the romantic birthday dinner he'd arranged. Candlelight and wine.

Chapter 37

The rains that fell along the Billabong, sparse to be sure, but enough to bring a haze of tender green to the blighted land, had spent their strength in double measure in the hidden valley some two hundred miles away. There could be no cattle-duffing in the wet, and the three occupants of the small one-room house were shut in together for days.

Arthur Melvin, as he still insisted on being called, raged like a caged animal. Whatever his other characteristics, he was a man who must be working and planning. That it not necessarily be honest work was not important. Driven by a desire for wealth and power, he knew his return here had been a mistake, just as his marriage to the Narvaéz girl had been. He scowled at her, thin, bedraggled, her blond hair dull and lifeless as she worked over the stove. It was her fault that he was stuck here in a backwater. Then his mind returned to the failures of these last months.

Cattle-duffing had proved to be not worth the effort expended. After the long dry, the mobs within hundreds of miles were slat-thin, mangy looking creatures. Most of the small, remote stations within several days ride had simply given up and sold out. Less than two thousand pounds rested in the cashbox, half of it belonging to the old man. Not that Melvin would have any qualms about taking all of it when he cleared out. But it wasn't enough.

He'd been thinking about Perth. He was not known there as yet. A bloke with a little money might get in on something big, then clear out for another country. He might represent himself as an investor. But first, he had to have a stake. A new name. He was considering that when Missie set his plate before him.

"Boiled beef again," he snarled. "Can't you do better than that?"

Once Missie would have spoken up, saying there was no other fare in the house, but she'd learned her lesson. It was better to keep quiet and try to stay out of his way—and that of the lascivious old man.

Her pregnancy seemed to repel her husband. It made her almost glad for it. He hadn't touched her—that way —in some time.

His hand closed over her thin wrist, twisting it, and her eyes filled with fear. Then he flung her away from him and dumped the contents of his plate on the floor. "Bring me something decent," he growled.

She carried his plate to the stove and filled it with food from the same kettles. Except this time, she arranged everything carefully, the beef cut in small pieces; potatoes laid symmetrically, a border of boiled cabbage around the plate.

"More like it," he grumbled. Missie knelt and cleaned the floor. This would have been her portion, after the men finished eating. But it didn't matter. She had little appetite.

Melvin went to the door after he'd finished eating. Grass had grown in ragged clumps, concealing the rails of the duffing yard, and the cliffs above ran rivers of red mud.

"The bloody rain!" Melvin raged. "The bloody flaming rain!"

After a deluge that lasted a week or more, the rain ceased altogether. The ground, after its three-year thirst, drank it greedily. Within another week, the soil was firm underfoot. Arthur Melvin announced that he intended to go on a short journey to determine the state of the rivers. If they were in flood, there would be no more cattle-duffing. Not that he cared. The job had been a bloody failure anyway. He planned to look around for something else.

He was going alone, he announced, taking some money from the cashbox. He might come back, and he might not.

Missie, ordinarily glad to see her husband leave, clung to him. He treated her brutally, but she was more afraid of the old man, his father. Only Arthur's presence had protected her from him thus far. The way he looked at her gave her shivers. If he put his hands on her, she would die. And now they would be left alone together.

Dressed in trail clothes, a suit of spotless whites in his swag, Melvin endured her embrace. He could afford to be generous, now that he was escaping this hole in the ranges. When she sobbed out her fears, he chuckled. Going to a box, he drew out an ancient pistol, loading a single bullet into it. He pointed it, playfully, at old Mick, grinning. Then he handed it to Missie.

"There you are. If he bothers you, blow his brains out. But remember, you've got to do it with the first shot."

Laughing uproariously, he picked up his swag, mounted his horse, and was off to freedom.

Posing as a squatter, he made his way from one small town to another, from one saloon to the next. "My shout," he would say, and the saloonkeeper would draw beer for everyone in the house at Melvin's expense. Since manners compelled each guest to return the "shout," the gesture served two purposes. It made Melvin feel important once more. And, when people were beered up, they tended to talk. He kept his ears open for opportunity.

The kind of information he was looking for finally came; not from a bar, but a brothel. He had stopped for the night in a town too small to be named. Feeling the need for a woman, he went to a house and paid for the services of a slim, half-Abo girl. He had paid for an hour. The hour stretched into a night, another night, another. The girl was impressed by the white-clad, apparently wealthy man. She matched his passions and endured his perversities as no other woman had ever done. His ego salved by her obvious pleasure, he led her into talking of her other customers.

Her desire to impress him made her mention the police guard who rode with the coach that picked up surplus funds from small town banks once a month, carrying the cash to the railhead. He came to her regularly, the second Thursday of each month. If Melvin were here next week—

"I'll have to move on," Melvin said modestly. "Business, you know. Tell me, do you accomodate the young man you mentioned—and the other guards too? Their jealousy would make them miserable traveling companions."

"Oh, no, there's only the one."

"And he is a lucky man." He reached out lazy arms toward the slim darkness of her. "Come here."

When he left the cheap room that smelled of stale perfume and lovemaking, he knew the exact route the money-carrying stage would be taking. He followed it, seeking an appropriate spot for an ambush. He found it in a wash, deep in sand, where the coach would be bogged down, the horses laboring. A nearby grove of trees and scrub would make an ideal place to wait until it had passed. A fallen tree at the far side would bring the coach to a halt. They would approach it from the rear.

Unfortunately, he would require his father's help; one of them to hold the passengers at bay, the other to pick up the loot. Then they would be off and away to the secret valley until the pressure was off. This just might be his ticket to Perth!

He would wait a week. Not this Thursday, but next. That would give him plenty of time. He debated returning for one more night with the girl, and decided against it. Whistling, he rode toward home.

Missie had endured some nerve-wracking weeks. Wherever she turned, the bewhiskered old man seemed to be there, grinning. She knew he was playing a cat-and-mouse game, believing that one day he would catch her without the weapon Arthur gave her. She carried it with her always, sleeping with it in her hand.

She had never fired a gun in her life, and didn't know if she could hit her mark if she did. Sometimes at night she thought of putting it to her forehead, pulling the trigger and ending her misery. But she couldn't bring herself to commit what she'd been taught was a mortal sin. Somehow, she managed to get through the days, knowing that when she dressed or bathed, those lewd old eyes were watching through some crack or knothole in the wall.

What would she do if Arthur never came back?

"Well, I be damned," her father-in-law bawled one morning. "Look what th' cat drug home!"

Rushing to the door, she saw a horse toiling down the steep path that led to the opening in the red cliffs. There was a white-clad figure on its back. Arthur!

A wave of gladness went over her. At least she was safe from the old man. She ran to meet him, but he ignored her presence as he slid from his mount, handing a

287

bottle of whiskey to his father. "There's going to be plenty more where that came from," he laughed. "I got on to something. We're going to be rich! Get that, you bloody old fool? Rich, by God!"

Missie watched the two of them, clapping each other on the back, capering like clowns. For the first time she could see a resemblance to old Mick in Arthur's features. How could she have been such a fool? Again, she thought of her family. Mama, Papa and Luka were safe, thank God. But what of the others, Ramona, Tamsen, Dusty, Nell—if they had died in the fire, then she had killed them.

That thought had haunted her ever since that dreadful day. But it still brought tears to her eyes. Unfortunately, it was at this moment that her husband noticed her. He swung an open hand, catching her across the cheek, snapping her head back.

"Stop your bloody blubbering. See if you can get some food on the table. I'm hungry. And get us a couple of mugs."

Missie sliced cold beef and garnished it with wild greens she'd gathered earlier in the day. The food went untouched, the two men emptying the bottle Arthur brought. He produced another. By nightfall, the men, father and son, were maudlin drunk, discussing plans for the robbery, their estimates of what the stages would carry, growing wilder as they talked. Both faces, young and old, were ugly with drink and avarice in the flickering light.

Finally, Missie crept beneath the blanket on the bed she must share with a drunken husband. She tossed, unable to sleep, dreading his coming to join her. She tried to blank out their tipsy conversation, then, to her horror, heard her name. They were discussing her.

"Hell, go ahead," Arthur laughed. "I don't give a

damn. She's just so much excess baggage now. Plenty of sheilas in Perth. I can bunk down in your spot."

She heard old Mick's shuffling footsteps as he stumbled toward her. For a moment she was paralyzed. Then she remembered the gun. She'd shoved it beneath her pillow when she went to prepare the meal.

Mick bent over her, grinning his toothless grin, and came nose to nose with the loaded pistol in her hand.

His recoil sent him staggering back into the room, where he crashed into a chair. His predicament brought a howl of laughter from his son. Cursing, Mick went to his own bed. Arthur, still laughing drunkenly, joined Missie. The alcohol, combined with the joke on the old man, had made him amorous. Missie endured his attentions with gritted teeth.

It was not possible to kill two men with one bullet, even if she knew how to aim.

Chapter 38

Three weeks later, the two men left; the old Mick and the young. They rode two horses and led two. These were to be hidden at a halfway point, to be fresh for riding on the way back. They also took the last of the flour to make dampers along the way, the remainder of the beef, and the majority of the potatoes. They would be home soon enough, and the girl didn't eat much, anyway.

She watched them go, hoping that they wouldn't return. She would probably starve, but that would be preferable to her life as it was in their company. In the meantime, she would enjoy their absence. She began to take stock of her situation.

An old rangy cow had somehow missed being included in their last drive of stolen animals to market. They had taken her half-grown calf. Missie had asked Arthur to herd the cow into an enclosure, and she'd managed to milk about a pint a day from the fractious beast.

She had boiled fresh coffee this morning. Taking the bag of grounds from the pot, she carefully spread them to dry. If they didn't sour from damp, they might be used several times. The chickens were gone, but there was some sort of grain in the shed. Pounded, it might provide some kind of gruel.

Worst of all, they'd left no firewood to cook with—or to heat the shack if an early winter brought a cold wind screaming through its splintered walls. They had also taken all the blankets. She took up the filthy kangaroo skin the old man kept on the floor beside his bunk and carried it to the river, washing it repeatedly until it no longer stained the water. Then she spread it to dry.

With a feeling of satisfaction, she returned to the hut. She'd been wearing some of Arthur's mother's old clothes that she found in the shed. The woman had been tall and big-boned, and the gowns wrapped twice around her frail body. In order to keep the hems from the floor, she had tucked the gowns at the waist, tying an apron to hold them in place—and to cover the gaping bosoms.

They were ugly things of muddy calico or black bombazine. But now, with the men gone, she would have time to take them up to fit. She could piece the leftovers together and make a sheet for the stained bunk.

That night, her freshly washed blond head close to the light, she stiched away, thinking how peaceful it seemed; and wondering why she'd hated such work at home.

In the days that followed, she alternated between her temporary state of happiness—and despair. The memories of that last day at Opal Station clawed at her. Unable to concentrate on anything else, she wandered the valley, armed with her gun. She learned to point it with unerring aim, her other hand supporting the wrist that took the strain of the heavy weapon.

"Bang!" she would say to a bush that took on the features of Arthur Melvin. Then, whirling, "Bang!" That bullet disposed of the old man.

If only they were real shots instead of imaginary

ones. If only she had more than one bullet to fire! What did it feel like to kill a man?

She found herself watching the chasm above that provided an entrance to the valley. They would return that way. There was only one path in. Occasionally, she would sight the gun at a pretend figure, a man on horseback on the ridge above. How far, she wondered, did a bullet fly? She'd had an avid curiosity about all things, but it was a question she'd never asked. She brooded on it, the need to know becoming an obsession. If she shot a man, he would have to be far enough away that she wouldn't see his face—

Arthur Melvin, nursing a bullet in the shoulder, could have answered his wife's question. He was returning to the secret valley empty-handed and alone, mulling over the failure of the stickup, wondering what had gone wrong.

They'd left the horses as planned, then camped for a week in the bush. No one could have seen them, nor would they have suspected their mission if they had. Under cover of darkness, they had traveled the last few miles and set the barricade across the path on the other side of the sandy wash. Then they erased their tracks and returned to the grove to keep watch. Within several hours, they heard the mail coach; the creaking of wheels, the jingling of harness, the shouts of the driver urging the horses on to greater speed.

Reaching the wash, the vehicle slowed. Melvin smiled to himself as it reached a near halt in the sandy bed. The tree fallen ahead, bogging sand to either side, there was no place it could go. Complimenting himself on his good planning, he took careful aim. The armed man beside the driver toppled and slid from his seat.

Then all hell broke loose.

From the windows of the coach came the rattling fire

of repeating rifles. The old man had stepped out of hiding when the guard went down. Arthur saw him fall, riddled with bullets. He left him lie and ran for his horse. Hell, he'd never claimed to be a hero, and his dad was bloody done for, anyway. But just then some bloke got lucky, aiming blindly at the movement in the bush. Fist clenched to his wound to stop the pumping blood, bent low over his horse, Melvin had escaped.

He rode hard, spurred by anger over his failure. There was no doubt about it; they had been expecting him. It had been a trap, a setup. But how? Who knew? Groping for an answer, his dazed mind finally found one: Missie. She must have overheard their plans, and found some way to get a message out. How she might have accomplished it, he couldn't guess. But it was the only explanation. He shifted in the saddle, groaning with the pain of his wound. He would proceed to beat her to death when——and if——he made it home.

He had no way of knowing that his own ego had been his undoing. The half-abo girl from whom he'd received his information had been in the profession since she was a child. Used and battered, she had come to take her occupation for granted. She went through the motions matter-of-factly, not feeling the need to remember a mans' face unless there was a particular reason: if he were a regular, like the police guard; or if he were a grand and wealthy gentleman.

Arthur Melvin was still on her mind when the guard stopped by the following Thursday. Thinking to impress him, she told him all about the man who had taken up her time for two days and three nights. "I told him about you," she said flatteringly. She went on to repeat the conversation almost word for word.

Billy-Boy Haines was rough and untutored, but he was far from stupid. There might be something up, and there might not. But it would be best to be on the safe side. He alerted his boss, who saw to it that the stage that left to deliver the cash to the train for Melbourne bristled with armed men.

It was late afternoon when Arthur Melvin arrived at the spot where the spare horses were tethered. Anger at Missie's supposed betrayal had held him upright for most of the way. But he knew he must rest for awhile if he was ever to make it home. He slid from his saddle, cursing as he crumpled to the ground. He had expected to return this far in triumph. Instead, his old man was dead; he was empty-handed, and damned near dead from loss of blood.

Setting his teeth, he crawled to the small spring that supplied the glade with water. He drank to ease his feverish thirst; then, tearing strips from his shirt, washed the wound and padded it, binding it clumsily with his good hand. Weak with the pain and effort, he pillowed his head on his uninjured arm, and slept.

The next day, he traveled on nerve. Part of the time he was out of his head, incoherent, but somehow he kept to the proper course. He had to reach the shack. Missie was there, and he intended to kill her. Missie, during the next day of journeying, somehow took on the face and figure of Tamsen Tallant. She danced just ahead of him, her chin held high, her dark eyes haughty.

"Bitch," he gritted through clenched teeth. "Bloody bitch!"

He followed the apparition across plains, through deep gullies, across riverbeds, wet and dry, taking no note of the scrub that tore at his clothing; the game that might have provided a meal to alleviate his faintness. Finally, seeing the wall he must negotiate to reach the cleft near the top, he knew he was almost there. He slumped in the saddle, letting the horse have his head. He would take him on in.

His eyes were closed as the animal negotiated the path, rocks slipping beneath its hooves, falling in a miniature shower to the plain below. Up, up and up. The climbing eased. They were in the airless corridor. The horse turned—

Melvin opened his eyes, and gave a strangled cry.

There, in the opening that led to the downward path, stood King, the aborigine, spear in hand. Frenzied, Melvin drew his pistol and shot.

King was untouched. He smiled, a horrible humorless smile, and carefully set his spear along a ledge. Then he disappeared.

There was no place for him to go. Arthur Melvin rubbed his eyes. It was only another dream. The fever. That's what it was. The fever. But the spear was still there. He rubbed again at his blurred vision. Only a crack in the rock, or a shadow.

He rode on, fighting a compulsion to keep his eyes on that crack, that shadow. He managed through sheer will until he reached the spot where the trail narrowed before it emerged under open sky. He turned to look as the snake struck, the shadow having become a living thing.

Eyes bulging, Melvin raised his hand to the side of his throat. In that moment, he knew he was going to die. He spurred the horse out of the gap, then reined in. A burning heat had spread throughout his veins. His throat was suddenly paralyzed, he couldn't swallow. His body was growing numb. And then it was cold. So cold—

Missie, in the secret valley, heard the shot Melvin fired in his delirium. Leaving the scrubbed hut, a pot of greens boiling on the stove, she went out into the yard. Only one man emerged from the corridor. Her husband. Where was the old man?

A thought sent her brain reeling. Arthur had killed him. They'd had an argument over division of the spoils, and Arthur had killed him! As deliberately as he'd set fire to Opal Station.

The pistol was in her hand. She raised it, supporting her wrist, sighted and fired.

At that exact moment, the venom reached Arthur Melvin's heart. He swayed in the saddle, slipped sideways, and fell. For a few moments, his hands scrabbled vainly at the rocky soil. Then he was still.

Missie's arm dropped, the weapon falling from numbed fingers. She'd shot a man in cold blood. Murdered him. Oh, dear God!

Suddenly she bent double with a slashing pain. Whimpering, she dragged herself into the house. Unable to make it to her bed, she sank down on the floor where she writhed in misery. It was not until some hours later that she regained consciousness and realized what had happened. She had lost the baby.

She managed to pull herself upright, moving along the wall to the bunk she'd shared with Melvin. There she lay for several days, alternating between vague dreams of Opal Station and nightmares in which Arthur Melvin wasn't really dead at all. He crawled down the hill and loomed over her, his face menacing. He crawled down the hill. He crawled down the hill. He crawled down the hill—

On the morning of the third day, she got shakily to her feet, weak from illness and loss of blood. Her first act was to go to the door and look upward. Melvin lay where he had fallen, his hair moving in the wind. She swallowed and closed the door against the sight. The important thing now was to regain her strength.

The pot of greens she'd left on the stove had boiled dry, filling the shack with a smell of scorching. The water pail was empty. God in Heaven, how was she to fill it again? The stove had gone out. She managed to get a fire going and made a thin gruel from a little of the remaining grain and some water left in a cup on the rickety table.

It wasn't until the next day that she regained enough

strength to go outside. Keeping her eyes averted from the thing above, she tottered toward the cow lot.

At best, the ancient cow had given little milk. Now, deprived of her calf, not having been milked or given water for several days, she'd gone dry.

Missie sank to the hard ground, leaned her head back and looked up at the sky. She'd managed so well until now, she thought, dazed. Perhaps God was punishing her for her dreadful deed. Suddenly, everything was going wrong.

Chapter 39

King squatted outside of the nulungery's cave-home. Courteously, he had paid his way here; hunting during the day, and sharing the fruits of his hunt. In the remaining hours, he merely waited. Though the wait was long in white man's terms, it meant nothing to King. A need to go home to his wife and child might have begun yesterday, or tomorrow. Yet the need was there.

The nulungery left his cave and came to squat beside him. "You still wait, my son?"

"I wait, my father."

"Your waiting has ended. It is done."

The nulungery stood, King following suit. For a long moment they looked into each other's eyes. "I thank you, my father."

"You are welcome, my son."

King reached for his spear and was off in the agile, twisting run of the bushman.

A little more than a week later, he came to the rock face where the twin pinnacles marked a hidden corridor. It was evening. Some inborn sense cautioned him to wait until morning. He managed to find a few witchetty grubs beneath the roots of acacia scrub, and he chewed on them slowly. Then, his hunger satisfied, he curled among the rocks to sleep, certain that the smell of death was in his nostrils.

The next morning, he climbed the rocky escarpment so silently that crows perched among the stones took no notice of him. Reaching the entrance, his feet lagged, the scent of death growing stronger. As he turned with the corridor, a red-tailed black parrot swooped down from overhead. Sweat began to shine on King's brow. The bird was thought of as carrying the souls of the dead.

Another step, and he halted. The devil-devil's body lay across the entrance. He could not cross it, for fear its spirit might enter his own body.

He lingered only long enough to recognize that the man had died from snakebite. Then he turned back the way he'd come, down the wall-face. He began to run in the direction of Opal Station.

Arabella Narvaéz, at work in the kitchen, was tired and cranky. Though Ramona could cook, somehow it had seemed important that she do it herself; to show that she could equal Tamsen's skill if she wished. But the biscuits she'd made for lunch were still on the cluttered table. None of the diners had taken more than one. Ramona had gone to take care of some urgent outside chore and Luka, as usual, had slipped away, leaving the clearing up to her.

Admit it, Arab said fiercely to herself. Tamsen can do anything better than you can, so why try! How she wished her sister would come home.

Her temper wasn't improved at the sight of old Wyuna waddling toward the house. She squinted. Wasn't that the man, King, with her? Odd, the way he'd gone on walkabout, leaving his wife behind. But she would never understand these abos.

The men were all out on the range, settling the cattle

Courtney had sent from Melbourne. But one of them was riding in, now. Juan? He intercepted the aborigines. Good. She didn't like to have them in the house. They looked so fierce and strange, they frightened her.

Juan stood for a moment, talking to Wyuna who gabbled and gestured, evidently translating something for King. Then Juan was running for the house, his face white as paper. Arab frowned, then she thought—Luka! Something has happened to Luka!

She stepped outside and was almost bowled over as he rushed past her, taking a rifle from the wall. "Juan, what is it?"

"Nothing," he said as he levered shells into the chamber. "Now get out of my way!"

Arab put a hand to each side of the doorframe, blocking the entrance. "Not until you tell me what this is all about!"

"Diós, Arab, this is no time for games."

"I'm not playing games! Is it—Luka?" Her face was pale as she thought of the dangers that plagued the station: snakes, the bush cattle—

"Luka's all right, I'm simply taking a short trip. I'll be back in three or four days." He tried to move around her, but she stood her ground.

"Then I've got to know what's happening. I'm not going to let you go rushing off with a gun like a crazy man! You have responsibilities here at home. If the neighbors need help, you can send one of the hands."

He stared at her, seeing a pretty, selfish woman who was pouting a little at the thought of being left for a time. All of them had gone through hell, yet they had insisted upon protecting her. Maybe it had been a mistake.

"I'm going after Missie. I'm bringing her home."

A wave of uncertainty passed over her small face. "Missie? But she's married, Juan! She has a husband to look after her. If they want to come for a visit—But if they're having problems, they'll have to work them out. It's none of our affair."

His expression as he looked at her made her flush. She knew what he was thinking; that she had never been a real mother to Missie, not as she was to Luka. Well, it wasn't true! The girl, with her abrasive personality, had been hard to get close to. It was a relief to know she was happily married, and had someone else to look after her.

"I just don't think we should interfere," she finished weakly.

"Then it might be a good idea if you knew the truth." His voice was cold, his eyes contemptuous. "Melvin's a four-flusher. He brutalized the child. Tamsen shot him. He carried Missie off and burned the station. King says he's dead, but I don't know! I just don't know! But he knows where they are—and if he's not dead, he will be!"

Arab reeled. "Juan, what in heaven's name are you saying? No one told me—"

Juan looked at her suddenly shrunken face unable to summon a trace of pity. His anger had burned it away. "Nobody told you because there wasn't anything that could be done," he said flatly. "And you would have gone into a fit of the vapors. We already had enough on our hands without that."

Setting the rifle down, he picked his wife up and put her to one side. Then he reached for the weapon and was gone before she could move.

Arab stood numb with shock. Ramona had come up as they talked. She could see by the girl's face that she knew, too, that she'd known about Missie all this time. Even Ramona! Why had nobody told her? Dear God, what kind of mother did they think she was?

Her face burned crimson as she realized that, whatever they thought, it was probably true.

She didn't recognize her own voice as she spoke to Ramona. "Please saddle a horse for me. I'm going with him."

Juan and King had already disappeared. Grimly, she lashed her horse, following a faint cloud of dust on the horizon. She caught them before they had gone more than a mile; Juan on horseback, King running before him like a hunting hound.

Hearing hoofbeats, Juan paused, and turned in the saddle. He was surprised at the sight of his wife, still in her housegown, petticoats and red hair flying. Did she think to stop him now? The look he turned on her was a forbidding one.

"I'm going with you," she said defiantly.

"You can't, Arab!" His anger had melted. He felt close to tears. Whenever he misjudged his wife, she came through like a trouper. "There's no telling what we'll find."

"All the more reason for me to come. Missie might need me."

Without another word, he kneed his mount ahead. King still ran, a black blur in the distance, moving on with a single-mindedness that Juan was to emulate.

They stopped that night, spending two hours at a brackish water hole. The weather had turned cold, and Arab shivered, almost glad when she was able to climb into the saddle again. Dawn brought sight of a flat dry plain. The terrain changed rapidly as they traversed dark, rock-filled gullies, rocky creekbeds and washes, moving through punishing scrub. The horses were worn out, stumbling and blowing, but King kept running, like a black arrow released from a bow.

That night they made a dry camp at the base of an

escarpment. With gestures, King managed to convey that they would spend the night here. In the morning, they would climb the rock face. With his hands, he sketched the corridor, swooping downward to show they must descend. Then he spread his arms wide to indicate that they would have reached their destination.

Curled uncomfortably among the rocks that, at best, offered shelter from the wind, Arab thought of Missie—just at the other side of the cliffs that stood like a wall between them. Another wall, she thought miserably, separating her from her thorny, brilliant child. Maybe this time she would be able to conquer both of them.

How had the frail girl survived this trip? She recalled Juan's words. *He brutalized the child. Tamsen shot him.* And she, herself, had woven her daughter's disappearance with a man she hardly knew into a romance, to ease her own conscience. Even daring to criticize Tamsen in a conversation with Em.

Juan's words echoed in her mind. *There's no telling what we'll find.*

Arab—whose mind had been occupied with ways to get Juan to move to Melbourne, with Luka's welfare, pretty gowns, a place in society—began to pray.

In the dimness of morning, King led the way to the top of the escarpment. There, he pointed out the corridor that led between twin red pinnacles. He squatted at the entrance, making it clear that he would accompany them no farther.

Juan studied him, then looked at the narrow fissure with some trepidation. He moved his horse ahead, shouldering Arab's mount aside.

"I will go first," he said. He adjusted his rifle so that it would be ready for use, and entered the rift in the rock.

A perfect hideaway, he thought, as his mount moved forward cautiously, hooves soundless in the deep sand that carpeted the base. Melvin had not come upon it by accident. He had known it was here. It was the sort of place an outlaw would use. There was no telling how many men he would find waiting at the other end of this tunnel, open only to the sky. They might even have a guard posted at the entrance. Dios! If he'd only insisted that Arab stay behind!

The corridor turned and a stench met his nostrils. His horse danced nervously in the narrow space. "Easy," he said, leaning forward to stroke the animal's twitching neck. "Easy—"

Then there was a square of light: the entrance. Juan pressed the horse forward, then reined in, sick with shock. A figure in white moleskins lay across the opening; a dead thing, swollen, obscene, fair hair fluttering in the wind.

Juan turned his mount sideways to block Arab's vision. "Go back," he said sharply. "Leave your horse if you have to. Go back to King."

Arab's face was pinched and white, blue about the lips. "I saw it, Juan. Don't try to protect me any more. Let's go on."

They forced their animals ahead. Prancing, nostrils dilated with nervousness, they stepped across the gruesome barrier. Juan and Arab found themselves high above a small hidden valley, lush grasses concealing jerry-built railed fences. There was water, a necessary factor for a duffing yard; and a small hut, its chimney smokeless, the grass growing up to the door seemingly untrodden.

"There's no one there," Arab said in a small voice.

Juan shifted his gun into position once more. "We'll see," he said quietly. "We'll see."

Chapter 40

Missie had not left the hut for several days. After finding the cow dry, she'd had vague thoughts of trying to butcher it. But one did not kill a cow with a kitchen knife or a stone. She found some roots that looked edible, and, fetching a pail of water, made her way back to the hut, stopping to rest every few steps. Later, she managed to drag in some wood for the stove, one chunk at a time. She boiled the roots and drank some of the warm broth. It did not stay down. Evidently she'd made a mistake in gathering them. And she was so weak. Tomorrow she would have to find something more nourishing. A small animal she could kill with a rock. A lizard, anything—

—tomorrow—

That night she dreamed again that the thing on the hill rose and came down the winding path; dead, but bent on revenge. She got up and laboriously dragged a chair to barricade the door. A kookaburra's laugh sounded, mocking, eerie, insane. Her fear lending a false strength, Missie added another chair to the barricade; the rickety table; a spare saddle; anything she could move was added to the teetering pile.

Then she retired to her bed, crouching there like a small fear-maddened animal, the empty pistol in her hand. The wind rose, whining about the hut like a lost soul as Missie tried to hold on to the remnants of her tortured mind.

In the morning, she'd reached a strange state of calm. Arthur and his father would soon be returning from their journey. The thought was frightening, but not as frightening as the dream she'd been having. The dream that her husband lay dead on the cliffs above. That he rose in the night and searched for her.

Someone had piled furniture by the door. She must have done it, though she couldn't remember. Her brow cleared. She'd probably bared the floor so that she could scrub.

She would do it a little later, after she'd rested awhile.

Then she was in the kitchen-dining-living room at Opal Station. Aunt Tamsen was cooking something at the stove. It smelled good, though she wasn't hungry. She would miss dessert anyway. Arthur would be waiting for her in the salt cedar circle. He would read poetry to her.

The day was passed in a pleasant haze of shifting patterns. She sat at her Uncle Dusty's feet, listening as he rambled through a story in his clipped, English voice. Papa was tired. She helped to pull off his black Spanish boots. Mama—Mama was somewhere with Luka. Missie felt an overpowering sensation of loneliness.

If she could find her copy of Clara Morison, she would read for awhile.

Then darkess came, and with it the nighttime horrors. A dead man screamed about the house, trying to get in.

Again she woke to a dim morning, and she knew that it had all been a nightmare. She could hear the sound of horse's hooves in the yard, the creaking of leather as two people dismounted. They had come home. Arthur and his father had come home.

Empty gun in hand, she shrank beneath the patch-work sheet she'd made, covered by the kangaroo-hide rug, making herself as small as possible. She waited.

Outside, Juan dismounted silently, and helped Arab down. Sickened by what they'd found on the ridge, terri-fied for Missie's sake, neither felt like speaking. Juan tried the door. It seemed to be blocked by something on the other side. He shoved again, shifting the barricade a little. Through the partly opened door he could glimpse a part of the room—a bed—a cowering figure with lank, drab hair—

"Dios!"

With a mighty heave he sent table and chairs flying. He was inside the door, kneeling beside the bed, the frail figure of Missie in his arms. She fought and clawed at him with one hand as he wrenched the pistol from the other.

"It's Papa, my darling! It's Papa! I've come to take you home."

He rocked her in his arms, tears falling on her once-bright hair, Arab standing helplessly by, wanting to touch them both, father and daughter. And finally the girl's small shuddering body relaxed. Her eyes closed in a restful, natural sleep.

Putting her back on the bed, Juan tucked the make-shift coverings over her and turned to Arab. "Dios," he whispered. "Arab!" Then his arms were about his wife and they wept together.

Finally over their first emotional shock, they began to take stock of the shack and its contents. The fire in the stove was out. At the back of the stove was a battered pot containing what looked like boiled, slimy weeds. The room was freezing cold. And it was clear Missie was starving.

Without a word, Juan went outside. He carried in wood and soon had a fire burning. Then he disappeared and was gone for a long time. Arab winced as she heard a far off shot, but continued with the job of putting table and chairs back into place. Soon he appeared carrying a bush turkey. Within minutes, he had it cleaned and Arab had it boiling for broth.

First priorities attended to, Juan disappeared again, embarked on a grisly errand. They would be taking Missie home. Perhaps not today, but tomorrow or the next day; as soon as she was strong enough to travel. The sight of that gruesome object at the only exit from the valley would be too much for her. Somehow the remains of Arthur Melvin must be removed.

He found a pick and shovel in an old shed, and rode up the trail, bile rising in his throat as he neared the body. Steeling his nerves, he forced himself to walk around it, inspecting it for cause of death. The stained and dirty strips of shirt fluttering in the wind indicated that the man had been wounded. Perhaps shot. But there was something else—

He turned, sensing rather than seeing the thing that slithered behind him, moving up the rock face of the corridor to rest on a ledge. Raising his rifle, he fired, and the snake's head disintegrated. Thinking of passing through that narrow spot such a short time before, he broke into a cold sweat. If the thing had struck Arab!

He looked at the dead man, comprehension dawning in his eyes. Now he understood.

The pick and shovel he'd brought were useless. Here, at the top of the valley, there was no loose earth, no rocks small enough to move. There was a drop off at one side of the trail's beginning: He might use his tools to lever the body over the edge. But the thought of it dropping down into the valley, disintegrating as it fell, made him sick.

He stood looking at the man, a problem even in death. The man who had treated his daughter so cruelly; who had burned Opal Station—

Fire!

For several hours he toiled, riding down into the valley and up again, his arms loaded with firewood. On his last trip, he went into the house and, without a word to Arab, picked up a tin that held a small amount of coal oil. He returned to the pyre he had built on the rocky outcropping between the pinnacles, and dashed the contents of the tin over it. Then he set it afire.

The smoke rose high. King, squatting on the other side of the escarpment saw it, nodding his head. Boss feller clever-clever. He'd taken steps to drive the spirit of the devil-devil away.

Arab watched from below, her hand to her throat. Juan was a tender, sensitive man. Yet he'd done what he had to do. Nauseated, she went inside.

That evening, Juan and Arab sat quietly. Arab looked up and put her hand on Juan's arm. Missie's blue eyes were looking at them. The frenzied expression was gone. They were filled with an awful sanity.

"I killed him, Papa."

Juan was at her side instantly. "No, you didn't, sweetheart."

"I shot him."

It was possible. The man's shoulder was bandaged. But if she did, the bullet she fired didn't kill him. "He died of snakebite, Missie," he said gently.

She shook her head, her eyes beginning to glaze with fever again. "I opened the door and saw him up there. I shot him, and he fell down! He fell down!"

"You shot from the doorway? Sweetheart, a bullet from that gun wouldn't carry half so far! You didn't do it! Do you understand? You didn't do it! It was the snake! I killed it today. It's still there. I can show it to you!"

"Oh, Papa!"

Missie threw her arms about her father's neck and wept soft, healing tears.

Now it was Arab's turn. She brought a small cup of broth and fed it to her daughter, sip by sip, her arm cradling the girl's head. Then she sent Juan outside while she brought a basin of warm water and laved the emaciated body, murmuring words of love.

"I lost the baby," Missie said suddenly.

Arab jerked in surprise, but kept her voice carefully controlled. "I'm sorry, Missie."

Missie's eyes welled. "It doesn't matter. It never seemed real."

"None of this is real," Arab said brokenly. "Just get better soon. We're going to take you home."

Missie's eyes slanted nervously toward the direction of the pinnacles. "Mama, I can't—"

"There's nothing there now, Missie," Arab soothed. "Your father—took care of everything. Now rest."

The next morning, Juan, hunting again, found Arthur Melvin's horse. Still saddled, reins dragging, it grazed at a spot beyond a bend in the river. Removing the gear from the poor creature, he rubbed it down. Missie could use his mount going home. He would ride this one. A pity if it brought her unpleasant memories, but it had to be.

Two days later, the coals of the fire on the cliff had cooled to ash. Juan raked the debris over the drop at the platform's edge, and covered the charred spot with sand from the corridor.

There was nothing left of Arthur Melvin.

When the small party left the valley, Missie didn't look back. Somber, unsmiling, even now that she was going home, she felt tired and old. She knew she would never fit into life at home again. Oh, perhaps for awhile, until she was better. Until the ravages of this past month had disappeared. But then she was going to Melbourne perhaps to Adelaide. She would try to find work. A newspaper, maybe. The contents of Melvin's cashbox would tide her over for some time.

She had to make a life for herself. Never in this world would she trust her love to another man.

She didn't smile until they descended to the other side of the valley and found King squatting where he'd waited these last days. He rose and studied her solemnly; then, as if finding everything to his satisfaction, ran on ahead, leading them home to Opal Station.

Chapter 41

The day Juan and Arab rode out so precipitously, Nell saw them go. She waddled to the main house, her jaw set with determination. There was a helluva lot going on around here that she hadn't been told. Something to do with that Missie-girl, or she'd eat her hat! She'd overheard a few words passed between Juan and Em's man. Not much. They'd clammed up when she showed. Now, with that abo, King, coming back; Juan taking off with a rifle and Arab after him like a scalded cat; she was sure something was up. And she intended to find out just what. Hell, she was part of the family!

She stamped into the house and pointed a sausage-like finger at Ramona. "Set!" she commanded. Ramona meekly obeyed, and Nell glowered down at the white-faced girl. "Now," she said, "lemme have it. Whut the hell is goin' on?"

Ramona searched for words, then burst into tears. In Nell's comforting arms, she wept out the story of the shooting, the way Missie had been abused. Still she ran away. It was Melvin who set the fire.

Nell looked suddenly old, but she nodded. "Figgered ez much. Dammit, somebuddy shoulda tolt me. I ain't one of them gawdam stinking violets! Maybe I could of—"

"There was nothing anybody could do. And Dusty was sick—Tamsen had everybody looking for her."

Nell hurt inside. Her Tamsen-girl was her favorite. And she'd not been there when she needed her most. No wonder she looked like a gawdam dishrag! She loved Arab's kids, all of 'em. Dusty was like her paw to her. And then that sonofabitchin' fire.

King had found Missie, Ramona went on to tell her. Papa had gone to bring her home. He told Mama what happened, and she'd gone with him.

Nell nodded grimly, remembering Arab's blatting about Missie's romantic elopement. It must of cut Tamsen up pretty awful, having to hear that guff. But Arab was paying for it now. "Missie," she said abruptly, "you figger they'll find 'er?"

"I don't know, Aunt Nell," Ramona admitted. "King just told them he knew where she was. He said Arthur Melvin was dead."

"Maybe somebuddy kilt th' sonofabitch an' done the world a favor," Nell snorted. In her long and checkered career as dealer and madam, she'd learned to size up a man on sight. She'd pegged Melvin as a gawdam phoney at first sight. Hell, if that fool girl just had some of her experience—

"Well, what kin I do t'lend a hand?" Nell set her hands on her ample hips. "Yer gonna have yer hands full."

Ramona hugged the old woman. "You've already helped, Aunt Nell. Thank you."

"Aw-w-w, hell!" Nell's look disclaimed her words, her expression softening as she looked at the girl she loved best next to Tamsen. Seeing her now, her big eyes shining with tears, she knew she'd been right all along. Ramona had been the ugly duckling of the family as far as Arab was concerned. Her eyes and mouth were too big, her button nose too small.

Nell reached out to tweak it as she'd done when the girl was little. She'd grown into the stunner of the lot, as Dusty would say.

"Keep yer pecker up," she said cheerfully. "Yer sis is comin' home. This ain't no time to'go makin' mountins outta moleholes! Now, le's git this gawdam mess cleaned up."

Rolling up her sleeves, Nell attacked the pile of dirty dishes Arab had left behind. When Luka finally came in, bewildered by her mother's absence, Nell took over there, too.

"You'n'me's agoin' over to my place, young lady," she said briskly. "We'll git us up a leetle game. Ain't set in on a good game in coon's age."

"Luka doesn't know how to play poker, Aunt Nell."

"The hell you say! Then it's about time somebuddy learned her somethin' useful!" Shaking her head at the way some folks neglected their kids, Nell led Luka toward her house.

To cover her worries about Missie—and about her parents, since there was no telling what kind of danger they were facing—Ramona threw herself into preparing the house for their return. Arab's efforts at housekeeping had been less than perfect. There was dust in the corners; spills of flour and sugar on the floor; the fireplaces in all the rooms were heaped with ashes; the kitchen stove needed blacking—

Denis Dugald, having taken over Juan's work, sent Boswell to help her. With the aid of the tidy little man-servant, everything was soon shining. Ramona turned to baking. The house soon smelled of fresh hot bread and pie, made from the remaining apples that had been wrapped so carefully and stored.

Dugald, leaving the homelike atmosphere to return to his quarters, walked across the bleak yard and stopped, suddenly struck with an idea. The valley had repaired itself after the rains, a lovely vista of verdant green. But the station itself, without the trees and shrubs that once surrounded it, was graceless, a blot on the landscape. He surveyed it thoughtfully.

The next evening, the tired jackaroos rode in. After supper at the bunkhouse, they began to dig a large crater immediately in front of the station. Ramona watched them, confused. What were they digging? A well? Was it something Papa had set them to do before he left? Denis Dugald appeared to be bossing the job.

Since the day they had quarreled, they had maintained a polite and remote relationship. He had not mentioned this project at the evening meal, and she certainly wasn't going to question him. Exhausted by her day's work, she went to bed early, trying to close her ears to the sound of digging.

She rose the next morning to find not one hole, but five. When Denis, Boswell and Nell came to breakfast, the big woman wasn't shy about voicing her opinion. "Like t'busted my gawdam neck," she exploded. "What the hell you doin'? Diggin' up th' place like that?"

"We'll fill them up tonight," Denis said, pacifying her. "The boys are coming in early—"

"Diggin' holes, fillin' em up! Ain't you sonofabitches got nuthin' better t'do?"

"Not at the present," he grinned, heaping his plate for the second time. Shaking her head in mystified exasperation, Nell followed suit.

The sounds of digging began again in the late afternoon. Ramona worked at preparing the evening meal. She was burning with curiosity, but she refused to dignify the mysterious project by appearing at the door. Moments later Luka appeared, coming from an afternoon with Nell. Her eyes were bright with joy.

"Come see," she said happily, propelling her unwilling

sister toward the door. "Oh, Ramona, you've got to see!"

Ramona rubbed her eyes. The holes were filled, as Denis had promised. And each held a tall tree. Denis and the hands were carrying water, tamping down the earth covering the roots with muddy boots.

The trees were not as large as those cut down when fire threatened the buildings. But they would be one day. And when Missie returned, it would look like home.

"Denis did it," Luka caroled, dancing. "It was his idea. It's a s'prise." She stopped suddenly. "Ramona, why are you crying?"

"I don't know," Ramona said, hands covering her eyes, tears leaking between her fingers. "I don't know."

During supper, Luka kept up her excited chatter. Nell gave her grudging approval to the job Denis and the hands had done. "Waste of time," she grumbled. "But that gawdam tree where Dusty useta set—Looks good. I c'n almost see the leetle bastard settin' there."

The meal done Luka went with Nell after pleading to be permitted just one more game. Boswell retired to his quarters. Denis seemed in no hurry to leave. He sat in a chair by the fire, smoking a pipe, his eyes on Ramona as she cleared away the dishes. Finally she turned to face him.

"I want to thank you," she faltered. "The trees—It was very thoughtful of you." Again her traitorous nerves betrayed her and the tears began to stream.

Denis was instantly on his feet. "Lassie," he said. "Dinna greet! Guid lord—If ye dinna like the trees—"

"I love them," she wept. "It looks like home again. Oh, Denis, I'm so worried about Missie—Mama—Papa—"

His arms were around her, her wet cheek nestled on his shoulder. "They will be all right," he comforted her.

"I gie ye ma wor-r-rd on it. Now ye munna cry! Nae mair tears—"

He lifted her face, dabbing at it with his kerchief. The action slowed, stopped as he looked down into her huge tearful eyes. "Wee love," he breathed. "Oh, ma wee love!" Then his lips were on hers, warm, gentle.

Ramona clung to him, dazed, the beating of his heart seeming to synchronize with her own; this thing she felt, like a warm blanket around both of them; this weakening of the knees, the need to press closer—Was this love?

He set her gently away. "I'll trouble ye nae mair the nicht," he said calmly. "I'll leave ye to think on't." And he was gone.

That night Ramona lay in a delicious haze of re-membering, unable to sleep. Suddenly an awful screeching sound brought her to her feet. It continued like the caterwauling of a wounded animal. Ramona, in her long nightdress, ran for the front door, followed by Luka. The winter moon shone full on a tall figure clad in tam-o'-shanter and kilts: Denis, with his bagpipes.

"A serenade," Luka said ecstatically. "Oh, Ramona, isn't it lovely!"

Ramona's lips twitched. Lovely wasn't exactly the word she would have chosen. Nonetheless, she snatched at a cloak, wrapping it around her for modesty's sake, and stood until the concert was over.

At last, Denis bowed grandly, and disappeared. Ramona returned to bed, to dream of that tall body against her own.

Nell, the next morning at breakfast, was none too generous. Next time Denis went on a toot, he might remember that there was decent folks abed.

"I wasna droonk," Denis said stiffly. "Tis said music soothes the ner-r-rves. I thocht tae gie the gir-r-rls a treat."

"It was lovely," Ramona said, borrowing Luka's adjective. "Though it *would* be difficult to sleep through."

"Then ain of you guid ladies will hae to wed me, tae stifle ma r-r-romantic nature." He avoided Ramona's eyes as he spoke, his ears reddening.

He's shy, she thought with amusement. His words were clearly meant for her, and they made her heart sing. If he asked her to marry him, truly asked her, what would she say? They'd had their differences, but wouldn't love change all that? Denis had grown up without a mother's influence—

That night, Nell and Luka outstayed him. When he finally took his leave, Ramona followed, offering to walk part of the way with him. As they walked together in silence, he wrapped his arm around her to protect her from the evening chill. Halfway to his quarters, they stopped, turned to face each other, and their lips met in a kiss that left them both trembling.

"Ye ken I'm going tae ask ye tae marry me, lass."

"Yes. Yes, I know."

"And when I do, will ye not say ay?"

Ramona couldn't think, her head still spinning from his nearness. Her answer depended on so many things. Her parent's safe return. Missie—

"Don't ask me now," she begged. "Give me a few days."

"Ay," he agreed in a disappointed tone. The moon shone down through the newly planted trees, dappling her face with leaf-shadows as she raised her mouth to his, Then she was running toward the house, needing to reach her bed where she might lie and savor the wonderful things that were taking place inside her.

During the next few days, Ramona floated as if in a dream. She was awakened from it by the appearance of old Wyuna.

"Four-feller come," she said cryptically. "Three horse, one black-feller."

Dropping her dish cloth, Ramona ran for the door. She shielded her eyes with her hand as the riders came into sight. Mama, Papa—and Missie. But a Missie she hardly recognized. She rode stiff in the saddle, as if held up by invisible wires. Closer, Ramona could see the girl's sunken cheeks and shadowed eyes. She swallowed a small cry of pity as she ran to meet them.

Juan dismounted and reached up to aid his daughter. With a small sigh, Missie toppled into his arms. He carried her into the house.

Chapter 42

Missie was abed for several days, no one but Arab and Juan allowed to tend her. Her small cot had been moved into her parents' quarters, where Arab hovered over her, refusing the others admittance. Someone might hint at Dusty's demise. The child had all she could stand for now.

Therefore it was a shock when Missie appeared at breakfast one morning, a robe over her bedgown. Immodest it might be, but she'd lost all modesty in the hut with her husband and the old man.

"Did you set a place for me?" she inquired, smiling.

Arab rushed to her like a clucking hen. "Missie! You shouldn't be out of bed."

"I'm tired of being an invalid, Mama. And I wanted to see everyone. Ramona, Luka—" She held out her arms, and her sisters ran to her, Luka laughing with pleasure, Ramona's dark eyes wet with tears of happiness.

"I've missed you," Missie said, hugging them.

Ramona tried to hide her shock at the feel of the girl's fragile body in her arms. She seemed so—breakable! But Missie didn't notice her sister's reaction. Her eyes were searching the room. They finally settled on

Nell, who lumbered to ·her feet to return Missie's embrace. "Well, hell," she kept blubbering. "Hell!"

Finally releasing Missie, blowing her nose, Nell subsided. Missie greeted Denis and Boswell with grave politeness. Juan brought a chair for his daughter, placing it between himself and Arab, and Ramona filled a plate for her.

Only eight of them at the table?

"Tamsen's gone to Melbourne," Arab said nervously. "She's having a wonderful time. There's a letter from Em. I'll read it to you after breakfast." Don't let her ask about Dusty, she thought. Dear God, don't!

The same thought was in everyone's mind. Nell, for once, had lost her gargantuan appetite. She watched Luka's plate. When the girl had finished, Nell rose from the table.

"Me an' Luka got us a game set up this mornin'. Dunno why I play with her no more. Leetle devil skint me last go-round. Lost my gawdam shirt."

"You shouldn't bet like that on a *pair*," Luka said consolingly. "Not when I had three of a kind. I bet Dusty wouldn't have!"

There was a dead silence, then Nell growled, "Well, if yer gonna play, le's git th' show on th' road." Gripping the girl's arm, she led her toward the door.

"I'll be back, Missie," Luka called in her clear treble. "I'll teach you how to play."

Denis rose too, thanking Arab and Ramona for a delightful meal. Taking his cue from his master, Boswell followed suit. When they had all gone, Missie looked steadily at her father.

"Dusty's dead." It was a statement, not a question.

"Missie, you should get back to bed!"

Juan waved away his wife's statement as he knelt

324

before Missie, taking her thin shivering body in his arms. "Yes, my darling. He is."

The cornflower blue eyes were dry, though the trembling didn't cease. "I think I've guessed it for a long time," she said simply. "It—it wasn't because of me?"

"Not at all," Juan lied. "I think he died because he was—too happy." He went on to explain about Dusty's marriage to Nell, and how the old man had simply drifted off in his sleep. Finally, he picked up the grieving girl and carried her to her bed, remaining with her until her golden lashes closed in a natural sleep.

Missie didn't mention Dusty's death again. When she rose from her sickbed next time, it was for good. Dutifully, she resumed many of her household chores. But in her spare time, she didn't join in the group conversation. Instead, she retired to her dormitory room to sit by the fire, going over the papers in her little box. She had been gratified to recover her precious notes, after fearing they had been destroyed in the fire. But when she returned to them she was amazed to discover how shallow her earlier characterizations had been. As she poured over them making notes here and there on margins, they began to take on new dimension.

At mealtimes, she noticed Ramona and Denis Dugald as she listened absently to Luka's chatter. The two of them seemed wrapped in a dream, their eyes often meeting. She saw the way they were compelled to touch each other at every opportunity—and her heart sank.

On a day that was warm for late May, she observed them in the yard before the main house. Ramona had been to the dairy room; Denis headed for the stables. They met, and it was obvious that Ramona yearned toward the man; that they might have embraced if it weren't daylight.

Throwing a cloak over her housegown, Missie went

to meet her sister. Ramona, seeing her, turned reluctantly from Denis and came toward her.

"I would like to go for a walk," Missie said. "Would you come with me?"

Ramona ran over her list of chores, mentally. She could spare a few minutes. And Missie wasn't strong enough to be allowed to walk alone. This was her first time out-of-doors.

First, Missie stood for a moment, looking down the valley's length. Only a few charred stumps remained to remind one of the fire. And even those were sprouting new green. The past was erased, over and done with, and the future held new promise. But Missie had suffered, and she intended to keep Ramona from making the same mistake.

She led Ramona to the area that had been her secret place. Only a small clearing surrounded by verdure marked the spot. In the brightness of the day, there were no ghosts to haunt the space. Missie was free. She drew a deep breath.

"There used to be salt cedars here, growing in a circle. I pretended it was a magic ring. I used to come here when I felt lonely. Dusty came, before he got sick. We'd sit and talk. Then it was—Arthur."

She went on, telling of those seemingly enchanted nights; the way they'd discussed books and he'd read poetry to her. How she had begun to love him, and he'd behaved so honorably in accepting that love.

Her voice grew harsh as she described the wedding, here, under the moon. Without embarrassment, holding nothing back, she told of the horror of the wedding's aftermath; his cruel treatment; the pain. She remembered little of their return to the house, except that Tamsen shot him. And throughout a long night and day, she'd managed to delude herself that she still wished to be Arthur Melvin's wife.

She told of returning to the glade; the way he'd set the fire; the long grueling trip to the hidden valley: Melvin's humiliation and abasement of her—beneath the leering eyes of the lascivious old man.

"Did you know I was going to have a baby? Did Mama tell you?"

"No," Ramona whispered. "No—"

"I lost it when I thought I'd killed him," she said drearily. "I used to dream that he got up and came down the cliff after me, all dead and swollen, his face falling away—"

"Missie! Oh, God, Missie!" Ramona held her sister close, feeling the tension in the thin, rigid body. "Don't talk about it! Don't think about it! You're home, now!"

"No I'm not, Ramona. This isn't home. I love Mama and Papa, but I don't belong here, not now. I'm not a child anymore. I've got to begin to make a life of my own."

She told of her plans to go to Melbourne. Ramona, listening, understood. Her going would leave an empty place. But hadn't she been thinking of going, too? When Denis asked her—

But Missie was still talking. She had loved Arthur, she said. The Arthur she thought she knew. If she had learned anything from her sordid experience, it was that emotional love clouded one's judgment. She had no intentions of ever marrying again. One never knew a man until it was too late.

"I don't think that's true," Missie. I think it was just—bad luck. There are lots of nice men in the world. Papa—"

"Papa's proven himself," Missie said.

"There's Uncle Duke—Uncle Dan—"

"Uncle Duke had proven himself, too. As far as Uncle Dan is concerned, do you think Aunt Tamsen's very happy with him always away from home? I'm not talking about married men anyway. I'm talking about someone you or I might choose for a husband. We have no way of ever really knowing!"

"Take Denis Dugald, for instance," Ramona said, her face flushing. "He couldn't ever behave like Arthur Melvin did!"

"Couldn't he? How do you know? I remember when he was killing the animals!"

Ramona's heart jolted at the memory. "He isn't doing that now!"

"But he did it *then!*" Missie reminded her. "I'll bet he would even kill a man! I heard him talking once about going after the Kelly gang!"

"I think it was all just talk," Ramona said miserably.

"You see!" Missie leaped upon her uncertain words with triumph. "You're not sure!"

No, Ramona thought as they walked back to the house, she wasn't sure. And Denis had asked her to walk with him tonight. She knew he had something to ask her. With Missie home, and Papa and Mama safe, she'd thought she knew what her answer would be. But Missie's words had left a gnawing feeling of doubt.

They returned to find the station yard filled with excitement, the family and the hands milling around the wagon of an old tinker who passed through once or twice a year, wagon jingling with pots and pans. He had passed through Jerilderie where the Station's mail had been accumulating for some time, and had volunteered to bring it along. There seemed to be letters for everyone. A large package contained a cloak that Arab had ordered long ago. It was intended for Luka, though the girl had several warm ones. On impulse, Arab spread it over Missie's frail shoulders, fighting tears at the girl's pleasure in the warm red material. Had she spared so little thought for this middle daughter?

Several of the hands had ordered much-needed boots. And there was an oddly shaped package for Denis Dugald.

It hae coom at last," he said in a pleased voice. "I sent frae it so lang ago, I thocht it wouldna coom!"

Tearing at the wrappings, he revealed the contents. A repeating rifle, twin to the ruined one.

Ramona's eyes met Missie's knowing ones. She turned on her heel, and went into the house.

That night was not one for walking under the stars. A cold wind had come up suddenly after the bright day. Ramona considered refusing Denis Dugald's invitation, but decided there was no point in putting off their discussion. Perhaps, she thought, shivering as she walked beside him, it was just as well that the weather didn't lend itself to romance. She would be able to think with her mind, rather than her emotion.

"Are ye cold, lassie?" He put out an arm to pull her to him, and she drew away.

"Why did you send for another gun, Denis?"

He stopped dead in his tracks. "So that is what is ailing you, lassie! You hae been grumping and glowering all the nicht! The goon hae naething to do wi' ye and me!"

"You didn't answer my question!"

She could sense his squirming as he sought for an answer. "I dinna ken," he said finally. "I hae always had a guid goon. It is a par-r-rt of me."

"A part of you I do not like."

His anger rose, but he tried to control his voice. "Ye needna fash yourself, lass. When we're wed, I'll do ma hoonting on ma ain."

"I did not agree to marry you," she said furiously. "And you've never asked!"

"Then I'm asking ye, noo!"

"And the answer is no!"

329

"Lassie!" He reached a hand toward her. But she had turned and fled into the cold blowing night.

In the main house, Missie had just stated her intention to move to Melbourne. Listening to their daughter, speaking so logically and with a new maturity, her parents were finally forced to agree. At least she would have Em there. And Tamsen, for a time. But she must promise to remain a few more days, until she was stronger. Missie, pleased that there would be no active opposition, agreed.

Ramona passed through the room without a word, and went to her own bed. She was sleepless for hours. When she finally slept, she dreamed of Denis Dugald, his features murderous as he stalked a helpless Ned Kelly with his new gun.

She had no way of guessing that, at the moment, Ned Kelly was far from helpless. He and his mates had come out of hiding, to steal a number of moldboards of ploughs from the neighborhood of Greta and Oxley. Then, in concealment in the Greta swamps, they had heated the moldboards until they were white hot, and hammered them into rounded shapes, using a green log as a form. The completed products were suits of armor, covering vulnerable portions of the body, complete with an iron helmet, fitting over the head like a metal pail, flanged at the shoulders. Each set weighed in the neighborhood of eighty to ninety pounds.

The acid test came when Ned's sister, Kate, arrived to bring supplies and news that they were being betrayed by Aaron Sherritt, an old and trusted friend.

Ned stood grim-faced, and went into the brush. Soon he returned, a lurching figure in an iron suit, looking like nothing human. Kate stood her ground, a small pretty girl, hard-faced after years of persecution. She was not afraid.

Ned Kelly's laugh rang hollow inside the iron mask.

"Shoot me," he said mockingly. "Shoot me, if you've got the nerve!"

Kate raised her pistol and fired, the bullet caroming off the armor with a pinging sound. Ned gasped at the bruising impact, then raised his voice in a shout of triumph.

"It works! The bloody thing works!"

Now they were ready. First they would kill Aaron Sherritt, informer. Then they would pull off the biggest coup of all.

Chapter 43

As the days passed Ramona's dream stayed with her. Ned Kelly's face, with its wounded eyes, remained in her mind: the persecuted, she thought. And Denis Dugald was on the side of the persecutors. She treated him with utmost politeness, deliberately keeping a distance between them. Sometimes she ached to forget their quarrel, to just touch him. But as Missie said, that was only a physical thing.

She and Missie were closer than they'd ever been in their lives. Ramona was surprised to learn of Missie's ambitions; Missie surprised to learn Ramona could understand them. They walked and talked together, much to Denis Dugald's dismay. He'd had second thoughts since the night he'd proposed at such an inopportune time. If only he had the chance to see Ramona alone—

Finally, a letter arrived from Scotland, from his father. He had outstayed his leave. Indulgently, his father gave him permission to remain until after Christmas. But then he must consider returning to take up his duties.

Denis crumpled the paper in his hand. It had read as if it were written to a callow youth, not a man! His mouth twisted wryly, as he admitted that was what he'd been when he left home. Coming here in his fine tweed suit, complete with manservant and bagpipes: a spoiled lad.

Well, his father was right. He had stayed too long, and he must face up to his responsibilities. A day, a week, a year, it made little difference how long he lived at Opal Station. Ramona had indicated that she wanted nothing of him. He would go down to Melbourne and make the most of the time he was free.

He approached Juan Narvaéz with the news that he was leaving, secretly pleased to see the unhappiness in the man's eyes at his words. "We will miss you," he said. Then his expression brightened with a dawning idea.

Missie wished to go to Melbourne. He could not get away at this time. It would not be seemly to send a young girl in the company of two men. But if Ramona went along. He had been worrying about his oldest daughter. She had seemed rather subdued of late. She too needed a change of scene.

"I would be happy to escort them," Denis said stiffly. He might as well agree, though he knew there would be little chance of Ramona accepting the offer.

He was quite correct. Ramona flatly refused. Only Missie's tearful pleading brought her around.

They set off on a cold blustery day toward the end of June. Arab's tears froze on her cheeks as she kissed her daughters good-bye. She had a forlorn feeling that both of them had outgrown her; that Ramona, too, would decide to remain in Melbourne and lead her own life. She would be left with Luka, the child she'd always been closest to. It wasn't that she had loved the others less, she thought disconsolately. It was that she had never thought they needed her. But it seemed that Missie had needed a mother most of all.

Juan put an arm around her as the two men on horseback and the wagon with its waving occupants, disappeared into the distance.

"I still think we should have taken them," she said defensively.

Juan sighed. "You know I can't leave now, not with Dugald going too. But I promise we'll go down for a visit—as soon as Dan comes home."

"*If* he comes home. Juan, I can't help feeling something's wrong."

"Then that settles it," he teased. "Your instincts are absolutely infallible. If you think things are right, they're wrong. If you feel they're wrong, they're right. I've never known it to fail."

She pushed at him in mock anger. Laughing, he led her back into the warmth of the main house. "Luka's still asleep," he whispered, raising his dark brows in a question. She nodded her agreement, and they entered their bedroom, closing the door.

The journey from Opal Station was slow and tedious. Dugald and Bosworth, on horseback, were compelled to keep their mounts at a slow pace, the wagon holding them back. Juan had carefully mapped out an itinerary for them. Winter travel was not so difficult at this time of year, and the trains ran on a chancy schedule. Rather than take a chance of being marooned for a week or more, they were to travel by horse and wagon all the way, moving by day, spending the night at reputable pubs or hotels he'd listed for them. The first night they would spend with the Smythes, the next at Albury. Then the next—

Luke, at the reins of the wagon, set as fast a pace as possible. It wasn't often a young hand had the opportunity to savor the delights of Melbourne. He and Missie carried on an excited conversation; but Ramona was unusually silent, especially when Denis turned back to see how they were traveling.

"Are you comfortable, Missie?" She would nod in happy agreement. "Ramona?" Here, he would receive no answer. She kept her face averted in cold disdain.

Well, let her sulk, domn the lass! He didn't volunteer for this job. It was practically forced upon him!

The long ride with too much time to think began to erode at his patience. When the lass needed him, there had been hugs and kisses. He tried not to think of those kisses, but they were etched into his mind. Then, with her sister and her parents home safe, she behaved as if he'd turned into a monster. All because of a gun! And she had spoiled his other. He thought of the tanning he'd given her then, the pleasure he'd felt smacking that soft yielding backside. And the kiss, after—

If she kept up her unwomanly behavior, he just might be tempted to do it again!

It was a tight-lipped young Scotsman who swung off his horse at the Smythe's station, reaching a hand to help the girls down. Missie accepted his assistance, but Ramona pointedly evaded him, skipping nimbly down and into the house.

Luke stared after her, open-mouthed. "Dunno what got into her," he said. "Never seen Miss Ramona act like that."

Denis sighed. It was going to be a long trip.

They had a slow start the next morning. They still hadn't reached Albury at dusk. Denis rode back to reassure the girls. "It shouldn't be long."

"I'm glad," Missie sighed. "I'm a little tired."

"But we can at least look forward to better company," Ramona said bitingly.

With an incomprehensible howl of rage—the cry of his clan—Denis shouldered his horse against the wagon, sweeping Ramona from the seat. Holding the struggling girl beneath an arm, he spurred his mount forward and was gone from sight.

"Oh, Dear God," Missie cried. "Luke! Stop them!"

"He won't hurt her, Ma'am," Luke said. Secretly, he

336

was enthralled. It was like something out of a penny dreadful. He was rather cheering for the bloke—

When he'd put sufficient distance between himself and the wagon, Denis wheeled off the roadway, and into the trees. There, he dropped his kicking burden to the ground and dismounted.

"Ye will hae to talk wi' me, whether it's to your liking or nae," he said hoarsely.

She backed from him. "Don't you dare touch me!"

"Dinna tell me what I da-r-re!" He put his big hands on her shoulders, shaking her until the dark hair fell over her eyes like a mist. "Ye've been behaving like a shrew! I'll nae put oop wi' it, do ye ken?"

Her foot connected with his shin. When he grabbed at her, as if he would turn her over his knee, she opened her mouth to scream.

"Nae ye don't!" He put a hand over her mouth. "Ye're going to listen—" He gave a surprised yelp. She had set her teeth in his thumb. He put his other hand beneath her chin, finger to one cheek, thumb to the other to pry her mouth away.

"In the guid Lord's name," he said, surveying his bleeding hand. "Ye are possessed of the very divil!"

The wheels of the wagon sounded outside their secluded spot. She broke and ran for it. Tearing a piece from his shirttail, he bound his thumb and mounted. The wagon was ahead of him now. He rode past to take the lead, stopping only long enough to issue a proclamation.

"Ye willna get free of this. Tis a lang way tae Melbourne. And we'll hae it oot before we get ther-r-re!"

Ramona was trembling, more from the sensations his touch had aroused, than from fright. Missie was frankly horrified.

"Did he hurt you? I told you he was like Arthur!"

"Oh, hush!" Ramona said rudely. "You don't know what you're talking about." Then, immediately contrite, she apologized. With all Missie had been through, the way Denis carried her off must have elicited bad memories.

For that matter, she had a few memories of her own. And she had to keep from remembering. But, like Denis said, it was a long way to Melbourne.

By the time they reached Albury, she had evolved a plan. Missie entered into the idea with delight, since it reminded her of one of Aunt Tamsen's adventures that she planned to depict in her book.

They rose in the night and dressed, then quietly slipped down the stairs and back to the stables. Luke was snoring there in the wagon, but they managed to lead the horses out and saddle them. Let Denis and Boswell try the wagon for awhile. They would be off and away. They would leave the horses, not at Wangaratta, but at Glenrowan, on down the line, and from there take the train into Melbourne.

There were two inns at Glenrowan. Ramona had heard mention of one, the Glenrowan Hotel, operated by a Mrs. Jones. They could afford to spend several days there, if the train wasn't running on schedule. It would take that long for Denis to find them. He would probably check out Wangaratta first.

Missie's cheeks were pink with excitement, but Ramona's mood was somber as they rode off into the night. Now that they were embarked on their adventure, it seemed like a childish escapade. Did she really want to run away without trying to resolve her problems with Denis?

She thought of the way he'd snatched her from the wagon, shaking her. He might even have—have *struck* her again. Setting her jaw, she spurred her horse forward.

A few days in the creaking wagon would cool his temper!

It was farther to Glenrowan than they'd thought. It was almost morning as they rode in, only to be met with the noise of rifles cracking. It sounded like a battlefield. "A celebration of some kind?" Missie ventured.

Timorously, they rode forward, only to be drawn up short as a man ran between them, grasping both bridles at the same time. They could see his white face in the darkness, even to the freckles that showed against the pallor of fear.

"What the bloody hell you women doing here! Git off the streets! Take cover!"

"What is it?" Missie quavered.

"Where the hell you been? Asleep? It's the Kelly gang! They're holed up in the hotel with about fifty prisoners. Hare's trying to blast them out!"

Ned! thought Ramona, a wave of panic rising in her breast. Oh, dear God, *what have you done now!*

Chapter 44

Ned Kelly and his friend, Steve Hart, had arrived at Glenrowan in the early hours of Sunday, June twenty-seventh. Tired of running and hiding, Kelly had decided to make the police come to him. First, Dan Kelly and Joe Byrne were dispatched to the Woolshed District, near Beechworth. There, they disposed of the informer, Aaron Sherritt, shooting him down at his own front door. After that, they raced to join their leader.

In this way, Kelly had planned to solve two problems at the same time. The news of Sherritt's murder would reach the police at Beechworth by midnight, at least. And a special train carrying policemen and the hated black trackers from Queensland would be sent up from Benalla, early on Sunday morning, only to be wrecked at Glenrowan.

Unfortunately for the Kellys, the four constables set to guard Aaron Sherritt suspected a trick, since there had only been the two members of the Kelly gang present when Sherritt was slain. They reasoned that the others must be in hiding, waiting to pick them off as they rode to give warning. They remained in the dead man's hut until seven o'clock the next morning. The story of the killing didn't reach the police station at Beechworth for eighteen hours, throwing off the timetable for the train's derailment.

At one o'clock, Sunday morning, Ned Kelly and Steve Hart reached the spot where they intended to wreck the special train. The line, three-quarters of a mile north of the railroad station, was on a curve, with an embankment ranging from thirty to fifty feet high. They tried first to remove some rails, using handspanners. But the nuts on the fishplates were rusted and immovable.

"Damn bloody things," Steve growled.

"Keep it up," Kelly cautioned his mate. Finally, hands half-frozen, he threw his own spanner into the bushes with a curse. By his calculations, the train was due any minute. Lying down, he put his ear to the frosted rail. Nothing. Hell, maybe they still had a chance—

They ran along the track to the gatehouse, down the line, bailing up eight navvies they found camped at the crossing. They were only pick-and-shovel men, they explained. The stationmaster, roused and taken prisoner, insisted that this was a plate-layers job. And there were only two in town—Sullivan and Reardon.

Sullivan, a single man, was taken easily. Reardon, however, had a family. It was necessary to take his wife and eight children along, to prevent their giving an alarm. Leaving Hart in charge of the prisoners in the gatehouse, a very worried Ned Kelly forced the plate-layers and an unwilling navvy ahead of him along the line. After an hour of fumbling, while Ned stood tense and alert for the sound of an oncoming train, a length of rail was removed.

Dawn broke, and there was still no sign of the train.

Kelly, at the edge of his nerve, but still displaying a surface bravado, herded the prisoners from the gatehouse to the Glenrowan Hotel. The weatherboard structure, on the western side of the railway line in a clearing of trees, stood about two hundred yards from the station. The bar opened on the front veranda. The remainder of the building consisted of a kitchen, dining room, and three small rooms, with a corridor running from front to back.

By eleven o'clock, some fifty prisoners were held within the hotel's confines. At one o'clock, the outlaws had been on vigil for twelve hours. But the train had not yet come. Mrs. Jones opened the bar. Her daughter served dinners. The occasion began to take on a festive air, becoming merry when someone produced a concertina. The outlaws joined in the jigs, sets and reels, whirling the ladies in time to the music, bowing gallantly.

Ned Kelly, finally realizing that his strength must be conserved, leaned against a wall and watched the proceedings with affectionate amusement. These were his people. Those he'd bailed up had become his friends. He saw a series of similar activities in the future; he would go from town to town, showing people he wasn't the monster he was made out to be. Then everyone would stand behind him. All wrongs would be righted: his mother would be released from prison to live like a queen; his sisters, Maggie and Kate, would be free to lead a decent life. No one would dare harass them—

He raised a glass to his lips, then set it down again. He'd already had his limit. He didn't dare go beyond it. The train would come soon, and he'd need all his wits about him.

Calling Joe Byrne, he sent him to check on his brother Dan, drinking in the bar. The man returned to say that he'd cautioned him, but that he was still drinking.

"Let it go," Kelly said indulgently. "Dan's all right. He can handle himself, drunk or sober."

A voice spoke at his side. Ned turned to see Tom Curnow, the local schoolmaster, bailed up earlier with his wife, child, and sister.

"I understand you're planning to wreck the train."

Having an audience, Kelly plunged into a description of his plan and how it was to be accomplished.

Curnow frowned. "Then what do you plan to do with the rest of us?"

"Let you go, of course. If you keep your flaming noses clean. I don't want to hurt anybody."

"Yet you're planning to murder those people on the special!"

"They're not human beings, man! Those are policemen! Black trackers! They've hounded me for a long time. They'll be getting their bloody deserts!"

"Some of them have wives and children," Curnow said quietly. "Have you never married?"

For an instant, the face of a girl flashed before Ned Kelly's tired eyes; A big-eyed girl with a mist of dark hair, begging him to go away and begin a new life—when it was already too late.

"I wouldn't bring a woman into my kind of living," he said bitterly. "My mother and sisters have been persecuted, treated like a pack of dingo bitches. Think I'd subject somebody I cared about to that kind of bloody treatment? My job's to make it safe for settlers and their women. I'll do it, by God! And I can't have a wife hanging around my neck, dragging me back."

"You're going at it the wrong way."

"There isn't a right way." The conversation went on for several hours, Kelly describing the nightmare his young years had been; Curnow stubbornly clinging to his theory that two wrongs did not make a right. Meanwhile the prisoners capered and danced, having a wonderful time.

At ten o'clock that night, his face gray with fatigue, Kelly was almost ready to admit defeat. He allowed some of his prisoners to return home to their own beds, among

344

them, Tom Curnow, with whom he'd established a rapport of mutual respect.

"Don't dream too loud," he cautioned Curnow, grinning as he shook the man's hand.

Thirty people remained. The party didn't begin to flag until nearly dawn. Ned Kelly, his brother and their mates, had been without sleep for two days and two nights. And apparently they had overestimated the efficiency of the police.

"They're not coming," Ned said morosely. "Hell, we might as well light out of this bloody place." He took the floor to tell the prisoners they might all return to their homes. And at his first word, there was the shrieking of a train whistle in the distance.

"This is it, boys!"

The four buckled on their armor, intending to shoot down any survivors of the derailed train. Then Ned Kelly raised his hand. "Listen!"

The train had stopped just short of the place where the accident was set to occur.

Curnow, after seeing his family home, had walked down the tracks carrying a candle and his sister's red scarf. Holding the scarf before the candle, he created a warning light. The locomotive, moving in advance of the special train of police, stopped. After hearing Curnow's story, the engineer blew warning blasts to halt the engine that followed.

Ned Kelly, leaving his mates, rode his gray mare to the scene. Dressed in his crude armor, he peered through the slits provided for vision, seeing the policemen tumble from the train. Let them come, he thought exultantly. Let them come! He rode back, tethering his mare in the bush, and rejoined his men.

The lights in the Glenrowan Hotel were extinguished, the prisoners warned that they would be shot if they tried to escape. Ned, Dan, Hart and Byrne took up their places in the shadowed veranda, overcoats concealing their armor.

The police were in for a surprise.

They couldn't know that Glenrowan's one constable, a man named Bracken, was among their remaining prisoners. He escaped through a rear door and ran with a warning to Superintendent Hare of the recently arrived police. The Kellys held the hotel. And they were wearing armor.

Superintendent Hare approached with his small army of sixteen men. The capture of Ned Kelly would make him famous. The euphoria he felt at the thought helped to overcome his fear, for he was not a brave man.

"Come out and surrender," he called. "You're surrounded."

"Surrender be damned," the answer came. "You can't hurt us! We're in iron!"

The words were followed by a volley of fire from the outlaws. One of the bullets struck the superintendent's wrist. He promptly withdrew from the battle.

The bullets of the police clanged against armor. It proved as effective as Kelly had believed, but it was cumbersome, the weight slowing the movements of the wearers. Only Kelly wore a helmet. He was an accurate shot, but the eye-slit made sighting difficult.

And he had not allowed for protection of arms and legs. In the three minute engagement, Ned was hit twice in his upper forearm. A bullet plowed through his foot, and a shotgun pellet lodged at the base of his right thumb. Joe Byrne was shot through the calf of the leg.

The outlaws retired into the hotel, where their hostages lay on the floor in terror as police bullets shattered windows and ripped through weatherboards.

"We're cooked, Ned," Joe Byrne said dismally.

"Don't be a bloody fool!"

Shuddering with pain, Ned Kelly tried to rearrange his thoughts. The plan had gone wrong, that was all. Now he must make a new one.

He would leave by the back door, mount one of the horses in the stock yard, and circle the police, outflanking them, drawing their fire. As they turned to face him, the others could pick them off at will.

His teeth set, he managed to crawl to the place where the horses were kept, but he could not mount. The weight of his armor, his rifle and ammunition, together with a shattered arm and foot, foiled his every effort. Cursing, he tried to load his rifle, an action impossible because of his injured thumb.

Mindless with pain, he lurched into the bush where his mare was tied. He was unable to remove his armor because of his injuries. Blood poured from his wounds, and he felt dizzy and faint. Crawling into the bushes, half-dead from loss of blood, revolver in hand, he drifted into a half-sleep, dreaming—

A girl ran toward him. A girl in a red woolen gown, a lacy shawl about her shoulders. "Ned," she called, "Ned Kelly!"

They sat together on a sun-warm rock. He could feel her nearness.

Then a chill wind rattled in the bushgrass, and it was cold, so cold!

And her voice called again, with an odd, furtive sound: "Ned—Ned Kelly—"

Another overrode it, bringing him awake. "Caught you," it said. "I heard you calling that bloody bugger! Who the hell are you? One of them sisters of his I heard of? You think he got away? Mebbe I better have a look-see."

Ramona moved away from the horse she'd seen and recognized. Kelly had loosed it from its tether and it now grazed freely. "I don't know what you're talking about," she said haughtily at the policeman who had appeared from nowhere, grabbing her arm. "Please release me."

This was no dream, Ned thought groggily. It was real. He managed to shift himself, to raise the gun in his hand and point it toward the place where he judged the man to stand. His eyes blurred.

Ramona! But what was she doing here? He couldn't shoot for fear of hitting her.

His movement had brought another gush of blood. For a moment he clung to consciousness with a stubborn will. Then he fell forward, face down.

He didn't hear the policeman order Ramona to accompany him, nor Missie's indignant arguing at the arrest of her sister. "I've got two of the gang," the policeman boasted to his superior. "They're either the Kelly sisters, or a couple of their girl friends. This one," he jerked a finger at Missie, "has been asking all kinds of questions. And this one was sneaking a horse around back, figuring to help."

"Hold them," his superior commanded. "We'll take them down to Benalla. Find out who the hell they are."

In the bush, Ned Kelly tried to rise, shuddered once, and then lay still.

Chapter 45

Missie and Ramona were taken to the Glenrowan railway station, where they were searched, none too gently, by a woman whose husband was being held in the hotel. The girls had carried only their reticules when they left the wagon behind at Albury. Each held two gowns. Missie's had, in addition, a pad of paper on which she'd already taken copious notes of the battle of Glenrowan. One page held a detailed drawing of the interior of the inn. She'd obtained her information from one of the local residents by posing as a reporter for a Melbourne newspaper. Anxious to see his name in print, he'd been more than willing to oblige.

Also among Missie's possessions was the small single-shot pistol Arthur Melvin had given her. It wan't loaded, but it was considered damning evidence.

The woman who made the search arrived at a conclusion: gowns, diagrams, the gun—Why these girls had planned to help the outlaws escape—by disguising them as women!

Missie spoke up in their defense, but was ignored. There was nothing to do now but wait. The woman's half-witted son kept running back and forth, carrying news of the battle. Ramona and Missie kept their faces plastered to a small window, trying to watch the hotel—each for different reasons.

"It's my fault," Missie said forlornly. It had been her idea to use the situation to her own advantage. Armed with a story like this, she could use it as a wedge in gaining employment at the *Melbourne Age,* or the *Argus.* To her surprise, Ramona had agreed with her, displaying a courage she didn't know her sister had. It had been she who had gone within the range of fire until she was removed forcibly.

"Let me talk to them," she'd said. "I think I can help."

It was Ramona who, on learning from an ancient resident that there was a rumor Ned Kelly had escaped, insisted on looking for him. It led to their arrest, but it was a brave thing to do.

"It's not your fault, Missie," Ramona said in a dead voice long after Missie made her statement. "I got us into this. Dear God! Will the shooting never stop!"

At five-thirty, the woman's son arrived with the information that there were now reinforcements on the scene. Sergeant Arthur Steele had arrived at Glenrowan, Superintendent Sadlier on his heels. Sergeant Steele had ordered his men to fire at anything that moved.

It was suggested that the prisoners held by the Kellys be allowed to leave the besieged building, but Superintendent Sadlier would have none of it, for fear some of them were in league with the outlaws.

In the distance, there was a sound of renewed continuous firing, and Ramona sagged a little, her eyes blank with shock. The female guard's lips twisted in a derisive smile.

"I don't wanna miss anything. Maybe you girls ought to get a good look too. See what happens to the kind of company you keep."

She ushered them outside where they could get a good view of the proceedings.

The firing was intense. Bullets whizzed through the weatherboards of the hotel. The prisoners inside screamed with terror, some with pain. At the sound of children crying above the din, Ramona put her hand to her mouth to control her nausea.

"Ned Kelly isn't in there," she whispered to Missie. "If he were, he'd stop this. Oh, God, the police are doing more harm than the outlaws!"

Missie had to agree. She'd planned her story to show the heroism of the law. Now, she was sickened at their actions. Through the next hour-and-a-half, vision partly obscured by gunsmoke and rising mist, they listened to a boy screaming in agony.

This isn't real, Ramona thought. I've died and gone to hell. Oh, Ned! Ned!

As if in answer to the cry in Ramona's mind, the thing in the bush moved. Heaving itself up with the aid of a sapling, it lurched forward, revolver in hand.

Seeing the towering figure materialize out of gun-smoke and swirling mist, a man cried out above the rattle of guns.

"My God, it's the bunyip! It's Old Nick!"

The firing ceased, the police turning to stare open-mouthed, numbed with fear before they scattered.

Finding shelter, they opened fire, bullets pinging off the apparition's head and chest as he came toward them, laughing. He moved coolly from tree to tree, firing his revolver in the direction of his enemies, his voice hollow as he mocked them.

"Fire away! You can't hurt me!"

It was Sergeant Steele, who had fired upon women and children, who took direct aim at the armored man's legs.

The gigantic figure toppled.

The senior constable who reached him first, tearing his helmet off, couldn't believe his eyes.

"It's him, Ned Kelly!" he shouted. "We've got him!"

Ramona swayed and Missie caught her arm. "I don't think he's dead," she said. "He moved—"

"Maybe it would be better if he were. It would be over."

Missie looked at her sister, wondering at the curious remark. Before she could answer, the half-witted boy was back. "They're bringing him here," he said, shrill with excitement. "They said to take the women over to the house."

The woman marshaled them along a path, but stopped as Ned Kelly was carried by, unable to control her morbid interest.

Ramona stiffened her shoulders as she looked at Ned Kelly's face. He closed eyes were blackened, his face ghastly white where it wasn't bruised. His armor and shirt had been removed. His chest was welted, his body blue with cold.

She was unable to hold back a small sobbing sound of pity. The battered eyes opened. One closed in an unmistakable wink. Dear God, the man's courage!

Imprisoned in a small stuffy parlor, Ramona and Missie had to rely on further bulletins from the half-witted boy. Kelly had asked to be carried to the door of the hotel on a mattress. He'd refused to ask his mates to surrender. They would never give up. Dr. Nicholson had insisted the prisoner needed rest. He was very weak, having sustained twenty-eight bullet wounds and shot wounds in his arms and legs. But it looked like he was saved for the gallows!

Ramona turned away, and Missie understood the sense of her earlier cryptic remark.

"I feel bad about it, too," she confessed. "At first, I

thought they were just outlaws, like Arthur was. I—I guess I just thought it would make an interesting story. But after what I've seen, well, I'm sick and angry! No matter how terrible the man was—"

"He wasn't terrible, Missie," Ramona said tiredly. "He—He's not much more than a boy. And if you knew what made him do the things he's done, what his life was like as a child—"

Missie's eyes widened. "You *know* him?"

"Yes." Ramona wiped at her eyes. "I know him. Oh, Missie!" She wept out her story in her younger sister's arms.

The boy came and went for what seemed hours, reporting the grim news. A telegram had been sent to Commissioner Standish, requesting that a gun and crew of gunners be sent from the Garrison Artillery by special train.

The plate-layers had repaired the line. A police special from Beechworth had arrived, bringing the total number of police to forty-six.

At least a thousand rounds of rapid fire smashed into the walls and clanged on the iron roof of the building in one wild burst of shooting.

At 10:00 A.M., after a siege of seven hours, Superintendent Sadlier agreed to allow the survivors of those imprisoned by the Kellys to emerge from the hotel—if there were any.

Twenty-five terrified men stumbled out and were forced to lie prostrate on the ground, their hands over their heads, after having endured seven hours under withering fire. From among them, the McAuliffe brothers, known to be friends of the Kellys, were separated. They too were held under guard.

Questioning revealed that Joe Byrne lay dead in the barroom, shot through the groin as he poured himself a drink. The two remaining outlaws were still wearing their armor, but they were morose, having learned of Ned Kelly's capture, and they had little hope.

The regular train from Melbourne brought more police. The total was now fifty-one. It also carried a priest, Dean Gibney, Vicar-General of Perth. Learning of Kelly's injuries, he insisted on giving him the last rites.

The next bulletin overwhelmed the deliverer. Eyes popping, the boy related that Ned Kelly's sisters, Maggie, Kate and Grace had arrived and were admitted to see him. "Then these aren't them," he muttered, pointing to Missie and Ramona.

"Didn't think they was," his mother said bitingly. "Figgered 'em for doxies, from the way they look. They was fixing to help that gang get free, so I'm holding them."

Ramona was so relieved that Ned Kelly had seen his beloved sisters that she could ignore the woman's words.

The day dragged on. The priest asked permission to approach the hotel; to ask Dan Kelly and Steve Hart to give themselves up.

Ned Kelly advised him against it. They would surely shoot before they recognized his calling. Maggie offered to go in his stead, but was forcibly restrained, the police certain she would join the outlaws in their shooting.

And the firing from within the hotel stopped, filtering away at some unknown hour, the silence unnoticed as the police continued to blast the structure with their guns.

At three o'clock in the afternoon, plans were formulated to set the building afire.

The woman guarding the girls had no intention of missing such a grand event. Marshaling them before her, she went as close to the battleground as she dared. Ramona shuddered as they watched Senior Constable Charles Johnston bring up a bundle of straw. He soaked it in kerosene; then, covered by heavy riflefire, ran in a low, zig-zagging movement to the south side of the hotel. He placed his bundle against the weatherboard near a chimney, and struck a match to it. The flames flared high.

Too late, someone remembered that a wounded prisoner of the outlaws still remained in the structure. No one dared to approach, for fear of being shot down.

It was the priest who walked alone through billowing smoke, ignoring the commands of Superintendent Sadlier to halt.

"In the name of God! I am a Catholic Priest! I am here to offer you your life!"

There was no answer. Joe Byrne lay dead on the barroom floor. In a room at the back were two bodies, composed for sleep, armor at their sides.

The outlaws were dead.

The priest called out the news, and the wounded man was carried out, only to die within minutes.

Almost instantly, the hotel exploded into a mass of flames. A roar went up as the walls and roof collapsed, revealing the bodies of Dan Kelly and Steve Hart as they burned to cinders.

It was determined that Dan and Hart had died by their own hand; a packet of poison having been found on the body of Joe Byrne. Byrne had been killed by a police bullet. The battle had endured for more than twelve-and-one-half hours.

Later that day, Ned Kelly, the McAuliffes, Ramona and Missie, were transported to Benalla by special train. The girls were placed in detention in a room of the jailor's home. Kelly lay in a jail cell, a doctor watching over him through the night. Captain Standish had arrived to oversee his notorious prisoner.

Word of wild threats being made at Greta against Ned's capture and the deaths of Dan, Hart, and Byrne had reached the Captain's ears. He was unable to rest until Ned Kelly was on the morning train to Melbourne. It wasn't until the next evening that the Senior Constable at Benalla found time to quesion Missie and Ramona.

He was inclined to believe their stories. They were clearly of gentler breeding that one would expect of an outlaw's choosing. But the evidence against them seemed sound, and he must do his duty. A stern man, he hammered at them, asking the same questions again and again.

"Were you acquainted with the accused, or the dead men?"

"No," Missie answered, a little too quickly.

The constable had a cunning mind. He picked up on it, but continued his questioning. If they were traveling through, why did they have so few possessions? Why did they pause in a town under siege? Most young ladies would have fled. Why did the younger sister pose as a reporter?

And why did she have a gun in her possession? Why did she carry a drawing of the layout of the hotel?

Missie stumbled through her answers, her face flushed. Ramona sat by, her eyes still indicating shock. She blinked as the man turned on her suddenly.

"Were *you* acquainted with the accused?"

She thought of the boy she'd met on the clifftop; the tragic letter he had given her, explaining his crimes; the man who had opened his bruised eyes at Glenrowan, still filled with courage.

She could not deny him.

She met the senior constable's eyes, her own focusing truly for the first time since the fire.

"Yes, I knew him. I knew him very well."

The sisters were remanded to a cell in the Benalla jail to wait until the constable could discuss their plight with a higher authority.

The next morning, the girls were escorted from the

jailor's home by a deputy, their heads high as they approached the prison. The small structure was surrounded by a crowd of people, laughing and talking, children darting everywhere. Surely *their* arrival wouldn't create such excitement!

The deputy pushed them forward, past the milling mob, past a photographer, his black cloth over his head.

"Oh, God!" Ramona whispered at the sight that confronted them. "Oh, dear God!"

The body of Byrne hung there, a rope passed beneath his arms, another about his waist; he looked very young, his eyes closed as if in sleep. A grinning boy posed beside him as the photographer recorded a souvenir picture. Artists from various newspapers sketched the scene.

Joe Byrne, little more than a boy, himself.

For a moment the girls stood transfixed. Then Missie, ignoring the deputy at her back, walked forward and put her arms around the body, turning to face the startled audience.

"Can't you leave him in peace?" she asked sharply. "You should be ashamed of yourselves!"

The crowd began to melt guiltily away. The girls were ushered to a cell.

Ramona took her young sister's hands; the hands that had touched a dead man. "Thank you for—for what you did. I'm proud of you."

"I'm not even proud of being a human being," Missie raged. "Those aren't people out there! They're animals! Oh, Ramona!" She began to cry, and Ramona held her, stroking her blond head with deep affection. If all women were as brave as Missie, thought Ramona, the world would be a better place to live in. The Ned and Dan Kellys, Joe Byrnes and Steve Harts, might have a chance.

Missie pulled her small tense body together and freed herself from Ramona's arms. "I'm going to write it

357

all down," she said fiercely. "The way the police acted at Glenrowan, shooting at innocent people. The—the thing out there!" She gestured toward the front of the jail. "And maybe the *Melbourne Age* will be interested in the story of two girls imprisoned on false charges! It's the one thing I *can* do!"

That night, Ramona lay on a hard cot, the moon through the window casting a shadow of bars on the opposite wall. She thought of Ned Kelly. He had spent the night in jail, perhaps in this very cell. It was like caging a hurt wild thing. She shivered with the cold, wondering if he'd had more than one worn soiled blanket to cover him.

She was startled out of her reverie as Missie said her name.

"At least," she said, "Denis Dugald won't find us. He'd never think of looking for us in jail."

Chapter 46

At Albury, on the morning after the girl's departure, Denis rose and dressed. Boswell was waiting to help him pull on his boots. Passing the room where Missie and Ramona slept, Dugald rapped on the door. Then the two men, the young Scot and his manservant, went down to the stables and shook Luke awake.

They returned to the dining room for the breakfast of steak, eggs and strong bitter tea that the inn provided for early departures.

The girls did not appear.

"Tis their way of getting even frae yester-r-day, nae doot," Denis said, flushing. Giving the innkeeper's daughter a coin, he asked her to rouse his traveling companions. She returned, big-eyed. The ladies were not in their room. Their beds had not been slept in.

With a muffled oath, Denis raced upstairs. The girl had told the truth. The room was empty, save for a small trunk they had carried up the previous night. A note lay on the closed lid:

Kindly deliver the trunk to the Courtney home in Melbourne, along with the remainder of our gear.

Shoving aside Boswell, who had followed on his heels, Denis made for the stables. There, he found a bewildered Luke scratching a tousled head. The wagon team was still intact. But he was unable to find the two riding horses among those sheltered in the stable. They could not have been stolen. He'd been here the whole bloody night—

Denis and Boswell looked at each other, comprehension dawning. It was clear what had happened. The girls had taken their mounts and ridden off, expecting them to follow in the wagon.

"They willna get away wi' this shenanigan!" Denis said, his jaw hard. "I swor-r-re tae deliver them safe and sound, and I'm bound tae do it!"

He sent Luke to hire two fast horses. The boy was to proceed with the wagon and its contents. "Nae hurry," he told Luke grimly. While Boswell questioned the hotel staff, Denis checked out other local accomodations. They might have attempted a ruse.

They had not been seen.

Satisfied that the girls had gone ahead to Wangaratta, the two men left Albury, riding at breakneck speed. Though they made haste, it was necessary to stop and inquire at every small inn and station along the way. Denis Dugald's anger increased in proportion to his worry. He looked at Boswell, pushing back his coppery hair.

"As far as I'm consair-rned," he exploded, "they can go tae hell!"

Boswell was quiet, knowing his man. If necessary, Denis would carry his search to the ends of the earth..

Their journey was plagued by misfortune. The rented nags were not as sound in wind and limb as they appeared. Boswell's cast a shoe. It was nearly morning when they limped into Wangaratta. They pounded at the door of the hotel. The dim-witted little maid who rose to let them in seemed to know nothing. Boswell, though uncomplaining, was gray with fatigue. They would need to acquire new mounts, and it was impossible to make inquiries about the girls at this hour, when there were few up and about.

They asked for beds and a meal.

After four hours sleep, they rose, Denis to question the hotel staff, Boswell to find some road-worthy horses. Denis learned two things:

The two girls had not been seen in Wangaratta. And the town was jumping with excitement.

Had he heard Ned Kelly had been caught? There'd been an all-day battle yesterday, at Glenrowan; the men had been wearing some kind of armor. Here, the speaker pounded his chest to indicate his own vulnerability. It hadn't done them any good. Byrne was dead; Hart and Dan Kelly burned up when they fired the hotel.

The Kelly girls were there too. He grinned and put his hands on his hips, mincing in imitation of a woman's swishing skirts. "You know what *they* are. And they say some more of Kelly's doxies showed up, just in time to see their hero took down a peg!"

"I know the Kellys," another man said angrily. "They'd have been good people, if they'd been let be! Wouldn't you fight back if you was pushed to the wall?"

A mumble of voices sounded as others in the speaker's audience agreed with his sentiments.

"It doesn't make no difference," the other said with relish. "Not now. If he recovers, Ned Kelly's going to find his neck in a noose."

Denis Dugald was no longer listening. He was thinking. He was thinking of Ramona's odd preoccupation with Ned Kelly, the outlaw. It made no sense. She was nae the type of lass to form a hero-worship for a criminal. But he supposed such things happened. Young Missie had gotten herself into trouble because of a wildly romantic imagination.

But suppose, he thought alarmed, the lass did know

something of Ned Kelly. *Kelly's doxies showed up, just in time to see their hero took down a peg!*

Guid Lord, not Ramona! Not his ain wee lassie!

Boswell brought the horses, and they raced toward Glenrowan.

There, they talked to an unpleasant looking woman and her son, who seemed to be short in wit. She described the girls who had been in her charge, and was free with her opinions. One had been sneaking in the bush, calling Ned Kelly's name. She'd known he was out there, all right. The other had a drawing of the Glenrowan inn and a gun. They had been taken down to Benalla.

Denis listened just long enough to be certain the two girls had been Missie and Ramona. Then, leaving the woman in mid-sentence, he rode off. She squinted after him. "Well, I never!"

The little fules, Denis thought furiously as he spurred his mount ahead. The wee bar-r-rmy silly sheep! They'd got themself into the broth this time, for certain! He should ride back tae Opal Station, dump the whole thing in their father's lap! He was nae responsible frae their misdeeds!

Boswell, seeing his young laird's eyes so hot with anger, rode silently. The blue blaze turned full on him. "Make haste," Denis said harshly.

"Ay," Boswell agreed. They raced roward Benalla.

The senior constable of Benalla was none too co-operative when he was roused at midnight by two dusty, travel-worn men. Yes, the girls were here. They were being held in custody until their stories could be checked. He would discuss it with them in the morning.

"Coostody? Ye mean they are in the jail?"

The man nodded and Denis Dugald grinned mirth-lessly. "Guid! I shall sleep this night. Mind, ye hold them there."

Then they were gone. The senior constable, confused and bewildered, went back to bed.

Denis and Boswell found a comfortable hotel, where they slept soundly for some hours. Then they rose, asking for hot water and breakfast to be brought to their rooms. Boswell took a neat black suit from his saddlebags. Denis shaved, and donned his kilts; an imposing figure; a gigantic warlike Scot.

"Aweel, mon?"

"Ye look gr-r-rand!"

This morning, the senior constable was ready to listen. He was impressed by the young Scotchman's appearance, and especially by his credentials; his father's name and title.

He sent for the prisoners to be brought before him.

The girls were tired and worn, after two long nights and a day in a jail cell. The hours had dragged, even Missie beginning to lose her optimism. Unkempt, disheveled, they were taken through Benalla at gunpoint.

Entering the senior constable's office, they stopped dead still. Denis Dugald stood to one side of the man's desk. Ramona's first flare of gladness died at the expression on his face. His jaw was squarely set and his blue eyes seemed to crackle with anger. Clad in his colorful costume, he seemed ten feet tall.

Ramona tilted her chin and looked away. Missie followed suit.

It was the constable who did the talking. Dugald had sworn on his honor that, to his knowledge, the sisters had never met Ned Kelly. They lived on a remote station on the Billabong. He was to see them safely to an aunt in Melbourne. They had run away at Albury, in childish defiance of his authority. Probably the incident at Glenrowan had appealed to Ramona, who had a passion for standing up for the rights of the underdog—Kelly, in this case. The younger girl fancied herself a writer, and had probably seen a glamorous story in the battle.

Deliberately, he made them out as rather silly, spoiled little girls with a yearning for adventure. The several nights in jail, he said grimly, would teach them a lesson. He agreed to accept full responsibility for them until he delivered them to the Courtney home.

Duke Courtney's name was also known to the constable. He would let the girls go, but he did not intend to let them off lightly. He harangued them for half an hour, telling them of the folly of their ways, admonishing them to cease their unladylike behavior. Now he would release them to the gentleman's custody.

Chastened and humiliated, Missie and Ramona accompanied Denis Dugald to the hotel, where they remained in their rooms until Luke arrived several days later. Then the small caravan moved on.

Denis and Boswell rode ahead. Not once did either of them turn back to inquire after the girls' comfort. It was just as well. Ramona was so angry that she hated Denis Dugald; and hatred was a feeling that was new to her. Missie had been right all along. She had saved her from a fate worse than death. It was hard to imagine that she had ever considered marrying such a surly, ill-tempered, overbearing brute!

As for Dugald, he too was simmering. He had only asked one question when he marched the girls from the constable's office to the hotel.

"I want the truth. Did either of you know Ned Kelly, or have any dealings with him and his people?"

Missie shook her head, but Ramona faced him, her dark eyes sparked with fire.

"I know him. I know him very well. And it is absolutely none of your business who my friends are."

It *was* his business, he thought morosely as he rode.

Very much his business. He had given his word to the constable at Benalla, the word of a Scot, a Dugald.

And he had been wrong. He had perjured himself.

When they reached the, Courtney home in Melbourne, Denis saw them to the door. Em opened it to them, overcome with surprise and delight. After her tearfully happy welcome, the young Scot refused her invitation to enter, and took his leave. His coolness went unnoticed in the general confusion as Duke, Vicki and Scott joined in the greeting.

Em stood back, finally, surveying her nieces and wiping her eyes. "I know I'm a fool to cry," she said happily, "but it's so good to have you here!"

Missie had been searching the room. "Is Aunt Tamsen out?" she asked finally.

Em looked stunned. "Tamsen? But she went home long ago. Duke had a wire—"

Now it was Duke's turn to look sick with shock. Juan had sent a wire to his office, since Em knew nothing of Missie's problems. It had read, *Missie home. Everybody well and happy.*

He had assumed the word *everybody* included Tamsen, and had conveyed that impression to his worried wife.

It would appear that he had assumed too much.

Chapter 47

Not until the MacDonnell ranges hove into sight, their colors changing with the moving sun, did Tamsen come alive. She had endured the grueling journey, the dragging miles measured by her camel's plodding feet, in a dazed state of determination.

Now that she was almost there, and would soon be reunited with her husband, she could begin to recall small details of the journey.

Luckily, her arrival at end-of-track had coincided with a shipment of freight to be transported farther by camel train.The young leader of the caravan, a man called Abdul, while he admired her with his dancing dark eyes, demurred at taking a woman along. There would be trouble with the men.

She drew her small pistol from a pocket of her traveling gown. "There will be no trouble," she said.

He grinned, a flashing smile that showed strong white teeth. He liked a woman with spirit. In his own mind, he hoped that she might make an exception in his case. It would be a long journey.

"We will see," he told her.

They left on a freezing morning in early June. Tamsen looked timorously at the camel she was expected to ride: a rather stupid looking beast named Zaida. The camel knelt, and Abdul helped her to mount in the rear of the double saddle. Across the front seat was a rolled tent, provided in consideration for her sex. There were also several blankets, and the small amount of clothing she'd brought along.

"Hooshta," the Afghan commanded.

She thought she saw him hide a smile as she nearly pitched over the beast's head. She soon learned to lean backward to allow for the animal's motions as it rose, rear end first, at an angle impossible for an upright rider to maintain. She also learned, when a camel was running, to post; to put her feet in the stirrups, elevating herself from the seat as English horsemen do. Unfortunately, she only learned it after several jolting rides that set the camel drivers slapping their knees in hilarious delight.

The fact that she could laugh at herself brought a touch of respect from the other members of the caravan.

"The lady who laughs," one bearded gentleman said, "and carries a gun."

Once the giant ships of the desert were underway, there was no more running. Laden with freight, nose-to-tail, the camels plodded steadily across the sand and gibber The journey became a thing to endure. Tamsen clung to the saddle, her cloak blowing in the freezing wind, sand stinging her eyes, deaf to all but the sound of creaking leather and camel bells.

There were stations every several hundred miles. At these, she would receive a rest that she could not find in the freezing little tent. There was tea in a china cup at Charlotte Waters. A hot bath at Crown Point.

They crossed the dreaded Depot sand hills in a windstorm, the Afghans leading the camels walking backward against the wind. They had left the flat gibber country behind. The sand hills were mingled with a red country, where there was desert oak, clumps of spiny spinifex, and mulga.

Then came the Finke, a broad river of sand that curved across the land, only a few puddles of water remaining where there had been a raging torrent earlier in the year. At Horseshoe Bend they traversed a seemingly endless stretch of sand hills that stood in ranks, fifty-foot high or more, their red sides pleated in waves caused by the erosion of the wind. A midday stop at Alice Well. A woman there. Children. A meal of salt beef and bread, and on again.

The last night out, she dreamed of her husband. He was sitting in a chair, turning blind eyes to her as she entered. Then he held out his arms.

The next day, the camel caravan moved through Heavitree Gap, little more than a hundred feet in width. They were now in the midst of the MacDonnell Ranges. Abdul dropped back to ride beside the woman who had withstood the rigors of a freezing journey. "There is Mount Gillen," he said, pointing to the left. "The river, winding before us, is named the Todd."

Tamsen blinked back tears. It looked like heaven, with its tall ghost gums and river gums. A plain stretched beyond to hills rising again to the MacDonnells. A small huddle of buildings in the distance was the little town named Stuart.

Beyond Stuart, on high ground where the MacDonnells began, above the spring in the riverbed, stood the telegraph station of Alice Springs, with its attendant structures.

Some time later, Ernest Flint looked up from his key to see a gaunt woman standing in the doorway. She was travel-stained, disheveled, but she stood with her chin lifted proudly, her eyes burning with a feverish intensity.

"I am Mrs. Tallent. Where is my husband."

He stared at her for a moment, not quite believing his eyes and ears. "You came," he said finally. "I had thought that Courtney—Is he with you?"

"I came alone."

He hesitated, then said, "He's here. I'll take you to him. Sit down for a little first. I want to talk to you." His mind was reeling. He'd sent the telegram to Duke Courtney. How much did the woman know?

"I know he's blind," Tamsen said, as if he'd asked the question aloud.

She wanted more than anything to go to Dan at once. But she'd come this far. A few minutes more or less would make no difference now. And it might be best to learn the details.

She took the chair Flint offered her, and accepted the cup of tea he poured with gratitude. Then she lifted questioning eyes.

Flint's face reddened. It was difficult to begin. He had stuck his nose into someone else's affairs like a prying old woman. Yet he'd had a reason. He liked and admired Dan Tallant. He'd seen the man's earlier wires to this woman, in which he stated his love and affection. Then Tallant had returned from Darwin, sick and worn, to find a message containing frightning news; and he'd tried to make his way home.

They'd found him, blind and half-dead in the burning sun, and brought him back to the station.

He thought of the way the man had broken down when, soon after, a wire came from his wife saying that all was well at home. He had wept, unashamedly. Then he'd dictated a cold answer. At her request to join him, he'd said, There is nothing for you here.

As far as she is concerned, he'd told Flint, I'm better off dead.

Then the wire came from Courtney. Tallant ignored

it. And after some weeks, he'd taken it upon himself to answer.

He sighed, wishing he could say what he had to say along the wire. It would be far easier than talking to this woman face to face. He pulled a chair to face her, and sat down, taking a small calloused hand in his own, feeling as if he were drowning in those huge dark eyes.

Taking a deep breath, he began. The wire about the missing girl, the burning of the station, that his wife needed him, had come in Dan's absence. He had been gone for some months on a trip to the Top End, to Darwin.

"But I didn't send—" Tamsen was silent. Luke again. He had wired both the Courtney home—and Dan. But he had meant well. She compressed her lips for a moment, then said, "Go on."

Dan had returned, very ill. His aides had taken sick in Darwin, and remained behind. His camel driver, Said, had died along the way and his aborigine guide had disappeared. He had staggered in, alone, to find word of the disasters at home.

"It was my fault," Flint said, his face twisted. "I had sent a copy to Darwin, keeping one here in case it didn't reach him. I should have thought—"

"It couldn't be helped. Go on, please."

They had put him to bed. When he slept, they thought it was safe to leave him. But he'd gotten up, out of his mind, and taken a camel. He'd tried to make his way home.

Tamsen leaned back, her eyes closed, slow tears leaking from beneath her lashes. Flint stopped, alarmed, but she merely repeated her earlier words.

"Go on."

Tallent made it to the desert country. He'd lain unconscious for a time at a water hole. His camel disappeared, leaving him afoot in the intense heat. But he'd had the wit to cut the telegraph wire. The men who worked along the line found him several days later. He was blind.

"Dear God," Tamsen said. "Oh, dear God!" After a moment, she said, "Take me to him."

"I don't know what kind of a reception you'll receive," the man worried. "He thinks you'll be better off without him. He—"

"He will see me," she said, her voice firm now. "I am his wife."

"Let me call Sam."

Leaving the key in charge of a man who looked at Tamsen curiously, but asked no questions. Flint led her to a small building constructed to blend with the rest of the station. Tamsen stopped, gesturing for him to remain behind.

She walked up the path, stopping before the little house. Flint, watching, saw her wipe her eyes and stiffen her shoulders. After a time, she took a deep breath and rapped at the door.

God, Flint thought. What a woman! He knew, now, that he'd been right in sending the wire.

He could not know how her heart jolted at the sound of Dan's familiar voice. Knees trembling, she forced herself to step inside.

The man who sat in the dim room was busy at something he held in his lap. Strips of leather. He was repairing a harness, doing it by touch. Oh, Dan, Dan! Always working at something! Dan, with his unquenchable energy—

But he was so thin, sitting there in almost-darkness, his head bent to his work. She forced herself to stand still, denying the need to rush toward him and pull that dear head against her breast.

When she didn't speak, he lifted his intent face. She

372

looked into dark, haunted, unseeing eyes and suppressed a cry of pain. "Yes?" he asked. "Who is it?"

"It's Tamsen, Dan. I've come."

He exploded from his chair, harness and rings clattering to the floor, his face revealing an incredulous delight, hands stretched toward her.

It's going to be all right, she thought moving toward him. She stopped, seeing his expression change to one of fury.

"Damn you! I told you not to come. You've got no business here!"

"Why, Dan?"

"I don't want you anymore," he said brutally. "I— I've got other plans. And—" he sought frantically for something hurtful to say "—And look at you! *You look like hell!*"

She gasped. Was it possible—No, those blind eyes were looking past her.

"I'm sure I do," she said quietly, "after that long journey. But you wouldn't know that, Dan. You can't see me."

His face went blank for a moment, then he turned from her with a sobbing sound of frustration, catching a foot in the harness he'd dropped. He fell heavily against a wall, and reached a searching hand until he found his chair. Tamsen kept her fists clenched to avoid helping him.

"They told you at the office."

"No, Dan, I knew when I came here."

"Then why did you come? My God, it's bad enough without you here to see me!"

She finally dared move to him, putting her hands on his slumped shoulders, feeling him quiver at her touch. "I'm here because I love you."

"But I don't love you. It's over, Tam. I've got a nice

373

place here, and I'm doing enough work to earn my keep. I don't need you."

Tamsen bit her lip to stop its shaking. "I need you. I've needed you for a long time."

"And I wasn't there. I'm going to put it to you straight, Tamsen. I lost my shirt in some speculation—"

"I know that, too."

He ignored the interruption, plunging on. "There's nothing in the bank. If there's anything left of the station, sell it. Take the proceeds and go to Melbourne, back to the States, anywhere. Pay Courtney a note I owe him. There should be enough left to—"

"I just got here, Dan. We can discuss that later."

"There's nothing to discuss." He ran his fingers through his hair, his face desperate. "Now, get out. There's a hotel of sorts in town, Flint will take you there until you're rested enough to leave—"

"I'm staying, Dan."

The words had a final sound. He gripped the arms of his chair. His pride dictated that he break the bonds between them. But now that she was here, he felt it faltering. Her touch still held the same magic. It would be so easy to forget he was handicapped; to let her lead him about like a child; a beautiful woman tied to a sightless man.

He couldn't do that to her. He loved her unbearably. And having her here, near him, unable to reach out for her—Oh, God, it was too much!

It would be kinder if blindness were accompanied by a loss of memory. Her face was clear in his mind. He could see the pure oval of it, the big dark eyes, the long straight hair that hung to her waist, silken beneath his fingers.

God, give him strength.

He bent, feeling about the floor for the harness he'd

374

been mending. Trying to still the trembling of his hands, he set doggedly to work, his attitude indicating that he did not wish to talk.

He'd had too long to sit in that chair and dwell upon his predicament. She had to get through to him somehow, break down the wall he'd built around himself.

Tamsen walked to the water bucket sitting on a small table and picked it up, clanging the dipper to indicate what she was doing, then went to the door. Her hand on the knob, she turned toward her silent husband.

"I don't think I told you," she said softly. "Dusty is dead."

She went out, shutting the door behind her, and leaned against it, tears streaming down her cheeks. It had been a terrible thing, hitting him with news like that. But at least she'd given him something else to think about.

Now she must give him time to recover from the shock. She went down to fill the bucket at the spring.

Chapter 48

Tamsen steeled herself to return to the little house. She pushed the door open quietly. Dan was still in his chair, his head back, eyes closed, face white as paper. The flesh beneath his eyes looked bruised. For the first time in his life, Dan Tallant looked—old. Then he spoke, wearily.

"I know you're there, Tam. All right, you win. We've got to talk. I have a new life, and the past doesn't matter, but it does. Fill me in on what's happened at—home."

Tamsen carried the bucket to its proper place, then knelt in front of Dan's chair, her eyes fixed on his face. In a low voice, eliminating the more unsavory details, she told him there had been a fire, that Missie had eloped with Arther Melvin—

"Sonofabitch!" he said, startled out of his depression. "Melvin? Missie's only a baby! The bastard!"

Ignoring his outburst, she went on. It had all been too much for Dusty's tired old heart. He had died peacefully in bed, and they'd buried him at Opal Station.

As she spoke, tears welled in Dan's haunted blind eyes and ran silently down his cheeks. Tamsen longed to put her arms around him, comfort him. But it wasn't time. He was coming back to life, and it hurt.

"That's it," she said finally, thinking of the horrors she'd omitted in the telling.

She left him to his thoughts and moved about the little house, picking up objects, straightening. Anything to keep her eyes from the suffering man. There was a screen in one corner, behind it a tin tub. A vague notion forming in her mind, she filled the black pot that swung on a crane over the fire. She had tried to reach Dan with the surprise of her arrival, with shock tactics, with talk of home.

Now she would try something else. Surely, her years as a madam had taught her something about men.

For a long time, Dan slumped, immersed in his sorrow for Dusty, his worry over the events that had occurred at home. He'd planned to put it all behind him, and he thought the wound had healed. But it hadn't. Dusty was his friend. Opal Station was his home. Missie, a sweet child to be protected from the likes of Melvin. And Tamsen—

Tamsen was his beloved, his wife whom he needed desperately. He'd thought he could shut her out. But nothing had changed.

He flinched at the sound of water striking metal. What the hell was she doing? A bath, of course, after the rigors of the trail. He couldn't deny her that. But later, somehow, he would have to make her understand that she must leave.

He heard the rustling of discarded garments; the fall of her heavy serge riding habit, a whisper of petticoats, underthings, chemise and drawers. He could picture the scene he had watched so many times before. Finally there would only be Tamsen, slim and golden despite her years, stepping into the water that would glisten on honey-tinted shoulders, pointed breasts—

His mouth was dry. He couldn't swallow as he yearned toward the girl behind the screen, the girl who had become a woman, but remained ageless in her appearance and in the arts of lovemaking. Damn her! Oh, damn her! He tried to close his ears against the sounds that teased at his memory.

There, the bath was done. She would be toweling herself dry. Now she was drawing a brush through damp, heavy hair. Every strand would stand alone, filled with the energy that emanated from her small body. He began to tremble as he heard her come toward him, hearing each step of her small bare feet. He drew a ragged breath. "Tamsen—Don't—My God, what are you doing!"

"This," she said.

She pulled him to his feet and leaned against him, her fingers working at his shirt until his chest was bare against her own naked body. His arms closed around her as she reached up, pulling his face down until she could reach his mouth. He tasted the sweetness of her as she melted against him; felt her softness, the burning heat of her that came from the very core of her being—and he was lost.

"No, sweetheart," he groaned. "No—"

Dazed, he felt her fingers at his belt. And then there was nothing at all between them. Tamsen led him toward the bed in the corner, a cot, but surely large enough for two people in love. Lying down, she pulled him down beside her, holding him, stroking his too-thin body, feeling the muscles quiver beneath her touch, arousing him until he pulled her to him with a strangled cry.

"Tamsen! Oh, damn you! I need you—Tam—"

Their coming together was an act of desperation, of muffled, incoherent words that ceased as passion consumed them with its mounting fire, a fire that thundered in their veins as they strove frantically to merge, one with the other. Together they reached their joy, so like a small dying, and fell from it into a darkness, satiated, at peace.

How long they lay, clinging to each other Tamsen

didn't know. It was enough to just exist. To know that they were together, touching: body, mind and soul.

Then Dan's long body was shaking with a shuddering sob. She felt his tears against her cheek—or were they her own? She wanted to soothe him, to talk to him, but this was not the time. Instead, she only held him close, comforting him with her body as he wept, a strong man's tears.

Finally, he sat up. "I'm sorry, Tam. I didn't mean to do—any of this. I couldn't help myself." He choked on the words and put his face in his hands.

She ran her hand along the brown back she knew so well. "I love you. I'll always love you. Whether you can see, whether you can walk. You're part of me. Do you think it's fair to take that part away?"

She asked him to remember the night before their marriage, when they had made love on a hill high above San Francisco. There had been a minister waiting for them on the wharf at dawn; the ship on which they would sail, in the distance. Their only music had been the lapping of waves. A pink glow had appeared in the east as they heard the final intonation.

"I now pronounce you man and wife."

"Can't you remember?" Tamsen whispered. "I promised to love you in sickness and in health. Don't deny me the right to keep those vows."

Then he was holding her again, kissing her, mouth warm and urgent, and they were back in time to a hill above the California city, stars wheeling.

First passion, and now tenderness. It was going to be all right. It was going to be all right.

When he finally slept, Tamsen lay awake for a long time, suddenly cold with fear. What if she hadn't found that telegram addressed to Duke Courtney? What if, for that matter, the man named Flint hadn't sent it?

Would she have accepted Ian Gregory's love? Have

lain with him like this? She couldn't have. She knew that now. But the long months of deprivation and rejection—Missie's leaving, the fire, Dusty dying—had driven her close to the edge.

The path of love was a very narrow one, she thought ruefully. But very beautiful. Yet it was easy to lose one's balance and tip over the brink: she, through emotional fatigue and need for reassurance; Dan, through pride. She had been blinder than he.

They woke in the morning like two young lovers, introduced to a new delight.

"The sun is shining," she said happily, leading Dan to the window. "See, you can feel it." After a breakfast cooked over the fireplace, she led him outside. It was the first time he'd left the house since his blindness. They followed a footpath leading between gum trees, down to the sandy riverbed where pools of clear water lay like sapphires.

"I can see it in my mind," Dan said. She hugged him, laughing.

"I wish I could have brought you with me," he said wistfully. "When I could see. There are so many things I would have liked to show you."

"You still can," she said with confidence.

She made a list of the places he mentioned and took them to Ernest Flint. The ghost gums on the road west; Simpson's Gap, believed to be haunted by the aborigines; Emily Gap, a water hole, eleven miles east of Stuart where the residents of Stuart swam; Standley Chasm, with its majestic, towering walls.

With borrowed horses, they began to ride, each time going a little farther afield. Tamsen was delighted to learn that the maps were not really needed. The sun on Dan's face led him unerringly in the direction he wished to go. He would point out the direction, and Tamsen would follow the red, mica-sparkled paths. Then he would move behind her, led by the sound of her horse's hooves that kept him to the trail.

They saw the ghost gums with their eerie luminous beauty, with Tamsen's eyes and Dan's memory. At Simpson's Gap they stood silent, feeling the spirits of the aborigines who had been massacred there long ago in a tribal war. They came to lovely Emily Gap with its craggy rock walls looming over a riverbed. They swam at Wigleys Waterhole. And finally, they made the long trek to Standley Chasm, over fifty kilometers west. Here the walls towered to the skies, glowing with colors of gold and red.

"Dear God," Tamsen breathed, after they'd made the long trek afoot, over rocks, through almost tropical vegetation. The gigantic rift in the walls might have been made at the beginning of the world. "I've never seen anything like this," she whispered.

"I felt the same way when I first saw it," he admitted. "And I wished you were with me."

"I am now, Dan."

The sun went down slowly, turning the walls of the chasm to a richer red with its reflected light. The two who lay on the soft sand below were filled with awe at the magnificence of nature's creation, which somehow was mingled with the depth of their love.

Tamsen, holding onto Dan's hands, looked at the world they were leaving behind with wistful eyes, making the most negative comment she'd made since her arrival.

"I wish you could have seen it all again," she said, her lips quivering.

"I did, sweetheart." He hugged her close. "I saw it through your eyes. And that made it all the more beautiful."

Early the next morning they left the little town of Stuart and began the long trek home. They were traveling with two families to Adelaide; then, from there, they would take ship to Melbourne, visit the Courtneys for a time, and then return to Opal Station.

As they rode, Tamsen watched Dan's spirit mend. Once more, he was browned by sun and wind, his massive shoulders filling out. He lost the fragility that had caught at her heart when she first saw him at Alice Springs.

She thought of the half-truths she'd told him; of the ruined valley she had left at Opal Station; poor little Missie. What had happened to the child?

She should have wired Duke Courtney when she reached the end of her journey. But Dan had filled her mind to the exclusion of all else. She prayed that Em thought her safe at Opal Station; that Juan and Arab still believed she was at the Courtney home in Melbourne. There would be time to explain when they arrived. Seeing Dan, they would understand.

In the meantime, she must protect Dan from whatever they might find. Sometimes, dear God, she even had visions of Ian Gregory waiting on the steps of Em's house, arms folded, gray eyes stern as he chided her for her behavior toward him. And she had behaved badly, she realized now: leading him on, letting him think his attentions were welcomed.

She shivered. The sooner they left Melbourne, the better. But they had to stop there first. She owed it to Em. And she intended to have Dan see a physician there.

They stopped for the night, and Tamsen cooked over an open fire, Dan describing the way she looked in his mind: her face was flushed, her dark hair swinging.

Smiling, she took away the pins that anchored her heavy hair, and went to him, letting him grip it in both hands. "I knew it," he said with satisfaction, tipping her head back so that he could kiss her. "I knew how you looked. You will never change."

After they ate, she spread their swags at a distance from the other travelers and lay close to him, hearing the thudding of his heart; the booming of the kangaroos as they ranged at a distance.

After he slept, her worries began again. Missie. The ruined station. The welfare of all those she had left behind, and for whom she had not spared a second thought in months.

And Ian Greory, waiting at Em's door.

Chapter 49

Contrary to Tamsen's worries, Ian Gregory was not waiting at Em's door. At the moment, he was approaching Government House, alone in his carriage. For a long time, ever since he had waited for the woman he loved over the ruins of a small dinner for two he had tried to remain apart from the social scene. Tonight, he had almost been ordered by the radical minister, Graham Berry, to attend. The ball was in honor of the new Exhibition Building to be completed within the coming year, and for a short time during the evening, a number of gentlemen would retire to discuss a great Exhibition to be held following its construction.

Perhaps he wouldn't be here to see the thing done, he thought morosely. For some time, he'd been thinking of chucking it all and returning to England.

He looked up at Government House. It stood on a high wooded plateau a mile from town, across the Yarra, where it overlooked the park and the river valley. It wasn't what he considered a handsome place, but it was large and imposing. There was a tower in the center, a hundred-and fifty-feet high, on which waved the Imperial flag. Around it were lodges, approaches, porticos—and then the vast reception rooms, the enormous official dining room and drawing room; and the ballroom, the biggest in the world.

Melbourne was so new and raw, despite the pretentious structures that had sprung up of late. Gregory sighed, thinking of his home in England; green lawns and sculptured hedges, overlaid with the peace of centuries. For a while he had dared to dream of returning there—with Tamsen at his side. When she had left so precipitously, he'd been certain that she needed time to think. He'd waited for her to come back to him.

But his last conversation with Duke Courtney squelched all hope. Tamsen, Duke said, had not gone home as they believed. Apparently, she had gone to join her husband.

Now he, Ian Gregory, must enter Government House; attend another of those bloody parties; be pursued by simpering maidens and a flock of damned old hens with unsightly daughters. He was tempted to turn about and return to his quarters.

He chided himself for his unkind thoughts. There were lovely girls among the Melbourne citizenry. And he'd been accepted everywhere most graciously.

It was no one's fault that the small, dark-eyed woman who had won his heart so completely would not be there.

He sighed once more and urged his horses onward. Might as well get this over and done.

Entering the house, he tendered his hat, stick and gloves to a small uniformed maid, and made his way into the ballroom, as usual, a seething mass of people. The temperatures of crowded bodies and glaring lights combined to form a stifling, almost unbearable atmosphere. Gregory mopped his brow, and moved unobtrusively toward the punch bowl where Graham Berry stood with a number of his underlings. Perhaps they might retire and have their discussion now. Then he could leave.

Berry acknowledged his presence with a nod and went on talking. The topic was not the Exhibition, but one of more current interest. The infamous Ned Kelly, the bushranger, had just received his preliminary trial in Beechworth. He'd been committed for trial, on the basis of evidence, at the Beechworth General Sessions to be held October fourteenth.

"I don't like it," growled Judge Barry, a member of the group. "If he is tried there, he will get off. And he's guilty as hell. I sentenced his mother, some of his family and friends. They're all a bad lot. I said then that I'd give him fifteen years if he ever came before me. Now he deserves to hang!"

"I think justice will prevail in any part of this country," another man said mildly.

Barry grunted. "The court was filled with *women*. Nine-tenths of the people of that area see Kelly as some sort of hero. Sentimental hogwash! Do you think they can produce a panel that will convict the man? No, I say the trial should be held here, where there is no prejudice."

"But I think—"

Ian Gregory didn't hear the remainder of the sentence. He had been watching a slight blond girl; a pretty little thing, too thin, and though dressed expensively, without the frills and gewgaws so popular among the ladies of Melbourne. A pair of wire-framed glasses on a pert nose framed big blue eyes. She looked like a child masquerading as an intellectual.

He watched her, amused. It was clear she was eavesdropping on the men's conversation. Finding his eyes on her, she moved away with a studied nonchalance. He watched as she crossed the room, keeping sight of the shining head until it paused. She was talking to another woman.

His heart bumped. Good God! Tamsen—

His face grim, he forced his way through the crowd. She owed him an explanation!

Missie reached Ramona's side. "I'm afraid they're going to have Ned Kelly's trial here," she whispered. "I just heard Judge Barry talking about it!"

"Would that be bad?"

"It wouldn't be good! I'll explain it all to you later."

Missie moved on. She had taken her writings to the editors of Melbourne papers, and she'd finally been employed, but only as a reporter of social functions. And only because the name of Duke Courtney, her uncle, carried a lot of weight. The wealth of information she'd written up about the Battle of Glenrowan, the treatment to which Joe Byrne's body was subjected, was ignored. The press was not sympathetic to the Kellys or their ilk.

So Missie had been reduced to writing of lawn parties, teas and balls; what had been served, who wore what, and who attended with whom. It was not the assignment she'd hoped for, but it was a foot in the door. And someday, she might have a chance to put her information to some use. In the meantime, she had an ear to what was happening. She knew that Ned Kelly had been brought to Melbourne after the battle, and placed in the jail hospital—in the same prison where his small mother was serving out her term.

She knew that his mother had been allowed to visit him for half an hour, but not the details of that visit. Only Mr. Castieau, governor of the jail, present through necessity, knew what had taken place during that emotional encounter. A kind and humane man, he refused to discuss it with the public or the press.

Tomorrow she would discover the details of the Beechworth trial. But in the meantime, she must move about the room, taking notes on the dress of governmental wives. She smiled at her aunt Em, surely one of the most beautifully gowned women in the room, and moved on.

Ramona, seeing an eager suitor move toward her as the music began, slipped away, entering a small reception room where she stood at a window looking out, her mind on Ned Kelly. She didn't hear the footsteps behind her. Then someone gripped her arm roughly, turning her to face a pair of angry gray eyes.

"Tamsen, damn you! You're not going to run away again—"

The voice died as the tall man who held her captive looked down with an expression of incredulity. The hair was Tamsen's, but the huge eyes were set a trifle further apart; the mouth a bit larger. A young girl: a lovely child, but not Tamsen.

"I'm sorry," he whispered. "I hope I didn't frighten you. I thought you were someone else."

She looked at him curiously. "I've been told I look like my aunt. I suppose, in the crowd—"

His face reddened. Ramona knew, intuitively, that this was the man she'd heard about. Em had insisted both girls stay at her home for a time, and had introduced them into Melbourne society. Picking up bits and pieces of gossip, she and Missie had questioned Em, who admitted there was something to it. An Englishman had fallen in love with Tamsen. For a time, she seemed to reciprocate. But then suddenly, she had gone. Em was certain she was with Dan.

"You are Ian Gregory?"

His flush deepened, and she felt sorry for him. He must have loved her very much, and it would be difficult for a proud man to face down the speculations that arose when she disappeared.

"I am Ramona Narvaéz," she said quietly. "Are you enjoying the ball? I am. I love to dance."

His brow cleared, and he extended an arm. "Then shall we?"

They returned to the ballroom, and they began to move in time to the music. Looking up into Gregory's grave gray eyes, Ramona decided she liked him. If Aunt Tamsen was actually attracted to him, she certainly had reason. She found herself talking to him as if he were an old friend. And Ian Gregory was surprised to discover that he was having a delightful evening.

Engrossed in each other, the two didn't realize the attention they were receiving. There was a buzzing of comment as guests, who hadn't noted Ramona's resemblance to her aunt, took note of it now.

Em, on the sidelines, saw the pair together and was shocked for a moment, seeing Tamsen. Then, recognizing the girl as Ramona, she thought, Oh, lord! She went in search of Duke, a little shaken. This was all perfectly aboveboard, of course. Ramona didn't have a husband in the offing. But Gregory was too old for her! And he might transfer what he'd felt for Tam to Ramona. It wouldn't be fair!

Duke Courtney was seemingly unperturbed at his wife's urgent whisper. "Don't be silly, Em. He's old enough to be her father. And they've only just met, I'm sure." Still, he found himself watching the couple speculatively during the remainder of the evening.

Perhaps the most disturbed was a tall young Scotchman in swinging kilts, his copper-colored head gleaming in the flickering light. His name alone was an entree to Melbourne's social circles, and he was staying with the Governor and his family. Therefore he was included on all guest lists, as were the Courtney nieces. This wasn't the first time they'd attended the same function. They'd kept at a distance from each other, speaking only when necessary.

But it was the first time he'd felt this strange sensation—like a sword had been plunged into his vitals. Surely it wasn't jealousy, he told himself. Whoever the lassie took up with was nae his affair! And if he took Ned Kelly from her ken, sae much the better. The mon was sure tae hang.

Still he was unable to keep his eyes from the dancing couple who seemed entranced by each other's company. He left early, the night having turned sour, and went home to dream of a gentle big-eyed girl he had once held in his arms.

Chapter 50

If it were not for the thought of Ned Kelly behind bars, the next weeks would have been among the happiest Ramóna had ever known. She and Ian Gregory had become the best of friends. He undertook to show her the city of Melbourne. Having lived in the outback most of her young life, her experience of the city limited to social affairs, she was in a constant state of wonder. It pleased Gregory to watch her childlike enjoyment of things he had taken for granted.

They rode the omnibuses, dropping threepence into a little glass box near the driver's seat. If they didn't have the correct change, they rang a little bell. Then they entered by means of a strap attached to the driver's foot; the strap was pulled again when a passenger wished to alight. Ramona found it thrilling to speed through the streets of Melbourne in the horse-drawn vehicles.

More frequently, they drove in Gregory's buggy through streets that became a riot of flowers as the Australian spring approached. As varied as the blossoms was the wave of humanity that thronged the streets: black coats and belly-toppers; swagmen, with their blanket-rolls; Chinese hawkers with their bamboo and baskets filled with exotic merchandise; policemen, newspaper runners, bank clerks, shop owners. Feathers, flowers, silks and gold ornaments, alpaca and plain garb clothed the citizenry.

They walked Bourke Street, that spot of excellent and cheap restaurants, where one might purchase soup, meat and pudding for sixpence. They attended Hosie's magnificent dining salon at the Academy of Music; the Theatre Royal, St. George's Hall, the People's Theatre.

On Saturday mornings, they 'did the Block' along with the rest of fasionable Melbourne. Collins Street was to Melbourne as Bond Street and the Row are to London, the Boulevards to Paris. It was a place to show off a new gown, to greet friends, to gossip.

That they constituted a good part of the gossip, a young woman replacing her aunt in the affections of the town's most eligible male, occurred to neither of them. Nor did they note a glowering Scot with copper hair who often followed behind them, scowling at their animated conversation.

The days passed, a shimmer of sunlight and lamplight. They attended a pantomime performed by a clown, and Ramona laughed delightedly, Gregory joining in like a giddy young boy.

On the way home, he was quiet. The thought had occurred to him that he wan't a boy, but a man past middle age. Sometimes he confused this girl with Tamsen, seeing her as a true companion, rather than a child to be entertained, a lovely, enchanting child. He would have to watch himself.

"A penny for your thoughts," she said, smiling up at him. The smile produced such a wave of emotion that he almost groaned.

"Just thinking what a nice evening it has been. I hope you enjoyed it as much as I did."

"It was wonderful," she breathed, eyes sparkling.

"And I was thinking that I'm not being fair, taking

up all your time. I'm sure there is some young man who—"

Young man? Ned Kelly, in prison. Denis Dugald, who was insufferable. A flock of others whose names and faces she couldn't even remember.

"There's no one," she said honestly. "But I don't want to take up *your* time, if you have other things to do. I appreciate what you've done for me, but—"

"Oh, God, Ramona! It's not that! You're so young—"

He swore as he yanked at the reins. Too late! A small white kitten had scurried beneath the buggy. There was a sudden squall—then nothing.

Ramona was out of the buggy in a flash, kneeling beside the little bleeding body, her eyes filled with tears. Finally she stood. "It's dead." He put his arms around her, holding her shivering body against his own for comfort.

"I'm sorry, little sweetheart. I'm so sorry."

"It couldn't be helped."

She lifted her flowerlike face with its great, swimming eyes, and before he could stop himself, he was kissing her. Not as one would kiss an unhappy child, but as one would kiss a desirable woman.

This was what he had been afraid of!

With a supreme effort, he pushed her away. His voice didn't sound the same as he said, "I will take it somewhere and bury it. But first I will take you home."

He wrapped the kitten's body in his coat and placed it at a distance from the road, then helped Ramona back into the buggy. They drove to the Courtney home in silence, the memory of a kiss between them.

"I'm going to be gone for a few weeks," he told her at Em's door. "I have some business in Sydney."

"I will miss you."

395

He put his hands to her shoulders, his kind gray eyes smokey with feeling. "I've never had a daughter, Ramona. I want to thank you for giving an—an old man—a few weeks of happiness. You're very like your aunt, you know."

"You loved her, didn't you?"

"Very much."

"I wish I were like her, but I'm not. Not at all. Oh, maybe I look like her. But Aunt Tamsen is strong and brave, like Missie. I'm not like her, not inside."

He knew she'd guessed his secret, that in these last days she'd become Tamsen in his mind. Maybe she'd even known it before he did. And she was telling him she understood.

God, if she were only a few years older—he, a few years younger.

Or if she were Tamsen, and free!

He bent and touched her cheek with his lips. "Don't ever settle for anything but the best," he said. And then he was gone.

She went into the house, her hand to her cheek, as if to hold that expression of love he'd left with her in farewell. The house was quiet, everyone evidently abed. She tiptoed her way to the room she shared with Missie.

Missie sat on Ramona's bed, a waiflike figure in a long bedgown. "I've been waiting for you," she whispered. "There's bad news."

Ned Kelly's trial, slated for October fourteenth at Beechworth General Sessions, had been changed. He was now to be tried at the Central Criminal Court in Melbourne. The new date set was October eighteenth.

If he were tried in Melbourne, he was certain to hang for his crimes.

Ramona wept, Missie in sympathy. And, some distance away, a strong man wept. Ian Gregory, true to his promise, buried the little white kitten. With it, he buried the past: his love for Tamsen, who had a husband; his love for Ramona, who had served as her substitute for a time.

He would go to Sydney and remain there until after the holidays. Perhaps by that time, Ramona would have returned to her home at Opal Station, and temptation would be removed from his way.

He rose at last, and brushed the soil from his hands. Stepping into his buggy, he took up the reins and headed for his empty house, a tall and somber man with lonely gray eyes. The most eligible bachelor in town.

Chapter 51

The departure of Ian Gregory for Sydney was duly noted in the Melbourne papers, along with the change of venue in regard to the Kelly trial.

Denis Dugald was a great reader of the news. His first reaction to Gregory's going was one of relief. Then it was replaced by anger. The fellow had courted Ramona assiduously. Now he was deserting her when she needed him most. He'd never understood the girl's relationship with the bushranger, Kelly, but he knew that the coming trial, with its inevitable result, would hit her hard.

For some reason, the thought of Ramona, her soft features melting in grief, twisted in him like a knife. He tried to remember his anger at the girl. Hadn't she forced him to perjure himself to release her from the jail at Bengalla? And he'd certainly received no thanks for it! She'd made a fool of him.

Still he could not forget the night he'd held her in his arms—and called her his wee love.

He lit his pipe and puffed at it savagely. Regardless of his feelings toward her, there should be someone at the girl's side. He had a feeling she wouldn't share her problems with the Courtneys. Apparently her parents hadn't known of her friendship with Kelly. Friendship? He hoped to the guid lord that's all it was.

But if he were to offer his support and aid her in any way, he must mend his fences. He looked musingly into the bowl of his pipe, as if he would find the answer to his dilemma there. He was still sitting there when Boswell came in and began, unobtrusively, to lay out his evening clothes.

"Boswell, I'm a dommed fule, but I intend to do something aboot it!"

Boswell managed to hide a smile. "Yes, sir," he agreed, as a proper manservant should.

Dugald looked at him suspiciously, but began to dress. He would find a way.

The opportunity came that evening, at a musicale held at Rippon Lea. Ramona stood near a doorway leading out to the grounds. A hand gripped her arm, and she was propelled outward to face Denis Dugald's angry eyes.

"Ye've been avoiding me," he said loudly over the music. There was a sudden lull, and she instinctively put her fingers to his lips.

"Sh-h-h!" she whispered.

"Dinna shoosh me," he whispered back. But he drew her farther from the doorway. "I maun talk wi' ye," he said. "Please coom—"

Ramona cast a glance back toward the doorway. No one had missed her. The music had begun again. And the warmth of his mouth still burned against her fingertips. "Very well, though I don't appreciate your high-handed methods," she said haughtily.

"Ah, lassie, I dinna mean tae t-r-reat ye badly. Can we nae be fr-riends? Please, walk a wee bit wi' me.

The magic of the soft, enchanted night, the husky sound his soft burred voice, pentrated her mind. She let him lead her, dazed, far from the house, over the arched bridge where a waterfall sang and the air was scented sweet with flowers. It was beginning again, the magic of his touch, the need for him—the *physical* sensations that Missie had warned her against. And she was powerless to help herself.

"Noo, lassie, ye're going tae listen." His voice stopped as he looked down into the pale face lifted to his own. Then he uttered a broken cry: "Lassie! Lassie! Wee love—"

And she was in his arms, every fiber in her body yearning toward him, her mouth as hot and seeking as his own. They clung in an ecstasy that sent the stars spinning and finally blotted them out altogether. It was he who stepped back at last, with a shuddering breath.

"Say ye love me, lass! Say it!"

"I love you," she said in a small voice.

He gave a great whoop and enfolded her again. His heart thundered wildly against her own as he lifted her from her feet. For a moment, they swayed together, then he placed her gently on the grass and lay beside her, pulling her to fit against him.

"We mauna do this," he moaned. "We maun gae back. I willna do a dishonor-r-rable thing."

"Please," she whispered mindlessly, "Please."

He got to his feet, stumbling a little. "We'll gae tae the hoose, announce our betrothal. Tell the Courtneys ye're tae becoom ma wee wife—"

"Not yet," she said, coming to her senses a little. "Wait."

"Wait?" He laughed her suggestion away. "We'll be wed at once, and sail frae hame! I canna wait! I willna!"

She sat up, smoothing her skirts and frowning. "We will be married at Christmas, or not at all."

For a moment, he answered her glare, then he laughed and lifted her to her feet. "Ye beat the Scots for stubbor-rness, ye do! But ye hae me oonder-r your thoomb! I'll do whate'er ye wish, lassie."

"Will you give me two hundred pounds?" She

blurted out the question and he stopped dead still, his cheeks blotched with angry red.

"Twa hoondred pounds? And frae what?"

"Ned Kelly's defense." She cowered back, seeing the blue eyes turn to ice, his huge fists clench.

"I should hae known," he said harshly. "It was tae guid tae be tr-rue! Ye were leading me on!"

"No, please, Denis, listen! I meant what I said. But—"

"Dinna say please tae me! Ye said it a moment, since! And it took all ma will tae hold back. Ye'd sell your body and soul for that cr-riminal, would ye not?"

She looked at him steadily. "If it would save his life."

He controlled himself with an effort, shaking his coppery hair back, the anger gone from his face. "I came tae offer ye ma help," he said simply. "If it means sae much tae ye, I'll not gae back on it. But I'll nae trooble ye wi' ma presence nae mair . . Ye'll be having a packet frae me in the mor-r-ning."

He turned on his heel and was gone. She sat still for a moment, realizing what he must have thought. That she'd offered her love in exchange for money. Rising, she ran back to the house. He had gone.

In the morning, as he had promised, she received a packet that held two hundred pounds. There was no note with it. She took it directly to Missie. Now, they could carry out their plan. In a short time, a four page pamphlet went to the printer. It was entitled, *Kelly's Defence (by a lady)*.

The pamphlet would be held, pending the outcome of the trail. Missie had done the best she could, even carrying a copy of the letter Ned Kelly had given Ramona prior to the robbery at Jerilderie from paper to paper. None would print it, all coming down solidly on the side of what they believed to be law and order. As one editor explained, if fifty, a hundred, or more young Australians had affiliated with the Kellys to change the power of the government and the rule of the privileged, the small brushfire they created might have become, instead, a political revolution.

As the days dragged, moving toward the trail, Ramona grew thin and pale. At night, in order to keep Denis form her mind, she went over every detail of her friendship with Ned Kelly; remembering the bushranger who had attempted to steal her horse, who had returned it, and confided in her; the boy who had finally turned on his enemies, his back to the wall. She read his Jerilderie letter, reread it. She thought of the many against so few at Glenrowan, of Joe Byrne's dead body, tied to a door and photographed like a—a trophy.

And always in the background was Denis; Denis with his warm mouth and loving arms; Denis who had come to Australia to hunt animals and who had considered hunting man.

Maybe it was justice that she had taken Denis Dugald's money to help save Ned Kelly. But that two hundred pounds had been the price of her happiness.

"Are you all right?" Missie stood beside her bed, her hand on Ramona's burning forehead. "You were making a whimpering sound."

"I must have had a dream," Ramona lied. She had not been asleep. She hadn't slept for a long time.

On the day of Ned Kelly's trial, there was yet another postponement. Kelly appeared in the dock of the Central Criminal Court at ten o'clock on Monday morning, October eighteenth. This time, court-appointed attorneys requested ten days grace, pleading that they must read and study documents pertaining to the case.

Request granted.

On October the twenty-eighth, Edward Kelly, bushranger and murderer, would appear before the same court to be tried for his life.

"I'm going to be there," Ramona said.

"Aunt Em would never approve."

"I'm going to go."

Missie hugged her sister. "I'm going with you!"

Chapter 52

Ramona and Missie were both at the trial. They had managed to get into the courtroom by the simple expedient of standing before the chambers since just after midnight on the day it began. Knowing Em would never approve, they had slipped from the house via the servant's entrance and stolen into town. Then, waiting in the dark shadows, the girls had huddled close, terrified at any sound of approaching footsteps. The larrikins who roamed Melbourne streets at night, in groups they called 'pushes,' could prove a danger to two unattended women.

For a time they waited alone. Then, with the dawn, the crowd began to arrive; the concerned and the curious. Larrikins and settlers; shopgirls and ladies of questionable virtue from the brothels on Little Lonsdale Street; criminals and drunkards from Little Bourke; the privileged and the persecuted, all pushing forward in a crush. When the doors were opened, Missie and Ramona were carried forward by a thrust of humanity.

They found seats in an inconspicuous place, where they would not be seen. They had no way of knowing that outside in the mob, Dennis Dugald stood, frustrated in his attempt to attend the trial. Fearing the girls might do something foolish with the money he had given them—

like plan a jailbreak—he had decided to come. But he had not had the forethought to arrange for a privileged entry—or to arrive early. He viewed the motley crew about him with some distaste. When a flashily gowned woman approached him, laying a hand familiarly on his thigh, he fled.

At ten o'clock in the morning, on Thursday, October twenty-eighth, Ned Kelly, twenty-six years of age, took the stand in the Central Criminal Court at Melbourne. He was specifically charged with the murder of Constables Lonigan and Scanlon, at Stringybark Creek. Judge Redmond Barry, who had already prejudged Ned as incorrigible had chosen the date of trial well. It was the anniversary of Stringybark Creek. Two years to the day.

Ramona shrank back in her seat as the prisoner was brought in. He bore no resemblance to the young bushranger, clad in a sheep-lined coat, who had leaped out at her, ordering her to "bail up." That man, though hurt, was vital, alive.

Now, clad in a dark serge suit supplied by his jailors, Ned Kelly was white-faced from his long illness. Helped to the stand, he sat stiffly. He might have been already dead, except for the eyes burning against his pallor. He didn't move as his Crown-appointed barristed, serving at a paltry fee of seven guineas a day, applied for a delay to further acquaint himself with the facts of the case. Permission was denied.

"It isn't fair," Missie whispered. "He really needs more time. And look at the prosecution smile!"

The jury was impaneled. Ramona craned her neck to see them, then glanced over at Ned Kelly. He had such a lonely look, sitting there. Ramona wished now that she had taken a seat in the front row. No man should be so alone.

She alternately rolled her handkerchief into a ball

and shredded it as the testimony began. First on the stand was Constable McIntyre who told of the shooting of Lonigan and Scanlon.

"I and Lonigan, at about five o'clock, lit a fire in the angle formed by two huge logs which crossed each other, and proceeded to prepare our tea. We were standing at the fire with one of the logs between us. Lonigan alone was armed and he had only a revolver in his belt. My revolver and fowling piece were in the tent. There was a quantity of speargrass five feet high about thirty-five yards from the fire, and on the south side of the clearing.

"I was standing with my face to the fire and my back to the speargrass when suddenly a number of voices from the speargrass rang out. 'Bail up, hold up your hands!' Turning quickly, I saw four men, each armed with a gun and pointing those weapons at Lonigan and me. The prisoner, who was one of the men, had the right-hand position and he had his gun pointed at my chest. I, being unarmed, at once threw my arms out horizontally. Lonigan was in my rear and to my left.

"I saw the prisoner move his rifle, bringing it in a line with Lonigan, and fire. Turning round, I saw that the shot had taken effect on Lonigan, for he fell. A few seconds afterward—"

"He's lying," Ramona whispered angrily. "They had only two guns among the four of them. And Lonigan dropped behind a log and took aim! Ned fired to save his own life, and those of the others!" She half-rose from her seat and Missie pulled her down.

"There's nothing we can do! It's McIntyre's word against Kelly's."

"But the letter Ned gave me—"

"I read it," Missie said forlornly. "But nobody will pay attention to it. Wait. Maybe something will come up."

The testimony continued. McIntyre told of the shooting of Scanlon and Kennedy; of his own escape. Ramona had a moment of hope when Edward Living, bank teller at Jerilderie, tendered a written statement Kelly had given him at the time of the robbery there, asking him to have it published. Judge Barry refused to have the statement admitted as evidence.

Witnesses came and went, Barrister Bindon managing only the most superficial attempts at cross-examination. Several times, the prisoner leaned forward, his features intent, as if he wished to interject a few questions of his own.

After an interminable day, the trial was adjourned until the following day.

Leaving the courtroom, the two sisters fought their way through a restless mob that had waited outside all the long day. Ramona was at the edge of tears.

"What do you think? Does he have a chance, Missie?"

"I don't think so. His only chance was to prove he shot in self-defense. You'll have to face it, Ramona. He'll be found guilty. But then, maybe we can help."

Cole's Book Store was still open. They darted in and purchased an armful of books apiece. Then they went to the Courtney home and gave their flimsy excuses to Em. They had risen early. It was such a lovely day, they'd bought food at a take-away stand, and breakfasted in a park. They had browsed through all the store, done a little shopping, eaten lunch downtown. They'd had a wonderful time.

Em cautioned them against overdoing. They both looked exhausted; Ramona at the edge of her nerves. And it wasn't seemly for two young girls to wander so much, alone.

"Take me with you, next time," Vickie begged. "It's dull here, without Cammie—Mama, may I go?"

"I don't think they'll be doing this again for some time, Em said dryly. "Then we'll see."

Missie and Ramona avoided each other's eyes. They must slip out again tomorrow without their aunt's knowledge. Too bad they couldn't tell her the truth; but she would never approve of what they were doing.

That night, Ramona dreamed of a dingo pup. It was coming toward her with its peculiar slinking gait. She held out her hand, a little uncertainly. Was it coming to be petted? Or would it snap at her?

A gun roared beside her ear, and the dingo fell dead. She turned to see a tall smiling man with copper hair. Then the dream-picture shimmered. Instead of a gun, he carried a rope with a noose in his hand, and he wore a black robe.

"We're going tae hang Ned Kelly," he said.

Then hands were on her shoulders, shaking her. "For heaven's sake, Ramona, wake up!" Missie's tense voice said. "It's time to go!"

Again they crept through the servant's entrance and out into the darkness. This time, a small group of people were already waiting when they arrived. The girls listened to the conversations around them, hearing Ned Kelly's praises sung. It helped to know that there were people on his side, even though the speakers were of the poorer classes, citizens with no political influence. If there were enough of them—

Each girl carried an enormous stack of the anonymously written pamphlets; *Kelly's Defence (by a lady)*. Timorously, they moved among the early-comers, selecting those who were most vociferous on Ned's behalf. To each, they gave a small number of papers to be distributed—if the trial went wrong.

"Sure, sis," a painted woman said, good-naturedly. "My old dad was a settler, like the Kellys. I growed up, watching him and my brothers get pushed around by the police. They wound up in jail, and—well, I had to eat. I figure Kelly struck a blow for all the rest of us poor damn bloody blokes."

The courtroom doors burst open and Missie and Ramona were swept inside by the throng. Again, they seated themselves in an inconspicuous corner. Ramona put her hand to her mouth, as she recognized a coppery head in the first row. Denis Dugald had used his influence with the governor to gain a privileged seat.

What was he doing here? Her dream of the previous night come back to her, full force. Had he come because he was curious? or because he wished to get his revenge —in seeing a man sentenced to death.

The court convened. After some preliminary skirmishing, no witnesses were called for the defense. Barrister Bindon relied on an address to the jury, pointing out discrepancies in the evidence.

The duty of the jury, Bindon stated, was to dismiss extraneous testimony, excluding everything but that which related to the alleged murders. McIntyre's information contained minute observations he could not possibly have made under such stress, therefore should be discredited. Only two men were alive after the fray, and it was a choice of believing the statements of one over another. The prison was not allowed to speak, therefore they had only McIntyre's word for what happened.

The prisoner had a great respect for human life, and had harmed none of his prisoners at Euroa or Jerilderie. He had had many opportunities for assassinating policemen if that were his desire. He urged the jury not to condemn the life of the defendant on the prejudiced evidence of a single man.

Ramona frantically studied the faces of the jurors during Bindon's exhortation. "They're thinking, Missie! He has them thinking!"

Then His Honour, Sir Redmond Barry, delivered his

summation. Edward Kelly, he said, was presented for that he, on the twenty-eighth of October, at Stringybark Creek in the northern Bailiwick, feloniously, willfully, with malice aforethought, did kill and murder Thomas Lonigan. Murder was the highest form of homicide.

He droned on, each word calculated to send Ned Kelly to his death, effectively destroying everyone of Bindon's arguments.

Then the jury was ordered to retire.

It took only half an hour for them to return with their verdict; thirty minutes that spelled torture to a man in the dock, and to two young girls in the back row.

The verdict was *guilty*.

"Prisoner at the bar, have you anything to say why sentence of death should not be passed upon you?"

Ned, who had been sitting silently, as if his mind were far from the courtroom, stirred and smiled mockingly. "It's a little late for me to speak now. I thought of speaking all morning and all day. But there was little use. Nobody knew about my case except myself. I wish I had insisted on being allowed to examine the witnesses."

He looked around the suddenly quiet courtroom. "If I had examined the witnesses, I could have thrown a different light on the case. I do not fear death. I fear it as little as to drink a cup of tea."

Ramona's lips moved in a silent whisper. "Oh, Ned! Ned! Don't do this to yourself!" But the man in the dock went doggedly on.

"I lay blame only on myself that I did not examine the witnesses yesterday. But I thought that if I did so, it would look like bravado and flashness."

A ripple of approval ran through the audience, and Judge Barry hastily donned his black cap to pronounce sentence. The usher shouted for order in the court.

"Edward Kelly, the verdict pronounced by the jury is one you must have fully expected."

"Yes, under the circumstances."

Again there was a shocked silence. The courtroom ritual did not allow for interruption at this point. The judge finally found his voice.

"No circumstances that I can conceive could have altered the results of your trial!"

"Perhaps not from what you can now conceive," Ned Kelly said calmly, "but if you could have heard me examine the witnesses, it might have been different. I know that I would have been capable of clearing myself of the charge, in spite of all against me."

A clamor rose up in the court. The judge, furious at the man's audacity, and the interruption of his trial, tried to regain the floor.

"The facts are so numerous and so convincing that no rational person would hesitate to arrive at any other conclusion but that the verdict of the jury is irresistible, and that it is right! I have no desire to inflict upon you any personal remarks, to aggravate the suffering with which your mind must be sincerely agitated—"

"My mind is as easy as the mind of any man in the world, as I am prepared to show before God and man."

Again a wave of shock ran through the courtroom.

"It is blasphemous for you to say that! You, who appear to revel in the idea of having put men to death!"

"I am not the only one who has put men to death. I would shoot a man if he forced me to do so. If I saw that he was going to take the life of an innocent person."

The judge decided he had had enough. Wishing to bring the strange argument to a close, he ignored Ned Kelly's voice, picked up his notes, and in a lofty tone, began to read.

"In new communities," he began, "where the bonds of society—"

Ramona was frankly crying now, as were many of the women in the audience. Strong men scrubbed at their noses with their sleeves. Many of them had pinned their hopes on Ned Kelly as their only spokesman. And few of them had the courage to stand up for themselves.

"Listen!" Missie said sharply. "I want to hear this. All of it!"

"Foolish, inconsiderate, ill-conducted, intemperate youths unfortunately abound. Unless they are made to consider the consequences of crime, they are led to imitate notorious felons whom they regard as self-made heroes . . ."

"I can't stand it," Ramona wept. "If he'd only stop!"

"A felon is as helpless and degraded as a wild beast of the field. He has nowhere to lay his head. He has no one to prepare for him the comforts of life. He suspects his friends, he dreads his enemies. He is in constant alarm, lest his pursuers should reach him.

"This is the life of the outlaw or felon, and it would be well for young men to reflect that the unfortunate termination of your life will be a miserable death!"

The diatribe continued, interrupted once by the prison. And finally, Judge Barry said darkly, "I have now to pronounce your sentence.

"You will be taken from here to the place from whence you came, and thence on a day appointed by the Executive Council to a place of execution, and there you will be hanged by the neck until you be dead, and may the Lord have mercy on your soul!"

"I will add something to that," Ned Kelly said quietly. *"I will see you where I am going!"*

The courtroom erupted into a noisy, crowding mass of dissension. Ned Kelly's trail had ended.

Denis Dugald, with a note from the Governor and the permission of Judge Barry, had entered by a private door. Now, for some reason, he felt uneasy. He had no wish to be closeted with the judge, or to compliment him on his decision. He had to admit young Kelly had been a decent appearing chap. And from the comments he heard about him, well-liked. Perhaps even loved. A Robin Hood of sorts. He could see why a young girl like Ramona might be drawn to such a man.

For a moment, he stood trying to make up his mind. Then he followed the mob through the door by which the general public had entered.

His heart stopped as he stepped out into the sun. At one side of the entrance stood Missie. At the other, Ramona. They were handing out some sort of paper to all who would take it. A printed tract.

He walked over to Ramona, who didn't seem surprised at his presence. She must have seen him, then. She had been inside, sitting through the horrors of the trial! Her cheeks were still wet, her eyes showing signs of tears.

Instinctively, he reached out his hand. "Lassie, is there nought I can do tae help?"

She shoved a pamphlet into his hand, and in the same dead voice she'd been using to others, she said, "Please take this. Read it. Thank you."

She melted into a cluster of bystanders. He waited for a moment, indecisive, then crumpled the paper in his hand, walking toward Government House. When he reached the comfort and privacy of his room, he spread it on a small table, smoothing away the wrinkles.

"Kelly's Defence," it read. And, in parentheses, (*by a lady*).

Chapter 53

Missie and Ramona walked toward the Courtney home, both of them numb at the grim sentence which would deprive a man of his life. Ramona's eyes were tear-stained and swollen, her face pale. She kept going over the evidence that was presented, comparing it with what she knew to be true.

"You've got to remember that he told you his point of view," Missie said gently. "Maybe it didn't happen quite the way he depicted it."

Ramona turned on her. "You call yourself a writer! You read the letter he gave me before the robbery at Jerilderie! Would you say it wasn't sincere?"

Missie thought of that letter, every word of it charged with emotion; an uninhibited outpouring of a human soul. It negated much of the testimony they'd heard today. It wasn't admitted in evidence, but surely some day it would be published, Ned Kelly vindicated— too late.

The girls were so devastated by the court's decision that they hadn't considered the impact of their absence on the Courtney household. Arms empty, no excuses at hand, they walked into a hornet's nest.

Vickie had risen before dawn, determined to join the girls if they slipped away for another outing. Finding their beds empty, she was furious. They had deliberately sneaked off without her! Mouth set in an angry pout, she went straight to wake her mother.

In a sing-song tattle-tale voice, Vickie recited her woes. Missie and Ramona were gone again, and they hadn't asked her to go with them. She always got left out of everything.

"What time is it?" Em asked, groggily, forcing herself to a sitting position.

"Three o'clock."

Three in the morning? And her nieces out on the street? Where would they go at this hour? She had a sudden horrifying thought. They had lied to her, yesterday!

She shook her sleeping husband. "Duke, wake up! I need you!"

From that hour, the house was in turmoil. Duke Courtney, though certain they would be home eventually, was infected with his wife's concern. There was no *reason* for their evasive behavior. Therefore, whatever they were up to, it could be nothing good. Ramona had always been a quiet girl, sweet, shy, more involved with her pets than with people. But Missie had managed to get herself into trouble before. He would have thought she'd learned her lesson. Dammit, if she'd got her sister involved in something—Em was afraid there might be a man—or men.

He searched the nearby parks, to no avail. When it came time for business to open, he cancelled appointments and sent his employees searching the downtown area, knowing that gossip would result, but it couldn't be helped. Finally, he went to friends among the police, asking that they keep an eye out for his two nieces—unofficially, of course. Thinking Denis Dugald might provide a clue, he called at Government House. The young Scot wasn't there. Boswell was unsure as to where his master had gone.

He began to wonder if, like Tamsen, they'd decided to strike off on their own. Maybe they'd gotten homesick. The thought of two girls making such a trip was rather frightening, but not impossible, since they could travel much of the way by train. At least, there were worse things they could have done.

But according to Em, they'd pulled the same type of disappearing act the previous day. He went home, scowling. He liked a peaceful homelife. And here he'd lost a day of work, and Em was at the edge of her nerves. They came home yesterday. They would be home tonight. And by God, he'd find out where they'd been and what they'd been doing, and he'd see it didn't happen again.

When the girls walked in that evening, they met a battery of furious eyes. "Where have you been?" Em asked, on the verge of tears. Duke stepped in front of her.

"I'll handle this," he said grimly. "Now! You were not in your room at three this morning. And probably yesterday morning also. I want to know where you were!"

The sisters spoke simultaneously. "In the park."

"Shopping."

"You are lying," Courtney said flatly. "I'm responsible for you. I'm going to send you home."

Missie's head jerked up. "I'm a grown woman," she said. "A widow. I can do as I please!"

"Not while you are under my roof!"

"Then I will find another place to stay! If you'll excuse me, I'll pack my things."

"No," Ramona said. "Uncle Duke, Missie, don't talk like this! It's my fault! It's all my fault!" She confronted her uncle, her chin quivering. "We've been to Ned Kelly's trial. We had to leave early to get in."

417

Courtney's jaw dropped. A courtroom where a murder trial was in progress was no place for gently reared young girls. No wonder they looked so wan and pathetic. He took a deep breath, quelling his temper.

"I'm sorry I spoke so harshly. We've all been quite concerned. This is a large city, with an undesirable element. Anything might have happened. I'm going to ask you not to do such a thing again."

Ramona turned great tragic eyes to meet his. "We won't. I promise. The trial is over anyway. He's going to die."

I don't understand it," Duke said to Em, after the girls had left the room. "Missie, yes, if she thought there would be an article in the affair. But Ramona,—She seems to be taking a morbid interest in this criminal."

"You said yourself that Kelly was not as black as he is painted; that you hoped he'd get off"

"They couldn't let him go. He's broken the laws. Any changes for the better have to come from improving our laws, not through violence. Kelly's a maverick, a renegade."

"And something of a hero," Em reminded him. "You know how young girls are."

He grinned. "Hell, young or old, they're all alike. I don't think I've ever understood a woman in my life! But I love them anyway."

Em smiled up at him, her eyes the color of blue morning glories, warm with love. He took her in his arms.

"Have you considered what I discussed with you last night?"

"Moving to San Francisco? I told you—"

"You told me you'd do whatever I wanted to do. But I know you love Melbourne, that you've put down roots here. And there are bound to be some bad memories of California. Your first husband committing suicide."

She looked at him with grave, honest eyes. "That's in the past. My future is with you. I will be happy where you are."

"I don't know if it's the right thing," he said moodily. "All I have to go on is a hunch. I sense a depression here, within the next ten years. My intuition tells me to sell out."

"And I trust your hunches."

He buried his face in her hair, the color and scent of ripe wheat. "We have lots of time, sweetheart. I'll talk to Dan about it when he gets back. It shouldn't be long." At the flicker of worry that tensed her body, he added soothingly, "And Tamsen will be with him. You'll see. I won't make any moves until everyone's settled. Right now, we've got to decide what to do about our two delinquent nieces."

The next morning, Ramona and Missie, guilty at their deception, promised they would be no more trouble. But Duke made them agree, for the duration of their stay, to go nowhere unchaperoned. In the day, they would be allowed the use of a buggy, but a driver must accompany them.

"I'm not meaning to be overbearing," he said. "It's just that I owe your parents some consideration."

Ramona, emotionally exhausted by the events of the trial, remained at home for the next few days. Missie attended afternoon teas, and a few evening functions along with Duke and Em. On Novemember fourth, she returned from a visit to her newspaper office, her face white.

The government, sensing the sympathy of the public for Ned Kelly had moved swiftly. The Executive Council of the Colony of Victoria, presided over by His Excellency, the Governor, George Augustus Constantine Phipps, Marquess of Normandy, acting with unprecedented speed, had fixed the date for the hanging of Ned Kelly at ten o'clock in the morning, Thursday a week, on November eleventh.

On November the fifth, the day following the decision, two thousand, five hundred people jammed the Hippodrome on the corner of Lonsdale and Stephen Streets. A mob, too late to enter, waited outside. The meeting had been called in aid of Ned Kelly, soon to be hanged.

Denis Dugald was one of the early arrivals. He found a seat, then let his eyes rove the hall, his heart sinking as he failed to locate two girls, one blond, the other with a mist of dark hair. Finally he was forced to admit that they, not interest in the Kelly case, had brought him here. And that he was almost sick with disappointment.

The chairman, a Mr. A. S. Hamilton, President of the Society for the Abolition of Capital Punishment, opened the meeting. Denis made himself listen. The man's speech was moving, though the young Scot disagreed with him in principle, believing such punishment—not in the case of Ned Kelly specifically, but in general,—proved a deterrent to crime.

Following Hamilton was a long address by David Gaunson, Member of Parliament, who had defended Kelly at his earlier trial. It was his contention that Kelly was not morally guilty of murder: that the police had gone to kill him, rather than make an arrest; that the prerogative of mercy, should be exercised in this case.

It was moved that a petition be taken to the Governor, on Kelly's behalf. The resolution carried, asking for the Royal Prerogative of Mercy, to save Ned Kelly from hanging.

Denis Dugald found himself signing the paper that

was handed throughout the auditorium. He cursed himself on the way home, for allowing the wiles of a wee big-eyed lass to affect his stern Presbyterian judgment.

It was Missie who brought the news to Ramona before it even appeared in print.

They said there were more than three hundred thousand signatures on the petition; that given time, there would be five hundred thousand.

They said the Governor refused to consider the petition, and the private plea made by Ned's sister, Kate.

They said the prisoner, in his lonely cell, was losing his courage, showing a yellow streak, crying and bemoaning his fate.

"That is a lie!" Ramona said stoutly. "A lie!"

The days stumbled on, each tick of the clock a minute; each minute an hour. And it was Wednesday, November the tenth.

Missie brought more news. Ned's sisters, and his brother Jim, just released from Wagga Wagga jail, were permitted to visit him briefly. And, at last, his mother was brought to him from her cell.

"She said," Missie paused and swallowed. "She said—"

"Go on," Ramona pleaded.

"She said, *'Mind you die like a Kelly, Ned!'* "

Dear God! Oh, Dear God!

And tomorrow would be the final day!

That night, as if he had been summoned by her need, Denis Dugald called, asking to see Ramona. He talked of trivial things, studying the girl's face, the dark-rimmed eyes, until Em went to fetch refreshments.

"I had to coom," he said soberly. "I felt like ye needed ma help. I canna but ask ye tae forgie the past. If I can be of ser-rvice—"

"There is something I want to do. Will you help me? You promise?"

He raised his hands, palms out in a helpless gesture. "Anything."

She moved closer to him, speaking in a rapid whisper.

"Guid Lord, lassie!"

"You promised—"

Dizzy with her nearness, his pulse leaping at the memory of her in his arms, he knew he was trapped, enmeshed in his need for her as he had never been with any other woman.

It was an impossible task she had set for him; a dreadful thing for the lass to wish. But he would try.

"I can't let him die alone," she said. *"Surrounded by enemies. I've got to be there."*

Chapter 54

On the day he was slated to die, Ned Kelly woke at five o'clock in the morning. He knelt in the dim light that filtered through his small dark cell in the old wing of Melbourne Gaol, and spent twenty minutes in prayer. Then he lay down again.

He had loved his mother and his family and friends. He had killed only to protect them. He couldn't believe that he was doomed to hell. But he had no idea what heaven would be. He smiled wryly, wondering if God would trust a bushranger to enter a city with golden streets and pearly gates.

It didn't matter. He would be miserable in such a place.

No, he thought, a just and loving God would tailor heaven to fit each soul. For his mother, one day, it would be a place to rest, a place without worry.

For himself? He shut his eyes, trying to imagine what had been most pleasurable in all his life.

He sat on a sun-warmed rock, with a girl beside him; a small, big-eyed girl in a red gown. Below them, the valley spread in a panoramic scene; a cluster of small buildings, sun glinting from their roofs; the humpies and wurlies of the abo settlement across a creek bed, where small oval pools glittered with opal fire.

Heaven is there, he thought. With a woman's shawl spread, and a feast of sandwiches, a tin of biscuits, dried fruit, a jar of cold milk. A pansylike upturned face, the touch of a gentle hand—

For a time, he had stopped breathing. It would be a picture to hold when he stopped breathing forever.

He rose at eight o'clock and waited. At a quarter to nine, a blacksmith was brought to remove his irons. And then, the priest.

Finally, he was taken from his cell, to be led to the condemned cell, alongside the gallows in the main building. Stepping into the garden that surrounded the hospital ward, he paused in a patch of bright sunshine, savoring it. His eyes fell on the handcart in which his body would be returned to the death house within the hour, and he looked at it for a moment in horrified fascination. Then his gaze lifted to the sky.

A rainbow bird swooped in pursuit of a dragonfly, the golden undersides of its wings gleaming.

He smiled at his warden and gestured toward a riot of blooming shrubs.

"What pretty flowers," he remarked. He strolled onward with a jaunty air, leaving the sun for the last time to enter the somber prison where the hangman waited.

The prison was quiet, but eyes watched through small barred windows as Ned Kelly took his final walk. He climbed the echoing metal steps that led to a walkway surrounding a second tier of cells. He was taken to the last cell on the right, where the mechanism that operated the trap was in his view.

The gallows, in the center of the new wing, consisted of a timber laid across the transept of the first gallery, with a rope attached; a bolt, or lever, operated the trapdoor where the condemned man would stand.

The last rites of the Roman Catholic Church were

performed by Father Donaghy, the prison chaplain, and Dean O'Hea, who had christened Ned as a baby.

Shortly before ten o'clock, Colonel Rede, Sheriff, and Mr. Castieu, Governor of the Gaol, appeared with the officials and members of the presss who had been granted admission. The hangman, a convict himself, a fit looking man with gray stubbled hair and carbuncled face, approached Ned's cell. The door was opened, and the prisoner pinioned.

"There is no need to tie me," he said calmly.

But it was done.

With a firm step, he walked toward the gallows. And no one saw the couple that watched from above.

"Ye'll be all right?" Denis Dugald whispered to his companion. The little figure dressed in Boswell's clothing, hair tucked firmly under his small round hat, had stifled a whimper as Kelly came into view.

"I'm fine," Ramona whispered back. But the hand Denis took in his own was cold as ice. He cursed himself for having let her press him into this.

It had taken some doing. He had used some pressure on the Governor of Victoria himself, making free with his father's well-known name. He had told the governor that his father, The Dugald, was most interested in prison reform. He was to take him a report on law and justice in Australia when he returned to Scotland.

Only an agreed upon number might attend? Then perhaps there was someplace he and his man might stand, unseen, to observe the deed.

A letter of request from the governor, plus a sizable bribe to a warden, had gained them this vantage point. Before dawn, they had been escorted to an empty cell in the third tier. When the appointed time came, they pushed the door open and came to stand in the shadows near the metal railing, to look down on the scene below.

Denis thought of those hours of waiting. Ramona's face, above Boswell's dark suit, had been the color of death. She had been silent, and so had he, though he wished more than anything to put his arms around her and comfort her.

At least it would soon be over.

"He won't know you're here," he said now, in a low voice. "Lassie, once mair, please, for ma sake—"

"I'm staying."

A sacristan held a crucifix high, priests chanting prayers for the dying as Ned Kelly stepped into place on the trapdoor. God, he was praying, don't let me show fear.

Above him, Ramona was making the same plea.

He raised his face upward, toward the vaulted ceiling, for just a moment, and she moved forward, tearing the round man's hat from her head, letting her hair fall.

She began to sing, in an almost whisper, the words losing themselves in the shuffling and chanting below:

"In bold defiance stand, my boys, the heroes of today. So let us stand together, boys, and shout again, 'hurray—'"

Dugald dragged her back from the railing. "Ye barrmy wee fule!" He hissed. She jerked free of him, and, tucking her hair back under the bowler, returned to the rail.

Below, the witnesses to the execution, were looking about rather nervously. The Ballad of Ned Kelly was known to all. Each of them could have sworn they heard a word or two of it, filtering through the priests' intonations. And none of them would speak of it, ever, attributing it to the voices of their conscience.

The executioner lifted his arms to pull the knotted rope over the condemned man's head and paused, startled

426

at the shining look of calm, almost joyous expectancy that the man's face wore.

"Ah, well," Kelly said conversationally, as if to someone on high, "I suppose it has to come to this." Then, as a white cap was pulled over his head and face, he sighed, saying his last words.

"Such is life."

The hangman stepped back and pulled a lever. The trap opened and Kelly fell through, the rope jerking taut with his weight, quivering briefly.

Ned Kelly was free, at last.

Denis Dugald had closed his lids as the hangman threw his weight against the lever. Ramona did not. She watched with great empty eyes until the witnesses left their posts.

"I want to go home."

Outside in his buggy, he tried to reach her, rubbing her icy wrists. "Dinna greet, so, Lassie. Like he said, it was bound tae happen."

"But it needn't have happened! He never had a chance."

He swallowed hard. "Ye must hae looved him very-ry much."

Her gaze swung to him with a look of startled surprise. "Loved him? You thought—! Yes, I loved him, because he was hurt. He was my friend."

His heart leaped. He had seen this same expression in the girl's face during the killing of the beasties that infested Opal Stations! Could it be possible—

"He never had a chance," Ramona said again, in a dull voice. "He never had a chance, so he fought back."

"'Tis the way of the wor-rld, Lass."

"I know, but it isn't fair!"

He continued to rub her chilled hands and wrists, and found a weal beneath his fingers. He slid the sleeve of

Boswell's suit upward, revealing a slim arm and hand.

"Ye've been hur-rt! Tis an angry scar."

She looked at him with an impenetrable expression. "I used to feed a dingo puppy. Someone shot him, wounding him. The next time I saw him, I put out my hand and he snapped at me."

"He might hae gone for your throat, lass! I hope he was put away."

"You killed him," she said flatly. "Now, please, I want to go home."

He let her out in a small alley that ran behind the Courtney property. He waited for her while she changed, in a woodshed, from the clothing she'd worn to the prison into more feminine garb. She took only a few moments, then returned to hand him the bundle of men's garments.

"You're going to be all right?"

Her luminous gaze transfixed him. "It's over now. There's nothing else to do."

He drove home, musing over the events of the morning. The execution had been an ugly thing. But the expression on Kelly's face, when he saw Ramona and recognized her song, was something he would never forget. For a moment, he had looked like Christ on the cross, with his pale face, the long curling beard.

Denis thought guiltily of the idea he'd had long ago of helping to hunt the man down. It had seemed an adventure then. But not now. Guid lord, not now!

He thought of the small hand he had held so recently; the ugly scar on a slim arm; the expression on Ramona's face as she told the story of how the weal came to be there.

She had been telling him something; a deeper meaning underlying the surface of her words. She'd been making a comparison.

The puppy had been tame until it was hurt. Then, it

retaliated. He remembered now the conversation of a night at Opal Station. He had mentioned the dingo that came toward him, like a wee, guid doggie. Then when he reached to touch it, it had growled and snapped. He had shot it, taking note of the scar that indicated it had been fired at before.

Ned Kelly might have been tame, had he not been hurt. But he and his were persecuted, and he had fought back. And now the outlaw was dead at the hands of man.

Dennis Dugal thought of his own life: the wee foxes turned loose and hunted to ground; the hares that sometimes screamed at a deathblow; of feathers drifting down, following the death plunge of a bright bird; the kangaroos, with their soft fur and inquisitive faces.

He finally saw himself as Ramona saw him, and he didn't much like what he saw.

Returning to his room at Government House, he replaced Boswell's clothing. The small manservant had not questioned him when he borrowed the things. He did not question him now, at their return.

"Boswell," he asked moodily, "have you ever hunted?"

"With you, sir."

"I mean frae yourself," Denis persisted.

"Nay, sir."

"Would you mind telling me why?"

"It doesna suit my station—nor my inclinations, sir."

Denis dismissed the little man, and sat for a long time with his face in his hands. Finally he rose and roared for his servant.

"Boswell!"

Boswell appeared from the small dressing room where he slept on a cot. "Ye called, sir?"

"Boswell, bring me ma goon!"

He would show the lass!

Ramona and Missie did not discuss the execution that day. Ramona was still suffering from shock, and Missie wisely refrained from questioning her. She did not know where her sister had been, only that she'd slipped out at dawn. Missie had covered for her, saying that she still slept, and then that she'd gone shopping with a friend.

She assumed that she'd been in a crowd outside the prison, waiting for the word that Ned Kelly was dead.

Late in the evening, a package arrived for Ramona; an oddly shaped parcel, brought by a messenger. The Courtneys crowded about curiously as she opened it.

A repeating rifle—its barrel bent in an arc.

Em looked at it helplessly, and than at Ramona's face. "What in heaven's name—" she began. But Ramona's face crumpled, and the floodgate of her tears was lifted at last. Sobbing, she fled to her room.

"If this is supposed to be a joke," Em said tartly, "I do not think it's funny!"

"It isn't a joke, Aunt Em," Missie said. "Oh, Aunt Em, I think I've made a terrible mistake."

She followed Ramona, without further explanation, leaving Em and Duke, Vickie and Scott, staring at a new repeating rifle with a curved barrel, wondering what in the world was going on.

The odd gift was not nearly as startling as what occurred later, at exactly midnight. A shrill blast of sound brought Em upright in her bed, fumbling for her robe. A scream? One of the girls—

The blast evolved into a sort of skirling music. Em rushed to the window. A tall Scotchman clad in full regalia stood in the moonshadows in the center of her lawn, bagpipes in his arms, tootling merrily away. Up and down the block of the sedate, proper residential area, lights were coming on.

Good Heavens! Denis Dugald! Was the young man tipsy?

Duke had appeared at her shoulder. "Damn it, Dugald!" he bawled. "What the hell do you think you're doing!"

Denis looked up and smiled, the moon touching on his copper hair. "Serenading ma lassie," he said.

"Well, di it in the daytime," Duke snapped. "Decent people would like to get some sleep! Of all the damned—"

"He ye no r-romance in your soul?"

"Not at midnight," was the answering growl. "And neither do my neighbors!"

The upraised features showed disappointment. "Then tell ma lassie I'll be by frae her in the morrning."

He disappeared into the darkness, and Duke slammed down the window, his face comical in its bewilderment. "Which lassie? Vickie? Ramona? Missie? Or—"

Em giggled. "It's certainly not *me!*"

"It better harn't be!" He held her close, feeling her heart beat beneath the thin nightgown. Finally she pushed him away.

You said there was no romance in your soul at midnight," she teased.

'So I lied," He picked her up and carried her toward their bed.

Ramona, in her own room, had appeared at a window, peeping through drawn curtains, hearing the bagpipes and the exchange of words between her uncle and the handsome figure on the lawn. She watched Denis Dugald go, yearning after him. Then she felt Missie's hand on her arm.

"I was wrong," Missie admitted. "I made a bad mistake in marrying Arthur and I was afraid for you. What are you going to do?"

Ramona put her hands to her face. "I can't think. This day has been so dreadful—"

"That was yesterday. Now it's already tomorrow. The beginning of a brand new day."

Chapter 55

Ramona was waiting when Denis arrived in the morning. Though she still showed the ravages of the day before, she looked delicate and lovely in a soft ivory traveling gown trimmed in deep rose, with a small rose-colored parasol Em insisted that she carry.

She had lain awake most of the night, not daring to dream that the damaged rifle meant what she thought it might. She knew he'd thrown away the old one. This had to be the replacement that arrived at Opal Station. Then appearing on the lawn as he did, and his words—" serenading ma lassie."

Missie was certain he'd ask for her hand in marriage. Would he? And if he did, what would she say? She lay, her heart in a tumult, as she feared that he would, and that he wouldn't ask her to marry him.

When he arrived, as he had promised, he was stiff and solemn, dressed in a conservative gray suit that made his blue eyes and copper hair blaze above it. Decorous in his greeting, he was gallantly polite to Em and Missie. With Ramona's permission, he would be taking the lass for a drive. They wouldna be gone for long.

He aided Ramona into the carriage, careful to touch only her small gloved hand. She settled back in a corner, feeling her pulse racing in an alarming fashion. He was a little frightening, so stiff and proper.

For Dugald's part, he was quite miserable. Maybe sending the gun like that had been a fool thing to do. He'd worried about it, too late. And then he'd done an unprecedented thing. He'd partaken of a wee drop of his own country's spirits. Feeling more relaxed, he'd followed it with another. The false courage it gave him led him to make a scene on the Courtney lawn. It may have even lowered the lass's opinion of him. Perhaps she only accompanied him now out of gratitude for yesterday.

Conscious of the girl at his side, his senses reeling at her nearness, he set his jaw grimly and drove sedately along the Melbourne street. And before either spoke, two streets away from the Courtney house, Ramona gave a little gasp. He followed her pointing finger. Two boys were engaged in fisticuffs on the grassy verge. One of them was young Scott Courtney; the other, a poorly dressed ragamuffin lad.

Denis drew the carriage to a halt and leaped out, separating the two. Scott scrubbed at a bleeding nose, the other boy's eye was bruised and swelling.

"Now, what the bluidy hell is going on?"

"I arsked i'm fer a copper," the ragged boy said sullenly. "And he called me a bloody mug."

"You called me a snob," Scott countered. "And he is a mug, Mr. Dugald. His father's in gaol, his mother's a—"

The young stranger's fists were raised again. "Ye'll say nothin' agin me mum!" he said threateningly.

"You'll wind up in jail too," Scott taunted. "One day you'll hang—like Ned Kelly!"

"Get into the car-r-riage," Dugald thundered. He hauled Ramona's cousin to the buggy and heaved him in, then returned to the other sniveling lad. "Why did ye need a copper?" he asked in a reasonable tone. The boy's

434

hand went to his pocket, and he held out a few pennies in a grubby palm. "I'm short fer a spot of breakfast," he said disconsolately.

Dugald's hand went to his pocket. He dumped a fistful of coins into the boy's hand. "I'm not gieing ye this. Ye'll wor-rk frae it." He scribbed a note. "Take this tae Gover-rnment House. Ask frae a mon named Boswell. He will gie ye a job.

Driving Scott home, he gave him a strict lecture. He had been born to a privileged class. He and his kind drove boys like the other to a life of crime. If the lad did grow up like his father, it would be because he'd not been given a chance.

He dumped him unceremoniously before his home. He was to tell Duke exactly what he'd done, honestly. And it had better tally with the facts, or he, Denis, would see him tonight.

Denis returned glumly to the carriage. It had not been an auspicious beginning to what he'd planned as an ardent courtship. He'd made a fool of himself over the gun, the midnight serenade—and now he'd shown her that he was officious, butting into the situation as he did.

He had no way of knowing that his eyes, as he scolded young Scott, had held the intense expression of Ned Kelly's, when he spoke of the need for justice. Or that he had echoed Ramona's own words, her own thoughts. She longed to put her arms about him and tell him so, but his grim exterior kept her in the corner of the carriage. Perhaps, she thought sadly, he didn't want her anymore. He probably regarded her as a silly little girl.

"I want to thank you for yesterday," she said in a small voice.

"It was against ma better-r joodgement," he said morosely. "It was nae place frae a lassie. I'll wager ye didna sleep well."

"No," she whispered. "I didn't. There—there was a great noise in the night."

His face flamed. "I maun apologize frae that. I thocht a wee drap would ease the day. I am nae accoostumed to spirits, and I fear I wasna maself."

Then he hadn't planned the bagpipe episode. Maybe he'd had a drop too many when he sent the gun, too. She'd read something into it that wasn't there—

She turned from him, watching the countryside roll by.

They drove eastward, where the high ground began to close in about the Yarra-Yarra, the surroundings becoming more beautiful as they climbed. They reached the Botanic Gardens, the Domain, as it was called when it was first begun. Here there was a lake and an aviary with hundreds of rare and beautiful birds; among them, songbirds imported from England; thrushes, linnets, robins, sparrows, blackbirds filled the air with their twittering.

Ramona half expected this to be their destination, but Denis drove on, beauty increasing as they followed the river's course past gardens and vineyards, shady groves of willows.

"I wanted tae tell ye that I'll soon be ganging hame," Denis said abruptly.

Ramona's heart sank. "I thought you'd be here at least until after the first of the year."

"There is naething for me here, and I am needed. There are cotters on our pr-property. The far-rm hae been oonder the hand of a manager these last years. It is rumored he hae not dealt fairly wi' them. Noo, they are ma r-responsibility."

"I see," she said in a small voice.

For awhile they rode again in silence. The road, following the river, turned with it as the Yarra-Yarra almost doubled in its course. Denis steered the buggy off the road, taking a faint trail. He halted the horse and

436

helped her to the ground, careful, again, to avoid too much contact.

"How beautiful," she whispered.

They were on a bluff headland. Below them, the river tumbled and tossed, broken into minature falls. As far as the eye could see, stretched a forest of green to be finally lost in the Dandedong and Plenty Ranges.

"It is like this in the Hielands at hame," Denis said. His arm went out and closed about her, an almost automatic gesture. Ramona felt the old weakness at his touch, her blood thundering in her ears. He tensed, then put her away from him, his hands on her shoulders.

"I'm ganging hame," he said in a rough voice. "Ma father sent me to Austr-ralia to gr-r-ow up. I think I hae doon so, but I maun have help. I wasna r-reared tae onderstond the common mon. I maun have help tae deal wi' the cotters, and sound advice. A woman in the hoose—"

Ramona listened as he stammered, his brogue growing thicker as he tried to say what he had to say. Her bewilderment finally turning into a warm glow at his last words. She looked into his face, set doggedly, a splash of color on his cheeks and the tips of his ears.

"I don't think I understand," she said carefully. "If you could tell me in fewer words—"

"Domn it, lass I'm asking ye to marry me!" he exploded. "Do ye no ken?"

The face she raised to him was shining with happiness, tinged with mischief. "I suppose, if the cotters really need me, I must say yes."

With a great cry, he caught her to him, nearly squeezing the breath from her small body. "Cotters be dommed," he said hoarsely. "I'm the ain who needs ye! Guid God, how I need ye!" She had time for one breath, and then his mouth was on hers. She felt dizzy, the blood in her veins turning to warm, melting honey. The view before her tilted, righted itself, tilted again as they strove to get closer, to become one.

Finally he led her to the shadow of a tree, and they sat down on the soft grass at its foot, still holding to each other.

"I want to love ye her-re and now," he said distractedly, "but tis against ma code. But I swear-r, if ye try tae escape me again—"

"Never," Ramona whispered. "Never!"

"The nicht at Rippon Lea," he said. "I thocht ye were mine. Do you r-r-remember? Noo, I'm afear-rd tae let ye go!"

The night at Rippon Lea. Indeed she remembered. The arched bridge, the singing waterfall, the flower-scented breeze; the magic of his touch that frightened her. She had been haunted by it ever since that time.

And she had asked him for two things: that their marriage be delayed until Christmas; and for two hundred pounds to be used in Ned Kelly's defense.

"I would like to explain," she said, looking up at him with honest eyes.

"Dinna bother, lass," he said huskily. "I know ye, noo. Ye had to get this other-r frae your mind. I was fear-ring tae ask ye tae marry me, thinking maybe it was twa soon."

"When you woke us last night, Missie said that— that the sad things happened yesterday. That it was already tomorrow."

"Missie is a wise young lass. Ramona—" his voice held a note of yearning. "Ramona—"

She raised her eyes, seeing the depths of love that shone in his, the ray of sun that penetrated the shade to touch his hair, turning the lock that fell over his forehead to fire.

"Denis!" She pulled his head to her breast, and

cradled him like a child; this great boy who had become a man, and whom she loved.

All day, they stayed on the bluff, and on into the gentle evening. When night fell, sweet and perfumed, they stayed on for another little while. One last embrace, one last kiss—and the stars still spun like silver comets in the sky at his touch.

Chapter 56

As Denis and Ramona left their trysting place to carry their glorious news to the Courtney home, another carriage was nearing the same destination. Tamsen and Dan had reached the last leg of their journey.

It had been a long and arduous trek, but they'd managed to complete it before the worst of the heat set in, the group they traveled with moving faster than the camel train that had taken Tamsen to her husband.

Now, coming from the small ship that had carried them from Adelaide, in a hired hack with a driver, Tamsen reached to touch Dan's hand. He was rigid, tense.

"We're almost there," she said softly. There was no answer.

She knew what he was feeling. In Alice Springs, he'd grown to accept his blindness, regarding it as a handicap, rather than a deficiency that made him less than a man. On the long journey to Adelaide, they'd traveled with people who knew him, knew his problem. But in Adelaide, no one knew him. He'd reverted to his depression for a time, feeling that people were pointing at him, seeing him as a curiosity: a man led about by a small, frail woman.

She'd insisted on staying there for several days, coaxing him to walk about the bright, well-planned city of about one hundred and sixty thousand people. The city itself had been fixed at an area of a square mile. It was surrounded by parklands. They visited the private market at one end of the small metropolis, the municipal market at the other, Tamsen describing everything in detail. They purchased gigantic meat pies and baked potatoes on the street, from the "saveloy man" with his portable, horse-drawn oven; pigs trotters from ancient women peddling them in wicker baskets. They drank coffee from the open-air stalls, made in charcoal-heated boxes, with funnels protruding from the roof, the price varying from one shilling to three shillings per cup, depending on its strength.

They walked, crossing the Adelaide Bridge at the end of King William Street; the Victoria Bridge at the end of Morphett; and the Albert at the end of Frome; all leading from the city to the parklands. They visited churches, and attended a church fete at the home of Sir Edwin Smith at Marryatville, Adelaide.

They visited a spiritualist, who advertised "solar harps, materialization of Beings of Unearthly Beauty, Cherubs in the Air, Stone-throwing by Unseen Agencies, Odic Forces," and other inducements, and left, laughing together. They tried a phrenologist, one of the newest crazes to sweep Australia, and discovered they were both of excellent character, well-matched in the amative zones —and were offered advice on the rearing of their children.

In the same spirit of fun, Tamsen insisted Dan visit Thomas Bastard's Turkish Bath. It couldn't hurt him, and something about the proprietor's name appealed to her. He obeyed, and they laughed for hours, quoting his poetic advertisement.

We'll go and take a Turkish Bath:
'Twill make you supple as a lath,
'Twill set you up from head to toe
And put your system in a glow.

"Are you supple?" she asked teasingly.

"Try me!"

And, a little later, he would ask, "Are you glowing?"

Dan's initial depression, his concern that he was an oddity, vanished in the warmth of their companionship. It had been a wonderful experience, the two of them alone in a strange city. But now, as their hired hack rolled towards the Courtney home, he was again despondent.

"I still think we should have wired them from Adelaide," he said jerkily. "I'm afraid it will be a shock, walking in on them cold like this."

"I told you, Dan! You don't *look* any different!" She smiled lovingly into his haunted blank eyes. "They'll be so glad to see us they won't notice until we've had time to explain. If we'd wired, they'd be expecting an invalid. You said you didn't want to be treated like one."

He forced a taut smile. "I suppose you're right, sweetheart."

"Relax." She put a hand to his dark, tumbled hair, pushing it back to reveal a tanned forehead. In spite of his infirmity, he had never looked so good. He'd regained his lost weight, the long smooth muscles again rippling beneath his shirt. Her hand left his hair, passed down over his muscular shoulders, his flat middle, teasing him.

He caught at it, laughing, and pressed it to his lips. "Remember, we're respectable, old married people. I may be blind, but they're not."

"We're here," she said, trying to hide her nervousness. She waited as he gave the driver of the carriage change she'd counted out for him. Then, slowly, she led

443

her husband up the walk. Taking a deep breath, she lifted the brass knocker, and let it fall.

She had expected Em to answer. The small figure that appeared in the doorway staggered her. For a minute, they stared at each other, unable to speak.

"Missie! Dear God, Missie! You're all right!"

"Aunt Tamsen—and Uncle Dan!"

Tamsen burst into tears, and Missie followed suit. Em entered behind Missie and called frantically for Duke. He came running, followed by Scott and Vickie. He stood for a minute, confused. The chaos created by three crying women, all asking questions at once, was mind-boggling. His face lit up as he saw his brother-in-law, still standing outside the entry.

He went toward the door, shoving past the knot of weeping females, a broad grin on his face. "Dan Tallant! Goddam, it's good to see you! Hell, don't stand there like a stranger! Come in."

Dan's mouth tensed. He put out a seeking hand, finding the doorframe, and stepped inside, grazing a shoulder as he did so. Duke looked at him, puzzled. Had the man been drinking? "It's good to have you home," he said heartily, extending his hand. For a moment, Dan stood still, then put out his own hand, bypassing Duke's extended one.

Shock hit Duke like a blow to the midsection as he looked into Dan's unseeing eyes. He drew a ragged breath, seeking to right himself, then put a strong hand on his old friend's arm and led him toward the study.

"Let's leave these women until they get their tears under control," he said, in what he hoped was a normal voice. "Never could stand the sight of a woman's tears."

Closing the door behind him, he maneuvered Tallant to a chair, drawing it up so that he could feel it against the back of his legs. "Sit down," he said genially. "We've

444

got a lot of catching up to do. I suppose you want to know how the station—"

"You know, don't you. It's obvious that I've lost my sight."

Duke sighed. He poured a small glass of brandy, which he placed in Tallant's hand, then one for himself. He stood with his back to his desk, leaning against it as he sipped at his drink and studied the man before him.

"How did it happen?"

Dan sketched it out for him in as few words as possible. He'd been ill, after a trip to Darwin. Returning home, he found a wire—sent by one of the hands, according to Tamsen—telling about Missie's disappearance, the fire, and saying that Tamsen needed him. He'd been off his head when he started home, and suddenly found himself blind. The illness, perhaps a heat stroke—He didn't know the true cause.

"The question," he said wearily, "is not what caused this problem—but what I'm going to do now. By selling the station, I can just about clear my debts, but after that—Well, what can a blind man do? I had hoped Tamsen would forget me. I tried to let her think it was all over between us. For a woman like that to be tied down to half a man! God, I wish I'd died!"

"Don't be a fool," Duke said roughly. Now the wires Tam had received, her brief fling with Ian Gregory, began to make sense. "We'll work out something. Em and I are talking about moving back to San Francisco. There are doctors there—"

Dan shook his head stubbornly. "I'll find something to do here. I'm pretty good at harness mending."

Duke scowled into his glass, swirling the smoky liquid as if he might find an answer there. Goddam Tallant and his pride! Well, he'd find a way around it, somehow.

In the room with the others, Tamsen suddenly came to her senses. She'd meant to shield Dan, to casually mention that he had a small visual difficulty at the present. And in the shock of seeing Missie safe and well, she'd allowed everything else to escape her mind. She had a vague memory of seeing him with Duke, moving toward the study.

Disentangling herself from Missie's clinging arms, she ran toward the study door, opening it. Duke leaned against his desk, facing her. "It's all right," he mouthed, soundlessly, gesturing for her to go. She closed the door quietly.

Dan's hearing, intensified by his disability, heard the opening and closing door. "Tamsen?" he asked with a wry grin.

"Tamsen," Duke chuckled. "Dan, you really didn't think you could get rid of her, did you?"

Meanwhile, Tamsen took the opportunity to tell the others of Dan's problem. Again, Missie and Em burst into tears. "It's all right," Tamsen comforted them. "Now, Missie, you haven't told me—"

"I'm a widow," Missie said quietly. "Arthur's dead. I'd rather not go into details tonight. You have enough problems of your own. Mama and Papa and Luka are at Opal Station. Ramona and I are here—

As if the mention of her name had triggered the action, Ramona flung the door wide, "Aunt Em, I—!" She stopped, her eyes growing huge as she took in the members of the group. "Aunt Tamsen!"

She flung herself into Tamsen's arms, Denis Dugald standing by, a rather sheepish grin on his face as the woman and the lass, both with long dark hair and big, heartbreaking eyes, indulged in a tearful reunion.

Finally, Ramona, remembering the news she'd planned to announce, stepped back to stand beside him, her small hand engulfed in his large one.

"You've come at just the right time," she said happily. "Denis and I have something to tell you."

From the expression in her starry eyes, the look of worship she directed up at the tall young Scot, Tamsen knew what her next words were going to be.

"Denis and I are going to be married. I'm going to be Mrs. Denis Dugald."

Duke Courtney and Dan Tallant came from the study to join in the congratulations. Dan handled himself well. With Duke's firm hand guiding him, he had no trouble greeting the young couple without disclosing his problem. As the party began to break up, Denis going home to Government House, Tallant found his hand on the familiar stair rail.

He smiled in the direction of Em's voice. "Same room?" he asked. "or is it occupied."

"The same room."

Bidding them all good night, he climbed the stairs without faltering, his habit of counting steps, feet, miles, coming to his aid without conscious thought.

Tamsen watched him go, holding her breath. She was proud of him. More proud than she had ever been. He would be brave enough to cope—with anything.

She turned again to look at Ramona's beaming face. She was glad her niece's wonderful evening would not be spoiled by news of her uncle's infirmity. They had all silently agreed to spare her the details until tomorrow.

Chapter 57

The whole family was shocked at learning of Dan's blindness, but within a few days, it had become an accepted fact. The hubbub of preparing for Ramona's wedding overrode everything else. Duke employed a station manager to relieve Juan of his duties for the coming month, sending him to Opal Station with a number of messages.

Tamsen and Dan had returned. Dan was blind, but was to be treated in a normal manner. They were to come at once, upon the arrival of Donald Fellows, who was to handle the station's affairs while they were gone. They must be sure to bring Nell, since this was to be a family reunion. Oh, and Tamsen requested that they bring her old cashbox. They were to come as quickly as possible, and remain until after Christmas—and hurry!

They didn't mention Ramona's engagement. That was something for a girl to tell her mother face to face, a fact in which Missie strongly concurred. In the meantime, invitations must be prepared, announcements sent to the papers. Arab was going to get her wish: Em was determined to make Ramona's the wedding of the year.

The first announcement appeared on November twenty-third. Denis Dugald found it, a lengthy item, telling of their engagement and wedding plans for Christmas Day. He arrived at the Courtney home, beaming, a number of copies of the same issue beneath his arm.

The two sat on a couch, heads together, poring over the article that somehow made the coming event more real. Ramon's face was glowing with happiness. Then it suddenly went white.

"Look," she said, pointing a trembling finger.

Judge Sir Redmond Barry was dead.

"I will see you where I am going," Ned Kelly had said.

"Denis—You don't think—?"

He took her in his arms without answering, since there was no way he could say, honestly, that Kelly's statement had not been a prediction. He considered himself a realist, a down-to-earth man. But in his background, the dark blood of the Celt lurked, steeped in superstition.

"Denis?"

"I dinna know, lassie. I dinna know."

He was left to brood on it alone, since his wife-to-be was soon caught up in a flurry of fittings and appointments. Her trousseau was to be Em's gift, the forlorn groom completely superflous in the planning, except for consultations on materials suited to Scotland where they would make their home.

The bridal gown was begun. It was to be of white, with a bell-skirt, scalloped at the hem with an edging of narrow ribbon. A small under-bustle would accent the tiny waist which would come to a point in front. Ramona's pretty shoulders would be bared in a deep, heart-shaped neckline, misted over with a full veil.

The gown would be "something new." For something old and something blue, she would wear a garter Cammie had worn at her wedding; it would also count for something borrowed. Her only ornament would be a jade locket Aunt Tamsen had had for years, a lucky piece. She remembered her taking it from her cashbox when she, Ramona, was a child. "I'll give it to you on your wedding day," she promised then.

The gown was finished. Ramona, clad in its shimmering beauty, stood still as the veil was put in place, the dressmaker kneeling to mark it for its fine hem. Em, Tamsen, Vickie and Missie, had gathered to admire the almost completed product when Missie chanced to glance out of the window.

"They're here," she gasped. "They're coming up the walk! Mama, Papa, Luka—Nell! Take it off! I'll stall them!

Ramona held out a hand. "Wait. I wanted Denis to be with me—but—Missie, answer the door and bring them up here."

She moved to the center of the room and stood waiting, her head high, her face radiant, arms at her sides, curving gently foward.

She waited, serenely, for some time. Missie had been caught up in a deluge of hugs and kisses. Crushed at last in a bearhug from Nell, it was a short space before she could even speak. Finally, she gasped, "Upstairs—"

They looked at her curiously, but asked no questions as they filed up behind her, Nell puffing along in the rear. Reaching the room she shared with her sister, Missie flung the door wide, stepping aside.

Arab stopped short, her slanting green eyes wide. As realization came to her, they glassed over, her lip beginning to tremble. "Ramona, you're not—You're not—"

The pause was broken when Luka pushed past her mother and ran toward her sister. "You look like a bride," she said. "Oh, Ramona! You look just like a bride!"

451

Ramona bent to place a kiss on the girl's soft cheek. "That's because I am one," she whispered. "Or will be. I'm going to marry Denis, Luka. On Christmas Day."

Arab was finally able to move. She had her arms around Ramona, around Tamsen, around Em, tears mingling with her laughter. Juan, trying to reach his daughter, finally shrugged, smiling at her over Arab's red gold head, indicating that he was saving their reunion for later. He left the room with mixed emotions; happy that Ramona had found someone as fine as young Dugald; sad that she wouldn't be coming home with them as he had hoped. Arab had missed her daughters dreadfully. Now Ramona would be far away, in Scotland. Missie—Missie was lost to them, too. Married, widowed, she was now an adult. She didn't belong in the outback, but in an area where she could feed her intellect. Books, lectures, those were the things she thrived on.

Ramona was going, Missie would not come home. And Arab was growing more unhappy every day, begging him to give up his work at the station and move to Melbourne, Sydney, Adelaide—anywhere.

He had been considering such a course of action when Dan returned. But now—he couldn't bear to see Arab pining away at Opal Station, and neither could he desert a blind man.

He met young Scott in the hall. The boy led him to the room where Dan Tallant sat, going over the Courtney harness with practiced fingers; a job he'd insisted on doing.

After their initial greeting, two long-time friends happy to be together once more, they got down to business. The station was in good shape. The fire, followed by rain, had brought a fresh greening of tender young shoots. The cattle Duke Courtney had placed there on a share basis were waxing fat. There would be enough profit to pay their debts, and see them into another year.

"Are you and Arab happy there?" Tallant asked suddenly. "Would you want to spend the rest of your life on the station?"

Juan stammered something to the effect that he was happy. "But you know how Arab is," he finished miserably. "She wants me to come to Melbourne, work for Duke."

"Duke won't be here. He plans to return to San Francisco after the first of the year. He wants us all to go with him."

"Then—you're going?"

Dan shook his head. "I won't be a dead weight," he said. "If you go, I will probably sell Opal Station, and open a small leather shop here. I think I can earn a living for the two of us, Tamsen and myself.

"Dios, man! We've been together all these years!"

"And you've carried the load when I've been gone. I'm settled now, and"—he grinned—"I think I'm beginning to like it. If you go, I sell; it's as simple as that."

"I don't know," Juan admitted. "I've got to talk to Courtney."

"No hurry. Why don't we just forget the whole thing until after the wedding. No need to mention any of this to Arab until then."

It was just as well. The house was so beset with confusion those last days before Christmas that no one could think a clear thought through. The previous day, it seemed nothing went right, but on Christmas morning all loose ends had been pulled together. Em, svelte in a fashionable costume of powder blue, was helping Arab, gowned in mist green, in dressing the bride. Tamsen left the room for a moment, going to the cashbox, lifting out the jade pendant. As she removed it, she heard a slither of paper in the bottom drawer. Frowning, she lifted it out. It was addressed to Nell—in Dusty's hand.

For a moment, she blinked back tears. When had the paper been placed there, and why? There was no time to look at it now. Leaving it on the bureau, she rushed to Ramona's room to place the pendant about the girl's slim golden throat.

"You look lovely," she whispered.

"Ten more minutes." Arab's eyes were misty.

That long? Perhaps there was time to peruse the paper, see what it was. For some reason, it weighed heavily on her mind. But she must check on Vickie, Missie, and Luka who were serving as attendants.

And to add to the confusion, Em's oldest daughter Martha had arrived, coming from her far off home, just in time.

Tamsen and Dan were the last to take their places in the seats reserved for the family. Em's drawing room was a bower of flowers, at this time in midsummer. Along the walls, servants, hired for the occasion, waved palm fronds to stir a breeze. Each lady carried her own fan of carved ivory and painted silks, moving it gracefully in time to the music.

A Christmas wedding, complete with hundred degree temperatures and blooming flowers.

With a graceful flick of her wrist, Tamsen opened her own fan, and Dan leaned closer to feel the breeze. Then the music changed its tempo, the attendants coming down the aisle, one by one. First Cammie, matron of honor, on her husband's arm. Then Duke Courtney escorting Missie; a blushing boy with Vickie; Scott, with little Luka, her slanting silver eyes glowing with an eerie beauty.

Again, the music changed. The fans ceased their motion, Arab uttering a little sob as the bride came down the aisle on her father's arm, a creature of mist and light, to stand beside a tall Scot in dress kilts. His copper-shining head bent lovingly toward his small dark bride.

Ramona and Denis: another joining of lives. I'm old Tamsen thought. And this is another thread in the web of years. Soon they will have children.

Her eyes wandered to the newly arrived Martha; her oldest child, near Luka's age, was a lovely creature with an odd Oriental look; the younger ones, two sturdy boys, looked very like their father. Martha seemed happy, though she was a little tired and worn; Martha, who had once seemed a version of her own younger self, now growing older.

Martha, intent on the ceremony, felt the brush of Tamsen's eyes and turned to smile at her. What does *she* see, Tamsen wondered. Is she thinking, like I am, that her Aunt Tamsen is aging fast? What will she look like, after so many weddings, funerals—

Dear God, what grim thoughts for a wedding day! She forced her gaze back to the young couple before the minister.

"Do you take this woman . . . ?"

"I do."

"Do you take this man . . . ?"

"I do."

Tamsen knew the words by heart. Only the brides and grooms changed.

"I now pronounce you man and wife."

Denis bent, gently putting back Ramona's veil, and kissed the mouth she raised to his. There was a hush, a long sigh, and the two turned to face the room as the Recessional sounded. Ramona glowed like a candle, a light from within.

Tamsen flinched as Dan's fingers dug into her arm. She turned to face him. He was white.

"I *saw* her," he whispered under cover of the music. "I saw her for a minute! A little blurred, but, oh, God, sweetheart, she looked like you!"

"Can you see now?"

He shook his head and her heart plunged. But at least it was a sign. She could begin to hope.

It wasn't until she began to help Em serve that she found Ian Gregory numbered among the guests. The mention of Ramona's coming wedding had been listed in the Sydney papers. He had cut short his visit, returning to find, to his surprise, an invitation to the wedding addressed in Duke Courtney's hand. Perhaps the man had addressed it automatically, using an old guest list. No matter, he would go. It would be a joy to see Ramona a bride.

He had not been in Melbourne for two days when a young lady, piqued by his earlier attentions to Tamsen Tallant, pettily told him the story of that intrepid woman, traveling all the way to Alice Springs by camel train, to find her blind husband and bring him back. He would be certain to meet him at the wedding.

Well, now they had met. Duke Courtney had turned, first white, then red when he walked up to them. "Gregory," he said to his one-time friend. "Good God! I thought you were still in Sydney."

"I wouldn't miss Ramona's wedding." He smiled, then looked to the tall man beside Courtney and back with a question in his eyes.

"This—I'd like you to meet my brother-in-law, Daniel Tallant," Duke stammered. "Dan, this is Ian Gregory, a representative of Her Majesty."

Ian Gregory studied the tall man, seeing dark long-lashed eyes that looked blankly at him from a strong face, slightly etched with lines of suffering. He was a handsome devil, with a mass of dark hair falling over his temples, a touch of silver at the sides. He shook hands, feeling strength in the grip that matched his own.

They chatted casually for a time, and finally Gregory excused himself. "I'd like to talk with you further," he said casually. "Perhaps next week?"

"A pleasure," Dan bowed.

Duke left Tallant in Juan's care for a moment and went looking for Em. "Why the hell did you invite Gregory?" he growled.

"I didn't. Was he on your guest list?"

Duke reddened. He'd handed it over for someone else to do. But how the hell was he to know the fellow wasn't in Sydney? The least they could do now was keep him away from Tamsen.

"Duke, I've got my hands full!" Em wailed. "Listen!"

Nell, in a corner, was holding an audience of quivering ladies enthralled. "So I figgered, after all them gawdam years of foolin' around, it wuz now er never. So I married the leetle sonofabitch on his deathbed. A bride an' a widder, all the same day, you might say."

"Too much champagne," Em whispered. "Duke, stop her."

The problem of Ian Gregory was forgotten as the Courtneys graciously coaxed Nell upstairs. Ramona wished to speak to her before she went away.

So it was that Tamsen, making certain that everyone had been served, looked up to meet a pair of sober gray eyes. Remembering their last meeting, and the way she'd left him waiting, she shrank. Whatever he had to say, she deserved it.

"I am glad to see you're back," he said in a dry voice. "I've just met your husband. A most interesting man."

She lifted her chin. "I think so."

He extended his glass. "Perhaps some more champagne?"

Her hand shook as she filled it, and she knew he saw it. "Ian," she said fiercely, "I want to explain—"

"Excuse me," he said. "I see Mrs. Sargood. I haven't spoken with her yet."

And he was gone, leaving Tamsen sick inside with a strange uneasiness.

There was music, singing, dancing, but she did not catch sight of him again. And finally Ramona came down the stairs in her traveling gown of sheerest, softest wool, so fine the yardage could have been drawn through her wedding ring.

Smiling, the bride tossed her bouquet. It was young Luka who caught it, to Missie's amusement and Vickie's disappointment. And then they were gone in a shower of rice, their marriage decorated with streamers. They would stay at a hotel tonight. Tomorrow, the family would congregate to see them off at the dock, on their way to Scotland and home.

That night, Tamsen turned the light low and began to undress, thinking of Ramona and Denis experiencing the wonder of their first night of love. She felt an ache of nostalgia at the memory of her own wedding night; the magic of knowing that she and Dan were sealed together forever.

Thinking what marriage meant, the shared joys and sorrows, she sighed, praying that Ramona would know only joy. Moving to the wardrobe, she hung up her things and took down a filmy gown, the lamplight gilding her slim body.

"Wait," Dan said from the bed. "Just stand there! Oh, God! Tamsen, I see you! I see you! Blurred, but I see you!"

She ran to him, cradling his head against her, tears falling on his face. Please God, oh, please, God—

"It's gone now," he said quietly. "But it lasted longer this time."

Lying in his arms, she wondered why she'd envied Ramona. This was the happiest day of her life.

The paper on top of the bureau had been forgotten.

Chapter 58

The turmoil in the Courtney household had not ended. In the morning, the family went en masse to the docks to see the newly married couple on their way. Ramona was radiant as she kissed the members of her family good-bye, clinging a little longer to Missie. Denis couldn't seem to stop grinning, his handsome face filled with pride as he kept his eyes on his little wife.

They boarded, and the ship weighed anchor. The family stood for a long time, watching until they could no longer see the beacon of the tall Scot's sun-fired hair.

Arab wept in her husband's arms. "It's so far," she kept saying. "So far! Juan, we'll never see her again."

"We still have Missie and Luka," he reminded her.

She wasn't comforted. In these last difficult months, she'd forgotten her preoccupation with her youngest child. She wanted them all. And now her family was breaking up—Dusty dead—

"I can't stand it," she sobbed.

He led her toward their carriage, knowing that she would feel better by the day's end. How different the sisters were! Arab, with all her feelings on the outside; Tamsen, who held hers in, and sweet, grave Em.

Yet he knew that Arab was the only woman for him in the world.

Tamsen, though she was overjoyed at Ramona's happiness, felt almost ill with the trauma of parting from the girl who had been like a daughter to her. The heat, now that the couple had gone, was enervating. She was glad it was over and done. She led Dan to the carriage they shared with Martha, Peter Channing, and small Petra, the Channing sons having gone with their grandmother.

"I want to sit by Tamsen," young Petra said.

"*Aunt* Tamsen," Martha corrected her, smiling. "In fact, it's Great-Aunt Tamsen."

Great Aunt! Oh, dear God! Again Tamsen felt the weight of years settle around her.

"She isn't *great*," the child said candidly. "She's little. And I don't think she's an aunt. Aunts are old."

Dan chuckled as Tamsen moved to allow Petra to sit between them, laying his arm across the seat to touch his wife's shoulder. It had become so important to him, this touching.

Reaching the Courtneys' home, the men retired to the study for another of their interminable business conferences, and Tamsen went to her room, removing her hat and veil. Her gaze fell on the paper she'd found in the bottom of the cashbox. In the excitement of Ramona's wedding, she'd completely forgotten it! She decided to search for Nell, who, rather than face the heat, had remained behind, napping while the others went to see the newly married couple off.

Tamsen knocked at the door and entered to find the big woman clad in her faded pink wrapper, its trimming of feathers long since molted. Her face was red, and she waved a bedraggled fan that, like the wrapper, had seen better days—in less genteel surroundings.

"Hotter'n hell, ain't it?" she said in greeting. "Seems like it gits hotter everplace we go. Mebbe I'm gittin' in training' fer the Hereafter. Hell, I ain't seen snow in a coon's age. Don't seem like yestiddy was Chrismus."

Tamsen felt a wave of nostalgia, remembering her childhood home in Pennsylvania. After Arab's birth, it had been a motherless household. But there were snowflakes falling like white stars, the sound of sleighbells—

Enough of remembering. "I found this in my cashbox," she said. "It has your name on it. Do you know anything about it?"

Nell looked puzzled for a minute, then her face cleared. "Hell, yes! The leetle bastard give it to me the night he passed on. Said to put it in a safe place, so I stuck it in there an' fergot it. Whut's it say?"

"I haven't read it, Nell. It's addressed to you."

"Dammit, Tam, see whut it sez. You know I can't read the damn thing without my specs!"

Tamsen hid a smile as she unfolded the paper. She had never seen Nell with glasses, and doubted she'd ever owned a pair. It was almost certain the bluff old woman had never learned to read, yet she had fallen back on the same excuse for years.

"It says, that in the event of Dusty's death, you are to call upon a Melbourne barrister. A Robert Curney. It gives his address."

"Whut fer?" Nell was uneasy. "D'you figger th' leetle devil got himself in some kinda bind?" She snorted fondly. "Be jes like th' leetle fart to die off an' leave me holdin' th' bag!"

"I don't think it's that, Nell. Maybe it's something like a will."

She snorted again. "Will, hell! Leetle sonofabitch didden have no reason fer one. Never had more'n two cents in his gawdam pocket. Drank it up. I say fergit th' whole thing. Can't be nuthin' but trubble."

"No, Nell. I think you should check this out. It might be important. I'll take you there, myself."

Nell's beady eyes widened. "Now? In this gawdam

heat? Hell, I can't even stand my drawers, let alone havin' to git gussied up."

An hour later, Tamsen and Nell were bowling along Elizabeth in Em's buggy, Nell complaining every foot of the way. When they located the address on the message, Nell assumed an expression of misery as she panted up the narrow stairs that led to a second-story office. It changed to one of indignant self-righteousness as Tamsen read the sign on the door aloud.

"Closed until after the holidays! Wouldn't you know!"

"Hell, I tolja so!" As far as Nell was concerned, they ought to forget the whole damn thing.

As the days passed, Dan's eyesight improved—or at least, the periods of time when he had some vision lengthened. The house was still full to overflowing, what with the Tallants, the Narváez family, the Courtneys and the Channings. Occasionally Cammie dropped by, happy for the chance to visit with her sister. She had a secret to reveal, and was waiting for the proper moment.

She still hadn't mentioned it on the day after New Year's. The Channings and their children were returning to their remote station, leaving in the morning. Em had fluttered about, insisting on sending along a load of supplies, as if keeping busy would ease the pain of seeing them, go. She saw them so seldom, and now Duke was talking about returning to San Francisco. Martha and Peter were happy here. This would be their permanent home.

Maybe, she thought, Duke would change his mind.

He hadn't. On the steaming afternoon of that last day, he called everyone together: Dan, Tamsen; Arab, Juan and Missie; Nell, all the members of his own family, down to the youngest grandchild. He hadn't said anything earlier, since he wanted this visit to be a happy one. He had sold his various businesses, except for a wool export firm. He planned to go into the import-export field in San Francisco.

He, Em, Vickie and Scott would be leaving in two months. He had discussed his going with Juan and Dan, suggesting they go with him, taking their families. They were as yet undecided, but the offer was open.

Arab paled. San Francisco held some ugly memories for her; something had happened to her there as a child, which she did not wish to remember. And there had been the year the banks failed; when Senator Alden, Em's first husband, had been innocently involved in the scandal. Juan, working for him, had been tarred with the same brush. Alden put them on a ship, sending Juan, Arab, Em and little Martha in search of Tamsen.

Then he had gone to a rented room and killed himself.

How could Em go back there! She looked at her sister's serene expression. How confident she must be in her love for Duke Courtney to forget the past and return to its setting.

Tamsen's face had reddened. She had gone back to San Francisco once after her marriage, and somehow the papers had got hold of her return, playing up the notorious Madam Franklin who had operated a brothel on Stockton Street; Madam Franklin, Tamsen's other self. And they'd published an old photograph that revealed too much.

For years, she'd been hiding away at Opal Station, trying to make herself into something she wasn't. And she'd almost lost Dan.

Could she face up to it again? The tales, the rumors, the knowing glances that followed her on the street?

She reached to squeeze Dan's hand. "Whatever you want to do," she told him quietly.

"I still don't know," he whispered back. "And neither does Juan. I turned him down, but now that I'm beginning to see——" He left it there.

It was Cammie who provided the unexpected opposition. "Mama, you can't go," she gasped. "I'm expecting a baby!"

Em made a hurt sound, and Martha jumped into the breach. "Of course she can," she said matter-of-factly. "I think it's wonderful. As for having a baby, that's your job, not Mama's. I wasn't going to mention it, but I'm expecting, too."

Missie sat listening with shining eyes. In San Francisco, there would be large newspapers, perhaps publishers; libraries, schools, where she could embellish the education she'd acquired from Papa and Dusty.

The conference dissolved into a gabble of congratulations and tears. And next morning the Channings were on their way home, laden with supplies from Em's storehouse and kitchen. Em watched them go, her heart too full for words. Martha was not Duke's child, nor Alden's. She'd been a child of rape. But that made her no less dear to Duke, nor to herself. She'd been a prickly girl in her growing up; unlike the calm Cammie and—she smiled at her analysis of her children—spoiled-baby Vickie. More like Arab's Missie.

She put her arm around Missie's thin waist, feeling a surge of love for the girl. She'd seen her eyes when Duke mentioned San Francisco. She would consider it a wonderland.

The Channings out of sight, they all turned back to the house. Duke had to see his barrister this morning regarding the sale of the house. The word barrister jogged Tamsen's memory, and Nell reacted defensively under her gaze.

"If yer thinkin' on seein' that lawyer feller today, Tam, fergit it. Hell, he's prob'ly still off on a binge. I got better things t'do, dammit."

"Get dressed," Tamsen said quietly. "We're going to town."

Again, they climbed the dusty stairs, Nell puffing and blowing like a steam engine. This time, the door was open. It led into a tiny cubicle with a door at the far end. A prim woman with a pencil thrust into her yellowing hair ushered Nell in, offering Tamsen a seat on a horsehair settee.

It seemed only minutes until the door opened and Nell's face appeared in the aperture. Her face was pasty white, her jowls quivering, the beady eyes dazed.

"Tam," she said in a hoarse voice, "Git th' hell in here! I needja!"

The barrister, Robert Curney, a small man who appeared to have been mummified and placed in a setting of dusty texts, looked as dazed as Nell. He cowered a little as she clumped back to her chair and dropped into it with little regard for its age.

"Read th' damn thing to her," she ordered.

Curney adjusted his glasses. *"I, William Winston Wotherspoon, being of sound mind—"*

"Oh, hell," she snorted. "Cut out th' crap! Git to th' facks!"

Cringing, a furtive eye on Nell, Curney skipped the preliminaries and got hastily to the point. The small English gentleman, whom this lady referred to as Dusty, had come to his office some time ago. It appeared that he was a member of a noble British family; a second son, his brother having inherited the title upon his father's death. A short time before this will was drawn, the brother had met his demise, leaving no heirs.

"Sir William—"

"Didja hear that, Tam? *Sir* William! I'm a gawdam lady!" Nell interjected.

Robert Curney pursed his lips. "Sir William had no desire to return, or to claim his inheritance. However, he

467

requested that I research the validity of his inheritance, and take care of the death duties. There will be more, of course, but—"

"List them bequeathses," Nell insisted.

Curney sighed. This was highly irregular. The man had left the majority of his estate, including a large manor—or a small castle, if you will—to a woman to be known as Nell Campbell, or Mrs. Nell Wotherspoon, whichever the case might be."

"Leetle bastard already knowed I'd marry him," Nell said fondly.

In addition to the home and estate, she was to receive an ample sum for life.

Each of the children of Emmeline Courtney and Arabella Narvaéz were to receive, outright, five thousand pounds, with the exception of Melissa Narvaéz, known as Missie, who was to receive fifteen thousand, to further her career.

Realizing that the dead cannot govern the living, he could only request that Juan Narvaéz and Daniel Tallant, with their families, accompany Nell Campbell, or Nell Wotherspoon, to her new home in England. In this case, they were to be salaried at ten thousand pounds per annum for their assistance in handling her affairs.

Should this course of action not meet with their approval, a lump payment of fifty thousand pounds should be bestowed upon Tamsen McLeod Tallant, Arabella McLeod Narvaéz, and Emmeline McLeod Courtney, the latter to receive her bequest in any case.

The monies should not be regarded as a gift, but as an honorable settlement of debts incurred by the deceased, over a lifetime.

At the close of the document was a personal note, again highly irregular. Barrister Curney read it with some distaste.

"I have know I am terminally ill for some time. I

want to tell you that I regard the McLeod girls as my daughters. I am not afraid of dying and if I can persuade the most wonderful girl in the world to become my wife, I shall die happily."

Nell was openly crying, her face red-splotched, her gigantic body quivering with the depth of her emotion. "Th' leetle sonofabitch," she kept saying. "the leetle bastard! Wooden you know he'd pull some gawdam stunt like this!"

Tamsen, who had sat through the whole reading in stunned silence, fought her way back to reality. She was alarmed at Nell's condition. She had better get her back to Em's before she had a stroke. She rose and lifted the old woman to her feet.

"Mr. Courtney will call on you for further details," she said hastily. "Duke Courtney."

Curney was vastly relieved. He had not met Courtney personally, but he knew the man moved in the nicer social circles. And anything would be better than the interview he'd just concluded.

Tamsen took Nell back to the Courtney home. No one was in sight. Probably Duke was still away on his errand, and the others resting through the heat, after their emotional morning. It was just as well. It would give Nell time to get herself under control. By mutual consent, they agreed to save the news until dinner that evening.

Tamsen helped Nell to her room, and washed the red, perspiring face. Finally she left her, tight corsets removed, reclining on the bed in the familiar pink wrapper.

When the door closed behind Tamsen, Nell opened one eye and looked at the ceiling. "Well, ye leetle bastard," she said affectionately to the small shadow that was always with her, "you done it agin! Jes' about th' time I think I know you, you hit me over the gawdam head with sompin' else! All you ever tolt me wuz you

469

wuzn't good enough fer them folks back home. Well, I'm goin' over there, an' I'm goin' to show them how th' cow et th' cabbage, damned if I ain't. An' I'm gonna be one hell of a lady, you jes' watch my dust!"

Having gotten that off her chest, she settled her chins on her ample bosom, and slept.

dropped one, finally managing to squeeze enough juice, then breaking the pitcher.

It was a full ten minutes before she approached the door again. She paused for a moment to listen.

"— and I hope you'll consider it," Ian Gregory was saying. "It would be the best course for all concerned."

"I don't know," Dan answered heavily. "Tamsen will have to be consulted. After all, it concerns her. All I want is what's best for her."

"Just promise that you'll think it over."

"I will," Dan answered in a tired voice. "I certainly will."

Tamsen flung the door wide and entered, setting down the tray she carried on Duke's desk with a crash. She placed a glass firmly in Dan's reaching hand, and turned on Gregory. "Serve yourself," she said crisply. "I don't want to interrupt anything."

She went out again, slamming the door behind her. As she'd feared, Ian Gregory had spilled the story of their brief affair, and Dan was being so—so damned noble. They were discussing her as if she were a—a bag of potatoes, to be handed to the highest bidder! She would have something to say about that! She went into the kitchen and swept up the remains of the pitcher, cleaning the sticky beverage from Em's shining floor.

She hoped they choked on the lemonade! She wished she'd put some ipecac in their bloody drink!

She heard the two men talking, and peered into the living room. Ian Gregory was at the door of the entry, obviously taking his leave. Dan had risen and followed him as far as the study door where he held onto the frame for orientation.

"You needn't see me out," Ian Gregory was saying. "And I'd like to get with you on this later in the week."

"I need a little time," Dan admitted. "It is a major decision."

"I will see you soon, then. Good day, and thank you."

"Good day. It has been a most enlightening afternoon."

The door closed behind him. Tamsen marched into the room and took Dan's arm, propelling him back into the study to the big chair.

"Sit down," she ordered. "Now, what was that all about?"

Dan looked astonished. "Did you hear any of it?"

"Not much," she said grimly.

His expression changed to one of eagerness as he launched into the details of Ian Gregory's visit.

Gregory had come to him with a proposition. Australia was a growing country, becoming sufficient unto itself. A number of citizens were dissatisfied to be mere colonists, ruled by Englishmen. For years they'd been strugglling to become a federation, a Commonweath.

"Do you follow me?" he asked suddenly.

Tamsen's knees had gone weak. She'd settled, dazed, to the floor before him, her icy hands clenched in her lap. Ian had not told him anything about those short weeks! He had not told him! There was a roaring in her ears. She laid her head against Dan's knee.

"I'm not sure," she whispered. "I don't understand what you're getting to."

At present, the States, which made up Australia, were divided, each a separate colony, under Bristish influence. But they were in the process of being drawn together by wire and rail. Take the United States, for example. Supposing each state stood alone, with interstate customs barriers; each state governed by a small elite ruling class, and those rulers influenced by a distant monarchy.

"Australia stands where the United States stood a hundred years ago," he said quietly. "It needs to become a united country, with a national pride. A vote for all men. Protection for the poor devils like the man Kelly that they hanged last November. There must be an end to class distinctions, religious bigotry; a united trade within its own boundaries, and with other countries. The move toward becoming a Commonweatlth has to come from within and without. They—they need a representative in England, as a liaison between Australia—and Her Majesty, the Queen."

"Dan, you're not saying—"

He nodded, his face darkening. "They think I'm the man for the job. I've traveled most of the country. I'm familiar with the telegraph; the railroads that are here and that will tie the country together in time; what a United Australia would have to offer. Good God, do you realize there haven't been any Bristish soldiers here for the last ten years? We're a sitting duck for any nation that wants to take over. Something has to be done! But it isn't a job for a blind man."

"You can do it. Dan." Tamsen was beginning to come back to herself.

He shook his head morosely. A group of citizens had gotten up a subscription toward sending a qualified man to speak for them. Somehow, they'd managed to check out his background with Washington, learning of his earlier activities in working for the country of his birth. But evidently they hadn't known of his handicap.

"You still have a mind," she said, "and a voice. Dan, it's important!"

There were other considerations. The money the backers of Federation managed to scrape up was negligible. There would be fare to England; living expenses. They would be reduced to a poverty level. A poor man would have difficulty gaining influence at Court.

475

They weren't poor! Dan didn't know it yet, but *they weren't poor!*

And mention of a move to England had come up twice in the same day! Oh, Dusty—beloved Dusty to the rescue once more! She began to laugh, with a note of hysteria that brought a hint of alarm to Dan's sightless features.

"We'll do it, Dan!" She paused. It was Nell's secret to tell. She would not deprive her of that. "I can't say how, but we'll manage. It's tailor-made for you, believe me!"

He was caught up in the spirit of her enthusiasm. For a long time he talked as she nestled against his outstretched legs, holding fast to one of his hands. For a time, he was his old self, vibrant, overflowing with thoughts and ideas; the conversation he'd had with Ian Gregory engraved in his brain.

Immersed in happiness, Tamsen didn't absorb much of what he said. It was enough to be here, with him, watching him seem to come to life before her very eyes. It was enough to know she held the key that would help him accomplish what he wanted to do. And that what she thought might be the end of their marriage had become, instead, a new beginning.

Then, like a snake in her Eden, a niggling doubt slithered into her mind. It seemed strange that this opportunity had come from Ian Gregory, the man she'd run out on without explanation. He was British. He'd told her he was considering returning home. Did he still believe he could win her from Dan?

"I would think Ian Gregory would have been a good choice," she said, her mouth dry. "I'm sure he might have influence with the Queen."

"I pointed that out, and he said he had been approached. But he's a native Australian now. England

476

holds bad memories for him. His wife died there, shortly after they were married. He thinks he should begin a new life here; marry and settle down. He even spoke of perhaps buying Opal Station."

Once more, Tamsen was glad Dan could not see. She felt silent tears coursing her cheeks; tears of relief—and of pain. Ian Gregory had talked of his home, so often; of an ivy-covered house and green, sloping lawns. Now he intended to remain here, in a country that was alien to him.

He had either loved her too little—or too much.

As Tamsen leaned against Dan's knees, listening to his dreams, Ian Gregory strode toward his rented home. The sun was still high, beating down on him with a furious intensity, but he didn't feel it. His mind was back in Duke Courtney's study, seeing the mingling of shock, fear and anger on a small lovely face. He had read her like a book. She'd thought he'd come to make trouble for her, and he had let her think it—a most uncharacteristic action. Revenge, perhaps, for that night he'd waited, his dreams dying as a supper spoiled and ice melted beneath the wine.

By now, she would know the nature of his errand. He hoped she would concur in the plan he'd outlined for Dan Tallant. He would like to think of her in a green and gentle land—

He clenched his jaw to discipline his thoughts. He did not intend to think of her at all!

He'd gone to a great deal of trouble to erase her from his life. Seeing her with her husband at Ramona's wedding, he'd known he'd been fooling himself; that his main attraction had been that he'd been there when she needed him.

After the wedding, he'd gone to Courtney's office and frankly stated his case. If Courtney said there was no hope, he intended to take on the job he'd been offered in England—influencing Her Majesty into declaring Australia a Commonwealth.

He smiled wryly at the memory of that visit. Courtney had not only given him the truth, he had delivered it spiced with a bit of choice profanity. He'd told him of Dan's business failure and how, in keeping it from Tamsen, he'd left her feeling alone, unwanted. How he'd rejected her, not telling her of his blindness; the rejection coming on the heels of the kidnapping of her niece, the burning of the station, the death of her oldest friend. "Hell," Duke said roughly. "No wonder she kicked over the traces. She's human!"

Then he'd launched into a description of Tallant's exploits: the way he'd saved a railroad through Texas to California; his work in Alaska; in the reconstruction of the south after the Civil War; in Hawaii.

And an idea had been born.

Tamsen would go to England with her husband. And he, Ian Gregory, would survive.

Entering his house, he looked at the bleak, unadorned walls, the furniture arranged so conventionally by his manservant. A womanless house. He needed a wife.

Sinking into a chair, he buried his face in his hands, the image of the sort of woman he would look for behind his lids.

She would be small, dark, with an oval face that held a nunlike purity. She would have long-lashed eyes, deep enough to drown in, and long black hair that was live to the touch. And she would look at him as Tamsen looked at Tallant—even if he were blind.

For a moment, his shoulders were racked with choking sobs. Then he rose and went to his bedroom, calling for his man. He caught sight of himself in the mirror.

Nothing had changed. The visage that looked back at him was that of a quiet, gray-eyed man in a conservative gray suit.

There was a ball at Government House tonight. He must change into something more festive.

Chapter 60

When the family gathered for dinner that night, Nell did not immediately appear. Tamsen began to feel a gnawing fear. She had looked in on the old woman earlier, and she'd been sleeping. But what if it had not been *sleep?* After the shock she'd had, her heart might have failed her.

She pushed back her chair. "Nell hasn't been feeling well. I'd better check—"

She was interrupted by a concerted gasp to which she added one of her own as she stared toward the doorway to the dining room, seeing the apparition that leaned nonchalantly against the frame.

Nell!

But such a Nell! Somehow, she'd managed to find a gown from those earlier days when she'd pursued a less-than-savory career. Of heavy black satin, completely festooned with strings of jet beads that glittered and shimmered in the gaslight, the gown was cinched in at the waist, and Nell billowed above and below. The neckline of the gown was low-cut, and Nell had corseted herself so tightly, in order to get into the dress, that her bosom rode high in the vicinity of her chin. Her face was red, perspiring, and happy, beneath an enormous feathered and beaded hat. In one hand, she carried a dainty parasol that matched the gown; in the other, a black fan, also trimmed in feathers, that she waved coyly as she posed.

Duke was on his feet. "Good God, Nell! You—what a surprise," he finished feebly.

"Lady Wotherspoon," she simpered, batting her sparse eyelashes at him. "Well, hell, ain't you goin' to invite me to set down? This looks like a soshul affair."

It was clear from Duke Courtney's face that he thought Nell had lost her mind. With a worried look at Em, whose expression showed that she shared his opinion, he moved toward Nell warily. It would be best to humor her.

"Of course, Nell. Let me help you to your chair."

"Lady Wotherspoon," she reminded him.

"Of course."

She swept to the table on his arm, and he seated her to the sound of creaking corsets, followed by a snap. Something had given way.

Duke went to his own chair, and Nell picked up a fork in one hand, a knife in the other, and beamed at the stunned faces around the table. Only Tam looked normal, a smile quivering at the edge of her lips. The others looked as if somebody had died! She was stumped, but only for a second. Then she realized what they were all thinking. A laugh rumbled up from her tightly laced middle, parting another stay, climbing higher and higher, mingling with snorts of helplessness. Her face was purple, her eyes streaming with tears. She looked at Tamsen who was also weeping with mirth.

"Oh, hell, Tam," she choked. "They think I'm nuttier'n a peach orchard boar! You tell 'em, I can't"

She went into another fit of laughter, her midriff touching the table, making the cups rattle in their saucers.

It was some time before Tamsen could regain her own composure. Finally, Nell's chuckles still punctuating her words, she managed to tell the story of their visit to the barrister's office, and what they'd learned there.

The first reaction to her news was one of relief that Nell had not lost her sanity. Then the wonder of it all set them quiet. Dusty had been a beloved friend, but he'd been a drink-sodden little man; he was obviously well educated—but a member of Bristish nobility? It was hard to believe.

When Tamsen convinced them it was indeed the truth, they each began to make private plans for their sudden fortune. Em and Duke, having no immediate need for the money, thought to bank it for a rainy day that might affect them or their children. Vickie drifted in a dream of pretty clothes; Scott thought in terms of cricket bats, perhaps a polo pony. Missie saw independence; schooling; the book she would write. And she knew whom she would dedicate it to.

Arab saw an escape from Opal Station. They wouldn't have to go to San Francisco. She saw Luka growing up in cultured surroundings, perhaps even being presented to the Queen.

Luka was not impressed at being an heiress. She was too filled with the joys of the day. The garden had been filled with butterflies.

Dan's thoughts were on Tamsen. He reached for her hand, his own trembling. "You knew this afternoon, then?"

"Yes, I knew."

Em followed the old hospitable custom of setting an extra place, should an unexpected guest drop in. More than one eye turned toward the empty chair beside Nell, expecting to see a small man, white hair on end, grinning at them, the gap of two missing teeth visible beneath his wispy moustache.

Finally, Duke left the table. When he returned, he carried a bottle of champagne left from Ramona's wed-

483

ding, and a tray of glasses. He poured one for each of them, then went to his place at the head of the table, extending his own drink toward the empty chair.

"To Dusty," he said in a choked voice. Misty-eyed, the others followed suit.

It was Dusty's evening. All his old exploits were gone over again and again, while Nell sat grinning with pride in her man. Missie listened with rapt attention. It would all go down in her book. Dusty had been modestly reluctant to talk about himself.

Finally, the party broke up; Duke promising to get further details from Robert Curney in the morning; Nell swearing that she'd melt down into a tub of lard if she didn't get out of them gawdamn lacings.

"Good night, Nell," the others called after her as she left the room. She paused in the doorway, elevating her nose, the feathers on her God-awful chapeau quivering.

"*Lady Wotherspoon,* to you!" She said in a lofty tone. And then she swept grandly away.

Tamsen grinned with delight. Nell, among British nobility? It would be something to see!

That night Dan and Tamsen talked for a long time, content with just lying in each other's arms. When she finally slept, he turned on his back, hands folded behind his head, as he stared at the ceiling with blind eyes.

The offer Ian Gregory had made him was a godsend. With something to look forward to, he felt like a man again. But from the moment he'd met him, he'd felt that Gregory was holding something back. And today, he'd discovered a truth.

For one brief moment in the study, he had been blessed—or cursed—with another return of vision. And he had seen clearly enough to discover Gregory's secret. The man was in love with Tamsen. And it was plain that she was aware of the fact. He wondered if there had been anything between them.

He would not ask. It was enough that Tamsen had come to him, brought him back to life after a long period in which he wanted to die. He needed no more proof that she loved him.

He put out a hand, tangling it in her long black hair. And, smiling, he slept.

The next morning decisions that had been made during the night were announced over breakfast. The Narvaéz and Tallant families would accompany Nell to her new home. The Courtneys stayed with their plans to go to San Francisco. Em had asked Missie to sail with them. She could enter a University in California, and they would be nearby. Dear Missie, small, thin and blond, so unlike Martha in appearance, but resumbling her in spirit.

Missie would be a link with the others. Em's eyes filled as she watched Dan and Tamsen, Juan and Arab in spirited conversation. They must make one last visit to Opal Station to pack their things.

Duke looked at his wife, his own eyes turning serious. "You're not sorry?" he asked in a low voice. "We don't have to do this. I can always change my plans."

She managed a watery smile. "Don't be silly! I don't care where we go, as long as I'm with you."

He thought of the way she'd walked beside him on the trail to the goldfields; the way she'd borne cold and privations before he struck it rich; the stillborn baby, buried in northern soil. And he knew that what she said. was true.

It was amazing, how strong she was; and her sisters, too. He looked over at Tamsen, such a small woman, but with a core of steel; and at Arab, a little spoiled, perhaps, a bit selfish. But even she came through with flying colors when the chips were down.

He'd never met Scott McLeod, their father, after whom they'd named their own son. The old man had died long ago, leaving three orphaned daughters to fend for themselves. He had heard stories about McLeod. Saint, drunk—the versions varied as to exactly what kind of a man he was.

But of one thing Duke was certain. He'd done a helluva good job in raising his daughters.

Chapter 61

Two weeks later, Juan and Arab, Tamsen and Dan, Missie and Nell, approached Opal Station. The place had been sold to Adam Jones of the Booradabie. Young Adam, having given up on Ramona, had married one of the O'Donoghue girls from the Mairn. It suited his father to set his son up on a neighboring property, the range to be mutually shared.

The jackaroos were to remain. Now the house had to be emptied for the new occupants, its contents sorted and packed for shipping.

As they neared the aborigine settlement, Tamsen was struck by the sight of the greenery across the creek. All signs on the fire were magically erased. Wyuna waddled toward them, her face split in a grin. "I tell you-feller come," she said. Missie asked after King and his family. They were gone. Long-time walkabout. She sensed they had returned to their early home. She would never see them again. But she would write about them someday: a story of a different people with human dignity.

There was little time for nostalgia. The rains threatened and they must do their packing and move out while they were able to make the journey. They all turned to wrapping their prized possessions in dish towels, packing them into bureau drawers to avoid breakage.

The job was finished sooner than they expected. Taking Dan's hand, Tamsen wandered with him through the early evening. The valley hazed into purple in the distance. A late sun touched the walls of the valley, painting them in tones of red and gold. Everywhere mallee and eucalyptus scrub sprang into new life like a resurrection. The pools of the Billabong reflected the valley walls and the new green of graceful, drooping willows with an opal's changing fire. The place had been truly named.

In the young trees Denis Dugald planted—God bless him for the thought—birds rustled, settling themselves for the night with cooing sounds. And from across the creek came the primitive singing of a corroboree.

"You're going to miss it," Dan said quietly.

"I suppose so. It seems like when we leave a place, we leave little pieces of our lives behind. We're getting old, Dan."

"Are we?" he said teasingly. "And here I'd thought of suggesting we spread our swags out here tonight! Moonlight and romance, love under the stars— But of course if your old bones can't take it—"

She leaned against him, laughing. For his sake, she told him demurely, she would try to endure it. Still laughing, they made their way back to the house where the jackaroos had prepared a barbecue for this, their last night at Opal Station.

That night, Missie could not sleep. Their beds were packed, and the various members of the group slept on blankets on the floors of their former rooms. The moon shining through Missie's window brought back vague, disturbing memories that finally forced her to a sitting position.

She thought of Arthur Melvin; not the brute who had mistreated her, but the man who had held her gently, poetry on his lips. The man she'd thought him to be;

tender, well-read, the sharer of her dreams. She shivered a little, remembering.

Unable to exorcise his ghost, she rose, pulled on a cloak and quietly left the house. There was a faint breeze, a scent of green things growing. She viewed the moonscape about her with new eyes. She'd seen Opal Station as a prison, holding her back, stifling her ambitions. But it was a lovely place. If only she hadn't been so intent on growing up, the time of going away would have come. And she would have enjoyed her younger years.

Her footsteps led her along the old familiar path, along the creek where the moon reflected in shallow pools, and to the salt cedar ring where she had spent her days in dreaming; where she'd found King and his family; where Arthur Melvin loved her, took her for his wife—and then treated her so cruelly.

The tall salt cedars were gone, now. In their place was a new barrier of tender green, almost shoulder-high. She parted it and stepped into the natural ring.

It was occupied. Dan Tallant lay on his back, his hard-muscled chest golden in the moonlight. Tamsen rested in the curve of his arm, her head on his shoulder. Her mass of dark hair was loosened, falling across her upper body to cover all but the curve of a shoulder and the slender arm that lay across Dan's chest. A blanket concealed them from the waist down.

For a moment, Missie was unable to move. They looked like a portait of young lovers—and Tamsen was over fifty, Dan even older than she. Why, she thought with wonder, did youth think romantic love was only for them? The beauty of the scene brought a lump to her throat.

Silently she backed away and left them to their idyll.

As she walked back to the house, she thought of the

book she intended to write. How ignorant she had been as she worked at it in those earlier days! It would have come through as the tale of a madam, glamorous, self-centered, admired by many men. And it would have been a false picture. This, too, was part of it: a woman who loved a man more than her life—even when he was blind. A woman who spent her lifetime caring for that man, for her sisters, and for one sister's children.

It was as if Missie herself had been blind. Now, since her own tragic experiences, she could see. And she could even begin to forgive Arthur Melvin. Like Ned Kelly, he'd been born to a life where he hadn't had much chance for success. Unlike Ned, he'd chosen a path of cunning, conniving, pretending. Until, finally, he degenerated into the thing he became.

Missie had almost reached the porch when she changed course. Her footsteps led her far from the house, to Dusty's grave. There, in the moonlight, she made a number of vows to him, and to herself. She would never again let her own self-interests blind her to the truth. The Tamsen of her book would be a courageous woman, self-sacrificing the noble. And, in her own life, she would try to be just such a woman.

Someday, she'd make Dusty proud of her. It was a promise.

Blinking tears from her lovely myopic blue eyes, she returned to the house. She had said her farewells to Opal Station. When she returned to Melbourne, there was only one more thing to do. She would go, alone, to stand for a few minutes in front of Melbourne Gaol, the place where Ned Kelly was hanged; where his mother was still incarcerated.

She would go over it all in her mind, fixing it there forever. Maybe someday she would be able to tell his side of the story. Ramona would like that.

She finally slept.

In the morning the small caravan was loaded—and waiting. Nell had not yet joined the wagons. After a scant breakfast, she had stumped off, muttering that she had one more gawdam thing to do, and she had not returned.

They could see her in the distance, seeming oddly shrunken as she stood beside Dusty's grave. Though the women were worried about her, they felt it best to leave her alone with her grief.

Nell stood silent for a long time, tears running along the creases of her screwed-up face. A lizard ran, unnoticed, across her foot, and a lorikeet swooped overhead, attracted by the feathers on her hat. In the distance, a kangaroo sat immobile, watching with curious eyes, a gray shadow against the green of a clump of speargrass. Nell saw none of it.

After a time, she began to speak in an almost conversational tone.

"Well, yuh lettle sonofabitch, I'm gonna do it. Wooden leave yuh here, effen I figgered you *wuz* here. Knowin' you, yer gonna be taggin' along, grinnin' like a gawdam monkey cuz nobuddy but me know's yer there. Won't even have t'pay yer gawdam fare. Oh, hell, I better git goin'—"

She took a step or two, then turned back, settling her hat more firmly on her head, squinting ferociously. "Dunno if you kin git hold of a bottle, where you are, but I wooden put it past you, yuh leetle bastard. You sure as hell better not git soused an' miss th' boat!"

She tramped back to where the others waited, and settled herself in one of the wagons, the feathers on her hat bobbing. The small train pulled out in silence. They were leaving too many memories behind.

It passed through the aborigine settlement. Tawny-

491

haired children, their naked bodies light with a powdering of dust, ran alongside them as they moved down the long red ribbon of road, leaving a life that had once seemed alien, but had become their own.

Chapter 62

The Narvaéz family, shrunken now to Juan, Arab and Luka, along with Tamsen, Dan and Nell, set sail for England in mid-March. The Australian summer was dwindling into fall. There had been a spell of rain, but today was clear and bright; Melbourne was scented with flowers; a cool wind at sea.

Em, Duke, their two younger children—and Missie, were not to leave for San Francisco for at least another week, while Duke tied up the loose ends of his business dealings. They were somewhere on the dock, lost in the faceless crowd. Tamsen and Arab waved frantically, in hopes that they might be seen.

It had been a sad parting. Luckily, Arab was too preoccupied with Luka to have time to break down. Luka, pale hair shining, silver eyes alive with interest and excitement, was enchanted by her surroundings.

A coil of rope, bigger than her waist.

A gull perched on a flag-mast.

A pelican wallowing in the sea, its pouch bulging with its breakfast.

The ship began to move, and Arab, tried beyond her nerves, joined Juan in leading Luka to their cabin. Nell followed shortly after. Only Tamsen and Dan remained to watch a young nation set in an ancient land slip away.

Tamsen clutched Dan's hand. She would not think of the years she was leaving behind; Opal Station; Dusty—

She would concentrate on the happy times.

The far shoreline was replaced with a vision of the red center of Australia. Behind her lids, she could see the blues and purples of the MacDonnell Ranges; the plains below them floored with paper daisies; the higher, more rugged ground starred with the pale delicate blues, lilacs and whites of rock isotopes; a field of tall yellow-tops sparkling against a background of purple hills; and in the night, the shimmering ghost gums, sapphire pools in a desert Eden.

With her eyes shut, she transported herself to the base of a chasm, Dan's hand in hers. Before them was a small blue pool. To either side, the walls towered to the skies, strained with the setting sun, in colors of red and gold.

A rift that might have been made at the beginning of the world. And two people, insignificant in the majesty of it, who might have been Adam and Eve as they slept in each other's arms in the soft sand at the chasm's foot.

There had been much talk this morning about returning some time. Perhaps Em and Duke would make the journey, since they'd left children behind; grandchildren. But Tamsen had the forlorn sense that they would not return, as they hadn't gone back to Alaska, Hawaii.

She felt a tear rool down her cheek. Before she could raise her hand to wipe it away, Dan touched it gently with a loving finger.

"Don't cry, sweetheart. And don't look back. We've got a whole life ahead of us."

She sought for a cheerful answer; then the significance of his touch dawned on her. "You *saw* me," she said finally. "You really *saw* me!"

"I've been able to see all morning," he said. "I didn't mention it because I didn't want to get your hopes up— and then I wanted to surprise you. I have to admit that you're a little blurred."

"Oh, Dan! Dan!" She threw her arms about him and kissed him, ecstatically, much to the amusement of several sailors passing by. "Thank God!"

He finally held her away, grinning down at her. "Don't get too excited. It's been coming and going, you know. So, while it's still with me, I'd suggest we retire to our stateroom. I want to see all I can while I can." After a pause, he grinned again. "My love, you're blushing."

Laughing, like a pair of newlyweds, they hurried to their cabin. As Dan undressed, something fell to the floor. He retrieved the object; then, at Tamsen's questioning gaze, held it out for her inspection. An opal, glinting with fires of red, green and gold as he turned it in the light. He had a pocket full of them.

"Someday these will be priceless when people see them for the precious things they are." He paused. "Sometimes it takes a while before people recognize the things that are of most value."

She blushed, realizing he wasn't only talking about opals. He saw the arms that lifted to him in invitation. A blur, but he saw.

When he loved her, the cabin walls disappeared and became a chasm lit by a fading sun that left them with a velvet night sky studded with stars.

In another stateroom, Luka slept and Juan comforted Arab who grieved over Missie's absence; a mother-daughter relationship that flowered too late. They would see her again, Juan soothed. In the meantime, she had Em to watch over her. Soon they would be in England, near Ramona.

In yet another shipboard room, Nell, now clad in her

faded pink robe, arranged her enormous bulk in a provocative posture and practiced listening—inside her ears —as Luka had taught her.

"Well, Dusty, where th' hell are yuh?"

In a moment, she blushed coyly, her small eyes twinkling with pleasure. The leetle bastard hadn't missed the boat.

Tamsen lay in Dan's arms; Arab turned to Juan; and Nell hugged her memories close as the ship sped toward their new destination on wings of love.